This is a work of fiction. Names, characters, places, and incidents are the product of the author's imagination or are used fictitiously, and any resemblance to actual persons, living or dead, businesses, companies, events, is entirely coincidental, with the exception of the names of the towns used and depicted.

THE 5TH

MIRANDA

A NOVEL

BY

J. PATRICK FLANIGAN

To my wife, Hildy

ACKNOWLEDGMENTS

I WANT TO THANK EVERYONE WHO WAS PART OF THIS EFFORT – ESPECIALLY MARILYN THOMAS – WITHOUT WHOSE ASSISTANCE THIS BOOK COULD NOT HAVE BEEN COMPLETED.

1

Sergeant O'Conner tried, without success, to again squeeze the fingers of his hand. His forearm still felt as though someone was pouring scalding hot coffee on it. Forcing himself to open his eyes, he could barely see bits of plastic and gray-black smoke hanging suspended in the air in front of him. But the pain was too much and although he tried not to he was forced to close his eyes again in a futile attempt to focus on making the pain go away. The newspapers would say that the explosion blew him thirty feet away from the car and had he not been standing next to the telephone pole, he would have been killed. None of that mattered to him now. All that mattered was that he felt tired and so very cold. He could now smell the odor of burning gasoline somewhere near him and he hoped – no prayed – he wouldn't be burned alive.

* * * * *

May was unusually cool and wet this year in Kansas City. Winter snow had now been replaced by rain. It was early Wednesday morning. The dark blue police car eased left out of the station lot and headed north toward the main cross street of town, several blocks away. Bowers Mill was one of those Kansas suburbs that had appeared in Johnson County after World War Two. As the Kansas City metropolitan area had grown, so had the town. Ten years ago there were 12,547 residents. Now there were 21,416. But as a town it was running out of room to grow, for it was surrounded by the towns of Lenexa, Shawnee, and Merriam.

A block from Colorado Boulevard, Patrolman Matthew Martin suddenly noticed a dark colored car on his right, parked behind the Four Aces Bar, which had closed an hour and a half earlier. Three years of experience as a patrolman had taught him that the Four Aces Bar and anyone in, near or around it was up to no good. Passing the entrance to the alley, he could see that the driver's door was open and someone was sitting behind the steering wheel. Patrolman Martin knew he had to go investigate why they were there.

"Be careful. Be careful." he repeated to himself as he glanced at his watch to note the time for his report. It was 3:25 a.m.

Momentarily stopping his Chevrolet at the intersection with Colorado Boulevard, he then quickly turned east. Just before the next intersection, Matt had finished requesting a backup unit. He first turned south on Bailey Street and then west into the alley, toward the parked car. Up ahead he could see the driver's side door was now closed.

Matt Martin didn't like the feeling he was getting. Not after what his wife had just told him while they were talking on the phone. She was up, as usual, with their new baby. Sherri had just told him three times to be careful, having checked his horoscope for today on the Internet. According to what she had read, Matt was to have a below average day and this worried her. What else was new, he thought, although that kind of information worried him too.

Ever since the baby was born, Sherri had wanted him to quit the department and she took every opportunity to press him to leave. She had been telling him for weeks she was afraid something bad would soon happen to him. He heard this every time he went to work. And with the baby here, Matt, too, was more concerned about his safety. Still, he loved what he was doing. Where else could a twenty-six year old have so much authority and fun exercising it?

Patrolman Martin pulled behind and slightly to the right of what he saw was an older model four-door Ford. He began to carefully look it over and saw it carried a Kansas license plate. In the left corner were the letters "WY" showing it was registered in Wyandotte County, the next county to the north.

"Wyandotte County, what an armpit," he said out loud as he hurriedly wrote down the tag number. He then began to speak into the microphone on his left shoulder.

"Unit 16 to dispatch."

"Go ahead 16."

"I need a registration check on Wyandotte County license plate: One, Zero, Three, Five, Bravo, Victor, Charlie. That's One, Zero, Three, Five, Bravo, Victor, Charlie," he repeated.

"10-4, hold for verification."

While he waited for an answer, Matt Martin picked his flashlight up off the seat beside him and slowly got out of his car. He winced when he felt the pain in his left shoulder, pain he had gotten from the extra weight he had started lifting at the gym. As he always did, he shrugged it off and then unsnapped his holster.

Gripping the handle of his 9mm pistol he began walking down the driver's side of the car parked in front of him, shining his light into the car's interior as he went. He was relieved to see that there was no one in either the back or the front seat. He stopped at the front of the car and began to methodically search along the back of the shops, which were on either side of the Four Aces, slowly moving the circle of light from one back door to another. Nothing looked suspicious. That was good because he could still hear his wife's voice warning him over and over to be careful.

Headlights now rapidly came toward him from the opposite end of the alley. Another police car quickly pulled up and blocked the abandoned Ford from the front. Matt saw that his backup was Webster O'Connor, the field sergeant on duty this shift.

Why him, he thought but before he could come up with an answer the voice of the female dispatcher came back on the air. She startled him, and instinctively he gripped his gun handle tighter.

"Unit 16. Unit 16."

Matt turned his head to his left, keyed the microphone on his shoulder and told her to go ahead.

"License plate Wyandotte County, One, Zero, Three, Five, Bravo, Victor, Charlie reports back as being registered to a 1983 Ford 4-door belonging to Thomas A. Gilley, 11631 West Nall, Kansas City."

Matt asked her to repeat the information and this time he finished jotting down the owner's name and address into a spiral notebook he had hurriedly taken from his shirt pocket. When he was finished he flipped it closed and put it back, being careful to button his pocket flap. No use appearing sloppy in front of the Sergeant, he thought.

"Where's the driver, Martin?" asked Sgt. O'Connor who was now standing next to him and peering into the empty car. As he spoke, the sergeant's right hand was tugging at the neck of his bulletproof vest. It must be too tight, Matt thought, that or the sergeant still needed to lose more weight.

"He could be inside," said the patrolman motioning with the beam of his flashlight toward the back door of the Four Aces Bar while at the same time muffling his laughter at his joke about the sergeant's weight.

Sergeant O'Conner nodded and then said matter-of-factly, "Try the door."

Matt turned off his flashlight and hung it back on his belt. There was now enough glare from the headlights of the two patrol cars for him to clearly see the back of the building. He took his gun out of its holster again and held it close against his side as he began moving toward the door. He came to a stop in front of it and, after hesitating for a moment, gently turned the protruding knob.

"It's locked," he said, turning back toward the sergeant, who had moved to the front of the Ford, where he stood pointing his gun at the same door. Sergeant O'Conner now used it to motion Matt toward the door directly east of where he now stood.

"Try the doors that way and I'll check this way," he hollered out.

Matt wondered why they even needed to keep looking as the sergeant had been so loud people four blocks away could have heard him. He declined to say anything and both men began to move along the back of the building, stopping in front of each door long enough to see if it was locked.

Sergeant O'Connor had finished checking his third door when he whistled toward Matt. Matt turned and saw him pointing toward a trash dumpster in the far corner of the parking lot that was across the alley.

"Check out the dumpster," the sergeant called out, again in a loud voice.

Matt didn't like this idea at all. He was still having trouble getting his wife's voice out of his head. She was starting to get annoying with her constant pleading for him to be careful. In an effort to get her to stop, Matt forced himself to concentrate on his search for the person he had last seen sitting in the Ford. He, or she, must be nearby, as there hadn't been enough time from when Matt had first seen the car to when he had come up behind it for whoever was there to have gone very far.

Still, as he began walking toward the dumpster, he could hear his wife's voice loud and clear again. No, Matt definitely didn't like the idea of searching any dumpsters. Not with today's horoscope, not with the insistent sound of his wife's voice in his head. He hoped they were both wrong. Police work like this was one of the reasons why Sherri wanted him to quit. He looked at the dumpster again. Maybe she was right, he thought as he took out his flashlight.

Matt began to follow its beam toward the battered green box that rested at an angle as it was missing a wheel. Just beyond it, he knew, was a large drainage ditch, a ditch that extended east and west for miles into the darkness.

Officer Martin kept his gun down by his side until he got within fifteen feet of the dumpster where he raised and pointed it toward the box. At ten feet he began to walk more slowly. Five feet away he leaned over and placed his flashlight on a low concrete wall that ran along the far side of the parking lot, carefully positioning the light so that it shone directly on the dumpster. In the background he could now hear the faint sound of water moving through the concrete ditch.

The last five feet he moved even more slowly, deliberately placing one foot in front of the other. Once beside the dumpster he stopped for a moment and carefully listened for any sound that would betray the presence of the Ford's driver. Try as he might, he heard nothing but the sound of water. After first taking a deep breath, he counted to three, then reached up, flipped open the lid to the container and proceeded to stick his gun into the darkness of its interior.

"Police! Put up your hands and come out!" he yelled.

There was no reply and nothing came out of the bin except the odor of beer and stale food. Looking for something to probe its contents with, he found an empty two-liter bottle in the corner nearest him. He picked it up with one hand and, still holding his gun at the ready, began poking through the trash. Bottles, cans and old food moved for him. So did dirty paper plates. But Matt's search of the dumpster found no owner of the vacant Ford.

Relieved, he holstered his weapon and then found several sides of a cardboard box to wipe an unknown liquid off his right hand. Congratulating himself on a job well done, he then walked to the sloped edge of the ditch and peered into the darkness. If the car's owner had gone down there, he knew he was long gone. Still, he had a duty to check it out. Matt turned to go pick up his flashlight when the bomb went off.

All he remembered later was that before him, in slow motion, the abandoned Ford lifted up in the air like a rocket taking off, tilted forward then headed back toward the ground before landing on Sergeant O'Connor's one-month-old car. It crushed its top, then its trunk, before tumbling to the ground behind it.

At least Matt thought he saw all this happen before the concussion from the blast blew him backwards. He did remember tumbling down the side of the drainage ditch. When he finally stopped he found himself on his side where he immediately began to feel something soaking through his clothes. He hoped it wasn't blood. With great effort, he managed to slowly turn over onto his stomach. From there he started to get up but fell backwards only to have the liquid begin soaking into his clothes again. Matt was having trouble seeing and there was also something wrong with his hearing, all of which he hoped was only temporary. Sherri was right, he was having a below average day.

The explosion blew Webster O'Connor back the way he had driven into the alley. Lying in a patch of gravel on the west side of the parking lot, he tried to remember where he was and why he was there. No answer came to mind. It was then that he felt the pain. Forcing himself to look down he saw something sticking out of his left arm, something that looked like a bone – his bone to be exact. The skin, which should have been covering it lay peeled back like it had recently been filleted. Blood – dark blood was everywhere. His eyes quickly fell on the elongated piece of metal that stood in the center of a sea of red that was his arm. Why was it there, he wondered. Then the pain came back again and ripped at his arm. He began to scream. Then what passed for reason took over and Sergeant O'Connor began to focus, just as his karate instructor had taught him, to block out everything that wasn't important. He would decide what was important and what was important was to stop the pain. He had to stop the pain. Taking his right hand, he reached over and gripped the jagged metal piece. It felt extremely hot as he slowly pulled it out of his arm. The pain caused him to scream anew as he dropped it on the ground beside him. Terrible pain now arose in three of his fingers; fingers that he guessed had been burned pulling the metal out. He couldn't stop himself now and he continued to scream even as he forced himself to fold the loose flesh back over his arm.

Ignoring the damage to his right hand, Sergeant O'Conner squeezed the loose flesh to his arm in an attempt to stop the flow of blood. Concentrate, he told himself, concentrate on what's important. He had to stop the bleeding or he might bleed to death. He wanted to close his eyes, not for long, but just for a little while. No, no, he kept repeating to himself, there wasn't time to sleep now. But he felt so tired and he began to wonder what a little sleep would hurt.

The tears running down his cheeks streaked pink lines into the blood on his face as he kept forcing his eyes to stay open in an effort to stay awake. From where he lay he couldn't see the smoke that had begun to curl out from under the Ford. Light grey at first, it rapidly darkened as the gas tank caught fire and began sending yellow flames up into the night sky.

Patrolman Martin had been spending his time struggling up the side of the ditch where he arrived just in time to see the Ford burst into flames. He then watched as lines of dancing yellow colored liquid quickly ran under his sergeant's car and it, too, caught fire. The heat was intense and he quickly rolled over and looked up at the sky to get away from it. He told himself he had to get over to help his sergeant, but now he couldn't remember which sergeant. Taking a deep breath, he began feeling all over his body for any sign that he was hurt. He did notice a small amount of blood on the palm of his left hand that had appeared after he had wiped it across his forehead. Probably glass cuts from the explosion, he thought. He wiped his hand on his shirt and then ran it across his forehead again. Relieved at finding nothing else, he then focused on the ringing in his ears. It was still constant and had not diminished. He hoped he wasn't deaf. Matt knew that was a distinct possibility as all sounds seemed muffled. Maybe it would turn out to be like the liquid which had soaked into his clothes, which, he had discovered, was only water.

* * * * *

The explosion was heard all across the northern part of Johnson County and parts of southern Wyandotte County. The force of the blast blew out all the windows in the two-block area surrounding the bar. Immediately the Bowers Mill police dispatcher began getting calls asking what had happened. She had no immediate answer. Sitting at her console in the windowless room she began a methodical questioning, between the calls, of all cars in service looking for information on what had happened. When it came to their turn, Units 16 and 7 did not respond. She tried several more times to reach them, but each time was no different than the last. They remained silent.

The Bowers Mill fire and police stations stood one block apart, separated by a small park, facing toward Northern Avenue. No one at either place had any trouble finding the site of the explosion. When they came outside and looked, the flames and smoke were clearly visible from both stations. It took the first fire truck less than two minutes to reach the alley.

They found Sergeant O'Connor lying motionless on the ground. He did not respond to any questions he was asked and began to fight with anyone who tried to touch him. They quickly gave up trying to explain to him what they were trying to do or why they were there. Two big firefighters appeared and, despite his protests, half carried-half dragged the sergeant away from the intense heat coming from the two burning cars. Once in a safe place, they stopped and one of the firemen tore off what was left of the sergeant's left shirtsleeve and began to wrap his arm with white gauze. Gauze which quickly turned red before it could be covered over again.

* * * * *

The Chief of Police was already awake when the phone rang. The watch commander didn't have much information on his two officers or how badly they had been hurt, but she did tell him they had both been taken to the hospital. She had no word on any other injuries or why the car they had been checking had blown up.

The Chief slowly hung the phone up and lay back down and began to stare at the bedroom ceiling. His wife turned over and asked what was wrong. He had nothing he wanted to tell her so he shrugged his shoulders and got up to get dressed.

The fires were out by the time he walked past the emergency equipment to where the two cars sat smoldering. Lieutenant Case crisply reported that both officers were now at the hospital and the preliminary report was that they were doing well. He also informed the Chief that a thorough search of the area had not produced the driver of the car or any motive for its being in the alley. That was the bad news.

The good news was that the car's license plate had been called in prior to the explosion and units of the Kansas City,

Kansas Police Department were now on their way to the owner's house to see if they could make contact with him.

* * * * *

Several miles away the sound of the explosion had abruptly awakened John Calloway out of a shallow sleep. He had rushed to the front door in time to see flames rising up in the sky off to the west. After watching them for a while they slowly began to die down. Closing the door, he turned on the television, went over to the sofa and sat down. There was nothing on about the explosion and he soon picked up a file on the coffee table in front of him and began to prepare for court in the morning.

2

The white house was in the middle of a block of similar white houses, all of which had been built in the early 1950's. A few were in need of paint but most of them had well-kept lawns. This neighborhood, unlike most other parts of Kansas City, Kansas, was not part of the city's slow decline. Streetlights stood on either side of the street at half block intervals, but their light seemed to drop straight down and cling to the base of each pole as though it was afraid to travel any further away.

The two black and white police cruisers that had suddenly appeared at the end of the street began to slowly move down Nall. The lead car was using its spotlight to search the front of each house as it passed by. Patrolman Eugene Noland had no luck finding what he was looking for until midway down the street. There he found 116–1 West Nall. Satisfied that this was the house, he pulled over to the curb and turned off his spotlight. The police car behind him pulled over and stopped near the end of the driveway. Both officers got out and hurriedly walked up the driveway toward the front door.

Patrolman Russell Gilbert stopped long enough to look in the garage window. In there he could see an older model green car sitting upon concrete blocks. He shined his light on the back bumper looking for a license plate. There wasn't one, but never one to be discouraged, he moved on.

Patrolman Noland had stopped and waited for the other officer. He now spit his gum out and buttoned up his coat against the cold spring air. Together the two men climbed the steps to the front door where Officer Gilbert, the first to get there, proceeded to knock. He paused for a few seconds, and not getting a response, knocked again. There was still no answer. He looked around but was unable to find a doorbell. Peering in the small window on the door, he hoped to see some sign of movement before he knocked a third time. This paid off for him as a light came on in a back hallway. It revealed a small balding man, clad in a dark colored robe, hesitantly looking from one corner of the living room toward the front door.

Thomas Gilley had retired five years ago after working thirty-two years on the line at the Ford plant over in Missouri. In his prime he could handle himself well in any situation. But not now. The arthritis in his hands had gotten to him. Even taking the medicine the doctor had given him was not enough to control his pain. So Thomas Gilley wasn't prepared to handle any trouble with whoever was at his door, but he first needed his glasses to see who was there. That was another problem - he couldn't remember where he had last put them down.

Exasperated with himself he settled for yelling toward the door, "Who's there?"

* * * * *

Eugene Noland was still standing outside looking in the window at the man standing in the hall. He tried the doorknob but it was locked and did not turn. Then he began

~ 13 ~

to shout at the cowering figure to open the door. "Police. We need to speak to Thomas A. Gilley," he shouted in an official voice.

The figure still didn't move. Instead, answering back, he said "I hear you. I hear you."

Tom Gilley was almost sixty-eight and had arthritis along with his vision problems. This meant he was slow to move across the living room carpet toward the voice at the door. Midway there he stopped to catch his breath and wished, for the umpteenth time, that he had stopped smoking twenty years ago. Looking up from where he stood resting, he was able to make out two faces looking in at him. When he finally got near the door, he turned on the porch light and could see that they were both wearing uniforms.

"What you want?" he asked.

One of the two faces answered, "Police. We need to speak to Mr. Thomas A. Gilley about his car---the 1993 Ford. There's been a problem with it."

"What problem?" he now asked before looking past the officers toward his driveway. His car was not there. At least he couldn't see the shape of his car out there, but he would need his glasses to be sure.

"Wait a minute, wait a minute. I'll be right back," he said as he turned and started to shuffle back across the living room, but in the opposite direction from the hall light.

Angered by his reaction, Officer Gilbert immediately began pounding on the door. At the same time he raised his voice and said, "Hey, come back here. We need to ask you some questions about your car."

The old man didn't say anything and kept moving. Officer Noland now tried to open the front door. It was still locked. Both officers realized they had to resign themselves to watching the bent figure move out of sight.

"Want to break in?" said Russell looking over at his partner and smiling.

Eugene Noland stood on the porch, shifting his feet from side to side, trying to keep warm. He was just now getting over a cold and had no desire to spend another couple of days off work if he got sick from standing on this porch. He momentarily hesitated, then shook his head and said, "We don't need that kind of publicity. But, we need to do something."

Russell Gilbert was about to say something else when the old man slowly came back into the living room. Seeing him, Russell began pounding on the door again and in his sternest voice said, "We need to speak to Thomas A. Gilley. If you're him – or even if you're not – open the door now. If we have to tell you one more time, we'll be forced to break it down."

"Can't hurt," he said under his breath. "How much slower can he get?"

The officer's threat had no more effect on the speed of the figure coming toward the door than anything else they had said or done. Finally, however, the two patrolmen heard the sound of the door being opened.

Tom Gilley felt the sharpness of the night air on his face as he stood looking at two uniformed policemen. He squeezed his robe tighter around his neck and tried not to breathe in the cold air. Squinting at the men standing in front of him, he wished, again, he could remember where he had left his glasses.

"I'm Tom Gilley," he finally said, "Now where's my car? What's happened to it?"

"Can we come inside?" one of them asked and then added apologetically, "Its cold outside."

Tom Gilley nodded and turned back away from the door.

"Close the door behind you," he snapped as the second officer came into the house, "you're wasting my heat." He had managed to shuffle back across the floor to his recliner where he was now busy lowering himself into its worn seat.

The lamp on the table beside the chair came on and cast a pale yellow glow over the room and the three men in it.

The two officers had stopped near the front door and were looking around the room. The furniture, they told each other later, was like the house, neat but worn. Nothing expensive. There were no expensive furnishings in this house, but it was apparent that someone took care of what they had.

"Anyone else in the house?" said Patrolman Noland. Waiting for the answer, he kept his eyes focused on the hallway from where the old man had first appeared and his hand on his gun.

"Just my son, Lonnie," replied the seated figure.

"Where's he?" asked one of the policemen.

"In the basement. In his room down there."

Patrolman Noland started to say something, but he decided against it. Instead, he asked how to get to the basement to check on the whereabouts of the other purported resident of the house.

Tom Gilley pointed to his left. He was still tired and pointing was easier than speaking.

At the top of the stairs Eugene Noland stopped and made no move to enter into the darkness below him. He strained to hear anything that would give away the location of the man who was supposed to be down there, but he heard nothing.

Patrolman Gilbert was still silently standing by the door. As Noland moved away he began to talk about what had brought them to this house at four o'clock in the morning. "Where's your car, Mr. Gilley?"

Tom Gilley had been wondering the same thing. It wasn't out front in the driveway. It wasn't in the garage either as he had gone to check in there before he had opened the front door. Truth was, he didn't know where it was now, but he knew it wasn't where it should have been. The thought of saying nothing crossed his mind, but, instead, he looked up at the officer and said, "It was in the driveway tonight when I went to bed. Lonnie, my son, was going out and was going to use it. I don't know where it is now."

Russell glanced over to where his partner stood at the top of the stairs. "Go see if he's here, but be careful," he said.

Eugene nodded and took his gun out of his holster. He found a light switch on the wall and flipping it, found that it worked. Then slowly he disappeared out of sight.

Russell Gilbert was now alone with the old man in the recliner, who was constantly squinting. He wondered why he wasn't wearing glasses.

Tom Gilley was barely able to see the clock sitting on the table beside him. It must be four a.m. as that was what the officer had said. Years ago, he remembered, he had gotten up at this time, five, and sometimes six, days a week to go to work. He could tell he was lightheaded and in response, he began to breathe more deeply, just as the doctor had said to do when he wasn't close to his oxygen bottle. He also wanted to go back to bed, something else the doctor had told him to do when he felt this way. Looking up at the officer, Tom Gilley blurted out, "I need to go lie down. I need my oxygen. That's why my boy Lonnie is living with me. He moved back here from Texas to take care of me." And then he added, "Left a good job too," just to make sure the officer knew his boy wasn't just another a freeloader near-do-well.

Russell Gilbert said nothing in response to all this information. He was too busy reviewing the facts. First of all, the old man could barely move. Which meant, secondly, it was highly unlikely that he was the person driving his Ford over in Johnson County tonight or any other night for that matter. Third, the son, now he was a different story. He ought to go run the son's record and wondered how far back it would go, for few people got out of this area without a record of some type.

Tom Gilley had stopped wondering about his glasses. He had just remembered he had set them down on the back of the toilet. Having solved that problem, he moved on and began to ask questions of his own – for he now needed to find out where his son was and why the police were at his home looking for his car.

After the old man began repeating them, some for the third time, Russell finally decided to answer several of his questions. He saw the veins on Mr. Gilley's hands stand out where he gripped both arms of his chair when told what had occurred behind the Four Aces Bar. While they talked Patrolman Noland could be heard coming up the stairs where he soon appeared in the hallway.

"He's not there," he said to no one in particular as he walked back into the living room. Russell had already figured out as much by his long absence. It was now time for him to be a policeman again and start asking questions, not answering them. He took out his notebook, then a pencil, and began by asking, "Where was your son going? Did he leave a telephone number where he could be reached? Who are his friends? Where do they live?"

Patrolman Gilbert paused between each question just long enough to record Mr. Gilley's answer before asking the next question about his son.

Tom Gilley had been steadily answering every question asked of him when he abruptly put his hands on the sides of his recliner and began to get up. "I want to check for myself," he said looking down at the floor. "He's home every night. He has to be here."

"There's no one down there," replied Officer Noland, who then continued on with the next question. "Did your son tell you who he was going to be with tonight?" he asked.

Tom Gilley had no answer and told him so. Meanwhile, he continued his struggle to get to his feet and upon hearing, again, that his son was not home became more agitated.

Russell watched the old man for a while and then decided to try and calm him down. "It's okay," he said. "I'm sure your son is all right. Remember I told you they didn't find anyone else in the wreckage."

At the thought of his only son being hurt or worse, Tom Gilley's breathing became more pronounced as he continued his efforts to get up. Frustrated by his lack of progress, he began to curse and this seemed to give him the extra energy he needed. Once on his feet, he paused long enough to take in a deep breath before slowly letting it out. This was one breathing exercise the doctor had given him, which seemed to work when he felt short of breath. He continued to stand still. When he began to feel better, Tom turned to his left and began slowly walking towards the basement stairs.

Officer Gilbert had been watching Mr. Gilley and knew he was doing the investigating not him. He moved to block the way to the basement while, at the same time, reaching out and placing his hand on the old man's shoulder. Watching the prolonged struggle to get up and the labored breathing that had followed had made the policeman concerned for Mr. Gilley's health. "Mr. Gilley, you need to sit down," he said in a firm voice before adding, "I have more questions to ask you."

Tom Gilley's right arm rose to push the officer's hand off his shoulder. It was up halfway when it dropped and he fell forward into the patrolman, who caught him and gently lowered him to the carpet.

Russell quickly felt the side of Mr. Gilley's neck for signs of a pulse. He managed to find one, but it was weak. "This guy's had a stroke," he said to Officer Noland.

Eugene nodded as he began speaking into his microphone requesting an ambulance. Then he bent down beside Mr. Gilley and, placing his ear near his mouth, listened for the sound of his breathing. What breathing he heard was shallow and jerky, that is, when he could hear it. Putting one hand under the man's neck, Eugene carefully tilted his head back as he continued listening. His training had taught him that if he waited any longer the old man would die. Gritting his teeth he first put out of his mind the origin and content of the dark coating on Mr. Gilley's tongue and began mouth to mouth resuscitation.

Patrolman Gilbert stood up to get out of the way as he continued watching the death scene unfolding in front of him. He moved near the front door, frequently glancing outside, hoping to see the ambulance that had been called. In the background he could hear the rhythmic sound of his partner counting out loud before he either blew into the old man's mouth or used both his hands to push on his chest. After a while the tension got to him and he said to the heavily perspiring officer kneeling on the floor, "God, I hope you can save him."

Patrolman Noland had no time to say anything in response. All he knew was that he was losing this guy. He put his hand on Mr. Gilley's chest again, but this time he couldn't feel a heartbeat. "Where's the ambulance?" he shouted toward the door.

"Coming, it's coming," was the quick reply.

"I need it now. Call again," he yelled as he continued to count. It was time to blow into Mr. Gilley's mouth before he started his count over again. Why, he thought, did he have to be the one to be here doing this. The old man was dying and there was nothing anyone could do about it.

Russell Gilbert called dispatch again and was again told that an ambulance was on the way.

Eugene Noland was now forced to stop what he was doing - he had to rest. He used the time to feel for a pulse on the thin wrist stretched out beside him. It was very faint. Sweat continued to roll off his chin and he watched as the drops fell, one by one, onto Mr. Gilley's robe. All he could hear was the sound of his own rapid inhaling and exhaling. And then there was the matter of the taste in his mouth. It was awful. Eugene prayed that whatever Mr. Gilley might have wasn't contagious.

"More pulse. I can't feel your pulse," he shouted at the man lying on the ground. He was mad at him for not responding. Off in the distance he began to hear a siren. Faint at first, the sound quickly increased. He felt for a pulse again and wondered when the ambulance would get here.

"Where is it? Where is it?" he shouted at the old man. "Damn you, answer me. You can't go now, help is almost here. Do you hear me?"

But no one was listening to him. His partner had gone outside to wait for the ambulance, leaving Mr. Gilley motionless on the floor. Suddenly, a strong odor began to rise from near Mr. Gilley's waist, an odor which Officer Noland instantly recognized. It was the smell of human waste, waste that was released when a person died. It was, he knew, the smell of the dead.

Eugene stopped mouth to mouth and sat down on the floor beside the late Mr. Gilley. "He's dead," he muttered to himself as he slowly clenched and released his hands in an attempt to work the pain out. Reluctantly, for he knew it was no use, he got back on his knees and began pushing on Thomas Gilley's chest. He continued on with the established routine until the first paramedic came through the door and pushed him aside. He then slowly got up and backed away so the woman beside Mr. Gilley could examine him. He sank down onto the brown sofa behind him. His own breathing was still so rapid he began to wonder if he needed the paramedics. He sat there and watched as the first paramedic turned to one running through the front door carrying a big black box and said, "Don't bother. This man's dead."

Patrolman Noland continued sitting on the sofa and catching his breath while he looked upon the late Thomas A. Gilley. He no longer had to wait for him to talk about his son. One question he didn't need answered was that Lonnie Gilley had a militia connection. Scattered around the basement, he had found militia pamphlets and newspapers. He wondered if the late Mr. Gilley had known.

As his breathing began to slowly return to normal, Patrolman Eugene Noland got up off the sofa and stepped around the people kneeling on the floor before walking out of the house. He didn't want to be in that room anymore. Here, outside, the air was cool and, unlike when he first arrived, this time it felt good. He pulled out his shirttail and used it to wipe his face. A religious man, he said a prayer for Mr. Gilley's soul on his way back to his car. He said no prayers for Mr. Gilley's son.

3

Lonnie Gilley couldn't believe his luck—it was twenty minutes after three in the morning and his father's car had decided to act up when they were almost at the house on the south side of the police station. Seeing the alternator light come on he had quickly turned onto a side street and then down an alley. From where he was he could almost see the police station. He brought the car to a stop and turned the engine off. The passenger said nothing as Lonnie got out and opened the hood. Why he decided to open the hood he wasn't sure, as he knew next to nothing about alternators. However, a glance at the engine didn't show anything that looked obviously wrong.

Sliding back into the driver's seat, he tried to turn the key several times to get the engine to start. The motor didn't respond. Lonnie got out again and quietly closed the hood. The car, he had concluded, needed more help than he could give it. His father had not driven it much prior to his coming back from Texas and that probably had something to do with it.

Lonnie stood in the alley and contemplated his next move. He knew he was in trouble, for there was no way to get this car and its contents to their destination – which they could clearly see - unless they pushed it. Not only was the trunk of this car packed with enough explosives to level all the businesses around him, but he had no way to escape the place where he now found himself. Try as he might, he couldn't decide what to do next.

Reflecting back, it had all seemed so simple when they first asked for his help. The passenger would handle the explosives and, indeed, had prepared them in such a way that they could easily be carried to the side of the station. All he had to do was drive the car. Nothing else. "Now," he asked himself, "what am I going to do?" Looking toward the far end of the alley, he watched a car coming down the main street toward his location. Seeing the car, he quickly got back in and tried the engine again. It was still no use. The oncoming car was now about a block away from the alley entrance when Lonnie saw its other lights. Not the headlights, but the bar lights on the top of the car. He swallowed hard and almost threw up as he blurted out, "It's a police car, what are the odds of that?"

The police car continued toward the alley where, half a block away, Lonnie sat frozen in his seat unable to decide what to do. The night air was no longer just keeping him awake, it was making him shiver. He stuck his hand into his back pocket to make sure he had his billfold. It was there. He also knew his new Kansas driver's license was in there too. He hoped the officer wouldn't take it away from him for he had only had it a week.

The two men in the car watched in amazement as the police cruiser drove by the alley apparently unaware of their presence. With an overwhelming sense of relief, Lonnie let out a low whistle. It never ceased to amaze him how fast his Irish luck could come and go. "Welcome back," he said softly.

After the police car passed by and out of sight the passenger hurriedly opened his door. Pausing momentarily, he exclaimed, "Let's go. He'll be coming up behind us in no time. He had to have seen us."

He said this as he fumbled to open the lock to the glove compartment. Succeeding, he reached in and quickly turned a dial on the small plastic box placed inside it. "We'll give it this long before it goes off. That'll be his reward," he said, flipping the switch next to the dial. Even though they weren't going to get to the planned target, he now felt satisfied that at least one officer would receive the Captain's greetings. Next time, he assured himself, it would be more. Slamming the car door as he got out, he took off running toward the far side of the parking lot opposite him. Halfway there he glanced to either side and didn't see Lonnie anywhere. Without stopping, he called out over his shoulder, "Come on. Hurry up. Let's go, we've got less than two minutes."

Upon hearing this familiar voice, Lonnie Gilley quit hesitating and grabbed the keys from the ignition. He carefully shut his father's car door before he took off running after the fleeing figure ahead of him. They stood at the top of what they later discovered was a drainage ditch long enough to see the back of the Ford suddenly reflecting light from an oncoming car.

Neither man needed to wait any longer. They knew who it was and together they slid hurriedly down the side of the ditch. Reaching the bottom, they began to run east. Behind him Lonnie he could hear the footsteps of his friend. Both men ran until they came to what looked like the entrance to a tunnel. Unable to see into its dark interior for any unknown dangers, either living or otherwise, they decided to stop.

"Think we should go on?" a panting voice asked.

"Are you kidding? We don't have much choice," came the tired reply.

"Where does it go?"

"You mean the tunnel?"

"Yeah."

"How do I know? At least it goes away from back there."

And with that both men fell silent. Lonnie squatted down as he tried to catch his breath. He vowed for the third time today to stop smoking.

The other man stood, bent over, with both hands on his knees. He kept spitting as something was stuck in his throat. He desperately wanted a drink of water, but knew he wasn't going to get one down in this ditch, unless, that is, he drank from the liquid running down its center. He didn't.

"Let's keep moving," said Lonnie getting up on his feet again. The pain in his side was almost gone.

The passenger reluctantly took his hands off his knees, straightened up and began to follow behind Lonnie into the tunnel, holding on to one of his belt loops.

As they started into the darkness a terrific explosion echoed behind them in the direction of their recently abandoned car. Immediately the inside of the tunnel filled with light. They had gone just a short distance further when this explosion was followed by a second one. Upon hearing this one both men stopped and turned around in time to watch the sky light up for a second time. "I don't know what that's all about," said Lonnie.

"Doesn't matter. That'll take care of at least one stupid cop," said the passenger.

Lonnie stared back in the direction they had come and said, "What about my car?" He got no answer.

The two men stood and watched as flames and smoke rose up in the distance. Then, almost as if by instinct, they both turned and began moving on through the tunnel. Once they reached the other side they began jogging down the channel. Sirens were soon heard off to the west. Here and there along either side of their path, lights in the houses they were passing came on. Once they even heard a door open and someone say, "What's that?"

"The war has begun," the passenger said when they stopped to rest again.

Lonnie nodded as he pressed his hand to his right side and hoped he wouldn't get sick from the pain. "How far before we get out of here?" he asked.

"Don't know – just keep going. We're not far enough away – not by a long shot. What would the cops do if they saw us walking along a street at this time in the morning? How about this as answers to their questions: 'I'm sorry officers, but we're lost, but in a hurry. You see we just blew up our car and we think – no hope – one police officer. So we're sorry but we can't stay and talk, need to go. Where you say? Why you ask? We need to get home quickly to change our incriminating clothes. Sorry, we have no more time to talk to you. By the way, please forget you saw us. Bye bye.'"

The passenger paused to catch his breath and then in a sarcastic voice said, "I don't think we have any choice but to keep on moving – no matter where this takes us."

With that he began moving forward and for the next ten minutes the two of them half walked-half trotted along in silence before stopping again. They rested this time, all the while as the passenger strained to hear any sounds that he felt were unusual. Comforted by what he didn't hear, the two of them walked on for about a block before he decided he wanted to climb out and see where they were. Lonnie followed as together they crawled up the side and out of the ditch. The street sign across the way said they were on 71st street. Motioning for Lonnie to follow, the passenger began walking west toward the convenience store they could both see off in the distance. It was still quiet and no cars passed them as they approached the lights of the store.

"Our luck still holds," said the passenger.

"Because our cause is just," retorted Lonnie.

They stopped by the outside pay phones at the store. Lonnie felt in his pockets for change and came up with part of the money needed to make the call. The passenger had the difference and made the call. The phone rang six times before it was answered.

"Yes, it's me," he said softly into the receiver. "Something went wrong. Come get us." He then listened to the person on the other end. When they had finished he began again. "No, we're at the convenience store on W. 71st. How long before you can get here?"

The passenger shifted the phone to his other ear and began to look up the street in the direction they had come as he waited for the answer. "That's okay," he finally said, "but hurry." And with that he hung up the receiver and looked over at Lonnie.

"How long?" asked Lonnie.

"Fifteen minutes," was the reply.

Lonnie removed his wallet from his back pocket, carefully looked inside and said, "Let's have some coffee."

The two men entered the store. The store lights, for some unknown reason, hurt Lonnie's eyes and he was forced to partially shield them so they could adjust to the brightness. At the same time he was doing this, he noticed a clerk was standing behind the cash register looking at the two of them.

"Where's the coffee?" asked Lonnie.

The clerk pointed toward the back of the store and said, "It's over there. The coffee's fresh." Then he asked, "By the way, did you happen to hear that huge explosion?" hoping that they had some more information on the big explosion he had heard earlier.

"No," replied Lonnie, shrugging his shoulders. "We just got off work."

The two customers began to walk single file back toward the coffee machine. As they passed by the register the clerk relaxed. Neither man looked dangerous, he said to himself and then deciding to be friendlier and less official said, "Where's your car?"

Lonnie smiled at the question, turned and said, "It broke down a couple of blocks from here." At least this one speaks English, he thought as he finished filling his cup.

At the counter after paying for their coffee, Lonnie casually asked, "Mind if we stand by the door and wait for our ride?" No, the clerk didn't mind, he was glad to have the company.

When the two men stopped by the door the clerk left the check stand and went into the cooler to stock the shelves. He periodically looked out through the cooler windows to see whether the two customers were still by the door. The first two times he looked they were still there, but the next time he looked, they were gone. Hurrying to the door to see where they went, he saw the taillights of a car turning east in the direction of the Interstate. "Hope they get their car fixed," he said out loud and went back to the cooler to finish with his stocking.

Before his shift ended at seven, a policeman came by and asked if he had seen anything unusual earlier that morning. The clerk was emphatic in his reply. Nothing unusual had occurred on his shift.

* * * * *

No other traffic was on the street as the light colored car with its three occupants drove east over the interstate. They turned north after passing through several stoplights and drove a short distance down a block before turning into the driveway of a small grey house. The three men quickly entered through the front door and walked into the kitchen. The driver removed the gun from his belt and put it on the kitchen table before he walked out of the room and down a hallway and got back in bed.

He had said very little to the others on the drive back from the convenience store. Lonnie and the passenger had done most of the talking. What they told him had confirmed his worst fears about the wisdom of the mission. Even if the Captain was a genius, no one could plan for every possibility. The next attempt would need a better plan.

The passenger wasted no time in taking the empty bedroom on the other side of the hall, leaving Lonnie with the couch in the living room. Lonnie looked at his watch before he took it off and laid it on the table in front of the sofa. It was four fifty-three. He couldn't remember when he had last slept. It seemed like months ago.

* * * * *

Sunlight streaming through a crack in the drapes hit Lonnie in the face and no matter how he turned his head he couldn't get away from it. At first he just turned over and tried to go back to sleep, but eventually, as it got brighter, he was forced to deal with the light. He finally took a pillow and put it over his head. That worked and he fell back to sleep.

Lonnie woke up again when the passenger lifted up the pillow and said, "We gotta leave. He's goin' to work."

Yawning, Lonnie looked over at the spot where the sunlight he had worked so hard to avoid was still managing to intrude into the room. "Where to?" he said. "My car's in pieces back in that alley. Is he going to drop us off there to pick up what's left of it?"

"That ain't funny, man. Come on, we'll go to my place first. There we can decide where you can go."

The driver of the car had come into the living room and, while they were talking, opened the drapes. Turning toward the two men he said, "It'll take me twenty minutes to shower and get dressed." Looking at the passenger he then said, "I'll drop you both off at your place."

Lonnie lay back down and closed his eyes, but not for long. The sound of the television made him sit up. Channel 3 was getting ready to broadcast the seven-thirty news.

The commercial had just ended and was now replaced by a reporter. Lonnie could see his father's car or, more accurately, what was left of it behind the reporter. The pieces were being loaded onto a flatbed truck. Several policemen could be seen stopping occasionally to pick up smaller pieces. What they planned to do with them, Lonnie didn't know.

Lonnie leaned forward and intently watched the screen. The reporter was now saying that no one had died, but that two policemen had been hurt in the explosion, one seriously. As he heard this, Lonnie felt his stomach relax. At least, he thought, no one had died. Now he heard the reporter say that the car was registered in Wyandotte County.

"My fifteen minutes of fame," said Lonnie looking toward the man seated beside him, who was busy rubbing one of his feet. The reporter continued on, "The owner died early this morning at his residence, while the police were there questioning him. Sources at Westhill Hospital tell Channel 3 that the man had a history of heart problems, which doctors believe was the likely cause of death. A police spokesman told this reporter that the police are searching for his son who reportedly lived with the dead man at an address on Nall in Kansas City, Kansas. The son is not considered a suspect at this time but is considered a person of interest."

Lonnie let out a low howl and sank back in the couch. The reporter kept talking, but he couldn't hear what she was saying.

"I can't believe it," he said before softly repeating himself again. "I can't believe it."

The passenger had come over by now and patted him on the shoulder. "That's a cold way to learn about your father. That's too bad. His heart must of just picked last night to give out … But I wouldn't put it past them, though, to make that up. You know, trick you to get your attention."

Lonnie had no response to this. He had turned his thinking to finding out if what was being said was really true. He ran to the phone in the kitchen. He had just finished dialing the number when, suddenly, a hand came from behind and grabbed the receiver and firmly pulled it out of his hands. Lonnie angrily turned and saw the owner of the house standing behind him.

"Can't have you do that Lonnie. Call could be traced," he said hanging up the phone. "You'll have to call from someplace else," he went on to say. Having finished, he stood with both arms crossed over his chest waiting to see what Lonnie would do next. Though not taller, he outweighed Lonnie by at least forty pounds.

It had all happened so fast that all Lonnie could muster up was a harsh glare to throw back at him.

Unperturbed by this look the owner continued to stand and watch his potential adversary.

"Don't do it Lonnie," he said as Lonnie began to reach for the phone again. "I can't let you call from here. No matter what it means to you. You can call from his house," he said gesturing toward the passenger who had been drawn into the room by the confrontation.

"It's okay, you call from my place," confirmed the passenger as he glanced back and forth between the two men.

Lonnie was still at a loss for words and could only look down at the floor. He had not been all that close to his father until his mother died. Then his father had sought forgiveness from him for his years of drinking and all that had gone with it. Lonnie hadn't wanted to forgive and it was not until after he had made his father pay enough of an emotional price for what he sought that he forgave him. Now Channel 3 was saying his father was dead. He had to know if it was true. He hated the owner of the house for not letting him call. "But don't get mad, get even," he said to himself as he pushed his way past the passenger and went back to the sofa. He wanted to cry, but couldn't.

The three of them left the house fifteen minutes later. Lonnie sat in the back seat of the car again. His anger grew as he mulled over how he had been treated in the kitchen and soon he was forced to bite his lip to keep from lashing out at the other two. The Captain always was saying that part of the success of any mission depended upon the strength of the men involved. He had to remain strong.

The driver had followed the back way to the Cedar Street address. The men in the front seat had spent most of their time talking about what they had seen on Channel 3. Lonnie sat in the back seat wrapped mostly in his thoughts but occasionally allowing their conversation to interrupt him. The more they talked, the more Lonnie became convinced that he would have to turn himself in to the police. As they reached Cedar Street, Lonnie spoke up and told them what had been on his mind.

The driver wasn't sure that was such a good idea and suggested Lonnie go south, to Arkansas, and stay at the compound outside Ft. Smith. There he could get a new identity and then disappear from sight. The passenger disagreed. He thought Lonnie should stick to the plan that had been agreed upon in the event something went wrong. He was positive it would work.

Lonnie listened to what they both had to say. Nothing in the plan, however, covered what to do if his father died. He knew he would have to go to the police, if for no other reason than to find out whether his father was really dead or if the police and Channel 3 were lying.

Lonnie was well aware that reporters made up stories about people for ratings. They were just like the police in their ability to lie to the people. Captain Walker was always talking about that and Lonnie believed in Captain Walker. All this passed through his mind before he spoke up again and said, "I'll talk to the cops. I'll stick to the plan and tell them that the car is missing and I didn't know where it was until I saw the news."

He finished his statement as the car stopped in front a small white house. Lonnie and the passenger said goodbye to the driver and went inside. "Remember the plan," were the last words Lonnie heard the driver say as he closed the car door.

Once inside the passenger headed for the kitchen. Lonnie followed behind and stood watching as he made a pot of coffee. Then they both sat at the table and talked about Lonnie's mounting problems while the coffee brewed on the stove behind them. Reluctantly, they again came to the conclusion that Lonnie would have to call the police and follow the plan. What had happened last night – some form of early discovery before the mission could be carried out – a worst case scenario – had been discussed many times at their meetings. Lonnie had even practiced what he would say if he got caught and had even undergone several mock interrogations by members of the group acting the part of police officers. Unfortunately, what he faced would be for real and would put this training to the test.

Lonnie opened the phone book on the table and searching for a phone number. Once he found it, he slowly punched it into the phone beside him. It rang several times before a stern voice on the other end answered, "Bowers Mill Police Department."

Lonnie hesitated. The dispatcher began to speak again when Lonnie interrupted her. "I want to speak to a detective about last night's explosion."

"Please wait," she said most officially.

The line was silent for what seemed like an hour when another voice suddenly interrupted his thoughts. "Investigations, Detective Stewart speaking."

The voice sounded so menacing, Lonnie started to hang up. Recovering his nerve, he said, "I'm Lonnie Gilley. I think you want to talk to me."

Detective Stewart gripped the handle tighter to keep from dropping his coffee cup. Quickly putting it down, he sat up in his chair and reached for the tablet lying on his desk. He then fumbled under his desk until he found the pencil that had rolled off onto the floor.

"Yes," he said several times and, when he was ready to write, added, "I, we, very much would like to talk to you." He forced himself to sound friendly and hoped he was coming across this way.

"I can be there in an hour," said Lonnie.

Bill Stewart considered this offer and then quickly disregarded it. Glancing at the number displayed on the phone, he said, "I'll be glad to come pick you up." Be friendly, he reminded himself, don't upset this guy, just be friendly.

"No, that's ok. I need to do some things first."

The voice on the other end of the phone sounded so matter of fact, Bill thought, it was like he was making plans with a friend. "Fine then, how about in thirty minutes? You think you can get here by then?" he countered, knowing he couldn't afford to let this guy change his mind. The sooner he got to the station the better.

"Thirty minutes," said Lonnie, repeating the time back. He hesitated as he thought about this request before he said again, "One hour." That was still the shortest amount of time he knew he would need before he would be ready to see this detective.

"Ok, one hour. We'll see you here in one hour then," said the detective. The phone went dead and Stewart sat at his desk holding the receiver in his hand while thinking about what to do next. That didn't take long and he quickly hung up the phone. With the help of a cross directory, he found the address that matched the number that had been displayed on his phone. It was no more than ten minutes from the station.

* * * * *

Lonnie felt satisfied and relieved with his call. In celebration he got up and poured himself another cup of coffee. The passenger was still sitting across from him and having listened to Lonnie's side of the conversation said, "You ready for what's about to happen?"

"Yeah," said Lonnie - quickly adding - "But I still need to go over again what I'm going to say." And with that he got up and went down the hall toward the bathroom. "I'm going to take a shower," he said.

He used the time while he waited for the water to get hot to search through a closet in a bedroom across from the bathroom. There he found what he was looking for, an old pair of jeans and a long sleeved shirt, although they both smelled of mothballs.

Lonnie was not quite finished with his shower when two black and white police cars pulled up in front of the house. Detective Stewart was the first to get out and he hurriedly walked up the sidewalk and then the steps to the front door.

The sound of the doorbell, quickly followed by a hard knock, caught the passenger off guard. Jumping up from his kitchen chair, his eyes quickly scanned the kitchen and living room for signs of anything that might be a problem. Satisfied there was nothing sitting out, he walked to the front door. He told himself there was nothing to be worried about and this thought relaxed him somewhat.

Opening the door, the passenger found himself face to face with a man about his height, of medium build, and with dark close-cropped hair. He had no mustache or beard, but was wearing a frown. The guy looked and acted like a cop. The badge he held helped introduce him.

"I'm Detective Stewart with the Bowers Mill P.D. Are you Mr. Gilley?" As he was speaking he tried to open the screen door and, almost as an afterthought, added, "May I come in?"

"No," came a fast reply followed by, "Where's your warrant?" The passenger now stood blocking the doorway and stared back at Detective Stewart as he awaited his answer. He ignored the man standing beside him and the two uniformed policemen on the sidewalk.

Detective Stewart didn't answer but, instead, looked past the man into the room behind him praying to see something illegal. There was nothing in plain view. No drug paraphernalia, no weapons, nothing. Still, many times in the past he had bluffed his way inside a house without a warrant and he decided to keep trying.

"Mr. Gilley called and we decided to come talk to him. How about letting us in?" Detective Stewart had kept his hand on the screen door handle and, finishing his request, tried to open it again. It was still locked.

"I told you no," replied the man behind the door.

The detective decided to change the direction this conversation appeared to be going. This time he politely asked, "Would you tell him the detective he talked to is here to see him?"

"Wait here," said the passenger, closing the door with a bang. Hurrying down the hall, he knocked on the bathroom door and called out in a low voice, "The cops are at the front door. I guess they couldn't wait to see you."

"All right, tell them I'm coming."

Before turning to leave, the passenger added, "Leave your old clothes. I'll take them out to the ranch and get rid of them."

"Is that smart?" asked Lonnie as he opened the bathroom door.

"Better that than have some lab tech examine them for traces of explosives."

Lonnie nodded. No clothes, no tests, no evidence. It was a good plan.

* * * * *

Bill Stewart stood outside the house repeatedly swearing under his breath. He had no legal way to get in the house. God only knew what was going on inside. Just to be safe, he had sent the two uniformed officers around to watch the back of the house. Bill now glanced again at his watch. Only three long minutes had gone by since the last time he had looked. It was time to knock on the door again. He did and there was no answer. He started to knock again when the door reopened and the same man appeared and said, "He's coming."

Detective Stewart again asked if they could come inside and, again, the man on the inside, this time more gruffly, repeated his desire to see a warrant. With no warrant forthcoming, he slammed the door in the detective's face.

This time Bill Stewart bit his lip. He knew it was too late to stop Lonnie Gilley from doing whatever it was he was doing inside. The detective could only imagine what that would be - Had he cleaned himself up? Were the clothes he had been wearing washed by now? Bill had told one of the officers to call for a warrant, so they could come back and search the house. But he was under no illusions. By then, he knew, it would probably be too late; as it would take several hours to get one.

The two detectives continued to wait on the doorstep for what seemed like forever. Roger Sumler, the overweight one, had finally stepped back down to the sidewalk and was smoking another cigarette. He had let his partner handle this part of the investigation without any interference from him – and it was not going well. Occasionally he would glance up and see Bill standing in front of the door. Roger ground out the butt of his latest cigarette then kicked the pieces into the bushes. "Knock again," he said as he came back up the steps.

Bill quit leaning against the door frame and knocked again. This time he was rewarded by the appearance of a different man. This one was of slighter build than the first man, but was about the same height. And he appeared to be nervous. Bill noticed that his hair, what there was of it, was wet. So his suspicions were right. So much for some of the evidence, it was gone for sure.

"Are you Mr. Gilley?" asked Detective Stewart.

"Yes," said the man facing him in the doorway.

Bill recognized the voice as the one he had heard earlier on the phone. "Can we come in?" he said, trying for the third time to open the screen door.

"No," came a forceful answer from behind Lonnie. The other occupant of the house then stepped up to the door in preparation to again block this attempt to come inside.

Bill Stewart knew he was going nowhere with this request. He would have to wait for his warrant. He thought about the two hurt officers, friends of his, and became angry that he couldn't get inside this house. He knew evidence was going to be lost. Looking at Lonnie, he said in a firm voice, "Will you come to the station with us now?"

Lonnie had thought through his prepared story again while in the shower. He knew, if he just stuck to it, they would be forced to quickly let him go. Besides, he knew he was going to have to talk to them sometime. Better now so he could get it over and then go see his father. The detective had been standing there waiting for an answer to his question, but Lonnie, instead, asked one of his own. "Is my father dead?" he asked, searching the faces of the two men outside the front door for some clue to the answer.

"Yes," the overweight detective spoke up and said. Roger had not waited for the detective standing beside him to speak because he could hear the hurt in Gilley's voice.

"What killed him?" asked Lonnie.

Roger realized Gilley was not going to go with them until his questions were answered. He'd answer his questions but would be brief in his response. "Heart attack. That's what we heard. I'm sorry to be the one to tell you."

Roger made sure to get that last part out. Gilley had to think he cared if they were ever going to get anything out of him – but he really didn't care. One resident more or less of

Kansas City, Kansas didn't make any difference in his life. Especially one old man. Roger put away his matches and took a long drag off his newly lit cigarette.

"I want to go see him," said Lonnie in a voice so low it could barely be heard by the people on both sides of the door. At the same time he wiped his eyes with one of the sleeves of his shirt.

Detective Sumler, wanting to end this blubbering as quickly as possible, said, "We'll take you to see him, but first you need to answer a few questions for us - about the car, for instance." He then stopped himself from saying more. There would be time enough at the station to ask all the questions he wanted. That thought made him feel happy for the first time today.

Bill Stewart, as if on cue, took over the conversation and said, "You're not a suspect at this time, Mr. Gilley. If you want your attorney to be present, you can call him and have him meet us at the station. Or we can talk here. But I think we'd be better off at the station since your friend doesn't seem to want us to come in." Bill then pointed in the direction of the man standing behind Lonnie.

Lonnie looked out at the men on the steps as he attempted to make up his mind whether to go or not. Both detectives acted as if they were nice, but he knew that wasn't true. If they were - they wouldn't be detectives. He wondered what would happen to liars like this one when the new government – his government - took control of the county. If at all possible he would personally see to it that these two got what they had coming to them for their service to the current government.

"Do you want us to come in or do you want to go with us to the station to talk," said Roger, having waited long enough for an answer. He was tired of this guy trying to jerk them around, dead father or not. Besides he needed to go to the bathroom.

Lonnie put one hand on the back of his neck and tried to think through his options. He couldn't let them in as the passenger had work to do. Besides, if there was one thing he had learned about the police, they were never his friend.

"I'll go to the station," he said, and then added, "It's going to be quick, I need to take care of my father. Which funeral home is he at?" Lonnie didn't mean to talk so much, but he was getting more nervous the closer it came to leaving.

"We'll find out for you," said the fat detective, adding for effect, "We'll see that you get there." He knew that if there was the slightest hint Gilley was involved in the wounding of the two police officers, he would never leave the station, not if he had anything to do with it.

There was nothing more for either side to say. It was time to go. Lonnie unlocked the screen door and stepped out into the bright spring morning. Feeling the chill in the air he began buttoning up the jacket he had also found in the closet. It didn't fit and he was forced to stop. A detective got on either side of him and together the three of them walked down the sidewalk to the police car. There they patted him down, for officer safety they said, before putting him in the back seat. As the door closed, Lonnie reminded himself how tired he was of back seats. Mad at this thought, he ignored their request to put on his seat belt.

No one spoke on the way to the station. Lonnie used the time to go back through for one final time what he planned to say.

* * * * *

The passenger waited until they were all in the police car before he stepped outside to watch Lonnie being driven off. He stayed outside long enough to check the street in both directions for anything that looked suspicious. Seeing that both police cars were gone, he went back inside and started to work.

The first thing he did was stuff Lonnie's discarded clothes into a black trash bag. He followed this by putting the clothes he had worn last night in the same bag and then he took a shower. When he finished, he thoroughly cleaned the bathroom.

Next, he vacuumed the carpet throughout the whole house. Once that was done he removed the filter bag and put it in the same black garbage bag.

It was now time to move into the kitchen. Here he used the bleach again, this time to clean the linoleum floor, followed by the stove, the kitchen chairs and, finally, the table. Satisfied with his efforts, he went back to the living room and cleaned both sides of the front and screen doors.

When he finished the screen door, he stopped long enough to look up and down the street again. Nothing looked unusual, but the thought of the police racing up to the door with a warrant made him go back over the kitchen and the bathroom again. When he finally stopped, he said out loud, "This place never looked so clean." He then watched at the front window for several minutes before deciding it was safe to leave.

The drive down Interstate 35 was uneventful. Periodically, though, he looked in the rearview mirror to see if he was being followed. He was relieved each time to see that he was not.

Turning down the narrow lane to Captain Walker's house, he was happy to see the familiar red truck parked beside the house. Since they had been told not to call him, no matter what happened on the mission, the passenger had taken a chance that the Captain would be at home. He pulled up beside the truck and parked.

The Captain had heard a car coming down the lane and was standing outside to see who it was that was coming up to his house. Recognizing the green car, he walked down the steps and out to the edge of the lane where he waited for it to stop. The passenger got out and the two men talked for a few minutes before opening the trunk of the car. The trash bag was hastily removed and, after first stopping at the barn, the two men walked out into the field beyond it and toward the trees in the distance.

Harold Walker held onto a two-gallon can of gasoline and a rake. His companion carried a beer flat and the black trash bag. Once inside the tree line, the two men walked on until they came to a clearing.

After the first fire died out they raked the ground and then burned what was left for a second time. The Captain then used the rake to gather up what was left and place it in the beer flat before they walked further into the woods. When they next stopped, the Captain took the end of the rake and used it to dig a small, but deep, hole in the soft earth. Once covered with dirt and smoothed over with the back of the rake, it was almost impossible to see where the remains of their fire were buried. "One good rain and it will be impossible to find," said the passenger.

Captain Walker only nodded as they walked back across the field toward the house.

4

Lonnie Gilley walked toward the entrance to the police station with the fat detective beside him. That's what Lonnie referred to him as because he couldn't remember his given name. The fat detective opened the door and together they walked through the lobby and stopped in front of a locked door long enough for it to be opened. A few steps beyond it was a room with a large rectangular metal table, tan in color. Around the table were arranged seven chairs. As he entered the room, Lonnie noticed that even the walls of the room were tan. And high up the wall, in front of him, were two windows made of the cloudy glass, like police stations always seemed to have.

Lonnie picked out a chair on the far side of the table and sat down. All police stations look alike he said to himself. He proceeded to look around for any cameras or mirrors on the walls. There weren't any.

Detective Stewart had now seated himself down on the opposite side of the table. The fat detective left the room to get coffee for the three of them.

Lonnie kept scratching at his elbow which, for some reason, was constantly itching. Bill Stewart quietly sat for a few minutes before getting up and slowly walking around the room. Occasionally he would glance over at Lonnie, but said nothing to him.

For his part, Lonnie moved back and forth in his chair and continued to scratch his elbow.

Finally the fat detective returned with the coffee. He handed Lonnie a paper cup that was three-quarters full. "Black, no sugar," he added. Lonnie took it and proceeded to take several small sips. It was exactly what he had asked for and as good as police coffee ever got.

Lonnie was ready to take another drink, when he abruptly stopped and put the cup back down on the table.

"What's wrong? Too hot?" the fat detective asked. Lonnie, again, wished he could remember his name. He decided he didn't really care what his name was, he was still a cop even if he was a fat one.

"No, just don't want anymore. Changed my mind," said Lonnie looking down at the cup. He couldn't bring himself to look at the detective, who always wanted to look him in the eye. What he didn't say was that he had just remembered a warning that they had all been given. The police in Bowers Mills were known to drug people to make them talk. "How stupid could he get?" he said to himself. He decided he wasn't any happier than the last time he had been in a police station. This one, at least, was cleaner than the one in Texas.

Detective Stewart abruptly started the questioning. "Lonnie, we just want to get a statement from you, that's all. You're not under arrest. You are free to leave anytime you want and no one will stop you. Do you understand?" Waiting for Lonnie's reply he realized he couldn't count the number of times he had given this speech. Only a few people, maybe no more than three or four, had ever gotten up and left at this point. But he got them later; it was always just a matter of time.

Lonnie had been startled by the Detective's speech, but now settled back in his chair, nodded, and said to himself, "What a liar." He could tell both detectives were trying to size him up. He was positive they couldn't read his mind and, besides, he didn't feel any different. Maybe they didn't drug the coffee this time. Maybe that came later.

"Where were you last night?" said Bill. He was tired of waiting and wanted to find out what this guy's story was going to be.

"I was with a friend."

So much for a home run thought Bill as he asked his second question. "Where'd you go?"

"To a couple of bars."

And from then on as soon as Lonnie answered a question, the detective had another.

"Any of them have a name?"

"Both are across the state line in Missouri," said Lonnie. He then went on to give their names, because he knew what was coming next. The fat one wrote the names and everything else he said down while the other one, who wanted to be called "Bill" waited.

"Anyone who'll remember that you were there?" said the fat one asking his first question.

"I hope so," said Lonnie looking him in the eye this time.

Roger Sumler nodded at the answer. It even sounded sincere to him.

The detectives now alternated asking questions. They asked mostly easy ones, general information type of stuff, nothing hard. After several more minutes of this, the fat detective excused himself and left the room.

Lonnie was now alone for the second time with the other detective, whose attitude changed as soon as the door to the room closed.

"What were you doing behind the Four Aces Bar?" he barked.

The tone of his voice caught Lonnie off guard and he gripped the underside of the table with both hands before answering. "I told you already, my car was stolen. I wasn't there." And having said that Lonnie rocked back and forth as he waited for the question he knew was coming next.

"Why didn't you call the police when you found out your car was stolen?" This question was in an even harsher and more sarcastic voice than the last one. As far as Bill Stewart could tell, Gilley's attitude hadn't changed. So much for the scare he had hoped his change in attitude would cause in the suspect. Maybe, he thought, Gilley was too dumb to be scared.

"I was doing some heavy drinking and the last place I could remember leaving the car was in the lot of the bar on 17th. When I went back outside to get my other pack of cigarettes out of it, it was gone."

"You didn't answer the question. Why didn't you call the police?" The detective stayed with his original question and waited for an answer.

"I don't know. I couldn't find the keys. And I couldn't remember if I had loaned it to someone or not."

Detective Stewart listened to the way his question had been answered and knew he had found an area where Mr. Gilley didn't want to go. "You couldn't remember?" he asked in the voice he used when he wanted to act amazed. Without waiting for an answer, he continued, "The car that belonged to your father. You couldn't remember if you had loaned it to someone or not? I don't believe you."

"I've loaned the car out before," came the quick reply, "and, besides, I told you I was drinking a lot last night. I don't drink and drive no more."

Bill knew this last part was probably true. Gilley's prior record showed two driving under the influence convictions, one three and the other two years ago. Another one in Kansas or Missouri and Mr. Gilley would have a felony to deal with.

The detective now growled out the next question on his list. "Who took your car?"

"If I knew that I would have called the police and told them," came the sarcastic response.

"When?"

"When, what?"

"When would you have called the police?"

"Well, before I saw the car on TV, I was planning on going back to the bar to see if, maybe, I had parked it someplace else.   If I couldn't find it this time, then I was going to report it stolen – or missing, I hadn't made up my mind."

Bill stopped.   He had heard enough for now.   He abruptly got up and left Gilley alone in the room without saying where he was going or when he was coming back.

Lonnie watched him leave and felt a sense of relief that the smart mouthed cop was leaving him alone for awhile.   He sat back in his chair and began waiting for one or both of them to return.   He remembered that at one point - early on - something the Captain had said had come to mind.   "Leaving a person alone in an interrogation room was an old police trick used to scare people into talking."   Lonnie already knew this from his own experiences but he vowed this wasn't going to work on him.

He began thinking about his father.   Was he really dead? Did his sister know?   Were the police telling him the truth? All these questions began to upset him.   He realized he needed a drink of something to get rid of the dryness in his mouth.   He caught himself staring at the cup of coffee still sitting on the table in front of him.   But the voice of Captain Walker kept repeating, "Watch out for the drugs."   He reluctantly put the thought of drinking any coffee out of his mind even though he didn't feel drugged.

The need for something to drink began to take over his thinking.   Finally, unable to stand it any longer, Lonnie got up and walked to the door, half expecting it to be locked.   It wasn't. Cautiously opening it, he stepped out into an empty hall where he saw a water fountain to his left.

This, he knew, would be better than taking a chance on drinking the coffee they had given him. At the Sunday afternoon meetings of the Covenant of Trinity Church, the Captain had spoken several times to the audience on police interrogation methods. Besides adding drugs to coffee, he said, they also kept people thirsty until they were forced to confess in order to get something to drink. "Well," thought Lonnie, "This won't happen to me now."

He took another long drink from the fountain before going back into the interrogation room. His mouth no longer dry, Lonnie was soon thinking about his father again. He knew he had to leave soon. Besides, he had come to the conclusion the police weren't too interested in what he had to say or they wouldn't have left him alone for so long. And when they had been there they weren't even asking him any hard questions. The questions the Captain and the others had asked him during his practice interrogations were much harder. Still, Lonnie was glad he had undergone the training. Even if, at the time, he had thought it was just as big a waste of time as high school Algebra had been. He now stood corrected and knew he was wrong.

Lonnie thought it had been about ten minutes that he had been left alone. It was then he decided he had waited long enough for the detectives to return. Pulling his jacket off the back of the chair, he had just gone back into the hall when he caught the sound of a door opening behind him.

"Where do you think you're going?" barked a familiar voice. Even so, Lonnie jumped at the sound and quickly turned to confirm it was the fat detective who was interrupting his plans.

"I'm leaving," Lonnie said. "Remember, you guys said I was free to leave at any time, so I'm leaving."

"Not so fast," said the detective who by now had managed to get around him and block his exit. "Why don't you step back in the room and let's talk some more." With that, he took Lonnie by the arm and guided him back to the seat he had just left.

Lonnie shrugged off his hand and sat back down. The detective named "Bill" was now standing by the door watching the two of them. Sometime during their walk back into this room he had also managed to come back from wherever he had been.

Both detectives now sat down and looked across the table at Lonnie. Detective Stewart began the new round of questioning. "Tell me why you did it?" he asked.

"Did what?" asked Lonnie, trying to act unconcerned by the new tone in the detective's voice.

"Why you bombed that bar," came the response, this time in a louder voice.

"I didn't bomb any bar," retorted Lonnie. "I already told you that."

"Yes you did," said the detective firmly. "I heard you say that, but I didn't believe you then and I don't believe you now. So are you going to tell me why you did it?" With each word he spoke, the detective's voice got louder and harsher.

Lonnie didn't reply. He concentrated on looking unconcerned. It was taking a lot of effort.

While he waited for Gilley to answer, Detective Stewart opened the drawer in front of him and frowned when he saw it was empty. "I need one of the forms," he said to the fat detective and got up and went back to his office. He soon found what he was looking for in the top drawer of his desk.

Detective Sumler said nothing to Lonnie while he waited for Bill Stewart to return. Most of the time he either looked down at his tie or up at the windows. He wanted a cigarette and vowed that the department's no smoking policy needed to be brought up and discussed, again, at the next union meeting.

Bill Stewart returned clutching a letter-sized piece of paper in one hand. Once he had seated himself again, Roger

Sumler looked across the table at Lonnie and said, "Lonnie, while I was gone earlier, I was on the phone talking to the county crime lab. Would you be interested in knowing what they told me?"

Lonnie knew it didn't matter whether he was interested or not he was going to hear it. He knew he had to say something and finally blurted out, "Okay, tell me." A weak feeling had already started creeping up his legs. He had told himself several times while the detective named "Bill" was gone, that he needed to get this interview over with fast.

"The lab's investigation shows that the ignition switch isn't broken."

Lonnie leaned a little more forward in his chair and said, "So what, I told you I might have loaned the car out to someone. What does that mean to me?"

"Well it means that even though this car was reduced to a burned out shell, the ignition system was found not to have been forced."

Lonnie's head started hurting and the weakness began climbing ever higher up his legs. Trying not to show any signs of fear he managed to calm himself down enough to ask, "So what does that mean to me?"

"It means," said the fat detective, smiling now for the first time that Lonnie could remember, "that whoever, meaning you, drove the car behind the bar had to use a key to start it. Not just any key, Mr. Gilley, but the key to that car's ignition."

"How could they tell that?" asked Lonnie, hoping he didn't sound scared.

"Sir, it's their job to find out things like that," said Roger as he looked directly into the eyes of the man seated across from him.

Detective Stewart could feel his partner kicking his leg and knew it was his turn to work on the suspect. "You're in deep trouble," he said in a voice so low Lonnie could barely hear him. He had also leaned forward to emphasize this point.

Having made it, he now sat back in his chair. It was time, he knew, to proceed on in a less menacing manner. "Why don't you tell me how many keys there were to that car," he asked matter-of-factly.

"I don't know for sure, but more than one," was the emphatic reply.

"Do you know what your dad told us, Mr. Gilley?" said Roger who was now holding a cigarette in his right hand and wishing the fine for smoking in the station wasn't so high.

Bringing his father into the conversation made Lonnie angry and he replied sarcastically, "Nothing would be my guess, since neither of you have ever talked to him." If this was all they had to act so tough about then the interview was almost over, he said to himself.

"Smart mouthed guys get no breaks, Mr. Gilley. Don't forget that," said Detective Sumler, no longer hiding his contempt. Not with two of his city's policemen in the hospital.

Lonnie was now the one to change his attitude and he asked hesitantly, "So what did he tell you?"

Roger put away the cigarette he had been playing with and leaned over and whispered something into Bill Stewart's ear. Getting up, he then announced that he was leaving to go call the lab again.

Bill Stewart had continued to sit and watch Gilley's body language while his partner had been asking questions. It looked to him like Roger's methods were having the desired effect. It crossed his mind that he liked playing the bad cop – that maybe, just sometimes – he was a bad cop. He waited for Roger to leave and then, as if this had been his cue, abruptly changed his expression and in a voice dripping with contempt said, "You're lucky. No one was killed. As it is both officers will recover. Why don't you stop all this and tell me about it? What really happened? Who was with you?"

"Nothing to tell. I wasn't there," replied Lonnie defiantly. He was tired---tired of the questions and tired of being here. It was time to go see his father.

Detective Stewart continued with his next question. "Sir, did you hear what Detective Sumler said about the lab report? I'll repeat it, in case you weren't listening. The ignition was found in the locked position. Only you had a key, that's what your father said. Why are you lying to us by saying there's a 'thief' out there with a key that fits your car? Do we look stupid to you, Mr. Gilley?"

Lonnie listened as the detective continued to unload on him. This was not what he had been led to believe or expected would happen if he were interrogated. Captain Walker had said to never admit anything. "Make them prove it all" he said, "Always stick to you story, no matter what." The problem, as Lonnie now saw it, was that he needed to know one way or the other about his father. "What about my father?" he asked, ignoring the questions the detective had just asked.

"Talk to me first and you can go see him," spat back Detective Stewart, detesting the blank look on Lonnie's face.

"I don't want to talk no more," replied Lonnie softly. "I'm going now. You said I could leave anytime." And with that he stood up.

The detective also rose up out of his chair. "Not any more, Mr. Gilley," he said. "You're under arrest for the bombing of the Four Aces Bar. That was your goal wasn't it, Mr. Gilley. Now it's time to tell me all about it. Let's start with who all was with you - besides that guy at the house we found you at this morning. We know he was part of it. Come on, tell me what happened. Then – then you can go see your father. You don't want to be in jail when they have the funeral, do you?" Bill had held onto the last question until he was convinced Gilley was ready to break. It had been his trump card and he now played it with relish.

"No—no I don't," said Lonnie. The numbness had now crept its way up into his neck and given his forehead a dull ache. "I swear to you, I didn't do it," he said. He wanted the detective to quit asking questions, even just for a minute, so he could clear his head. But he wasn't getting his wish.

"The key, Mr.Gilley. What about the key?" Detective Stewart could sense the suspect was weakening. It was just a short time before he would break down and tell everything.

Lonnie was now having trouble remembering what the answer was to this question. Was there an answer to this one, he asked himself. He couldn't remember. "I must have left them on the counter in the bar on 17th." That was all he could come up with. It would have to do.

Bill Stewart leaned back in his chair and knew he was getting someplace. "Come on Mr. Gilley, I haven't got all day. Neither does your dad. Come on; tell me what you were doing there. Why the Four Aces? Is this part of your militia group's plan?" He carefully watched Gilley's face after he had asked the last question and was not disappointed. Gilley hadn't thought he knew of his participation in a militia group. Criminals never ceased to amaze him even after all these years.

Lonnie could feel the increasing pain behind his eyes. He tried to concentrate again on what it was Captain Walker had told him to say - but he could barely recall any of his talk. "I wasn't there," he finally managed to get out between his clenched teeth. "Look, I already told you. That's enough. I don't want to answer questions anymore. I want to go."

"Look yourself," yelled the detective from across the table at the suspect he knew was close to breaking. "I've got someplace to be in five minutes. If you don't start talking about what really happened, I'll send you out to sit in the county jail in Olathe until I get finished. And that could be awhile. Talk to me, now, and you can start making arrangements for your dad. It's up to you, sir." He had ended his statement with increasing distain for Lonnie Gilley. So much so that his last words sounded harsh – even by his standards.

The door suddenly opened behind them and the fat detective called out for his partner, breaking the tension in the room. "Think about what I just said," said Bill as he got up and left.

Stunned by what had just gone on, Lonnie watched in relief as the door closed sharply behind the detective. His head was now throbbing and the room felt hot and stuffy. He laid his head down on the table and gently rolled it back and forth hoping that would ease the pain. It didn't. It was fresh air he needed and he now told himself to just get up and walk outside. But before he could do anything Detective Stewart came back into the room. This time he didn't sit down but, instead, leaned up against the wall near the door.

"Gilley, this is it," he said. "You either tell me everything now or you're going to jail. Once there you can forget about your father's funeral, because I'll see they make the bond so high you'll never get out. And, in my way of thinking, anyone who tries to kill two police officers deserves to miss his father's funeral."

Lonnie had slowly raised his head off the table as he listened to the detective. He knew he couldn't – no, it was more wouldn't - take any more questioning. He needed fresh air. He needed to find out about his father. He had to leave. No one had told him where his father was – what hospital or, if they were to be believed, what funeral home. He had to know the truth. He felt responsible for his father, whether it was to take care of him when he got out of the hospital or to bury him if he was dead. His sister and the other family were all down in Arkansas and couldn't possibly know what had happened. It was his responsibility to tell them. He placed his head back down on the table as he began to speak. "I'll tell you," he said. The sharp pain behind his eyes still refused to let up, even upon his offering to betray the cause.

"Well, it's about time," snorted the detective, pulling himself away from the wall and approaching the table. Now he laid on the table the paper he had been holding, stepped back and said, "Mr. Gilley, you need to listen to what I am about to tell you. You're under arrest for the bombing of the Four Aces Bar."

"Look at the form in front of you. I'm going to explain to you your *Miranda* rights. You need to follow along on the paper as I tell you what's on it. One, you have the right to remain silent. Two, if you choose to speak, anything you say can and will be used against you. Three, you have the right to an attorney during questioning. Four, if you cannot afford an attorney, the Court will appoint one to represent you. Five, you can stop talking at any time."

Lonnie tried to follow the form, but it didn't make any sense to him. The detective continued talking and Lonnie decided not to interrupt him, as it would only take up more time.

"Having read and understood these rights, if you are fully and voluntarily giving up those rights, you need to sign right there," he said, pointing to spot where Lonnie was to sign his name. At the same time, the detective handed him a pen.

Detective Stewart stood and watched as Lonnie signed his name where he had been told. He then picked the form up and laid it at the end of the table nearest the door.

Turning back he said, "So tell me what happened."

Lonnie sighed, thought back to the last time he had seen his father alive, and then began to tell some of what happened. He said he was alone in the car behind the bar but not that the Bowers Mill Police station was the real target. He also left out that he belonged to the Covenant of Trinity Church and by extension was a member of the 138th Kansas Free Militia.

By now Detective Stewart was sitting down, taking notes. They took a break after fifteen minutes to allow Lonnie to go to the bathroom and get a drink of water.

Once back in the interrogation room Bill Stewart had ten or so further questions to ask Lonnie, who had grown increasingly anxious to finish as time went on.

The answer to the last question was at ten-forty. Detective Sumler had by now come back in the room, but hadn't asked any questions. He was content to spend the time playing with another cigarette.

Immediately after ending the questioning, the two detectives took Lonnie down to the booking area to be transferred to the jail. He was told to empty his pockets onto the desk in front of him and sit in the chair beside it. Each item was placed in a gold colored envelope after its description was written down on a piece of paper by Detective Sumler. When he finished writing down the last item he closed the envelope, stapled the inventory form on the front of it and left it on the desk. Lonnie was then fingerprinted and had his picture taken. Detective Sumler ended the process with a call to dispatch to request an offer come and take the prisoner out to the Adult Detention Center in Olathe.

When asked, neither detective was able to tell Gilley what his bond would be and for this they both said they were sorry. What they didn't mention was that the District Attorney's office set the amount of all bonds, often listening to the recommendations of the police officers involved, or that they were both going to insist that it be high because two officers had been injured.

Lonnie now sat handcuffed to a long wooden bench waiting to go to jail. The patrolman who came to take him was immediately taken from the booking area by the two detectives when he arrived. Lonnie could hear the three of them talking in the next room but couldn't make out what they were saying. After that conversation ended, the patrolman came back into the room alone and, without saying anything to Lonnie, immediately got on the phone. It was while the three of them talked together that Lonnie decided that he wanted a copy of what he had signed in the interrogation room. If the lawyer he hired on this case was like all his others, he would want a copy of everything. When asked after he got off the phone, the uniformed officer saw no harm in that request. He looked through the paper work that he had been given until he found the form. Photocopying it, he added it to the list on the inventory sheet and put it in the envelope which he later handed to a deputy at the jail.

* * * * *

Once processed into the jail, Lonnie was told to sit once more, this time on a long wooden bench in the booking area and wait for his 1:30 arraignment. He sat next to two other prisoners who had also just been brought in and tried to eat the sandwich a guard had given him for lunch.

He was the first prisoner to go into the small, brightly-lit room where he was handed a copy of the State's complaint listing the charges against him. He hadn't, though he tried to read it before his name was called and he stood alone in front of the camera. It didn't matter because Judge Oliver read it to him. He discovered he was charged with four felonies: Count one, criminal damage to property over $25,000; Count two, arson with major damage; Count three, aggravated battery on a law enforcement officer; Count four was the same as Count three except it was a different officer. The Judge then went on to explain the maximum and the minimum sentence he could receive if he was convicted of each charge. Finally looking at the computer monitor on his bench, Judge Oliver asked Lonnie how he wanted to plead to the charges.

Lonnie Andrew Gilley pled not guilty to each charge. When asked if he could afford an attorney or if the Judge needed to appoint one for him, Lonnie told him he could afford to hire his own lawyer.

Lonnie was about to ask the judge for the amount of his bond when Judge Oliver announced that it was set at $100,000. Lonnie's hope of being released quickly disappeared as he knew he didn't have that kind of money. He wasted no time in asking to have the bond lowered, telling the camera into which he was staring that he needed to find out about his father, of whom he was unsure of whether he was alive or dead. But no matter which was true, he added, he needed a lower bond to get out of jail.

Judge Oliver could be heard over the monitor asking the Assistant District Attorney about Lonnie's prior criminal record and was told it was mostly misdemeanors. The ADA went on to say there were no failures to appear in court at any hearings on his record either He did manage to get in that he was sorry to hear about Lonnie's father, but that didn't stop him from asking that the bond not be lowered. Judge Oliver was quiet for a moment. So quiet that Lonnie was about to speak up when the Judge finally announced that while he, too, was sorry about Mr. Gilley's father, the bond would remain at $100,000. He finished by saying that the case would be continued for one week and would next be heard in Division 2CR. Lonnie's first court appearance ended with Judge Oliver telling him to bring his attorney with him to the next hearing. The deputy standing outside the arraignment room quickly motioned for Lonnie to get away from the camera, whereupon he was replaced by a short, bald man who needed a bath.

Captain Walker had always said that if anything went wrong with the plan or any of them were taken to jail that bond would be posted when the amount was known. What he hadn't said was when it would be posted.

When the other two prisoners had finished their time in front of the camera they were all three taken back to the booking area. Lonnie asked for and was shown a list of bonding companies. He picked out a name and called one. Ten minutes later a bondsman was sitting on the other side of a glass partition explaining to Lonnie that on a $100,000 bond he would need $10,000 in cash. Plus, he then went on to say, he would also need to have sufficient property to cover the total bond before his company would commit to signing for Lonnie's release. Lonnie glumly thanked him and said he needed to think about who could be his cosigner, because he didn't have that kind of money or property. He didn't bother to call another bondsman to see if he could get a better deal. Lonnie didn't have the $10,000 cash required and didn't know anyone who did.

He reluctantly resigned himself to waiting for Captain Walker. Although he was growing increasingly more skeptical, if Captain Walker said bond would be posted, bond would be posted. But when, that's what Lonnie wanted to know, when he would get his bond.

* * * * *

Lonnie Gilley spent less than twenty-four hours in jail. But it was long enough to miss saying a final goodbye to his father, whose body had been taken to Arkansas to be buried. It was his sister who had come up and made all the arrangements. She told him all this in the letter she left for him at the counter in the jail lobby. A deputy brought it to him that Wednesday night, just before nine p.m. Lonnie read it three times before carefully folding it and placing it in the pocket of his orange shirt, the one they had given him to wear. He spent a restless night and sometime before dawn he managed to cry about his father's death.

At eight-thirty on Thursday, a bondsman came to the jail and asked to see Lonnie Gilley. Fred Billings, owner of Comfort Bonding, brought with him the paperwork that needed to be filled out in order to get Lonnie released. He began their meeting with a series of questions, the answers to which he wrote down in the appropriate spot on his forms. When they finished he told Lonnie that once he was out he was to call his office every day, starting tomorrow. This, he explained, was a condition of his taking the bond. Lonnie didn't need to ask why; all bondsman wanted to make sure you didn't leave town.

Lonnie sat in the booking area until a deputy sheriff came in and told him he was free to leave. Well, almost free. First, he had to exchange his orange jail uniform for the clothes he had been wearing when he was arrested. Next a different deputy took him into a room where the deputy checked off each item on the property list against its contents of the envelope before having Lonnie sign that everything was there. The same deputy then opened a locked door and told Lonnie to walk to the end of the hallway where there would be the doors that led out of the building.

It took thirty minutes before Lonnie found himself standing outside of the jail. His eyes darted up and down the street but to no avail, for he didn't recognize any of the vehicles parked in front. There was no one waiting for him, contrary to what the bondsman had told him. A strong feeling of loneliness came over him again. Lonnie reluctantly sat down on the steps that led up to the sidewalk and waited. What else was there to do, he reminded himself, he had no way to get anywhere.

The morning air was cool and he was soon glad he was wearing a jacket. While he waited, he began listening to the birds. It was easy to do since there were no trains going by. A set of railroad tracks ran behind the jail and from his recent experience Lonnie knew trains were noisily going up and down them at all hours of the day and night. He wouldn't miss the trains and that, he knew, was another benefit to being out of jail.

He had been sitting there for several minutes when looking up, Lonnie saw a red pickup at the Santa Fe intersection just north of the jail. He immediately recognized both the truck and its driver. Turning south onto Kansas Avenue the truck slowed to a stop in front of the jail. By this time Lonnie was at the curb and he hurriedly opened the passenger door and got inside the Captain's truck.

Harold Walker took Interstate 35 south toward Gardner. He exited at Westridge Road and continued on south for several more miles until he eventually got to his ranch. Once safely in the house, Captain Walker handed Lonnie two newspaper clippings. The first one was about the bombing, which he scanned and quickly put down. He didn't need to read any more clippings about the bombing, he already knew too much about it. The other one was his father's death notice. Lonnie read this clipping several times.

When he was finished he began to tell the Captain the story of what had happened since Tuesday night, the last time they had seen each other. The Captain was particularly interested in what Lonnie had told the police. He went back over Lonnie's statements to them until he felt satisfied he knew everything that Lonnie had said to the detectives. But with each succeeding time that Lonnie repeated his story, Captain Walker frowned a little more.

Lonnie finally finished his second interrogation in as many days. He was exhausted and needed to sleep before he went home. The Captain eventually dismissed him after giving him directions to an upstairs bedroom where Lonnie discovered, unlike the jail, the bed had no sheets. He crawled into it anyway and quickly fell asleep.

It was two-thirty when he woke up. He found Captain Walker in the kitchen where, after eating a sandwich, the two of them left for Kansas City, Kansas. Close to three thirty they pulled into the driveway of Lonnie's house. Neither one had talked very much.

Lonnie took the spare key from its hiding place and let himself in the front door. The house didn't look any different than when he had left it on Tuesday night. If it were only Tuesday again he thought to himself. He turned and waved to the Captain while telling himself that everything was okay. Closing the door, he crossed over and sat in his father's recliner. They had spent a little time on the drive here discussing the need for Lonnie to get back to his regular routine. Lonnie knew that was true, but first he had to cry again.

5

The clock on the wall said it was 3:30 a.m. and John Calloway had just been awakened by the sound of a large explosion. He continued to lay in the darkness until he heard the sounds of sirens off in the distance. This drove him to get up, whereupon he put on his robe and hurried to open the front door. Off to the west he watched as flames lit up the night sky. He watched for a minute or so and when they began to disappear, he closed the door and turned on the television. There was nothing about the explosion and, quickly bored by infomercials, John turned it off. Picking up the Walker file from off the coffee table, he began rereading the report the social worker had prepared for court.

One of John Calloway's roles as a lawyer was to be a guardian *ad litem*. As a GAL, as they were called, he represented children in juvenile court in cases involving abuse or neglect. It was his job to act in their best interest, even if they sometimes had a different idea of what that meant. Originally, he had planned on taking these cases only until his practice got better. He needed the money and the county always paid on time – not all his clients - then or now - were as reliable. As the years passed his practice got better, but, by then, he couldn't quit – sometimes he was able to make a difference in a child's life – a difference he felt that was worth the money he lost by taking these cases.

He had been appointed to this case around the first of March, John wasn't sure of the date. He happened to be in the hallway outside Judge Baker's courtroom on one of the Judge's "bad" days. Judge J. Robert Baker frequently had bad days. He was now fourteen months from retirement and many attorneys prayed that the time would pass quickly.   On that Monday afternoon the attorney who had been appointed to be the GAL for Gerald Walker was late for the first hearing on this case. This first hearing was to decide whether Gerald would stay where the state had placed him on the preceding Friday or would be allowed to go back home with his parents while his case was being resolved. For Gerald this meant the difference between being in the direct care of the State of Kansas or being released back to his parents on the terms and conditions set out by Judge Baker.

Luckily or unluckily, John was still uncertain which was more accurate, Judge Baker had been on the bench for several minutes waiting for the assigned lawyer to appear when he left the bench while at the same time telling the Assistant District Attorney to go find an attorney who wanted to work. Martha Fulton stepped out into the hallway just in time to see John, who was on his way to the drop off some papers at another Judge's office on the same floor. She smiled and motioned for him to follow her back into the courtroom. John, she knew from experience, could handle working with the Judge when he was in this kind of mood.

Once back in the courtroom she handed him a petition, which outlined the facts that had brought Gerald Walker to this place and time. John scanned it and noted that Gerald had gone to school last Friday with bruises on the back of his legs. These bruises were noticed by his gym teacher who asked where he got them. Gerald told him his father had hit him with a belt the night before.

Gerald was promptly taken to the principal's office where the Department of Social Services was called to report the abuse. A social worker came to the school within two hours and interviewed Gerald in the nurse's office. Based upon what she saw and heard, she decided to remove him from his parent's care for safety reasons. Gerald then spent the weekend in a group home not only for his protection, but because the state had no foster parents available to take care of him.

The petition also went on to give some biographical information on the father, but nothing on the mother except her name. John knew the address where Gerald lived was in extreme southwestern Johnson County somewhere near the Miami county line.

Holding his copy of the petition John walked back out into the hallway and called out the names of Gerald's parents. It wasn't necessary. There was only one person there and he stood up when his name was called. He looked to John to be about thirty-five.

"I'm Harold Walker," said the man as he walked toward John.

"Is Ralene Walker with you?" John asked.

"No. Who are you?" came a swift and hostile reply.

"I'm John Calloway, your son's new guardian *ad litem*," he said, holding out his hand for Mr. Walker to shake it. Mr. Walker just stood there. John didn't have the time or desire to make an issue of this lack of courtesy and continued on, "Have you seen this petition?" he asked, holding out his copy for Mr. Walker to review, "It sets out the state's facts as to why your son is in custody."

Mr. Walker pushed the paper away and in a voice now filled with anger exclaimed, "I don't need no state paper. I'll tell you right now, I want my son back home. This court's illegal and without authority to keep my boy from me."

John heard some of what Mr. Walker was saying while he was taking note of how Mr. Walker was dressed. It was not the usual clothing worn by parents when they came to court. Mr. Walker was wearing both camouflage pants and a camouflage shirt. In one hand he was clutching a brown hat. Not the kind duck hunters wore; it was more like the kind of hat worn by the military, the type with a floppy brim.

While John had been cataloguing all this, Mr. Walker had not let up. He was now expressing his disgust with the Kansas state government. This disgust included the heritage of many of its elected officials.

John continued to ignore his comments and began again. "This hearing is about the temporary placement of your son. It's my job to represent his best interest. I can understand your feeling on having him taken..."

"What makes you think you can understand anything about me or my boy?"

"...out of school and placed on Friday," said John, finishing his sentence.

Having unsuccessfully interrupted John, Harold Walker had begun moving his right arm up and down like he held a hammer. The force he put in this motion made John wish he were back in the safety of the courtroom, but he knew he had to continue talking to Mr. Walker.

"Look, Mr. Walker, you have the right to have an attorney to represent you. If you can't afford one, you can fill out a financial affidavit to see if you qualify for court appointed counsel. I'll be glad to get a form for you if you want one."

"I don't want a lawyer," was his reply. "I am my own lawyer. That school should never have called the police and I'm going to sue them for that. Ask Gerald. He'll tell you the truth. Well, have you asked him about what really happened, Mr. Lawyer?"

Before John could answer, Martha came back into the hallway and told them it was time to come in the courtroom as Judge Baker was ready to hear the case.

The Judge started talking as soon as John sat down. On the left side of the courtroom was a television monitor showing a short, thin boy with dark hair. John looked down at the date of birth on the petition and quickly figured his age at ten years old, plus or minus a couple of months.

"Will the parties state their appearances," began Judge Baker.

"State by Martha Fulton," said the Assistant District Attorney.

"May it please the court, the minor child, Gerald Raymond Walker, appears by video from the Turner Facility with his court-appointed guardian *ad litem*, John David Calloway," said John before sitting back down to listen as the roll call continued.

"May it please the court, Anne Hubert for the Kansas Department of Social Services."

Looking down from the bench Judge Baker peered over the top of his glasses at Harold Walker who had seated himself behind John Calloway. "You're the father?" he inquired.

Harold Walker nodded and Judge Baker continued on with the hearing.

"The purpose of this hearing is to determine the temporary placement of this young minor. This does not mean the allegations in the State's petition are to be construed as true - that will be decided at a later hearing. At this time, the central question that will occupy our discussions today will be what is the best temporary place for this young minor to reside, given the State's resources and his needs."

Having said this he looked over at Martha Fulton and said, "What is the State's recommendation?"

The Assistant District Attorney was slow to get up and Harold Walker took the delay as an opportunity to speak.

Without rising he looked up at the Judge and said, "I want my son to come home. It doesn't matter what the State wants – you can't keep my child from me; I have rights."

Judge Baker was not by nature or reputation a pleasant man. He also did not allow disrespect for the legal system, as he defined it, to occur in his courtroom. Attorneys and all others permitted in his courtroom followed his rules; one of which was, "You may speak only when I call on you." The Judge was swift to educate Mr. Walker on this rule.

However, the effect of this knowledge on Mr. Walker was minimal.

"I said I want my son back," retorted Mr. Walker, ignoring what he had just heard from the Judge, this time in a louder voice.

Judge Baker was not accustomed to having to repeat himself to anyone in his courtroom. Not after twenty-three years on the bench. He looked over the top of his glasses at Harold Walker again and, lowering his voice, said, "I told you earlier, sir, that one of this court's rules is, 'You may speak when I call on you.' Should you fail to follow this rule again, I will have you removed from the courtroom. Do I make myself clear?" Judge Baker finished but continued glaring at Mr. Walker.

Harold Walker had his rules too. One was that the present court system in Kansas was illegal. He ignored the Judge and said, "This court's illegal and is not representative of the people of this county. You are holding my son as a prisoner against his – and my - wishes. I now demand, as a sovereign citizen of this county, that you release him." He still remained seated behind John and when he was finished he glared back at Judge Baker.

John knew he was in-between a bad situation and one that was about to get worse, but he couldn't move his chair any further to get away from the coming storm. He had helplessly watched the Judge's face turn red.

But just before the Judge could get any words out, Martha Fulton rose to her feet and began speaking. "Judge, I have another hearing in fifteen minutes. If we can move on it would be the State's position that this child is—"

"Just a minute, Ms. Fulton," said the icy voice on the bench, turning then toward where Mr. Walker was sitting. "I'm not going to tell you again. You have stretched my patience as far as I'm going to allow you. I order you to stop talking – NOW. You will remain quiet and speak only when I call on you. One more outburst and I will send you across the street to sit in the jail for thirty days. Have I made myself clear, sir?"

Judge Baker's tone was one that had caused many an experienced attorney to meekly sit down and reputedly at least one to rush out of the courtroom and into the bathroom. Harold Walker knew none of this as he sat facing the Judge.

Having made his point, Judge Baker looked back toward the Assistant District Attorney and nodded for her to continue.

"Judge, this ten year old was found on Friday with bad bruises on the back of his legs. As you know, he was removed by Anne Hubert and placed at the Turner facility the same day. This is not the first time, Judge; this boy has been the victim of abuse. There have been at least three other times when bruises were found on his arms and legs. However, until last Friday, Gerald has always denied that his father was responsible for any of them."

Harold Walker had slowly risen to his feet while the ADA was talking, but Judge Baker looked at him and he slowly sat back down.

Martha went on, "The Gardner police and Anne Hubert interviewed Gerald and took pictures. No foster family placement could be found, due to the usual shortage of foster parents, so he went to Turner. I also want to bring to the court's attention that I have a report from his school stating that he's had more than five unexcused absences this semester. There's the possibility that a truancy count will be added to this petition based on the statute regarding school attendance. So based on all this, Judge, it's the State's position that he be placed in the temporary custody of Social Services and they be given the authority for suitable placement. It's also the State's position that he should remain in out-of-home placement until it is found that it's safe for him to go back there."

Judge Baker thanked the ADA and then looked at the woman seated in a chair behind her. She was wearing a blue blazer, a light violet colored blouse and a knee length black skirt. "Ms. Hubert," he said.

Anne Hubert rose as the Judge called her name, and as she did, John turned in his chair to get a better view of her. She was thin, almost too thin, John decided, with straight brown hair that came down to her shoulders. He knew her age because he had once asked her; she was thirty-two. He didn't ask her about her legs, he already knew they were great. She wasn't wearing her contacts today; instead she was wearing a pair of wire-rimmed glasses. What John did want to ask her, but was afraid to, was whether the rumor that she was in the process of getting a divorce was true or not. He was encouraged to see she was not wearing a wedding ring.

"Judge, it's SRS' position that Gerald be placed in a foster home."

Her slight Texas accent had always appealed to John and he smiled as he listened to her speak.

"As Ms. Fulton said, I interviewed Gerald on Friday along with a detective with the Gardner Police Department. Gerald told us that his father had hit him several times with a belt the night before. I observed the bruises that were found on his legs and also one that was on his back."

When she finished, Judge Baker asked, "Where do you plan on placing him?"

"We have a potential foster care placement here in Olathe. We are hopeful that we can quickly find something back in his school district, but with the shortage of foster parents and Gerald's other problems, we were fortunate to find a family here in town."

"What other problems?" said Judge Baker as he looked through the petition.

"Gerald has been getting into other kids backpacks. No one's said he's stolen anything, but this is of obvious concern to us. He has also been aggressive toward other students. Not threatening, but as one student put it, 'He's annoying.'" Anne Hubert then said, "Our position, again, Judge, is that Gerald be placed outside his home for now."

John Calloway looked at her for a moment longer and then turned his chair and faced the Judge while awaiting his turn to speak.

"What is the guardian *ad litem's* position?" inquired Judge Baker when he finished writing in the court file.

"I concur with the DA's office and SRS, Judge. Given the facts as I know them now, I think he needs to stay right where he is until he's placed in a foster home. Although Turner is large, Gerald's as least safe there until the father can decide whether or not to contest the allegations in the petition."

"I contest them," said a voice behind John.

Judge Baker said nothing to Harold Walker this time.

Having heard from everyone, Judge Baker then ruled that Gerald should remain in the custody of Kansas Social Services until the next hearing, which he then set out thirty days.

6

Bill Stewart had taken several calls from the Assistant District Attorney while she was preparing the charges against Lonnie Gilley. None were substantially troubling or difficult, mainly clarification of some of the statements in his initial report.

The ADA was pushing to get the complaint on file with the Clerk's office so they could arraign Mr. Gilley at 1:30 this afternoon. Her first call had been to ask him to fax out his initial report she could prepare the list of charges. They had both agreed that the publicity in this case was such that the complaint needed to get on file, even if it meant not following normal procedures. They had also agreed that Bill would fax out his final report as soon as it was finished and approved by someone higher up.

The ADA's final call had been to thank him for helping her and to say Mr. Gilley would be charged with four felonies.

Hanging up the phone after the last call, Detective Stewart felt good. He had obtained a confession from Mr. Gilley which, more importantly, was voluntary. Now to him, not all of what Gilley had said sounded true, but enough of it did to lock up this case.

Bill Stewart knew Gilley, or more accurately his lawyer, would probably plea-bargain away some of the charges, but not enough to avoid his going to prison. There was also enough information in his report to support a high bond, one that would guarantee Mr. Gilley's appearance at all court hearings should he manage to get himself out of jail. Besides, unless he was wrong and Mr. Gilley was rich, a high bond would keep him in custody until he was convicted and sent to do time in a real jail. For Detective Stewart had no use for the Johnson County Adult Detention Center. Just calling the county jail by that name was just one reason he felt it was too much like a country club – and for criminals no less.

Bill Stewart began putting together his final report just after he left Mr. Gilley in the booking area. Several telephone calls from the ADA had interrupted him, but otherwise he was well on his way to finishing it when he got a call to go out and investigate the theft of some office equipment. He hesitated and started to call his sergeant to ask that another detective be assigned to the case, but then didn't; after all, he reasoned, he'd had such a productive morning so far there was no use creating a problem. Besides, he knew he could get the final report done today if needed, but if the ADA was able to work with his initial report, he could finalize it tomorrow.

Detective Stewart finished taking the theft report a little after four o'clock. Because it was late in the afternoon, he decided to take advantage of his status and its flexible working hours and go home. He would finish the report on Thursday.

* * * * *

Bill Stewart got to work at 8:15 a.m. The first thing he did every Thursday was to water his ivy plant. It wasn't growing well, but he couldn't tell that to his daughter. She had been so excited when she had given it to him for Valentine's Day that he had already resigned himself to buying another one if this one died.

That done, he then listened to his phone messages. A couple of them needed to be returned immediately. It was 9 a.m. when he completed the last call and began to work again on the final Gilley report. It only took thirty more minutes for him to finish. His reports always took longer to complete than those of the other detectives because Bill Stewart was a "hunt and peck" typist on the computer keyboard. However, with this report he spent several extra minutes carefully going over it one last time. Satisfied with its detail, he printed it out and signed his name at the bottom of each of the six pages. With the file and the fresh report, he went into the sergeant's office and placed it on his desk for him to review and sign off on it.

Bill found the signed report on his desk when he came back from the bathroom at around 11:30. He was at the fax machine preparing to send it out to the District Attorney's Office, a fact he would later recall over and over, when he decided to review it one last time. He was halfway through it when he came to the Constitutional Rights form; the one Gilley had signed prior to giving his confession. At the top of the page was the heading, in capital letters, which said "Statement of Rights." It was followed by a list of the *Miranda* Warnings. Below that was another heading, again in capital letters, called the "Waiver of Rights Statement". Looking at the form he knew for some reason something was not quite right. He couldn't pinpoint what, but there was definitely something wrong with the form. Then it suddenly dawned on him why. This form had only four *Miranda* warnings on it, not five. The fifth *Miranda*, the one about the right to decide at any time to not say anything more, was missing.

"What's this?" he said out loud in an astonished voice.

Roger Sumler glanced up at the sound, and then went back to his phone conversation.

"Oh no!" Bill exclaimed, still standing by the fax machine holding the report in his right hand.

This time Roger put a hand over the end of the phone and said, "You're making too much noise. What's wrong?"

"Come here," came the anxious request.

"This had better be important," said Roger before removing his hand and telling the person on the phone that he would call them back in a few minutes. Getting up, he walked across the room to where Bill now stood holding out a piece of paper for him to read.

Roger took a quick glance at it then said, "So, what's the big problem?"

"Look at it again," said Bill with more emotion than the last time he spoke. "Look at the Statement of Rights section," he said.

Roger held the paper, but hadn't read very far when he stopped and looked at Bill. "What's this?" he said, slapping the paper with his free hand.

"I don't know, but it's serious," replied Bill angrily as he saw the disgusted look on Roger's face.

"I hope you know this will can the Gilley confession and I don't even want to be in the building when you tell the Chief. You know what he told you after the last incident." And with that Roger dropped the paper beside the fax machine, crossed his arms and waited for an answer.

Bill didn't respond, in fact he couldn't even look at the other detective. He picked the form up and slowly read it to himself again. He hadn't needed to be reminded of the Chief's warning. "I won't lose this one. This case is too good," he said after several minutes.

"Who did this?" he demanded, looking straight at Roger. "I thought we had gotten rid of all the old forms."

Roger shook his head but said nothing. He remembered the Zook case and knew Stewart's career couldn't withstand another major screw-up. No one who had been with the department back then could forget that case. Zook was a prominent accountant who lived in Bowers Mill. The victim was his neighbor, who was married to one of Zook's biggest clients. Her feud with him was over some tax work he had done for them the previous year – tax work that involved an obscure provision in the tax code. Whatever it was Zook had done for them - Roger had thankfully forgotten most of the case - had been disallowed by the IRS. The woman was so irate about the way Zook had handled the matter; she had filed a complaint with the Kansas Accounting Board.

Zook's copy of the complaint came in the mail that morning. When he came home for lunch, as he usually did, he discovered it and stormed over next door to demand an explanation from Valerie Bartlett. From that point on the facts became muddled. Depending on whom you chose to believe, either Mrs. Bartlett was killed as Webster Zook defended himself from her attack or she died by his hands while he was in a rage.

Either way, Mrs. Bartlett was dead and Detective Stewart was put in charge of the investigation. Like the Gilley case there was the potential for a high profile trial and Bill was under a lot of pressure to get the evidence to the crime lab. He was in so much of a hurry to do so - that he failed to check the back door to the Bartlett house to make sure it was locked before the detectives left for the night.

As his luck would have it, sometime during the night two neighbor kids, curious to see what had happened, went in through the unlocked back door. As they later said at their Juvenile Court hearings, one thing led to another and they soon decided to trash the place. This included the crime scene. The result was Zook's attorney was successful in his arguments that evidence that could have been favorable to his client's defense was lost. Mr. Zook avoided a murder trial and, after some more maneuvering by his attorney, eventually pled guilty to aggravated battery for having hit Mrs. Bartlett with a lamp.

Officially it could never be proved that Zook was guilty of, at the very least, second-degree murder. But what had been proved – in the public's eyes – was that the Bowers Mill police department was guilty of having badly mishandled the case and that mishandling had let someone go free who many residents believed had committed a murder. Once the plea agreement had become known, the mayor had been bombarded with so many complaints that he summoned the Chief to a closed door meeting to explain what had gone wrong and what he was going to do to make sure it didn't happen again.

The Chief came back from that meeting, called Bill into his office, and on the spot placed him on suspension, union or not, without pay for four weeks. He also warned Bill never to do anything again that could result in his being summoned to another meeting like he had just come back from.

Someone was saying something in the background and Roger shook his head to put the Zook case out of his mind.

"Okay, okay, I know what to do," said Bill. He was now over at his own desk, beside an open drawer. He finished reading the Constitutional Rights Form he had taken out to make sure it was the correct form and not one of the old ones. The department had been obligated to change their old form several months ago in response to a new Supreme Court ruling. The Department was told to get rid of all the old forms as they were constitutionally defective. However, apparently not all of them had been destroyed.

Taking the form Gilley had signed and the new form Bill walked over to the paper cutter, where he studied the signed form one last time before carefully arranging the new form on the cutting surface. He then swiftly cut it into two pieces just below the place where the five *Miranda* warnings were listed. He picked up everything and took it with him to the copier. Here he placed the correct part of the form on the glass plate before laying the original form over it. Closing the copier lid very slowly, Bill then pushed the print button. The machine made a single photocopy, which Bill quickly picked up and carefully inspected. It looked perfect to him. There wasn't even a line to show where the two forms had been placed one on top of the other.

Bill looked at Roger, who had followed him around the office, curious as to what he was doing, and said, "You didn't see this."

"You bet I didn't," replied Roger. "But what are you going to do with the original? You can't put it back in the file."

"It'll never see the light of day," said Bill, removing both papers from the copier glass and leaving the room. He was gone for several minutes. When he did come back from the bathroom he wrote a new cover letter and then faxed the finished report out to the District Attorney's Office. "Thank God that's done," he said when the machine showed the transmission was complete.

Detective Stewart's cover letter told the sad news. He was faxing out only a copy of the Constitutional Rights form which he had, luckily, made early on. The original, unfortunately, could not be found anywhere. Detective Stewart promised to continue looking everywhere for it until it was located. It had, he had gone on to write, to be somewhere in the station as it couldn't have gone far.

7

John Calloway woke up and found himself on the living room couch again. For the last three nights he had fallen asleep while watching TV. There had been a time when his wife would have awakened him and told him to come to bed. But those times were no more, not since last June when Janet had moved out.

That was only one of the reasons why he had been sleeping on the couch this Tuesday morning. The other was because he was representing Gerald Walker. Gerald wasn't the problem; in fact John thought he was a good kid. It was just the luck of the draw that he had been born into a family that had Harold Walker as a member. The rumor was that Harold Walker was the head of a militia group. And, if that wasn't true, if nothing else he acted strange enough to be the leader of a militia group. So for some reason, John wasn't exactly sure why, he felt safer sleeping in the living room several days before court hearings in Gerald's case. John knew it was illogical, but it didn't matter, he was still going to sleep out here.

The Walker file was still spread out on the table in front of the couch. It contained, among other things, a brief history of the family. John knew it by heart. Harold Walker had been a postal employee who quit his job the day his supervisor had written him up over a confrontation he had had with another employee, who was Korean, about his religious beliefs. That confrontation had occurred at the Bowers Mill post office and the police had to be called to forcibly remove Harold off the government's property. He was also known to be one of the leaders of a fundamentalist church that advocated the standard brand of white supremacy which, as usual, believed in the inferiority of Jews, Catholics, and blacks. The "Trinity of Hate" as some of Harold's fellow employees had come to call these beliefs.

There were also rumors his church had formed a militia to enable its members to become more active with those beliefs. Calls were supposedly being made by the church leaders for acts of violence to further their shared vision of an all-white, protestant Christian America.

In support of this belief, two of the church's long-time members had just, within the last month, been convicted in a Johnson County Court of severely beating a middle-aged black man. He had suffered the misfortune of having had his car break down on Interstate 35 at the extreme southwestern edge of the county. According to the news reports, the two convicted men were on their way home from a Wednesday night church service, one paper referred to it as an indoctrination session, when they saw him standing beside his disabled car waiting for his wife to come pick him up. They stopped, taunted him for a few minutes, and then attacked him with a shovel. County detectives tried, but were ultimately unsuccessful in linking the church's leaders to the attack. The two men had consistently refused to say anything so that part of the investigation went nowhere.

It was shortly after this incident that Harold had gotten into a confrontation with the Korean. He had initially denied doing anything wrong until two of his fellow postal employees said they had witnessed what had happened. Rather than face any kind of disciplinary action, Harold Walker had walked off his job and never gone back.

Ever since he left the postal service, Harold had farmed for a living, producing corn and milo crops on the twenty acres of land surrounding his house. Harold appeared to devote the balance of his energies to his church and its principles.

His neighbors had, when asked by the authorities, reported that some of the people who came and went from Harold's place looked like they were involved with drugs. The sheriff's department had been very interested in that news but, despite their efforts to do so, had been unable to confirm it. No one around Harold Walker or associated with his church would talk about him or what went on at his place. These same neighbors, when interviewed by the sheriff's department, went on to express the opinion that he was using his ranch for paramilitary training in furtherance of his church principles.

John hadn't really wanted to know all this information, but had found it throughout the reports in Gerald's file. Personally, he was reluctant to discuss religion with anybody and, especially, with people who were fanatic about it. However, as Gerald's GAL it was his legal and ethical duty to do an independent investigation of Gerald's case. This automatically brought him into contact with Harold Walker and, by extension, his religious beliefs, which beliefs he was constantly presenting to John.

John had thought enough about the Walker file for today. Tuesday was his day to be the Bowers Mill Public Defender. He never got tired of doing it. Municipal Court work was a haven from the rest of his practice, which seemed to be populated with arrogant attorneys who always wanted their own way. Besides, practicing law was generally boring to him, the same old thing over and over until he wanted to throw up. But not his job as the Public Defender.

John felt himself drifting off in thought and, catching himself, began speaking to the gray cat looking up at him from the floor. "Time to do some work around here," he said, and with that picked up his blanket off the floor and threw it toward the other end of the couch.

Leaning over he picked yesterday's mail up off the coffee table and saw another letter from Janet's attorney. He didn't have to open it. He knew it was another nasty gram about the status of his refinancing efforts on the house, which he and Janet had bought while they were married. She had wanted to sell it during the divorce, but John liked it and when their property was divided he kept it and in exchange agreed to pay her her share of the equity.

The divorce agreement had given him six months to get a new mortgage, pay Janet her equity, and get her name off the original loan. This had proved difficult for John to do because he just couldn't seem to find all the documents necessary for the mortgage company to determine if he qualified for a new loan or not, but he was now almost finished. In the meantime, the six months had quickly come and gone. The result was that letters from her attorney had started arriving about every two weeks threatening to take him back to court.

"I know I need to refinance," he said to the cat who had followed him into the hallway. As always, the cat failed to say anything but he did however rub up against John's leg.

At eight-twenty a.m. John Calloway backed his small Ford station wagon out of the driveway. He liked this car even if it was six years old. To John it was serviceable and got great gas mileage, but it hadn't been nice enough for Janet. She hated to be seen in it on the weekends, which was the only time she ever rode in it. The other part of the problem was that she wouldn't – refused was the better word – drive her car, which was newer. Whenever he suggested she drive she would always reply, "That puts miles on my car and, besides, you're the man, it's your job to drive us." He had never liked Janet's attitude about sharing her car, but then again, toward the end of their marriage, he hadn't liked her attitude about much of anything.

The twenty minute drive from his house to the Bowers Mill Municipal Court took John north on Interstate 35 to the 71st Street exit. From there he drove west to the city hall building.

Bowers Mill's one and only public defender pulled into the city hall parking lot and, as usual for a court day, saw it was full. Since there was no place to park in front, he switched to his alternate plan and drove around to the back of the building. History had told him it was not generally a good idea to park behind the building, as only regular city employees were supposed to do this, but John had figured out an exception. He pulled into the parking space for deliveries, his regular back-up spot, as he knew the city discouraged deliveries on Tuesday since it was a court day. Because the back doors were always kept locked, John walked around the building to the front entrance.

Bowers Mill was on the site of a raid by William Quantrill and his band during the Civil War. There wasn't a town here in June of 1863, just a collection of houses. Quantrill had dispensed a harsher justice on five of the people who lived there than was allowed by the current city laws. No forfeiting their lives and having their houses burned down. The current city prosecutor, a law school classmate of John's, had proposed that type of resolution in several of John's cases. Only once was he tempted to accept it on behalf of his client.

The city hall had been remodeled three years ago and still looked new. It contained two wings separated in the middle by the city council chambers – chambers that doubled as the Bowers Mill Municipal Court on Tuesdays. As he entered the building, John could see that the courtroom was full. A line of people were standing in the main aisle waiting to see the Judge, who was seated at the far end of the room.

John turned to his left and walked into the west wing of the building. Opening another door he walked through the clerk's area and out into a short hallway, past the pop machine and into the council chambers. John always walked this way to prepare himself for what came next and, no matter how any times he did this, he was never entirely ready for it.

The usual Tuesday pandemonium came into view as he entered the room. Almost immediately a voice called out, "Mr. Calloway, would you come here, please?" It belonged to Judge L.W. DeVon.

"Sure Judge," he said, moving through the second line of people waiting to see the prosecutor. Stopping in front of the Judge whom he saw was, as usual, not wearing his robe. The Judge always said it made him too hot. After fourteen years as Judge he wasn't often asked why he didn't wear it and, anyway, the robe was in the process of falling apart from old age.

Judge DeVon pushed several case files across to John while saying, "This is Mr. Coleman. He has a ticket for driving on a suspended license. I appointed you to his case and told him to talk to you since a conviction will carry an automatic five days in jail."

John took the file and motioned for his new client to follow him back the way he had come. John again past the entrance to the clerks' area and then continued on down another hall to the office he and the Judge shared. At one time he had been given an office to use, but the city was growing so fast he had soon been asked to give it up. With no other vacant offices, he was told for some unknown reason that he could share an office with the judge.

Richard Coleman's case was relatively simple and within a few minutes John had found that the reason his license was suspended was that he needed to pay off several tickets in Wyandotte County. Once paid this ticket in Bowers

Mill could be amended to a traffic violation that didn't carry a jail penalty. Richard had taken some notes on what he needed to do and happily left knowing there was a way he could avoid jail when his case was resolved.

Having taken Mr. Coleman back to the courtroom, John stood in the doorway long enough to call out the person's name on his next file. A small black woman got up from the bench where she had been seated and followed John back to his office. Here they discussed why she had slapped her sister at a restaurant. In the end, they agreed to talk again in two weeks. This would give Rosaline Saunders the chance to talk to her sister. Rosaline was positive her sister would drop the charges. John explained several times without success that it wasn't up to her sister anymore whether or not the charges got dropped, but Ms. Saunders continued to believe otherwise.

The first part of John's day was taken up with plea-bargaining. At some point during the morning, depending on the police department, the prisoners being held in the county jail in Olathe were brought in to be taken, one at a time, before Judge DeVon. Here they either said they were guilty or innocent to whatever charge they had picked up in the city. If they said they were innocent, a date for their trial was set and the amount of their bond was reviewed by the Judge. However if they pled guilty Judge DeVon sentenced them right then. Trials were supposed to occupy the balance of the day, although most cases got resolved without a trial.

The main reason there were few trials was that the city prosecutor didn't want to spend any more time at court than necessary. He worked for a private law firm that represented the city in all its legal matters, not just in municipal court. The city had used this firm for twenty years and ever since John had been handling cases in Bowers Mill the city prosecutor had been Lawrence C. Houston II. He had been in John's law school class, although, back then, they didn't know each other very well. It was only after John began getting cases in Bowers Mill that they got to know each other better.

John had met Judge DeVon through the attorney he had worked for during the summer after his second year of law school. Judge DeVon and that attorney had a case together and John had helped get it ready for trial. After he was sworn in as a lawyer, Judge DeVon had started appointing him to some of the city's indigent cases. Over time John had begun to receive the bulk of the appointed cases in Bowers Mill. Two years ago, when the city decided it was cheaper to hire just one attorney to handle all of the cases, John was offered the contract. He gladly accepted.

Janet, his ex-wife, had always wanted him to give up working for the city. "Quit wasting your Tuesdays. They don't pay enough over there," she was constantly saying.

To which John always replied, "We need the money. Besides it's sometimes the most fun I have all week. Where else can I go and hang out with other lawyers, hardly work at all, and get good deals on most of my cases?" None of this ever made any difference to Janet. She was now gone, but he still had the job.

Law had always been presented to him as a profession, whatever that was supposed to mean. He'd heard so much about "the profession" at home that when he graduated from the University of Missouri he decided to work for a bank in downtown Kansas City, Missouri, not go to law school. After four years of going nowhere, he decided that going into the family profession wasn't such a bad idea after all.

He had gone to Washburn Law School in Topeka. They didn't move there because Janet had a good job in Overland Park, the largest town in Johnson County. So he carpooled the sixty-two miles to Topeka five days a week and never missed a day of class. He also was able to keep his part time job in the computer department of a small bank where he had gone to work the summer before he started law school. Between work, school and commuting it was with great effort that he graduated in the middle of his class. He could have gone back to the family firm, his dad had offered him a job, but Janet said she couldn't live in Carthage, Missouri. She said it was too small and there was nothing to do down there. She had jokingly suggested, at least John thought she was joking, that he could move there and come visit her on weekends. Since their divorce he had thought on several occasions that his life might have been better had he followed her suggestion. Maybe then they wouldn't have gotten a divorce.

Court for John, this Tuesday, was going along smoothly. Rosaline Saunders had left and was in turn replaced by Bruce Lina. He was nineteen and evidently had missed the message that possession of marijuana in Kansas was illegal, this despite two trips to Juvenile Court for the same offense. Bruce believed, among other things, that "the law outta be changed because marijuana is just like alcohol. Besides I'm not hurting anyone."

John concentrated on reviewing the police reports and managed a nod here and there as Bruce continued talking. The reports said the marijuana joint laying on the passenger seat when Bruce was stopped for a burned out taillight at two in the morning. This fact, coupled with Bruce's attitude toward the police after he was stopped, all of which had been duly recorded in the officer's report, gave John little hope of winning the case at trial.

John told this to Bruce and instantly regretted his decision. He not only had to listen, again, to Bruce go on about the need to legalize pot, but, in addition, to all the reasons he knew the case should be thrown out of court. When Bruce finished they went back into the courtroom and set the case for trial because, "I didn't have that much on me. I know they singled me out. I could have just been given a warning about the taillight. Besides, I never gave them permission to shine that flashlight in my car."

John did as he was asked and hoped Bruce would be more reasonable when he next saw him. First time marijuana convictions, at least in the Bowers Mill court, resulted in forty-eight hours in jail. John hated for any of his clients to go to jail, especially if they could avoid it. He hoped Bruce would let him explain the other options before trial.

Back in the courtroom, Judge DeVon was now waiting for something to do. He watched as John and his client both got their copy of the notice showing the trial date. As John's client walked toward the back of the courtroom, the Judge motioned for John to come over. "What's going on Calloway?" he asked.

"The usual, Judge, you know, some handholding here, a trial there."

"Speaking of which, we have a Mullin trial today. He's trying another driving under the influence case. It's at ten, I think, if we can clear out the backlog first." And with that he looked out at the people still waiting to see the prosecutor.

John laughed. He was glad he didn't have to suffer though another one of Mullin's performances. He'd watched Joe's first attempt. It was awful. What Mullin lacked in skill he attempted to make up in bravado. He might have fooled his client, but he didn't fool anyone else. "Shall we talk about more pleasant things, Judge, like lunch?"

"We should. Where do you want to go? I suppose we ought to look at my coupons first." Judge DeVon then pulled out a wad of coupons from his left shirt pocket. He started going through them, describing, as he always did, what each one was good for and from what restaurant. He stopped and handed one to John. "How about the Williams Deli," he asked. "We haven't eaten there in a while. This is a buy one, get one free deal."

"It's expired Judge," said John handing the coupon back to the Judge. Over the years John had learned to check the expiration date.

"Well, let's go there anyway," said the Judge.

"It's okay with me L.W., but we should check it out with Larry." Larry Houston had taken a break and was now standing beside John.

"It's William's for lunch, Larry. All right with you?" John knew the answer to his question already, as Larry was never interested in deciding where they ate, only how much it cost. Larry was okay with William's, just as John thought. His only question was when they were going to leave.

"Depends on how fast you can move them," said the Judge, looking out at the people seated in the courtroom.

The three of them now laughed. Last summer Larry had been able to quickly settle all the cases on the morning docket several times. The three of them had then gone out and played nine holes of golf before getting back to the city in time for the afternoon docket.

"Watch this," Larry said as he motioned to Joe Mullin to come over. Larry turned back toward the Judge and began to recite the plea agreement that they worked out on the ten o'clock DUI trial.

John moved away while this was going on and stood by Kendall Masner, an almost permanent fixture in court on Tuesdays. "Kendall, how you doing today?" he said.

"Fine, just fine," came the reply. "Just waiting for my case to go to trial," he said motioning to the ticket he was holding.

Kendall was always doing fine because he had four months left until his retirement from the police department and he was counting the days. He could, and would, if asked, tell you exactly how much time he had left - down to the minute.

"Another speeder?"

"Always," replied Kendall. He was one of the three motorcycle officers in the police department. He worked traffic enforcement which meant he wrote hundreds of tickets a year.

Kendall started to say something else when the

prosecutor motioned for him. With nothing else to do for now John stood against the wall and watched what was going on in the courtroom. He spoke to several attorneys who had come in and were impatiently waiting for Larry to finish, for the court process had ground to a halt until this speeding ticket trial was over.

8

It was now Thursday morning and John was sitting in a phone room down in the county law library, which was on the first floor of the courthouse. He put his briefcase down and called his office. Going into his voice mail, he began to listen to his current messages. The second one had come in late Wednesday afternoon from a Lonnie Gilley, who left his phone number and asked John to call him back as soon as possible. John wrote down his name and telephone number then moved on to listen to the next call. Once he had finished, he began the process of calling people back. His third call was to the 281 prefix, which John knew from experience was in Kansas City, Kansas. A male voice answered the phone before the end of the first ring and said, "Rockland's."

"Lonnie Gilley please," said John.

"Just a minute," was the rough reply before he was placed on hold. While he waited, John began looking over his file for the hearing he had in ten minutes.

"Lonnie Gilley," said a voice that John recognized from yesterday's message.

"Mr. Gilley, John Calloway. You called my office late yesterday afternoon."

"Yeah, I did. I've been charged in Olathe and I need a lawyer. One of the guys here used you on a traffic ticket and he gave me your number."

"Well, thank him for that," said John before going on. "What charges do you have?"

"They charged me with blowing up a bar in Bowers Mill, but I…"

"Stop," said John interrupting him before he could say anymore. "It's probably not a good idea to talk about this on the phone." Besides, John was well aware of this case as it had been all over TV for the last two days. Two policemen injured and a fair amount of property damage. It would be good for his career to represent this guy, but he wondered what they would say in Bowers Mill if he ended up being hired. John didn't have an answer for that and so he dismissed this thought - at least for now.

"When can you come see me?" John asked, opening his appointment calendar.

After some discussion, they agreed to meet this coming Saturday morning at nine a.m. The conversation ended with John asking Mr. Gilley to bring any paperwork he had with him to their meeting. The call had taken longer than he expected and heading upstairs, John Calloway barely made it in time for his next hearing.

* * * * *

John Calloway parked in the front lot of his office building shortly before nine on Saturday morning and hurried up the steps. Standing outside the entrance to his office suite was a man which John hoped was Lonnie Gilley. His hair was cut short, but what John noticed more than anything else was the he smelled of machine grease. It was the same odor he had to smell every day at the plant where he had worked during summers while going to college at Missouri.

John introduced himself and shook Mr. Gilley's outstretched hand. He then led the way back to his office where he motioned for Lonnie to sit in one of the chairs in front of his desk. Lonnie Gilley sat down in the one closest to the door.

As he always did, John began by asking for any papers that the client had remembered to bring. Mr. Gilley quickly pulled an envelope out of his pant's pocket and handed it across the desk to John who took out the folded papers and opened them up. The first paper was the state's complaint, listing four charges. This caused John to reach over for a statute book on his bookcase, open it and look at it in several places.

Satisfied with his review, John turned his attention to the next piece of paper in the stack. It was a Bowers Mill Constitutional Rights form. He'd seen hundreds of them. He glanced at it long enough to see that his client had waived his *Miranda* rights.

The last thing he picked up was the bond receipt. Mr. Gilley must have some rich friends; a $100,000 bond required $10,000 in up front money. He would remember this when it came time to discuss his fee. Putting the bond request on top of the other papers, John looked across his desk and began by asking, "When's your next hearing?"

"This Wednesday at three," said Mr. Gilley.

John opened the appointment calendar on his desk. "I can be there," he said, "but I won't write in this court date until we've worked out my fee."

Lonnie didn't say anything to this; he just nodded and waited for Mr. Calloway's next question. He was not to be disappointed.

"So tell me what happened?" asked John, leaning back in his chair as he prepared to listen to the answer.

Lonnie Gilley began talking but was cautious in what he said. He told John what he thought it was safe to say, but was careful to leave out anything that wasn't in his police statement.

When Lonnie finished, John sat up again and asked his first lawyer-type question. "How long were you parked behind the bar, Mr. Gilley? By the way, you can call me John." He was tired of hearing his last name repeated over and over. Besides, most people, he'd learned over time, liked to call their lawyer by his first name.

Lonnie answered the question, ending it by saying, "You can call me Lonnie."

"Why here, Lonnie?" asked John next. He was careful with new clients and tried to ask open-ended questions so they would do most of the talking. It was his way of seeing what kind of witness they would make if they were to testify at trial. He got the same answer that had been given to Detective Stewart. Among other things, including the Four Aces Bar being on a main street, Lonnie said he didn't believe there should be bars as they caused so much misery for people. This was a belief that he had found through prayer at his church and, he reluctantly added, from his experience with his father. Bars, he had come to believe, were agents of corruption and had to be stopped by any means from spreading their evil.

Like Detective Stewart had done before him, John asked, "What church do you belong to that believes as you do?"

"The Covenant of Trinity."

John was surprised by the answer as he recognized the name. "Aren't they the church that is..." and here he paused to decide how to best continue, "...well, let's say, somewhat against people who are not Protestant and white."

It was Lonnie's turn to sit up in his chair. He cleared his throat before saying, "That's not true. We follow the true teachings of the Bible."

The answer came too quickly and John felt it had been rehearsed. He decided not to pursue Lonnie's religious beliefs any further, he could already tell they were beyond where he stood and so he went on to his next question. "Did your church leaders or anyone else, for that matter, who goes there tell you to blow up this bar?"

"No," was the swift reply, rapidly followed by, "I have strong beliefs about bars. This particular place is on a main street where its owners are trying to corrupt people. It's doing the work of Satan, by taking people's minds and money, trying to hook them on evil and stop them from finding eternal salvation."

John had already heard a rendition of this and knew the conversation was headed back to where he didn't want to go – a discussion about religion. He'd heard enough to know that this guy had bought the program his church was pushing. John was getting the feeling Lonnie was a loose cannon, but the name of the church had sounded so familiar to him that he decided to ask a few more questions about it to satisfy his curiosity. "Exactly where is your church?" he asked, then added, "Isn't it southwest of Olathe near the Johnson county line?"

"Well, that's close. It's just in Douglas County," answered Lonnie.

John now remembered why he had heard of this church, but to be sure he asked, "Is Harold Walker one of your leaders?"

"Why yes," said Lonnie sitting up in his chair again. "How do you know that name?"

John didn't want to go any further, so he replied, "Let's just say that I'm acquainted with him through some business dealings."

Lonnie took this answer in, thought about it for a moment, then suddenly pointed a finger at John and said: "You're his boy's lawyer."

"Lonnie, I can't say anymore. Let's say that I know Harold Walker and I'm familiar with your church."

Having said this, John changed the topic and began a discussion of the options he saw for Lonnie. "I see three ways you can go with your case. First is trial. Tell the State we'll see you in court. A great idea in some cases; in your case not even a good idea. Too much emotional value for the DA by putting the injured officers on the stand. The jurors would get to hear what happened and the officers, believe me, would play it to the hilt. So, at least for now, we can forget that option."

Lonnie nodded in agreement.

"The second option is plea bargaining. I haven't talked to anyone in the DA's office to find out who's handling the case and that will make some difference, but not much, because any offer in this case will have to be cleared at the top first. This will, hopefully, deter some of the more zealous ADA's from going too far to the right on the law and order spectrum. You know banishment to Australia, public beatings, the kind of punishments they would like to bring back. Just kidding," said John with a little laugh after seeing the look on Lonnie's face.

Relieved that Lonnie was smiling, John continued, "My guess is that they'll want you to plea to the arson count and one other charge, probably an aggravated battery on one of the officers. The more seriously hurt of the two, I would guess. It'll all depend on if they believe your story about not seeing the police car. If they do, maybe they'll have you plea to the criminal damage to property over $25,000.

Sorry, but I'm thinking out loud here. However, no matter what, there'll be probation for at least two years. And don't forget the restitution. They'll have you paying back several insurance companies for fixing all the damage.

Your next question should be: 'Would I do any time?' That's the question I'd ask, so I'll answer it for you. Yes. How much, I don't know."

Lonnie waited until John finished, then asked, "Give me a guess on how much time they'd want from me," he said.

John reached for another statute book and leafed through it until he found what he was looking for near the middle of the book. "It could be up to 60 days of 'shock time', time to give you a little taste of prison, although you'd serve it here at the county jail, or it could be between twelve to fourteen months in prison. If you get that you're on your way to a real jail, not the country club we have here."

Lonnie said nothing to all this, so John proceeded on to the last option. "The final option is to apply for diversion. With it, you're charged with a crime, but not convicted. It's a privilege, not a right. Don't even think about it. Rarely does anyone with a felony get diversion. But with a case of this type, forget it; it's not even an option. I wanted to tell you about it because someone you know is bound to bring it up. So I'm finished with the options as I see them. It's your turn – do you have any questions for me?"

Lonnie had several. John told Lonnie his estimate of how long it would be before the case could go to trial. He explained the option of diversion in more detail; although he repeated several times that it wasn't an option. He then discussed why Lonnie wouldn't be eligible for house arrest, but would have to serve any time imposed by the judge in jail.

They next discussed John's belief that Lonnie should try to have the statement he made to the detective suppressed, explaining to Lonnie that meant not allowing the DA's office to use it at trial, because the detective used Lonnie's father as a bargaining point. "You can go see him when we're through; we don't know if he's dead or not. Statements like that appear to me to be improper," John went on to say.

The room was silent as Lonnie thought through what he had just heard. Not hearing any more questions, John changed the conversation to the last topic that had not been discussed – money. "It's time to discuss how all much this will cost," he said after waiting to see if there were any more questions.

"That was going to be my next question," replied Lonnie.

"Eight thousand for a plea, fifteen thousand for trial. If you wanted to appeal it would be extra. I know that's a lot but I'll take payments. My usual arrangement is half up front and the balance in thirty days. But it's all somewhat negotiable," said John matter-of-factly.

Lonnie listened intently to all he was being told and when John finished said, "Well, I don't have that kind of money. Now, all I have is $3-400 that I can get my hands on – right now – that's it. But let me do some talking over the weekend and I'll get back to you on Monday. I'm pretty sure I want to use you but I need to talk to some people about coming up with the money."

There was nothing else either of them had to say. John picked up the papers and handed them back to Lonnie who put them back in his pocket. He also took one of John's business cards and put it in the envelope with them.

The two men quickly walked back to the reception area where, after shaking hands, Lonnie left. John had a gut feeling that Lonnie would be back to hire him. Maybe not on Monday but next week. Back in his office he wrote in Lonnie's name and the Wednesday court date in his appointment calendar. However, just to be safe he wrote them in in pencil.

* * * * *

Lonnie left the lawyer's office and drove out to Harold Walker's ranch. When told who he had just come from meeting and wanted to hire, Harold had a hard time containing his anger. His first question to Lonnie was, "Did he say anything about my son?"

"No," replied Lonnie. "He said nothing about him or you. All he'd say about you was that he knew you. That's all."

"Alright, so tell me what you talked about," growled Harold Walker in an official voice, satisfied that Lonnie knew nothing about his own case. Lonnie could tell this was going to be another interrogation like what he had just gone through at the hands of the lawyer.

"Well, don't use him. He's no good," Harold Walker said after listening several times to what Lonnie had to say. Then he added, "I'll get you someone better on Monday."

Having said that, Harold changed the conversation and said no more about John Calloway.

9

Bill Stewart enjoyed his weekend even more than usual. He and his wife went out by themselves on Saturday night, leaving the kids with her mother. Sunday they each took a child to a soccer game in the morning and then, Sunday afternoon, the whole family went to a movie. He would have good news to tell the marriage counselor when they saw her next Wednesday. She had been encouraging Bill and his wife to spend more time together for quite some time.

So it was that Detective Bill Stewart arrived at work Monday morning, just after eight a.m., in a good frame of mind. Walking toward the station, he saw the officer who had transported Lonnie Gilley coming toward him. "How'd it go with Gilley last Wednesday?" he asked, coming up to him.

"Nothing to it. Routine trip," answered Josh Rider.

"No problems of any kind?" Bill enquired, hoping for something unusual to tell his partner.

"Just one, but it was minor – nothing I couldn't handle. He asked for a copy of what he had signed when he decided to talk to you. I found it on the desk with your report. I photocopied it and put it in the inventory envelope. Other than that, he was quiet all the way out to Olathe."

"That was good," said Bill as he continued on into the station, but it was all he could do to put one foot in front of the other without stumbling. "Thanks for handling that," he finally managed to call out over his shoulder.

"Just doing my job," answered back the patrolman.

Once in his office Bill fell into his chair and continued asking himself what he could do about what he had just heard. If Gilley showed that form to any competent attorney he would recognize the error in it immediately. Add to that finding the altered one in the DA's file, which would show up when the police reports were requested by Gilley's attorney, and it would be all over for him. He would be fired, and that would be the least of his worries. He would be charged criminally. Then there would be the inevitable lawsuit for violating Gilley's civil rights. Bill had tried off and on since he discovered the original problem last week to quit thinking about what he had done. All that had suddenly changed. He was now trying mightily to keep himself from getting any more depressed and from throwing up.

Roger Sumler had arrived and was standing in the doorway. Seeing Bill was deep in thought, he threw a pencil at him.

It bounced off the desk, startling Bill and causing him to look in the direction it came from.

Roger saw the blank stare on Bill's face and said, "Hey, we need to go."

The sound of Roger's voice helped Bill focus his eyes on Roger even though the effort was making his stomach feel funny. "We need to go?" asked Bill, slowly repeating the words he thought he had just heard.

"Yes, Bill, we need to go. Remember. Eight-thirty, the meeting. The one we have every Monday at eight-thirty."

"Oh yeah. I need to talk to you Roger, it's sort of important."

"After the meeting. Now are you coming?" Roger shook his head at his partner's behavior, turned and began walking toward the conference room.

Bill still sat at his desk. He went through his desk drawers until he found the aspirin bottle. Whereupon, he took two of them followed by a quick drink of water from the hall fountain. He then joined the other Bowers Mill detectives already gathered in the conference room – the same room where he had interrogated Lonnie Gilley.

Bill managed to follow what was going on at the meeting – a meeting which seemed to last forever. Only occasionally did he think about the Gilley matter. His conclusion after each time was that he had to get the form back.

The meeting lasted one hour. Once it was finished, he left the building with Roger to continue their investigation of a series of burglaries at an apartment complex on West 84th Street. They had to go back to obtain statements from several of the victims who had agreed to a meeting at nine forty- five in the complex clubhouse.

Roger had just started the car when Bill, having contained himself until now, blurted out, "He has a copy of the original rights waiver form." Roger didn't say anything and continued backing the car out of its parking place.

Not getting a response, Bill spoke up again, but this time in a louder voice, "He has a copy of the original rights waiver form."

"You mean the waiver of constitutional rights form," said Roger sarcastically. Then, with a disgusted glance at Bill, he said, "You're in a world of trouble if that form ever gets into the wrong hands."

"Don't you think I know that? We've got a big problem here."

"You certainly do. Don't try to tie me to what you did."

"Au contraire," said Bill. "If I go down, you're going down with me. There were two of us there when the form disappeared. That's conspiracy to obstruct justice, in case you've forgotten."

Roger had nothing more to say and continued driving to their appointment. Finally he spoke up again. This time, though, his voice had lost the sarcasm it had held earlier. "OK, OK, so what can be done to remedy this mess? This could mean ruin for us both, including jail on the criminal charges."

"Don't forget the civil suit for violating his civil rights," Bill glumly added.

Both men lapsed back into silence as they continued on toward the apartment complex. It was Bill who finally spoke up and said, "We have to get the form back."

"Do you know what you're suggesting?" asked Roger. "You're risking everything."

"Yes we are, I know. But what choice do we have? I'm not going to watch my life go down the toilet because of this. Besides, how was I to know it was the old form," said Bill as more of a statement than a question.

"Did you ever think about reading it first, before giving it to Gilley?" replied Roger, who had regained some of his sarcasm back.

"That's not funny," said Bill.

"How do we go about unringing the bell, that's the problem. What's your answer to that?" said Roger as he turned the corner onto 84th Street where he could see the apartment complex up ahead.

"The answer is to go to Gilley's house and get it back," said Bill, somewhat surprised by his own suggestion.

"Just like that," said Roger. He then began speaking in a high-pitched voice, "Oh, it'll be so easy. I can see it now. We knock on the door and when Mr. Gilley opens the door and happily invites us in, we'll say, 'Could we please have back the copy of the form you signed? Here, please take this one in its place along with our apologies. It's the form we meant to have you sign - but we were wrong. Thank you anyway - again.'" Roger couldn't conceal his amazement with this proposed solution; the cure would kill the doctors instead of healing the patient, he thought.

Bill ignored what he had just heard. "We need to do whatever is necessary to get that form back," he said, more to convince himself than for Roger to hear.

"Suppose he's already gone to a lawyer. It may already be too late," offered Roger.

"I said we do whatever is necessary to get that form back," said Bill again, this time looking over at Roger to make sure he got the point.

Roger had another question that needed an answer. "How far are you prepared to go to get it back?" he asked.

Bill had been thinking about this since he first realized the potential repercussions that could happen if the substitute form was discovered. He first thought about the twelve years he had invested in the Bowers Mill police department and then about his wife and kids. The decision was easy to make then; he wasn't willing to let that be taken away by a criminal who had voluntarily admitted to his crimes. Yes, he probably should have looked at the form more closely, but that kind of mistake could happen to anyone. That there was even the slightest chance that Gilley could go free after what he had done; that had to be prevented. He had to repair the damage, that was all there was to it.

"I told you," Bill said, opening the door to get out, "I'll do whatever it takes to get that form back."

Roger felt a sense of dread as he played out in his mind several scenarios involving Bill's phrase, 'Whatever it takes.' He might be part of this, but he still had a sense of right and wrong. As he entered the clubhouse, Roger wondered for how long he would be able to keep up that distinction.

10

For the past six weeks Roger Sumler had not been called out on a case after he got home. His wife was surprised, then, when he came home and told her he and Bill Stewart had to go out this Monday night for a couple of hours. Just as they finished dinner, the doorbell rang. Bill was, for once, on time.

The two men went back over their plan as they drove into Wyandotte County toward the Gilley house. A part of it had been for Roger to bring his wife's cell phone. As they got closer to the Nall address he now used it to call Gilley's home. They had concluded early on that it was better to use Roger's wife's phone rather than one the police department issued in case something went wrong with their plan. There would then be no record of any calls by them to Lonnie Gilley – that is if anyone bothered to check up on them. Both of them were relieved when no one answered.

They had initially considered, and then quickly discarded the idea of directly confronting Gilley about the form. After considering numerous other options, including calling him back in for questioning, they had finally decided the best and safest way to get the form was to break into his house and take it back, that is, if Gilley had left it there. They still didn't have a plan if he carried it with him or left it somewhere else.

As they got closer to where they were going, they began discussing where to leave their unmarked car so that it would attract the least amount of attention – as little as a white Ford could that looked like a police car. They decided to park down the street, if possible. They happily congratulated themselves on this decision when they turned onto Gilley's street and saw it was poorly lit. The fact that there was a light across from the Gilley address wasn't going to be a problem either. It gave off a pale yellow light like it was in the process of burning out.

"Thank God for East Berlin," said Bill. They both laughed at the commonly known nickname for Kansas City, Kansas. It had been given this name years before by the police in Johnson County because it was poor and looked like it that had been bombed out after a war. Besides it was next to Johnson County, the richest county in Kansas, which was affectionately called West Berlin.

They couldn't see any lights on in the Gilley house as they slowly drove past it and hoped this meant no one was home. Bill finally parked on the opposite side of the street three houses away from Gilley's. Before opening the car door, he reached up and turned off the dome light. No use, he thought, in alerting the neighbors to the presence of a strange car parked on their street.

Leaving Roger in the car to handle any emergencies that might arise, Bill began walking back down the street toward Gilley's house. He soon crossed the street and started up the driveway. Stopping in front of the garage, he looked in and was relieved to see it was empty. Continuing up to the front door, he peered through a small windowpane and was happy to see no lights were on in the back of the house. Still unsure of whether someone was there or not, Bill tried knocking on the door and as he did, he hoped the sound wasn't so loud that one of the neighbors would come outside to investigate the noise. Nothing happened. He decided to knock again, this time a little louder. Still no one answered. Bill now tried the doorknob. He fantasized on how nice it would be if the door were unlocked - he could just walk in and look around. But it wasn't, so he knew it was time for him to find another way inside.

Bill quietly walked back the way he had come and then started to go around the side of the garage toward the back of the house. In the back, they had decided, there would be less chance someone would hear or see what he was about to do next. But before he did, Bill looked back toward the car. He couldn't see any movement inside, but he knew Roger was there, watching the street and waiting for him to get back. On the off chance that the KCK police were to show up, the two detectives had decided to say they were looking for Gilley to talk to him again. They both hoped the police didn't come while Bill was in the house. They had no story that would satisfactorily explain why they were there.

Bill turned down the side of the garage and immediately saw a side window. On a hunch, he decided to see if it would open. Placing his fingers under the bottom of the window, he slowly began pushing upward and, to his surprise, the window moved. He quickly looked around and continued pushing until the window stopped moving when it was about two-thirds of the way open. No amount of effort on his part could get it to go higher. He paused again to look around for anything that would show he had been discovered. But luck was still with him, no lights came on and no one rushed out of any of the surrounding houses to demand to know what he was doing.

Having satisfied himself that everything was okay, he stepped into the garage, turned and slowly closed the window behind him. It was then that he remembered to put on the blue latex gloves that were in his coat pocket. They were standard issue and were in all the Bowers Mill police cars for the protection of the officers when working accidents and crime scenes. What better time than now to wear them he thought to himself as he pulled on each of them.

Carefully, he began walking across the concrete floor toward what he hoped was a door into the house. He wasn't disappointed. Bill held a flashlight in one hand, but was afraid to use it – there were so many windows in the garage. In the faint light that filtered in from outside he began searching for the doorknob. Slowly turning it, he was rewarded by the sound of the door beginning to open. God, he knew for sure now, was on his team tonight.

The smell of what Bill called 'old people' now filled his nose and made him gag. He always remembered that smell from his grandmother's house and never seemed to get used to it. Looking around, he found himself standing in the kitchen. He was able to make out a stack of dishes piled up next to the sink. Their outline was fairly visible from the light coming through the window behind the sink. Bill wanted to close the curtains on either side of it, but decided that would be a no-no as one of the neighbors might notice. Burglary, he had come to realize, was more work than he had originally thought.

Holding his watch up in the moonlight, he saw that ten minutes had passed since he had left the car. He had to hurry. He and Roger had previously agreed that Bill would be gone for no more than twenty minutes. Time was starting to work against him.

Lonnie Gilley had told Bill during his interrogation that he lived in the basement. This was probably where the form was if it was here. Still, he had to do a quick look around the rest of the house just to be sure it wasn't sitting out somewhere else. Moving out of the kitchen he entered the living room and quickly searched it, again using the dim light from the feeble street light across the street. He didn't find what he was looking for in there or, for that matter, in either of the two bedrooms that were down a hall.

Bill had just finished looking around the back bedroom and was headed back through the living room when the reflection from a pair of headlights bounced off the wall behind him. His heart started pounding and his T-shirt became damp almost instantly. He froze where he stood and, out of habit, reached for his gun. But just as quickly as they had appeared the lights faded away as the car backed out of the Gulley driveway and out into the street. Bill took this opportunity to rush over to the side of the picture window in the living room and peer outside. He could see the headlights belonged to a car that had just finished parking in front of the house next door. He watched as someone, who looked to be sixteen or seventeen, got out of the car and walked up to the house, disappearing out of sight. Bill now shifted his view enough to look back up the street at his car. There was no way to know if Roger felt like he did at this moment.

Satisfied he hadn't been discovered, Bill moved away from the window and back toward the kitchen where he had passed the door to the basement. Unwilling to take a chance with the flashlight, Bill groped about until he found the railing and began his descent into the darkness below. It was so dark he couldn't see anything, so he concentrated on listening for any sound that might indicate the presence of someone down there.

This thought soon became too much to think about and Bill stopped momentarily and let go of the rail. Using this free hand, he took the flashlight out of his pocket and turned it on. That continued his luck because he then found himself on the next to the last stair. Before him was a large open area with no windows. Moving the beam from the light around, it soon fell on a sparsely furnished area off to his right. There a bed with a dresser that didn't match and an overstuffed chair were sitting on top of a fairly large piece of carpet. At one end of the bed was a table with a small television on it, its single antenna covered with a crumpled piece of aluminum foil. "Gawd, they don't even have cable down here," he said out loud.

The light then fell on a washer and dryer sitting in another corner. Finally, shelves filled with magazines, boxes of Christmas ornaments and several small appliances lined the wall beside the bed.

Reassured that no one was down there except him, Bill took the final step and walked over to the TV table. Scattered over one end of it was a pile of papers, including several unopened envelopes addressed to Lonnie Gilley. Bill looked through the pile but found nothing that even remotely looked like the waiver form or, for that matter, any of the other papers that went with Gilley when he left the police station.

He went over to the dresser and began looking through the papers lying on top of it, but, again, none of them were what he was searching for. However, as he started to open the top drawer, he saw a business card in an ashtray. It had the name "John D.Calloway, Attorney at Law" printed on it. He knew of Calloway, he was the public defender in Bowers Mill. His office address and the usual parade of numbers were also on the card. Turning it over, he saw nothing was written on the back. Apparently, though, Gilley had been to see a lawyer. He carefully put the card back where he had found it and grimly hoped they were not too late to get the form back.

A quick search of the dresser drawers and then under and around the bed also failed to turn it up. Bill reluctantly came to the realization that the form was not there; but where was it - that was now the pressing question. One thing for sure, they would now have to go visit Calloway's office. He knew Roger would not be happy to hear this news.

Bill turned the flashlight off at the bottom of the stairs and carefully climbed back up to the first floor. He then left the same way he had come into the house. Standing outside of the now closed garage window, Bill stood there long enough to take off the blue gloves. In the process of putting them back into his pocket, he saw the outline of his footprints on the soft ground. Using his right foot, he smudged them over and then quietly walked toward the front of the garage. He stopped again, this time to look toward the parked car that had scared him earlier. Satisfied that it was empty, he began walking back to his car.

Detective Stewart took one last look around to see if anyone was watching him before hurriedly opening his car door. To his relief, Roger was still sitting in the passenger's seat – playing with a cigarette.

Without saying anything, the detective started the engine and, with great effort, made himself slowly drive up the street. Roger had started asking questions the moment his partner had gotten back in the car, but Bill waved them off until he had satisfied himself that they weren't being followed.

"I didn't find it," he said as they headed back the way they had come into Wyandotte County.

"All that time in there and you didn't get it?" exclaimed Roger.

"I looked everywhere, it just wasn't there. It may be at the attorney's office," said Bill in a dejected voice.

"What attorney?" shot back Roger as he finished his cigarette.

"John Calloway."

"You mean the public defender? How'd you find that out?"

"I found his card in the basement."

"I thought you were there to find the form," said Roger, still unhappy at hearing the results of the search.

"I looked everywhere, it just wasn't there. It may be at Calloway's office," said Bill hopefully and continuing to keep his eyes on the road he added, "We have to check Calloway's office. Back at the house when that car turned in the driveway, I'd have told you I was done looking for it. But that was then and this is now." The decision he had just pronounced gave Bill a headache. This time he knew he couldn't do it by himself. Roger would have to come in with him.

They drove back into Johnson County and continued on the highway until they got off at the College Boulevard exit. Here they drove east, almost to Metcalf, before turning onto a side street where they knew the building they were searching for was located. They pulled into an empty parking lot and stopped near the building entrance. There was no need to hide anymore; they were back in their county. Here, if anyone challenged them, they could always say they were on official business.

The lobby, like the parking lot, was empty when they entered the four-story building. The list of tenants was posted on the wall opposite the elevator. John Calloway's office and those of several other attorneys was listed as being in Suite 105.

The entrance to the office they wanted was on the same side of the lobby as the tenant listing. Out of habit, Roger tried the front door; it was locked. The two detectives then followed the hallway that led away from the building entrance. They continued a short distance down it to where they found an unmarked door that had to be the back entrance to Calloway's office.

Stopping in front of it, Bill looked up and down the hall as he put back on the blue latex gloves that he had taken out of his coat pocket. He tried the door handle - it didn't open. But then he bent down and carefully studied the lock and the area around it for a moment.

"The frame was put in backwards. See - the bolt's exposed. Watch this," he said as he straightened up and proceeded to take out his wallet. "What's it to be, the gasoline or the store card? I know, choose one," said Bill holding out the two cards toward Roger.

"Don't you think we should get on with this?" said Roger angrily. "After all, we are in the middle of a crime."

"Sorry, but I've been so tense, I thought it would help to lighten things up," said Bill. Quickly putting away one of the cards, he took the other one and placed it between the door and the exposed bolt. Pushing down on the card he used his other hand to pull on the door handle at the same time. It readily opened. Bill let out a sigh of relief and looked over at Roger and said, "Who says TV doesn't teach you anything?" Then he started to laugh, but quickly caught himself.

The good news to Bill was that this time he didn't feel nervous. After all, he had been in a similar situation less than an hour before and, just like before, the area in front of him was dark. This time, however, he immediately used his flashlight to find a light switch and turn on the lights.

"No one will check on us," he said confidently. Then he added, "Anyone who might see us will think we work here. Now let's find Calloway's office."

They were standing in a short hallway near the open door to an office that looked like it belonged to a secretary. Roger went in and over to the phone. "Here it is," he said pointing to a piece of paper sticking out from under it. "It's thirty-four."

"What's thirty-four?"

"That's his extension. Got it off the list of extensions here. Thirty-four - that's Calloway's extension." Roger then picked up the phone, pushed the intercom button and pressed the two numbers on the dial pad. Off in the distance a phone began to ring.

"Brilliant work. Crime suits you Roger," said Bill as he followed the sound down a hallway to an office where he saw a red light blinking in the dark. "That's enough, I've found it," he said over his shoulder in a loud whisper.

Bill reached in to the now silent room and ran his hand along the wall until he touched the light switch. He flipped it on as Roger came up and joined him. Together they found themselves looking into a small office. On the wall in front of them was an oil portrait of a man, probably a relative of Calloway's. A bookshelf and a low file cabinet were to the left of the door and on the wall behind the desk were hung several diplomas and certificates.

"Where do you want to start?" said Roger after finishing his look around the room.

"Why not with that?" said Bill pointing to an appointment calendar that lay open on the desk. He went over and picked it up, then turned the pages back to the previous week and started scanning the entries. And there it was, penciled in on Saturday at 9:00 a.m., Gilley's name and telephone number. Satisfied with finding that entry, Bill then turned the pages forward looking for the next entry with Gilley's name. There wasn't one. He checked it twice to make sure, then put the book back where he had found it and turning to Roger said, "I found where they had a meeting, but nothing else after that."

Roger had remained in the doorway and watched as Bill went through the calendar. He now pointed toward the file cabinet and said, "Check in there to be sure there's no file."

Bill moved over and opened the top drawer. He thumbed through the files until he found the "G's". There were only four files under that letter, none of which had Gilley's name on it. Satisfied there was no file, he closed the drawer, but just to be sure he opened the bottom one. The files in there were also alphabetized and picked up where the top drawer left off. That was it, except for the desk, which Bill proceeded to search. He found nothing there either. "Nothing in here," he said triumphantly. "Let's go find his secretary's desk."

As Bill went by him Roger turned off the light and began following behind him into one of the secretarial cubes that filled the open area outside Calloway's office. They both stood in a cubicle looking at the desks for something that might show if part of this area was used by Calloway's secretary. They found nothing.

They proceeded over to the next cubicle which, like the last one, contained two desks. Nothing on either desk had Calloway's name on it. On the corner of one of the desks, Roger saw a black plastic box and on a hunch picked it up and opened the lid. It was filed with 3x5 cards, all with the initials "JC" in one corner of each card. Roger knew only one attorney in this office had the initials "JC" – John Calloway. He nudged Bill in the side with his elbow as he looked through the cards. Lonnie Gilley's name, however, was on none of them. He closed the box and made sure he placed it back on the desk exactly where he had found it. Secretaries, he knew, had a sixth sense that told them when someone got into their stuff.

"I don't think he hired Calloway," said Roger. "At least he's not in the case index," he added, pointing to the box after he was sure it was back in its right place.

"That's too bad," said Bill, "You know what that means – we may have to break into another office."

"Well it won't be tonight, I've had it," said Roger, turning to go back the way they had come. "I'm getting out of here."

Bill fell in behind him and they started back toward the door they had come in originally. As they drew near it, they suddenly heard the sound of a key being inserted in the lock. Terrified, Bill grabbed Roger's coat and pulled him back and through an open doorway just as the door opened.

They found themselves cowering in the law office library, listening as the sound of footsteps came toward their hiding place. Bill began to panic and he reached for his gun. Holding his breath, he tightened his hold on the grip as he waited for whoever was coming down the hallway to appear in front of him. But abruptly and without warning, the footsteps began to fade away and soon the noise of a vacuum cleaner could be heard.

"Cleaning man," whispered Bill as he took his hand off his gun.

The two detectives edged out of the library and out into the hallway. Keeping their eyes in the direction of where the sound was coming, they saw no one and then ran to the door. The sound of the machine could still be heard as they quietly closed the door behind them. Rapidly walking across the lobby, they left by way of the entrance they had so confidently entered earlier. Once outside, they fell into a casual walk as they made their way to the car.

"He hasn't got it," Roger said once they were back in the car.

"That's apparent," replied Bill as he started the car. He was drained and could tell his shirt was soaked - again.

"What's next?" asked Roger hesitantly. He hadn't wanted to get in this position, one where he had to ask this question, because he was afraid of the answer.

"Gilley's next court appearance comes up this Wednesday. We'll go see if a lawyer enters his appearance on his behalf," said Bill.

This was an answer Roger didn't want to hear. It wasn't the one he was afraid of but he knew had to hear that answer too, so he asked, "And if no one does?"

"Then we may be forced to have a meeting with Mr. Gilley to discuss the missing form," said Bill matter-of-factly.

"And if he does have an attorney?" inquired Roger in a low voice. Low, because, he had just heard the answer he had been afraid to hear.

"You're asking too many questions, Roger, for a man that has just committed at least two felonies. You know the answer, second verse same as the first." And with that Bill turned on the radio to break the tension in the car.

11

The two detectives arrived at the forth floor reception area of the District Attorney's Office just after two-thirty. The booking tape they carried with them had been requested earlier in the week by one of the ADA's, whose trial assistant came out and took it from Roger. Finished with the reason that allegedly had brought them out to Olathe, the detectives took the stairs down to the third floor and the Division CR2 courtroom. There was no one in there. They decided to sit in the corner on the far west side of the courtroom, next to the windows, and wait for the three o'clock docket. Within five minutes, people began coming into the courtroom and it steadily filled up as it got closer to three. The two detectives looked at everyone who entered, but Lonnie Gilley was not among them.

At precisely three p.m., a door on the left side of the courtroom opened and the administrative assistant walked in and asked everyone to rise. Following closely behind her was Judge Katherine Ruth, who went up the two steps to her chair, and then told everyone to be seated.

She called the first case by its number, following that with the defendant's name. No one answered, so she called the case a second time, and still getting no response, ordered a bench warrant for the defendant's arrest, revoked his current bond and set a new bond that was double the old amount. This procedure was followed in the next two cases. Judge Ruth was now ready for her fourth case in five minutes on the bench.

The fourth defendant and her attorney both rose when her name was called. Everyone having put their names in the record, the court began the process of scheduling the next court appearance based, in part, upon what the lawyers wanted to have occur. As this was being done, Lonnie Gilley hurriedly came into the courtroom. Without looking to either side, he quickly walked forward and sat down on a bench near the front of the courtroom. From the opposite side of the courtroom the two detectives watched Lonnie as he nervously waited for his name to be called.

Judge Ruth finished writing her notes in the court file in front of her. Then, carefully placing the closed file on top of her stack of completed cases, she picked up the next file and opened it. Looking up, she called out the case number and the defendant's name: "10-A-1758, Lonnie Andrew Gilley. Appearances please."

"State by Brandon Thorwich," said the ADA who barely rose out of his chair as he spoke. No attorney entered an appearance on behalf of the defendant. The detectives looked at each other and smiled.

Judge Ruth didn't bother to look up and called the case number and name again. This time she looked up and saw a man standing. "Are you Mr. Gilley?" she asked, somewhat exasperated by having to call the case twice.

The man nodded and answered, "Yes."

Motioning him toward the podium, she said, "Mr. Gilley, you need to come forward and speak your name into the microphone so we can get your appearance on the record."

Lonnie pushed open the gate separating the public section of the courtroom from the rest of it and hesitantly walked to where the Judge had pointed. Judge Ruth patiently waited until he spoke his name into the microphone, then asked in a stern voice, "Where's your attorney? Judge Oliver's notes indicate that you said you would bring one to this hearing."

"I haven't hired one yet," was the sheepish reply.

"These are serious charges Mr. Gilley," said the Judge, looking down at the file again. "I also see you declined the services of the Public Defender's Office. Are you sure you can afford to hire an attorney?"

"Yes," replied Lonnie.

"When?" asked Judge Ruth. She had been doing criminal cases too long not to ask this question. If she didn't push them to act, she knew many defendants would procrastinate forever.

"I have an appointment this Friday with Alexander Collins," said Lonnie somewhat defensively.

Hearing this, Bill took out a piece of paper and wrote down the lawyer's name. He knew of Alex Collins. Collins represented many people considered to be right wing nuts. He was also known not to cut corners and he wasn't one to pull the trigger immediately, that is, go to trial quickly. But, when he did go to trial, he was an above average trial attorney, and for that reason Bill was impressed by Gilley's choice.

Judge Ruth raised her hand to forestall any further talking by this defendant; besides, she'd heard enough. "You need to get a lawyer, Mr. Gilley. I'm continuing this case for two weeks for you to hire one, be it Mr. Collins or someone else. However, you need to have an attorney with you when you come back, because your case will be set for a probable cause hearing at that time."

The two detectives had heard enough and left the courtroom while Lonnie was still at the podium. They took the stairs down to the next floor and went out the south exit of the courthouse. On their way down the steps Roger quietly said; "Well, he doesn't have a lawyer yet."

"But he will," said Bill. "We must arrange a visit with Mr. Gilley before he has the opportunity to see Mr. Collins – who's all too capable of hitting a home run with the form if he gets the chance to read it."

Roger felt sick as he heard what his partner said. This feeling seemed to be happening more and more whenever he thought about what he was doing in the Gilley case.

"I'm not so sure we should do that, Bill. How will we get him to talk to us voluntarily?" he asked, hoping the answer would be gentle on his stomach.

Bill glanced over at him and said, "We'll find a way. It's down to him or us. I know who's more important to me. How about you?"

It was hard for Bill to tell if what he was saying was producing the desired effect on Roger so he went on, "You're free to go home anytime and tell Rachael – and the kids – not to worry, but unfortunately you're expecting to be indicted soon. Then you can look forward to several years away from them. That is – if you're sent some place where you can be protected from the inmates, otherwise you can tell your family 'good bye forever,' before you leave."

Roger gritted his teeth as he forced the words out between them. "I still don't like it," he said, putting his hand on his churning stomach.

Bill was tired of shoring up his partner's resolve. "Well, get used to it," he said. "You're in this as deep as me, too deep to get out now without getting badly burned."

They had been walking to their car when Bill turned and looked back at the courthouse. "Let's wait here for Gilley," he said.

"Why?" asked Roger as he finished lighting a cigarette.

"Don't start acting stupid, Roger, you know why," sputtered Bill. "If you're still nervous, you can go to the car and wait for me there. I, on the other hand, want to see where Gilley goes after he leaves the courthouse."

Bill had stopped beside the cornerstone to the old courthouse which, for reasons he had never figured out, was on the lawn near Cherry Street. Roger didn't have the energy to fight any more and he went on back to the car to wait.

Bill leaned up against the cornerstone and watched the people go in and out of the courthouse. He didn't have long to wait before he saw Lonnie Gilley come down the steps and continue on along a sidewalk that cut diagonally between the courthouse and the administration building to the south of it. Bill watched as he crossed over to the far side of Cherry Street and on toward the public garage which was a block east of the administration building.

Hurrying back to the car, Bill backed out into the street and drove slowly south as he kept Gilley in sight. Seeing Lonnie enter the garage, he pulled into an empty parking spot beside the administration building and waited.

Lonnie Gilley was inside the garage for only a few minutes before he drove out and turned left. Stopping at the corner, he turned right and continued over to Kansas Avenue. When the light changed he turned south toward Interstate 35 - two miles away.

* * * * *

Bill Stewart was in no hurry to catch up to the car in front of him. He kept far enough behind it to just keep the car in sight. He lost sight of it once, but sped up until he saw it pass by the Olathe Municipal Court building on the way to the highway entrance.

Twenty minutes after leaving the courthouse in Olathe, Lonnie Gilley took the Westridge Road exit off Interstate 35 and continued driving south. At 221st Street he turned right and drove west on a dirt road for two miles before turning south again, this time down a narrow lane at the end of which stood a house that was partially hidden behind a stand of trees. Parking beside the red pickup truck, Lonnie Gilley hurried up the steps and entered the house. He saw neither the white car that passed slowly by the entrance to the lane nor the man with the binoculars who watched him as he climbed the steps.

12

Lonnie's meeting with Alexander Collins, JD, was to be Friday at eleven. It had been arranged by Harold Walker who had then told – more like ordered – Lonnie when and where to meet him. Like John Calloway, Alexander Collins asked that Lonnie bring all his court papers with him. These papers were now upstairs lying on top of the dresser in the bedroom where Lonnie Gilley was now staying.

It was Harold Walker who had suggested that Lonnie stay at his ranch after he was released from the Johnson County jail – and Lonnie had quickly agreed. He felt safer at Captain Walker's house given what he had just been through.

* * * * *

Lonnie opened the front door and saw Harold Walker sitting on the sofa. Spread out on the table in front of him were the parts to a handgun. He was clutching a cloth in one hand and holding a part to the gun in the other.

"How'd it go?" said Captain Walker, looking up at Lonnie and continuing with what he was doing.

"Okay," said Lonnie, "my case was continued for two weeks so I could get a lawyer."

"Alex Collins is a good man. Better than the other lawyer you went to see – John Calloway. Collins will take care of you. He thinks like us," he said with emphasis on the "us" before carefully putting down the gun part he had been cleaning and picking up another.

Lonnie nodded in agreement, just as he did every time the Captain talked about his case. He knew now that he should have checked with Captain Walker before going to see John Calloway. After the mistake that experience could have been, the Captain had made him promise that he would do what was right from then on. So, on Friday, he would go see the lawyer that Captain Walker had arranged to represent him.

And tonight – tonight he was going to church to thank the congregation for having paid his bond and also his lawyer. Things – life – had been better since he had come back from Texas and joined this church. He vowed that once these charges were behind him he would pay them all back. He continued standing as he asked, "What time do I need to be ready to go tonight?"

Without looking up, Captain Walker replied, "We'll need to leave by 7:15."

The Captain's son, Gerald, who had been on the floor absorbed in a television show, heard this part of their conversation and spoke up. "Can I go, too?" he asked.

"Not tonight son, maybe next time," said Harold. "Tonight we're going to have a long service. Besides, you know your cousin's coming over."

"I don't like Robin anymore. All she does is talk on the phone," replied Gerald.

Harold had heard this complaint before. And now, just like all the other times, he said, "Son we've talked all about this. Every time you tell me you like having Robin here – no matter what she's doing. You know you have plenty to do before bedtime, like homework for one, that don't involve her."

"Yes daddy," said Gerald, continuing to look at his television show.

Harold put this newly cleaned gun part down and picked up another one. Looking over at Gerald, he went on, "Now go set the table. We need to get supper ready if we're going to leave on time."

Gerald got up off the floor and went around the corner into the kitchen. Lonnie moved over and sat down in the recliner near one end of the sofa.

Glancing first in the direction his son had just gone, the Captain then lowered his voice and said, "Did you follow my orders?"

Lonnie, too, kept his voice low as he answered, "Yes sir, I did. No one followed me here," he replied.

"You've got to be careful Corporal Gilley. The cops will go to any means to learn about our business."

Lonnie nodded as the Captain continued, "They're part of the illegal government. You know what they did at Ruby Ridge - those people there didn't have a chance."

The Captain was forever telling his congregation about the need to be careful and to always watch out for the occupation troops, as he referred to the police. The congregation meant the members of the Covenant of Trinity Church. It owned a building about half a mile west of the Johnson County line, just far enough into Douglas County to be free from prying eyes. Services were held on Sunday mornings and Wednesday nights. Its forty-five members considered themselves to be true Christians, who believed the Bible was written for God's chosen people, the white race. All others had no place in their church or, for that matter, even using the Bible. They considered it desecration for the Mexican race or Negroes to even think that the word of God applied to them. Catholics were not welcome either. In fact, they had no place even being in Kansas. It was God's will that they, as members of the true Church, rid Kansas of all of them. Jews were not even worth discussing.

There were other Covenant churches whose beliefs were the same as the Trinity Church. As a group they had once used the Internet to keep in touch with one another, but within the last year they were forced to stop when the commander of one of the Illinois churches was charged by the federal government with sending what they called "terrorist material" over state lines. To get around this problem, the churches devised a messenger system whereby computer discs were exchanged between churches every two weeks. Though still in constant contact with each other, each Covenant Church was now considered separate from the others and sovereign over its own matters.

Sundays after church services, a rotating group of members met at Captain Walker's for military training. These were not large groups, but small gatherings of no more than seven or eight people at a time, as Captain Walker had decided that the smaller numbers were less likely to draw the attention of outsiders.

This branch of the Covenant Church had been founded five years ago. Its establishment had been one of the reasons that Harold Walker's wife had left him. Ralene Walker had trouble accepting the rigid rules that covered most aspects of member's lives. However, it was the open prejudice that was hardest for her tolerate. Even if she was from Arkansas, a state not known for tolerance, she had been taught by her family to respect people and look for similarities not differences. She had forced herself to endure her husband's constant ranting and ravings, as she called it, but when his opinions had started to affect their child - this she could not accept. She started to take Gerald with her when she left Harold, but he had threatened to hide Gerald from her forever if she tried to take him then or in any divorce proceedings. Ralene, reluctantly, agreed to leave him behind but, in exchange, she extracted from Harold his promise not to discuss his religious beliefs around Gerald or involve him in any aspect of his Church. Harold had kept his word for the most part – with the lone exception of military training. This he decided was not a religious issue, but the right of a father to do for his son. Gerald, therefore, took part in the training exercises every Sunday and had done so since just after Ralene left and went back to her parent's house near Rogers, Arkansas.

On Wednesdays it was not unusual for one or more of the members of the church to be invited to Captain Walker's for dinner. He used this time to impress on the invited dinner guests the need to keep the church and its teachings central in their lives. But tonight only the three of them ate at the kitchen table.

Robin Brown got there a little before seven o'clock. She came through the front door carrying a blue backpack slung over one shoulder.

Gerald greeted her from the living room floor where he was now lying down watching another show. They both knew that the backpack meant that, unlike other nights, this one would be quiet as Robin had homework to do.

Hearing the front door open, Harold got up from the kitchen table to see who was coming into the house. Seeing it was Robin, he came out and asked how her mother, his sister, was doing as he walked toward her. Barely listening to her answer, he then told Robin he would be back by 10:00 p.m. and closed the front door behind him as he left.

Robin went into the kitchen and called for Gerald to come help her clean up. He was given his regular job of loading the dishwasher and then taking out the trash, jobs Robin had him do every Wednesday.

Robin started the dishwasher and then picked her backpack up off the floor and put it on the kitchen table. Settling into one of the chairs, she soon had papers and books arranged around her. Periodically she would pick a book up, read in it and then write something down in the open notebook in front of her. She had been working for about forty-five minutes when Gerald ran into the room and said, "There's a car coming down the lane."

Robin put her pencil down and got up to see who it was. As she stood looking out one of the living room windows, all she could make out was the car's white color as it pulled up next to her car and turned off its lights. She watched for someone to get out but no one did, although Robin could see two people in the front seat. The passenger was a large man who was smoking a cigarette. She didn't recognize him as anyone she knew.

"What'll we do?" asked Gerald who was standing beside her.

"I don't know," said Robin. She felt nervous, but not overly so. "They're probably some people from the church coming by to pick up or leave something on the way to the service," she finally said.

"Shouldn't we call the sheriff?" asked Gerald eagerly.

"No," came her quick answer to his question. Her Uncle Harold had always told Robin that in the event of any trouble she was to call her mother first. She looked at the car again and then left Gerald to watch it while she went to the kitchen phone to follow his instructions. Her home telephone was busy so Robin hung up, waited a few seconds, and tried again. This time was no different than the last – it was still busy.

She was starting to get a little more nervous and hurriedly went back to the window to see what, if anything had happened in her absence. She could see the large man was still in the passenger seat. He and whoever else was with him had been sitting out there for almost five minutes without making any attempt to get out of the car. This coupled with the fact she couldn't reach her mother was starting to bother her.

"Why don't they get out?" she finally said in frustration.

Gerald didn't have an answer; but, instead, had a question of his own. "You want me to get one of daddy's guns?" he said looking up at his cousin.

"No, no guns," said Robin. "You know what he told you."

"I know he said I'm not to handle any gun unless he's here. But this is different" volunteered Gerald.

"No guns, Gerald," she said again. Determined to talk to her mother, Robin told Gerald to stay where he was and to holler out if anything happened, while she went back to try and get her mother on the phone again. The line was still busy. Robin stood holding the phone in one hand, not knowing what to do, when Gerald cried out for her to come back. She dropped the phone and rushed back to the living room just in time to see the driver get out of the car. At the same time, she saw that the passenger was in the process of getting out also. The two men appeared to be talking to each other, but upon seeing Robin standing in the window they both turned and looked up at her. This made Robin very scared and she grabbed Gerald's arm and pulled him closer to her. As she did, the two men began walking toward the front of the house.

Looking down at Gerald, Robin motioned for him to go towards the back door. She tried to join him, but couldn't make her feet move. Outside she could now hear the sound of footsteps coming across the porch. They came to a stop and there was no sound out there – nothing. She was straining to hear something, any sound that would tell her where the two men were, when a knock on the door made her cry out.

She turned to leave but before she could move any further away, a second knock interrupted her. Out of the corner of her eye she saw her cousin was now standing by the back door watching her. This at least, she thought to herself, was good.

Someone knocked on the door again. This time she saw that the thinner of the two men now stood in front of one of the living room windows looking in at her and pointing toward the door.

The sight of him made Robin yell to her cousin to open the back door as she ran to join him. Robin grabbed his hand and together they stumbled down the steps and across the driveway toward the barn. She stopped at a gate just long enough to unlock and fling it open; then, grabbing Gerald's hand again, she pulled him with her as she ran into the field and toward the distant fence line. Behind her she could hear a loud voice ordering her to stop. Robin turned around long enough to see that the two men were standing in the driveway looking in her direction, before she turned back and continued running across the plowed ground.

Fifty feet from the fence line she slowed down to catch her breath and look back at the house again. She was unable to see if anyone was following them, but immediately realized that it wouldn't be hard to do so as their footprints could clearly be seen coming across the wet field. She and Gerald walked the few remaining feet to the fence, climbed in between the strands of barbed wire, and ran into the trees beyond where they were quickly hidden in the deep shadows.

"If we keep going that way, we'll come to 221st," said Robin whispering into Gerald's ear as she pointed to the north. Gerald nodded in agreement. He couldn't see where she was pointing because it was so dark, but he knew which direction she meant.

The two cousins had stopped to catch their breath again. All the while they kept glancing toward the light on the horizon that told of the location of the house. As their breathing returned to normal, they moved out onto the old cow path that ran between the edge of the trees and the fence and began walking toward the road. Stopping occasionally, they then listened for any sounds that might indicate they were being followed. They also periodically looked out across the field searching for any signs of movement. Each time they neither heard nor saw anything.

The cousins were as careful as they could be not to make any loud noises and this slowed their way along the path. Robin led and Gerald, for the most part, followed behind her. Sometimes he would walk beside her but the thickness of the brush and the narrowness of the path made that difficult.

They had been walking for several minutes when suddenly a beam of light suddenly crossed the path ahead of them and continued on into the forest. Robin froze in her tracks. Stunned, she looked toward the house and watched as the beam seemed to bounce along toward the fence. Absorbed in watching the light, Gerald had continued walking until he ran into her back.

He was just about to say something when Robin put her hand over his mouth and in a low whisper said, "Be quiet. They don't know where we are."

As she spoke the light ahead of them rose and then fell. Robin knew this meant the owner of the flashlight was now over the fence and would soon find the cow path. It was just a few feet inside the fence line and would be impossible to miss. Robin had not yet moved from the spot where she had first seen the light. Her mind was racing with thoughts about what would happen to them if they were found. Two voices could now be heard talking in the darkness ahead of them. She tried to listen to what they were saying but it was difficult. She strained and heard as one of them started speaking again, this time close to where she stood.

"Listen. I think I hear them."

"Where?" asked the other one.

"Over there," came the answer, "Didn't you hear a branch break?"

"Well, I heard something. But how do you know it's them?"

There was no immediate answer to this question, but Robin knew they were talking about her. In the first move she had taken since seeing the light, she had stepped on a branch, which had immediately broken. She knew it was now only a matter of time before the light would find them where they stood if she didn't do something quickly. She decided not to let that happen. Reaching down while keeping her eyes on the light, she grabbed Gerald's arm and gently pulled him off the path and down beside a tree.

"What was that?" said one of the male voices.

Robin held her breath and tried to move closer to the tree. She could feel Gerald trying to do the same thing.

"Sounds like a forest noise," replied a different voice. "Why don't you go check it out to be sure?"

"Yea, right, not me. I'm not up for that, but it sounded like movement in that direction." And with that, a beam of light broke through the darkness and went just over the top of Robin's head. At the same time she could hear the men beginning to move through the brush in her direction.

"Look! Here's a path," exclaimed one of the voices.

"See any footprints?" asked the other.

The light now swung away and she rose up enough to see it move up and down the path.

"None," came the reply.

"We'll have to split up and check this trail out," said the voice behind the light. And with that a second light appeared.

"I'm not so sure that's such a good idea," said the closer of the two voices.

"Afraid of two kids, are we?"

"Shut up, which way do you want to go?"

Before she could hear the answer Robin felt Gerald gently pulling on her arm. She turned away from the lights and saw him crawling on his hands and knees deeper into the forest. Robin knew she had no choice but to go after him. Together the two of them crept further into the darkness. Behind them the voices had fallen silent.

After what seemed like several minutes Robin grabbed one of Gerald's pant legs and he stopped and waited for her to come up beside him. Cautiously they then turned to see if they could locate the owners of the flashlights, but saw nothing in either direction. Both lights had disappeared and this prompted Robin to pray their owners had given up and left.

The only light was coming from the house whose outline they could barely see off in the distance. Suddenly, a shadow passed in front of the outline. Robin started to gasp, caught herself, and began to point toward what she had just seen.

Gerald reached out and quickly pulled her arm back down, then leaned over and whispered in her ear, "They've turned off their flashlights. You can hear them, if you're quiet."

They sat in silence for what seemed to Robin like an hour and heard nothing, when off to the right came the sound of a low whistle. Almost immediately and directly in front of them there came a reply followed by two flashlights coming on simultaneously. The whistles were replaced by voices, voices that Robin immediately recognized as voices she had heard earlier. She almost felt relieved to know it was them and not someone else.

"No dice, I didn't find anything. Did you?" said one voice.

"Nothing. I have no idea where they went after they got into the trees."

"Forget it then. If they're still out here I'd be surprised. They're probably on their way to that farmhouse, the abandoned one to the east of here that we saw the other day. Let's go back to the house. What we want may still be there."

The other man agreed as the two flashlights began to retreat back across the field. When Robin was sure they were far enough away that they couldn't see her, she stood up. Gerald quickly followed. They stood watching the house and hoping to see a car leave as they worked their way back to the cow path.

Once there Robin said in a normal voice, "Let's go to the road."

It took them ten minutes of careful walking with frequent stops before they came to a barbed wire fence that separated them from 221st street. Gerald had no sooner begun to crawl between two of the strands of wire when a bright light appeared on the mailboxes across from the ranch entrance, immediately followed by a car which then turned onto the road in his direction. Gerald stepped back through the fence and he and Robin disappeared back into the woods again. They stopped this time beside a large maple tree and watched as the car slowly came toward them – that is until a beam of light flooded their side of the road. Instinctively, the two cousins dropped to the ground and back onto the wet leaves. As they watched, the light grew brighter and brighter as it searched along the edge of the open field toward the tree they were lying behind.

"Do you think they saw me?" asked Gerald.

Robin had wanted to put her hand over his mouth, but didn't because she was afraid that whoever was in the car would see her. She settled on stammering out, "Shhh! Stop talking," in a very low voice.

They both fell silent as the car continued on toward them, its spotlight still probing the side of the road as it moved forward. As the light crept past them, Robin raised up just enough to see it was the same car that had been parked in front of her cousin's house. A short distance past their tree the spotlight went out and the white car picked up speed.

"They're gone," said Robin as the sound of the car faded off in the distance. She then jumped to her feet and ran to the fence in time to see the taillights of the car grow smaller and smaller until they disappeared over the top of a hill.

Uncertain of whether it would come back or not, the cousins decided to stay where they were for now. They did this until they felt the cold again. This convinced them they had waited long enough and they climbed through the wire and ran back to the house.

Robin had a strange sense of dread as she walked across the porch toward the front door. She couldn't see that anything was wrong but what, she wondered, had those men wanted. She looked in one of the windows, half-afraid that she would see someone staring at her, before letting out a sigh of relief when she saw no one in the room. Going back to the door, she tried the handle but it was still locked; just as she had left it.

Gerald continued to follow Robin as she went around to the back door. It, too, was just as she had left it – standing wide open. Robin stopped at the back steps and debated with herself whether to go up and into the house or just wait somewhere outside for her uncle to return. Standing there, though, she realized how cold she was and that made the decision for her. Reluctantly, but for his own good she knew, she left Gerald in the yard and climbed up the stairs alone. At the kitchen entrance she stopped and listened for any sound that would reveal the presence of someone in the house. Hearing nothing, she yelled to Gerald that it was okay to come up as she went over to the phone.

Her mother fell back into her chair upon hearing her daughter's story and she apologized over and over again for having been on the phone when Robin had tried to call. She then promised she would never be on the phone again. As she hung up to come over and get Robin she told her daughter to run back into the field again if any vehicle came down the lane without blinking it lights twice.

Robin followed her mother's instructions and then stood by the front window with Gerald by her side and waited. Fifteen minutes went by and she was just about to call her mother again when a car turned into the lane and blinked its lights twice as it rapidly came toward the house. Robin ran out the front door. Trisha Brown quickly came to a stop and jumped out of her car to hug her daughter.

"I'm sorry. I'm sorry. Are you all right, sugar?" Trisha asked as she looked over her daughter for any signs of injury.

"I'm okay, mom," said Robin, brushing the tears away from her eyes.

Putting her arm around Robin's waist, Trisha immediately felt the dampness of her clothes. "Let's go inside where it's warmer," she said. "You can tell me again what happened and I promise not to go crazy this time." They both laughed.

Trisha put the loaded shotgun she had carried in with her down beside the sofa and listened as her daughter told the story again. She shook her head and had a hard time stopping crying after Robin had finished telling what she and Gerald had done to escape from the two men.

* * * * *

Harold Walker got back to his house ten minutes later than usual and in stony silence listened to his niece tell him what had happened while he was gone. Midway through her story, he got up and left the room. He came back carrying a big, blue handgun, which he laid down on the coffee table before asking her to go on. When Robin had finished, Harold thanked her for being so smart as to take Gerald and run into the woods. What followed were several questions from Harold regarding the car, after which Robin gathered up her things and prepared to leave.

Trisha took this opportunity to pull Harold into the hallway where she demanded to know what was going on at his church. "That has to be what brought those men out here," she said before stopping to wait for his answer.

Harold admitted there was a chance she was right and that his being a member of this church may have played a part in what happened.

"Well, no more," said Trisha. "My daughter's not going to go through what happened to her tonight ever again. Your church is your business, brother dear, but my daughter isn't getting mixed up in it. From now on you can bring Gerald over to my house."

Harold could do no more than nod his head in agreement. He, too, had decided it wasn't safe for his child to be here – unless he was here also. And even then, he was having doubts as to whether it was safe.

Waving goodbye to his sister and niece, he hugged Gerald one last time and sent him upstairs to go to bed. When he was sure Gerald couldn't hear him, Harold turned to Lonnie and in a voice filled with disgust said, "They were here to see you."

"They couldn't have been," said Lonnie defensively. "We took my car."

"It was you, alright; you must have been followed out here."

"No. Never," countered Lonnie, quickly adding, "No one has ever followed me out here; I'm not stupid. I've been careful."

"Well, is anything of yours missing?" asked Harold, changing the topic, although he still knew what had happened had a connection to Lonnie Gilley.

"I don't know, I hadn't thought to check, but I'll go see," said Lonnie, disappearing up the steps. He was gone for a few minutes before coming back down into the living room. "Doesn't look like they were in my room. Nothing's missing there," he said, sitting down in the recliner.

"I know how people like that operate, this house could be bugged," said Harold looking around. "They may even come back. But I know one thing - this will never happen again. Not in my house, not here. No, they won't do this again. The government can't terrorize me or my boy. Not as long as I'm alive."

Harold had now worked himself up into a rage. He had done a good job of not letting his anger out around his sister, but he couldn't hold it in any more. Not when the reason for what happened tonight wasn't clear. "It could be they're watching the church or have some more questions for me, like the last time they were here." But, as he said this, he knew it couldn't be true. After thinking it over, he knew it had to be Gilley they wanted; why he didn't know, but it had to be him.

"It could be about the church," echoed Lonnie after listening to Harold. Speculation on this possibility took up half an hour of discussion and yielded no resolution. However, Harold did decide that tomorrow he would contact some of the most loyal church members and tell them what had happened tonight. Lonnie, for his part, was to go to work as though nothing had happened – and say nothing to anyone.

This having been decided, Harold excused himself and went down the hall to his bedroom, leaving Lonnie alone in the living room. When Lonnie was sure Harold had gone to bed, he got up and went into the kitchen. It took going through several drawers before he found what he wanted. He laid the duct tape on the stairs and quietly opened the front door before going outside to his car. When he came back in, he took the tape with him as he made his way up to his room.

For his part, Harold waited until he heard Lonnie going upstairs. When he heard his bedroom door close, Harold silently walked down the dark hall to the kitchen and picked up the phone. He had spent enough time thinking about what he was about to do; it was now time to act.

13

Gerald Walker's clock radio woke him up at the regular time and, as usual, he crawled out of bed long enough to go over to the dresser and hit the snooze bar. Laying back down he thought about last night again. Here in the daylight he wasn't scared. He did know he had to tell his friends what had happened. They would no doubt agree with him that this was the most exciting, dangerous and greatest adventure anyone of them had ever had. Then old thoughts on moments of last night came back to him and he felt scared.

Gerald soon heard voices coming from below and, reluctantly, he made himself get up. On his way downstairs, he could hear his dad and Mr. Gilley talking loudly. They both fell silent as he came into the kitchen and saw both men sitting at the table, each with a coffee cup in one hand. Gerald went over and hugged his father who, in turn, put one hand on his son's shoulder and tried to rub his head with his other.

Lonnie watched all this while he ate the last of his toast. Finished, he got up from the table and while putting his plate in the sink said, "I'll be late if I don't get going" before leaving the room.

The sound of Lonnie climbing the stairs had started to fade when Harold looked over at Gerald and said, "Son, how would you like to go to your mother's for a time?"

Gerald shrugged his shoulders and hoped his father didn't see that his hands were trembling. "I'll go if you say its okay," he said matter-of-factly. It was taking a lot of effort for Gerald to keep from smiling and he looked over at his father again to see if, this time, he had noticed anything. Gerald was relieved to see his dad wasn't even looking at him.

"Yeah, I want you to go", said Harold. "I called last night and she's on her way now. So there's no reason to go to school today. But you'll need to start packing pretty soon so you'll be ready."

"Should I call my teacher?" Gerald asked as he began to eat his cereal.

"No, I'll take care of telling the school."

"How about Mrs. Cahill?"

Harold couldn't remember who she was and was forced to ask, "She's the bus driver, right?"

Gerald nodded.

"I'll tell her too," he said.

"And Anne?"

"No," said Harold raising his voice upon hearing the social worker's name. "No, she's not to know where you've gone. Nor that lawyer either."

Harold looked at his son to make sure he was paying attention, then went on, "You can't tell them two, son," he said and just to make sure Gerald took him seriously added, "They'd put you back in Turner again if they knew you were about to leave. Don't you understand that?"

Gerald didn't have an answer to his father's question, but continued looking down at his bowl of cereal.

Harold wanted to find out if Gerald understood what he was saying and repeated, "Understand?"

This time Gerald replied, "I understand, it's all because of the two men who were here last night."

"That's part of the reason," said Harold.

Gerald had some questions he wanted answers to, but dared only ask one of them. "When will I come back, Daddy?" he asked apprehensively.

Harold Walker thought about how he was going to answer this question for a long time. He knew the two men who had come to the house had to be government agents of some type. Because they had come once, they were most likely coming back. Maybe they knew about the Miami County project. Whatever their reason for coming the first time, he knew Gerald wasn't going to be here when they came back. Harold finally looked across the table at his son and said, "You'll be with your mother until I come and get you. It could be a week or a year, I don't know. But however long you're there, remember, you do as she tells you. You hear."

Gerald squeezed the seat of his chair with both hands as he managed a nod; knowing if he didn't hold on, he would start shaking even more than he was already. He continued listening to his father tell him what to take and what to leave behind.

Looking up at the clock on the wall, Gerald saw it was 6:55. He knew that Brad, one of his best friends, would be leaving his house shortly to go wait for the bus. He really wanted to talk to Brad before he left and decided to ask his father if he could.

"Can I tell Brad I'm going?" he asked.

"No, son. I told you, you can't tell anyone" came back the answer. Harold didn't want to talk anymore about who was going to know, so he said, "Anyone you tell might lead those men to you. You don't want to see them again do you?"

Gerald shook his head and got up to go pack his bag. He was just starting up the stairs when the door to his room opened and Mr. Gilley came out. Stopping, he watched as Mr. Gilley quickly walked across the hall and quietly closed his bedroom door behind him.

Gerald turned to go tell his father, then stopped and continued on up the stairs making as much noise as he could. He'd decided that he would find out on his own why Mr. Gilley had been in his room.

Gerald had just put his new jeans in his suitcase when he heard a door open, followed by footsteps in the hallway. Those footsteps stopped outside his room and a voice he recognized said, "I just wanted to say good-bye before you left for your mother's. By the way, where's she living now?"

"Purty, Missouri" said Gerald looking up to see Mr. Gilley.

"Is that near her folks in Arkansas?"

"I think so," replied Gerald, who was now putting socks in with the other clothes.

"Well I hope I see you again soon," he said and with that Mr. Gilley left and went down the stairs.

Gerald waited until he heard Mr. Gilley's car start, then got up and closed his door. It was now the time to search his room – the rest of the packing could wait. Mr. Gilley had hidden something in here and Gerald was going to find it. After searching the places he thought it could be, Gerald began to believe he might be wrong. He was now down to his last few places where he thought something could be hidden in his room.

Gerald started with his dresser. One at a time, he pulled out the two lower drawers and checked over and behind each one without finding anything. He then pulled out the top drawer and began his search. He had just made the decision to put the drawer back when his hand hit something. Dropping to his knees he turned it over and saw a brown envelope attached to the underside with tape the same color as Mr. Gilley had carried with him when Gerald saw him leaving his room. Wasting no time, Gerald reached up and began pulling on one of the ends of the tape.

14

Lonnie backed his car around in the front yard and drove down the lane before turning east onto 221st Street. He picked up speed as he started the two mile drive to Westridge Road. At the crest of the first hill the sun hit him in the face and he pulled down the visor. When he did he saw flashing red lights in his rear view mirror. "Now what", he said out loud, "I couldn't have been speeding."

Reluctantly, he pulled over at the bottom of the hill and watched as a white Ford pulled in behind him and stopped. Someone in a suit got out and came up to his window just as he finished rolling it down.

"Lonnie, we need to talk to you," said a man who leaned his head in the open window and looked around his car.

"A little far from home aren't you?" he asked Detective Stewart.

The detective didn't answer but, instead, said, "You need to get out and come with us."

Lonnie continued to sit in his car. "What'd I do?" he asked, unsure of why he had encountered the detective on this road at this time of day.

"Nothing," said Bill Stewart, "we just need to talk to you some more, that's all."

Something didn't seem right and Lonnie asked, "Are you taking me to the station?"

"Yea, that's right. Now get out of the car," demanded Detective Stewart, tired of Lonnie's questions.

Lonnie hesitated then took the keys out of the ignition before opening his car door. He still thought something was wrong, but what else, he decided, was he to do – after all, they were the police.

"Just a minute, I need to search you to make sure you don't have any weapons on you," said the detective. Once he was finished Bill took Lonnie by the arm and led him back to the Ford. "He's got nothing on him," he said to Roger, who was standing beside the open passenger door.

"What about my car? Are you going to leave it here?" asked Lonnie.

"No, we'll move it off the road," said Roger, "but I need the keys."

Lonnie tossed them across the car to the fat detective who then started walking toward his car.

"You need to turn around so I can handcuff you," said Bill, still holding onto Lonnie's arm.

"Why?" asked Lonnie.

"Policy," was the curt reply, followed by, "We have to cuff anyone who we put in a car. So turn around."

Lonnie stood still and then asked, "Am I under arrest?"

Irritated by another question and in a hurry to get this done before someone came down the road and saw them, Bill Stewart said, "No, just relax will you, the ride won't be that long."

Lonnie still had that funny feeling but turned around and put his hands behind his back. The thought of refusing to go crossed his mind, but he decided against it. He had tried not talking at the station and these same guys hadn't taken kindly to that. It didn't look to him like they would be any happier if he tried it again.

Bill helped Lonnie into the back seat and began driving east. Lonnie turned his head as they passed by his car and saw the other detective begin following them.

Both cars had gone about half a mile along 221st Street when Detective Stewart turned onto a side road and drove south toward a farmhouse off in the distance. As they came upon it, Lonnie saw that boards covered its windows. The car began to slow down and Lonnie watched as his car passed them before turning into the driveway ahead of them. It pulled up and eventually stopped by the barn behind the house. The police car also turned in, but it stopped beside the empty house.

Lonnie was now sure something was wrong. When they stopped he angrily said, "Why are we here? Why did you stop?"

Bill kept looking ahead and watching as Roger walked back toward his car. He tried, with some success, to ignore the questions coming from the back seat.

"Hey, I'm talking to you," said Lonnie as he began kicking the back of the front seat. "You said you were taking me to the station. Why are we here? Answer me!" he shouted.

This was too much for Bill. He turned around and, looking directly at Lonnie, said, "We're going to talk here, so shut up."

The words felt as if they were cutting through him and Lonnie, seeing the other detective was now beside the car, said to him, almost pleading, "You need to stop this and take me to the station."

Without responding, the fat detective threw down his cigarette and opened the car door. Reaching in, he grabbed Lonnie's arm and began pulling him out of the car. Lonnie responded by jamming both his feet under the front seat. Joined by Detective Stewart, their combined force quickly had

Lonnie out of the car and on the ground where he continued to struggle.

"Get up," said Bill, "Get up - or things will get worse for you."

"Not until you tell me why you're doing this," said Lonnie. "You'll both be fired once I file my complaint, so, if you know what's good for you, you'll let go of me - now." Lonnie was trying to crawl along the side of the car out toward the road. He hoped someone coming by would see what was happening and stop to help him.

"Ok, Lonnie, you win," said the fat detective. "We had wanted to talk to you here so it would be easier for you to go on to work, but if that's the way you want it, we'll go to the station." And with that, the detective, whose name Lonnie could never remember, suddenly let go of him. "Let him up," he said to Bill.

Lonnie lay on his side behind the Ford looking up at the two detectives standing over him as he tried to catch his breath. He felt safer now, less scared. But he was still going to file a complaint against them - even if nothing more happened.

"Help me up," said Lonnie. When they didn't move quickly enough, he looked up and shouted, "Get me up off the ground. You can't treat people this way."

The detectives looked at each before reaching down and pulling Lonnie up off the ground.

"Now clean me off," he demanded. "Then take me to the station."

Detective Stewart began brushing off Lonnie's shirt while the other detective stood watching. When he was finished with the front of his shirt, the detective told Lonnie to turn around so he could clean off the back.

Lonnie did as he was told and found himself now facing the side of the house. The sharp blows of the detective's hand on his back began to sting. "Hey; stop it, that hurts," said Lonnie, his anger returning at this treatment.

"I'm sorry," came back the reply. Bill then took hold of one of Lonnie's arms and with his other hand began brushing off the back of Lonnie's neck.

"Are you almost done?" asked Lonnie he waited for the detective to finish.

"Just a little more to do," said the detective just before be rammed Lonnie's head into the side of the house. Lonnie staggered trying to regain his balance. But before he could accomplish this, Bill Stewart shoved Lonnie's head into the wall a second time, causing him to drop to his knees.

"Get up," said Bill, jerking on his handcuffs. Lonnie offered no resistance as he was pulled up off the ground. The two detectives then proceeded to half-drag, half-shove Lonnie around to the back of the house. Here Lonnie began struggling once more, but was rewarded for this effort by a blow to his ribs and he immediately quit. He opened his mouth to cry for help but, just as quickly, he closed it for he knew his cry would not go far enough.

They stopped dragging Lonnie when they got him up on the back porch. The big detective held onto him while the other one kicked open the back door. It banged against something and came back toward him as he started to go inside. Bill put his foot out and the door hit against it. This time the door swung back and stopped.

The big detective then pulled Lonnie inside where they found themselves standing in the kitchen. Most of the cabinet doors stood open and a large, stringy cobweb hung down from the light fixture in the ceiling. They stood together on one side of the dark room as the fat detective lit up a cigarette. The smell of its smoke quickly filled the room.

Lonnie said nothing. He glanced back outside and waited, not knowing what was going to happen next. A strange sound soon caught his attention and he looked down at the floor in time to see a cigarette butt being ground out on the linoleum.

Bill Stewart had used this time to calm down. When he saw that Roger was finished smoking, he looked over at Lonnie and asked, "Where's the paper?"

Lonnie didn't have any idea what paper he was talking about and told him so.

"The one you had the officer at the station photocopy for you," came back the reply.

"I've got it, but why do you want it?" asked Lonnie.

Bill laughed at Lonnie's question. "We need to see it," he said and continued on, "just to verify something, because, well, something happened to our copy."

Lonnie couldn't believe all this was about a piece of paper. "Take me to the station and I'll tell you, when we get there, where it is," he said, confident that once he got there and told someone about what had happened to him, these guys would get what they had coming to them.

"No, we're fine where we are," interjected the fat detective, who was now directly in front of Lonnie. "So, now it's time to tell us where it is," he said.

"I want to go to the station first," was all Lonnie could think of to say. He couldn't bring himself to look up at either of the detectives after saying this, so he looked away and focused on the light entering the house through a crack in the boards covering one of the front windows. He didn't hear the next question because his attention became focused on the cloud of smoke that began swirling in from outside. Lonnie suddenly realized it wasn't light he had seen outside the house, and turning to the two detectives, yelled, "Fire!"

They both turned and saw not only the smoke but several thin yellow flames through the narrow opening. Roger ran to the front door and started pulling on the doorknob. When it didn't open, he threw his weight against it. It still didn't move although the wood started cracking. He hit the door one last time and then peered out through the crack in the window. "It's getting worse," he said before turning and running back through the kitchen and on out the back door, hollering for Bill to follow him.

Bill grabbed Lonnie by his arm and the two of them went out the back door and around the side of the house. There, in the front yard, they encountered Roger beating the spreading flames with a branch he had broken off a nearby pine tree.

"Help me get the flames out," he shouted toward the two men standing at the corner of the house.

Bill quickly let go of Lonnie and ran over to the edge of the fire and began stomping on the burning ground with his feet. Seeing that the flames were going out, he ran to the edge of the driveway, scooped up some dirt, and threw it on the remaining fire. He went back and repeated this several times, until he was sure the flames were out. He then stopped and watched as Roger turned the branch in his hand over several times looking, apparently, to make sure it was not on fire.

Satisfied it wasn't on fire, Roger threw it down and reached in his pocket for his pack of cigarettes.

Bill looked on in disbelief. "Haven't you caused enough problems?" he asked. "Can't you leave those things alone for a while?"

"What do you mean – it was my fault the grass caught on fire?" replied Roger angrily.

"That's exactly what I mean. How else could this have happened?" said Bill.

Roger was silent. "Let's go talk to Mr. Gilley again," he said sharply as he shoved the pack back into his pocket, "I want to get this over with."

Gilley. Upon hearing this name, Bill spun around and looked toward the corner of the house. Gilley wasn't there. "He's gone," he said running over to look down the side of the house. Gilley wasn't in sight. Bill continued running until he reached the back porch. "Check in the house," he yelled at Roger, who he hoped had been following behind him, as he continued up the driveway toward the barn.

Almost immediately Bill shouted, "There he is," and began pointing toward the wooded area beyond the barn. He began chasing after Lonnie hoping to stop him before he got too far into the woods. "Last night's mess," he said to himself, "wasn't going to happen again; this guy wasn't going to be as lucky as those kids had been."

Bill started to tire as he struggled through the thick brush that kept blocking his way toward the ever disappearing figure ahead of him. Suddenly there was the sharp sound of wood breaking, followed by a high pitched scream that went right through the detective. Both ended with the sound of a thump.

"What happened?" hollered Roger from a distance behind Bill.

"I don't know, one minute he was there and now he's gone." Bill replied.

"Gone? Where?" shouted back Roger.

"I don't know; I can't see through this brush. The last place I saw him was over that way," said Bill, pointing ahead.

Roger caught up with him and both men hurriedly walked toward where Gilley had been last seen. Bill stopped several times and each time motioned for Roger to be quiet as he listened for any sound of Gilley. All he heard was the sound of their own breathing, nothing else. Near where Bill had last seen Gilley, the two detectives found the path he had made going through the brush. They followed it a short way until they came upon a hole in the ground which looked to be the opening to an abandoned well. Stopping at its edge, they could see that a cover of some kind had once been in place over it, but all that was left of it now were pieces of broken and splintered wood. The two men tried to see into the blackness below, but not even the light from several of Roger's matches was enough to show what was down there.

"Go get the flashlight out of the car," said Roger. He had heard enough speculation on Mr. Gilley's whereabouts, it was time to make sure one way or another if he had fallen down there or not.

"You go get it. If it wasn't for you we wouldn't need it," retorted Bill.

"Look, I'm tired. If you want to wait for me, fine, I'll go get it. But it might be a while," said Roger.

Bill didn't want to stay here much longer for he felt it was just a matter of time before something else occurred. "Alright, I'll go get it," he said. "But I want you to know I'm through with you. When this is over you can find a new partner to abuse, but it won't be me."

Roger narrowed his eyes as he spoke directly to Bill, "You think this will be over, do you? It will never be over, so you'll have me to contend with for a long time to come. Now shut up and go get the flashlight."

Bill said nothing. Instead, he took off jogging for their car.

"Be careful," came a warning from behind him, "no telling if there are any more of these holes around."

Upon hearing this, Bill slowed down to a walk and began to closely watch the ground in front of him. He returned with a flashlight and handed it to Roger. Turning it on, Roger pointed the beam down into the opening. Far below him lay the twisted form of a man partially covered in water.

"Think he's alive?" asked Bill as he gazed down at the lifeless figure.

Roger shook his head. "No, he's not moving, he's dead. Look at the way he's laying, his back's broken. Probably died instantly."

"What about the handcuffs?"

"Forget them. Nothing we can do about them now, besides we have no way to get down there."

"How do we explain this then?" asked Bill, starting to go beyond worry and into what he hoped would be a controllable panic.

"We came out here to ask him some questions and he tried to get away from us. We finally stopped his car here and cuffed him. Then the fire happened, why we don't know, and, while we were fighting to put it out, he escaped. We looked for him everywhere, including in the house, and even came upon this hole but, even using matches to see down it, never saw him. So we left. End of story. Some truth, some lies – all believable. Now let's go."

"Go where?" asked Bill.

"Back to the house. He didn't tell us what we needed to know, so maybe Harold Walker can be persuaded," said Roger.

"Do we just leave him here?" asked Bill.

"That's the general idea," said Roger. "We're still 'looking' for our missing prisoner. You know, I bet he's just up the street here, hiding in a house on the south side of the road."

Having said that, Roger turned and began walking back toward the driveway. He stopped at Gilley's car long enough to search it. Just as he suspected, the paper wasn't there. However, before he walked on to his car, he took Gilley's keys out of his pocket and tossed them into the brush. At least when the car was found it would look as though someone had left it in a hurry.

Roger looked back and saw Bill slowly coming out of the brush. His coat was muddy and there were dark stains on the knees of his pants.

"What happened to you?" asked Roger as Bill approached their car.

"I tried to see if he was still alive. I found a tree limb. I was able to reach close to him, but I just couldn't quite touch him."

"What'd you do with the limb?" was the only question Roger felt he needed to ask after hearing this.

"I threw it back in the brush," said Bill. "Don't you want to know if he's still alive?"

"No, I told you he's dead, broken back," said Roger, who then turned and spent the time it took to drive back to the Walker house looking at the scenery.   Sooner than Bill wanted, they came to a stop behind a red pickup truck. As they got out Roger spoke up again and cautioned Bill, "Don't tell him anything more than you have to."

They had just started across the porch toward the front door when it opened and Harold Walker stepped outside. "Who are you and what do you want?" he asked in a menacing voice.

Roger Sumler reached in his coat pocket and pulled out his badge.

"Cops, I should have known," said Harold disgustedly. "Were you two here last night scaring my boy?"

"Not us," snapped Bill.

"Same type of car," said Harold looking toward the man who had just spoken.

"Lots of white cars; you ought to know that," said Bill sarcastically. "Can we come in?"

"Only if you got a warrant, you ought to know that," retorted Captain Walker.

"No," said Bill, "we don't 'got a warrant'."

"No warrant, no entry," said Harold as a smile crossed his face.

"We can get one," said Bill casually. "By the way, isn't Lonnie Gilley staying here?"

"Don't know anyone named Gilley and, if I did, I wouldn't tell you," said Harold as he turned to go back inside.

"That's funny," said Bill offhandedly, "the bondsman said you posted his bond."

Harold stopped.   Before he could come up with anything to say, Bill leaned over closer to him and in a loud whisper said, "He says he lives here." And in an even louder voice went on, "Can we talk inside now? Or do you want to go down to the station for a couple of hours while we discuss your memory loss?"

"I don't want you to stay long, my son's home sick," Harold said holding the door open.

The two detectives went into the house and found themselves in the living room. Immediately Roger pointed toward a suitcase sitting at the back of the room and said, "Who's leaving?"

Harold looked over at Gerald's bag and replied, "I'm sending my son to his mother's."

"Looks like you expect him to be sick a long time," said Bill, "Where'd you say your son was now?"

"Upstairs," Harold answered. "I told him to stay in bed until his mother gets here."

"That also where Mr. Gilley stays?"

"Yeah."

Bill looked over at Roger and then back toward Harold Walker. In the same loud whisper he had used on the porch he said, "Mind if we go see both of them?"

"I'll want a warrant for that," said Harold looking toward the stairs.

"Now Mr. Walker, let's not get so upset," interjected Roger, moving up beside his partner. "Perhaps I can clarify matters for you."

"How's that?" asked Harold.

"Well let me tell you a few things and, perhaps, the need to visit his room will become clearer. Since you just lied to us about knowing Mr. Gilley, we're naturally concerned for his safety. So for that reason alone, we need to check out his room, and there are other reasons."

Something didn't sound right to Harold and he asked, "What other reasons?"

"We want to see his room Harold, to check on Mr. Gilley's safety," said Bill moving closer to him.

The anger in the detective's voice was such that Harold took a step back from him. "I don't like the way you're talking" he then said, "I want a warrant. You don't have one, so get out." And with that he started toward the kitchen to use the phone.

Bill followed behind him and using his same whisper repeated his request, "We want to see his room."

"I don't know who you're talking about," shot back Harold. "Now get out of my house."

"You're a liar."

Hearing that, Harold clenched his fists, turned and began walking toward Bill. He stopped about six inches away from him and said, "I told you to get out of here. Didn't you hear me?" As he finished, he saw movement out of the corner of his eye and looked upstairs in time to see his son pulling his head back in his room.

"I've had enough," said Detective Stewart, "turn around, you're under arrest for obstructing."

Harold started to resist, but both men reaching for their guns made him change his mind. Besides, he knew it would be better if they were gone before Ralene got there. "I'm filing a complaint," he said as he turned around and put his hands behind his back.

"We'll help you," said Roger as he put his cuffs on Harold. "Now come on."

"What about my son?" said Harold as they began walking toward the front door, "Can't I even say goodbye?"

"Sure thing. Call him to come down here."

Harold turned toward the stairs and called out, "Gerald, it's me. Come give your father a hug and a kiss. I have to go now."

The three of them stood waiting but there was no reply from upstairs.

"Can't you ever quit lying?" said Bill.

Roger kept listening for any noise that would indicate someone else was in the house, but he didn't hear anything. Still, he thought to himself, if it were true the son was here. He stopped the thought. He didn't want to think what might have to be done if the boy were here. "Go check upstairs," he said to Bill. "We'll be out in the car."

They didn't have long to wait for Roger had no more than put Mr. Walker in the back seat when Bill came out the front door shaking his head.

"He's lying again," he said. "There's no one upstairs; both rooms are empty. You ready to go?"

Roger nodded as he finished lighting his cigarette.

Standing beside the car Bill leaned in the back window and screamed in Harold Walker's face, "I hate liars. Do you understand me?"

Harold managed a smile as he continued to look straight ahead. "Let's get this over with," he said. "I want to get my complaint on file. Besides, I've got things to do this morning and I can't be gone that long."

"No. You won't be gone that long," said Roger looking over at Bill.

15

Thursday morning began as had the last few days - cloudy and cool. The sun briefly came out from behind the clouds just as John Calloway got off Interstate 35. Seeing this, he hoped the paper was wrong and that it would be warmer today.

John greeted the new receptionist when he opened the office door. Stopping beside her desk he opened a drawer and took out the contents of his folder. It was a mix of the usual, telephone message slips, what looked like replies to letters he had previously sent out, advertisements for legal education seminars and one envelope addressed to him in longhand.

John set the other mail down on the desk and put the envelope up to his nose. "Ahhh, nothing like the smell of money," he said before roughly opening one end. His eyes caught the amount written in the corner of the check and he said out loud, "Thank you."

Jena was busy with a phone call and didn't hear his joke. He felt sorry she had missed it as he picked up his mail and walked back toward his office.

He had been a part of this group of lawyers for eight years, starting when he had clerked for Bretton Jenner during the summer between his second and third years of law school. He had taken a leave of absence from his job at the bank in order to work for him. Although his clerking job paid less than the bank he had been amply compensated ever since then by the contacts he had made with this group. They weren't a firm, he didn't have the grades to go down that road, but they had an expense sharing arrangement. The office had space for eight attorneys, but the eighth office never seemed to get rented. It was this office that he had used up until he left in August to go back to both school and the bank. During his last year in law school John continued to work on special projects for Bret and for some of the other attorneys in the group when they needed help.

When he graduated the following May, the attorneys had offered him a deal; he could practice out of his old summer office, at half rent, until they found someone to take the space at the regular rate. Then he would be given the right of first refusal. John jumped on the offer – mainly because it was the only one he had. He had worked full time while in school and that was reflected in his grades. He ranked in the middle of his class which meant he was 'free to choose his own career path', as the phrase went, in looking for employment. The half rent arrangement lasted for a year and a half until Bret came in one Friday afternoon and told John that he had to start paying full rent or would have to leave.

John remembered this, for some unknown reason, on his way back to his new windowless office. That is, if you could call a converted storage room a new office. It had been remodeled a couple of years ago and then given to a secretary to use. Nine months ago he had been given the choice of giving up his old office and moving in there or being kicked out altogether for being four thousand dollars behind in rent. He chose the converted storage room. Now he was current on his rent and, despite himself, had grown to appreciate his new space. No more staring out the window and daydreaming. Not much anyway, at least at the office, not since his divorce had become final. No, John worked more now. It was that or go home and he found out rather quickly he would rather work than be alone at his house.

John started this Thursday by returning telephone calls and so it went for much of the morning. Between calls going out, there were calls coming in, the day's new mail and a break to visit with two of the attorneys about the University of Missouri's football schedule in the fall.

Back in his office after this discussion he heard his name being paged for a telephone call. Jeff Hartman first introduced himself as principal of the Rural Johnson County R-4 Consolidated Grade School. Then, without pausing, he came straight to the reason for his call, "Gerald Walker is absent from school today."

John flipped to a new page on the legal tablet on his desk and wrote Mr. Hartman's name. "Do you think something's wrong?" he said as he finished writing his client's name at the top and the time the call started.

"Yes, I do, and so's his teacher. Gerald was looking forward to school today because this was his day to start taking care of the class gerbils. We've called his house several times and there's no answer."

John shook his head and wondered why he was getting this call; perhaps, he thought, this guy didn't have enough to do. "Maybe he's sick and his father has him at the doctor's," he said.

"He's not. I talked to his bus driver," said Mr. Hartman.

John looked at his watch. About a minute had gone by and he was ready to end this call and get back to real work. "His bus driver?" He didn't try to contain his disbelief as he repeated back what he had just heard.

The principal went on, "Yes. Gerald talks a lot to the bus driver, Mrs. Cahill. He rides up behind her seat every day. Anyhow, she came to see me when she got to school today. She thinks something's wrong. Besides, his father would never let Gerald miss school without calling to tell us why, not with the court system being involved."

That last part sounded true to John. "Why don't you have the police go check?" he asked.

"The Sheriff's Department you mean," corrected Mr. Hartman. "We've called them before and they won't go out and check on what they call 'attendance cases'."

"Sound's like you believe it's more than that," said John, "Why don't you call and tell them about your concerns?"

"They won't do anything - Not without more. Their policy appears to be if you think something's wrong, go find out. Then call us. We've tried before to get them to go out and check on students before and, for one reason or another, they won't do it."

John decided to change the conversation and asked, "How many times have you called Gerald's house?"

"Three. The last time was just before I called you."

John now hated this call and didn't want to ask the next question, but knew he was trapped, "What is it you want me to do?" he said, forcing out the words.

Without hesitating the principal asked him to go out to Gerald's house and see if anything was wrong. "I hate to ask you to do this, but I feel very strongly something needs to be done."

"I don't know, it's forty-five minutes to his house from my office," said John looking at his watch again. This four-minute phone call seemed to be lasting forever.

Jeff Hartman hadn't anticipated this response and it made him angry. He quickly said, "Mr. Calloway, look, you're his guardian *ad litem*. You have a responsibility to act in his best interest."

"That's only in court," shot back John, but he knew Hartman was right. As Gerald's guardian he had an obligation to act in Gerald's best interest, even if that meant going out to his house today to see why he wasn't in school. He apologized for his last statement and ended their conversation by promising to call Mr. Hartman after he found out more about Gerald's absence.

John hung up the phone and got the Walker case out of his file cabinet. Flipping through it, he found the telephone number for Anne Hubert and called her, hoping that she was in her office, as he really didn't want to go out to the Walker house by himself.

John let out a quiet sigh of relief as Anne answered her phone. She, too, didn't want to go check on Gerald. She wasted no time informing John that Jeff Hartman had called her earlier with the same story he had just told John. Her response to Jeff had been that, because of her schedule, it would be late afternoon before she could get out there. In the meantime she had called Gerald's house several times, all without success.

It took John several minutes of heavy persuasion before Anne agreed to change her schedule and go out to the Walker house with him. In the end they agreed that John would pick her up at twelve-thirty and that they would make a quick trip out there. "I have to be back by two," she repeated several times. "I have a case planning conference involving a very problematic family situation, I just can't be late for it," she said before their conversation ended.

It was a little past twelve when John left his office and drove west on College Boulevard to the highway entrance. The sun was now back out and one of his favorite songs started playing on the radio. Joining in on the lyrics he accelerated through the gears to his usual cruising speed.

Twenty minutes later he left Interstate 35 and continued driving west to Anne's building. He sat in the lobby for almost five minutes before Anne made her appearance. She immediately apologized for making him wait, saying that a coworker had held her up. John's mental image of this was of a hooded figure with an armload of bad cases that she forced Anne to take from her.

* * * * *

Their first date had been six weeks ago. She had talked about her divorce over that first dinner at one of those expensive restaurants on 119th Street. Her marriage had lasted for six years before she got divorced late last year. It had started downhill just after she and her ex-husband, Ben, bought a new house. Anne found out she was pregnant a week before the closing. They were thrilled. But, unfortunately, she miscarried two months later. She was devastated at the time, and even telling John caused her to start crying, but not as devastated as Ben. Ben Hubert had always worked a lot, but after the miscarriage he began to work even more - or so Anne thought. One night he came home, said he was moving out, and ended the conversation by saying there 'might be someone else.' Anne slapped him and then threw a package of frozen peas she had started to fix for dinner at him. Ben's response had been to turn and walk out. They didn't talk or see each other again until the day of the final divorce hearing. Anne tried numerous times to contact him until her attorney called and said that Ben had let it be known, in no uncertain terms, she was to stop it and leave him alone. After that message Anne went back into therapy.

Anne had moved out of their new house and into a small apartment in the northern part of the county after Ben filed for divorce – she knew she couldn't afford to keep the house, not as a social worker. Ben didn't want the house either and so they sold it. A month after the divorce was final he transferred to Dallas.

Through a mutual friend, Anne had heard that a female engineer who had worked in the same Overland Park office with Ben had also transferred to Dallas. Her source had gone on to tell Anne they were now living together and the rumor was that they were going to get married this coming September.

John felt sad for Anne as he listened to her, but her story was like several of his current divorce cases. In reality, they were all sad for one reason or another.

John quit thinking about their first date when he saw Anne coming down the hall. She was wearing a short green skirt that showed off her legs. John couldn't help himself and he stared at them as she approached. He felt bad about doing this, but they were so great he told himself to get over the guilt.

They left in John's car and he got back on Interstate 35. The sun had stayed out and that, combined with being with Anne, made him feel happy. When they had been on the road for a few minutes, John got back to the business at hand. "Did you try calling the house again?" he asked.

"Three or four more times. Still no answer," she replied.

"What's your take on what's going on?"

"I don't know. I talked with his teacher after you called. Gerald didn't complain yesterday about feeling sick, or anything else for that matter. How about you, what's your guess?" she asked, looking over at him.

"I don't have one. All I know is that this isn't the day I wanted to do this. But we'll soon know," he said, glancing down at her legs again. He didn't hate himself this time.

They continued traveling west until they saw the Westridge Road exit. John left the interstate here and turned south. The first few side roads they passed were gravel, but after that they became dirt. Anne picked up John's cell phone and punched in a number as they passed the third dirt road.

"No answer," she said putting the phone back in his console.

"You sure you dialed the right number?"

Anne nodded and said, "I have it memorized."

"How about a work number, do you---." John stopped himself. There wasn't one. John took his right hand and, using his thumb and little finger, held them up to his ear like a phone. "Hello, is Mr. Walker there? Yes, the one who doesn't believe in the Constitution of anything. You're right, he's the one who also doesn't believe in work either; he'd rather be at home playing with his storm troopers." He then looked over at Anne for her reaction and saw she was laughing.

Harold Walker had told John early on that he grew crops on his land. But John hadn't seen any indication of that on his one and only visit out to his farm. Sorry, he reminded himself, he meant ranch. On the Kansas side they were all ranches. Less than twenty miles to the east, in Missouri, that's where they were called farms. Harold Walker had sarcastically pointed this out to him when John had called his place a farm.

"There it is, 221st Street," exclaimed Anne, pointing to a sign up ahead.

John stepped on the brake and shifted into third gear before turning west onto a dirt road. "It's about two miles down," he said - then added, "I think."

"On the left," said Anne. "Just before Evening Star Road. I've been here before, remember?" She then picked up John's phone again and tried the Walker number. "Still no answer," she said after it rang for a while.

John kept on driving. He soon came over a hill and past where the trees on his left ended and then opened up into a newly plowed field. Seeing this, he knew the entrance to the Walker ranch was just up ahead, near where a white car sat parked on the north side of the road. John slowed as he drove up on the car and passed a man walking toward it. John couldn't see his face as the man had turned his head and was looking off the road. John turned into the lane toward the Walker house and immediately stopped.

"Why are you stopping, the house is down there." said Anne, rolling down her window to smell the air. It was heavy with the scent of newly blossomed flowers mixed with the smell of fresh dirt.

"I want to see something," said John, getting out of the car and walking back across 221st Street toward a row of mailboxes. Anne watched him in the side mirror until he disappeared from her view. A group of purple wild flowers beside the lane caught her eye and her thoughts drifted to Friday and the weekend. If the weather in southwest Missouri was going to be like this, the camping trip with John would be fabulous. She had started to think about what she was going to wear when the sound of a car door being opened startled her. Looking over, she watched as John got back in the car.

"There's mail there. Not much, so it must have been picked up yesterday," he said as he drove toward the house at the end of the lane.

The Walker house was surrounded by several enormous trees; trees which helped keep the heat off the house in the summer. They also partially blocked the house from people passing by on 221st. It looked like it had the last time John had been here. The second story still needed some wood repair and the whole house was due for a coat of paint. On the left side of the lane, across from the house, was a large drum of gasoline mounted on a steel rack. Behind both it and the house, a hundred feet or so, was a faded red barn with its doors closed.

John drove past the house, made a U-turn and came to a stop beside the gas drum he had just passed. There were no vehicles parked anywhere around.

"Who wants to get out first?" he asked.

Anne looked at him, smiled, unbuckled her seat belt and opened her door. "I'm taking the phone with me," she said, picking it up and holding it tightly in her left hand.

"Why? No one could get out here for at least half an hour. Look how long it took us – it's worthless," said John.

The harshness in his voice surprised him and in a calmer voice he said, "I'm sorry. I don't know why, but this makes me a little nervous."

"It does me too," said Anne. She had by now walked around the car to where John was and they stood together for a moment looking at the house. There were no lights on and the only sound came from the wind. Anne waited for John to start walking toward the house. When he didn't, she nudged him with her elbow and asked, "What's next John?"

"I guess we go see if anyone's home," he said. "Let's try the back door first – if any door's unlocked that will probably be the one." Looking over at Anne he said, "You know I really don't want to do this. "Please God," he said now looking up at the sky, "please don't let us step in a pile of it."

"Amen," said Anne as they both began walking toward the rear of the house.

They said nothing else to each other and had gone about half way toward the back stairs when John spoke up. "Wait here," he suddenly said. Anne needed no further urging and quickly stopped.

John finished the rest of the distance alone and once at the first step, he turned back toward Anne. She saw him looking back at her and waved. He waived back and then slowly climbed the stairs until he stood in front of the screen door. The handle didn't turn when he tried it. Next he tried pushing the door open and that didn't work either.

"We'll try the front door," said Anne seeing that he couldn't get in the house this way. She was glad John had asked her to go with him. Had she come out here by herself she would have left the moment she saw the house - this was no place to check out alone. They could call her anything they wanted to, coward, whatever, she decided, but that wasn't going to change her mind. There was something wrong here, she could just feel it.

John retreated back down the stairs, and together they walked back around to the front of the house. Anne had reached over and grasped John's hand. It made her feel safer. In her other hand she continued holding the cell phone; she couldn't see walking around out here without it – regardless of how long it would take the police to get here.

They climbed the front steps and then stood on the edge of the porch looking at the front door ten feet away.

"Do you really want to do this?" asked Anne.

"No, not really, but I told Hartman I'd call back and let him know what I found out," replied John.

"Suppose the door's locked?" she asked.

"If it's locked we'll look around a little; you know, in the windows, maybe check out the barn. Then we'll get out of here," John said. He had no desire to break into the house and was secretly hoping the door was locked. Somewhere off in the distance he heard a car starting.

Anne, too, had heard the car start. "I don't like this place. It's giving me the creeps," she said as they stood there.

"This isn't in my job description either," replied John. "So let's get it over with quickly."

Still holding hands they walked across the porch together. When they reached the closed door, John grabbed the door handle which, to his amazement, turned.

"This is trespassing at a minimum," said John grimly, then added, "If Harold Walker finds me in his house, he'll have every charge available filed against me - It'll be the end of my career."

All of this was lost on Anne. She couldn't understand why he was worried. It was Gerald that was important here, not Harold Walker. Having heard enough of his potential legal problems she said, "Let's find Gerald," and walked into the house.

"Okay, maybe I'm exaggerating a little," said John quickly following her.

"Gerald, Gerald, are you here?" Anne now called out as she walked toward the back hallway to check out the two bedrooms. John caught up to her as she entered Harold's, which was just as messy as it had been on John's visit. The other bedroom was the same, too, still filled with boxes and miscellaneous furniture. They stood in the hallway looking into it for a few moments. Anne lowered her voice and whispered, "Gerald's room is at the top of the stairs."

"Why are you whispering?" asked John. "If anybody is here they already know we're in the house."

Anne couldn't think of anything to say, so she turned and went back through the living room to the stairs that led to the second story. She continued to hold on tightly to the phone as John went up the stairs ahead of her. The first thing they noticed was that the door to Gerald's room and the one on the opposite side of the hall were both closed. John put his finger to his lips as he pointed toward Gerald's room.

Anne held her breath as John slowly turned the doorknob and began to push open the door. It barely moved. He pushed again, this time harder than before. The door moved a little, but still not enough for him to get into the room. Stopping for a moment, John looked at the partially opened door. Suddenly, and with all his force, he hit the door and kept pushing until, finally, it opened wide enough for him to stick his head inside the room.

Gerald's room was in shambles, with furniture scattered about and what looked like his desk in a pile of pieces by one of the windows. Turning his head, John could see that a mattress and box springs were keeping him from getting inside. With a little more effort he was able to squeeze himself through the opening. Anne followed and together they looked around the room or – rather – what was left of it.

"What hit this place?" asked Anne.

"I have no idea, but this is awful. Look at his model airplane --- the World War Two bomber --- its been smashed to pieces, almost like someone stomped on it to look inside."

Anne had seen enough and called the sheriff's department. The dispatcher promised to send someone out immediately. Closing up the cell phone again she joined him in searching the room. They didn't find any traces of blood but, more importantly, there was no sign of Gerald.

John stood in front of a dresser whose empty drawers were scattered around it. Something hanging from underneath one of them caught his eye and he bent over to get a better view. There, attached to the bottom of the drawer, was a torn piece of manila envelope stuck to a strip of duct tape. John didn't see any writing on it.

"In the movies this is suppose to be the clue that solves the mystery," he said to Anne as he straightened back up.

"That's not very funny," replied Anne, who then added, "I'm going to search the room across the hall." She then squeezed back out the bedroom door and went across the hall. That door opened easily and she found herself looking at the same kind of disarray that she had just left. She quickly shouted out to John, "Look what happened here!" followed by, "Come see this."

She immediately heard the sound of someone coming across the hallway. John entered the room and saw the same devastation he had just left behind in Gerald's room. "Maybe it would be better to go outside and wait for the police," he said, after a quick look around failed to produce any sign of Gerald.

"We can wait here," said John letting out a sigh of relief as he walked out on the porch.

"No, not me," said Anne. "I'll be in the car. This place isn't safe, something bad's happened here." And with that she ran down the steps and out to the car.

* * * * *

It was shortly after two when the dark blue Ford turned into the lane and drove down to where two people stood waiting for it. After making his own quick search, Deputy Toulon decided that he needed more help. A possible kidnapping was not something he could handle alone.

By the time the sergeant who responded said John and Anne could leave, it was four-thirty.

Neither of them had anything to say as they drove back to Anne's office. Parking beside her car John looked around first before he reached over and gave her a hug. "I'm sorry about Gerald," he said. "I know they'll find him."

"I hope so---what a depressing afternoon," sighed Anne. "I even missed my two o'clock case plan." Exhausted by what had taken place at the Walker house, all Anne wanted to do was go home and lie down. She managed a give John a wave as she closed her car door.

John followed her out of the parking lot and north on the interstate toward Overland Park. It was then that he realized they had planned to have lunch after leaving the Walker house; but that had never happened. Deciding to get something to eat before going back to his office, John pulled off on one of the exits. Anything, even burgers, sounded great for dinner.

As he unlocked his office door John heard his phone ringing but, by the time he got to it the call had transferred to his voice mail. He started to listen to it but decided to eat first - the call could wait. After finishing, he began locating the files he needed for tomorrow's court appearances. He was putting the stack in his briefcase when the phone rang again. This time he answered it.

"Is this lawyer Calloway?" asked a voice that he could barely hear because of what sounded like diesel motors in the background.

"Yes it is," he said, "but speak up, it's hard to hear you over the noise."

"Is this lawyer Calloway?" asked the woman again, this time in a louder voice.

"Yes it is. Thank you, I can hear you better now. What can I do for you?"

"You're Gerald Walker's lawyer, aren't you?"

That question got John's attention and he reached for a legal pad. If this was going to be a ransom call, he could only write down her demands; he didn't have a recorder hooked up to his phone like some of the other guys in the office. He also knew he wasn't getting paid enough to get involved in any ransom negotiations.

The woman continued, "Lawyer Calloway, Gerald's in trouble."

John carefully chose his words then asked, "What makes you say that?"

Ignoring his question, she went on, "He needs your help." Her words came from a voice that, to John, seemed to be void of any emotion.

Still being careful with his words, three questions rapidly tumbled out. "How do you know? Is he with you? Did you take him?" Then catching himself he stopped and waited for her answers.

A long pause followed. He started to worry that whoever she was would hang up. John spoke up again hoping she wouldn't, only to have the woman interrupt him, "He's with me - I picked him up today. But Mr. Calloway – he's in danger. He saw one of the men from last night."

Relieved that she wasn't asking for a ransom John now had a new set of concerns. "What men? What danger?" he fired back. The lack of answers to any of his questions was starting to frustrate him, so John decided to go for broke. "Did you kidnap him?" he asked.

"No!" came the indignant reply.

John felt a wave of relief come over him as he waited for her to go on but, again, the woman was silent. He grew concerned again that she was about to hang up but, this time he didn't wait as long to say something. "You know the

Sheriff's Department is looking for Gerald. You need to call them immediately."

"Mr. Calloway – Mr. Calloway, I didn't kidnap Gerald. I'm trying to tell you something. Will you please just listen and quit asking so many questions." the woman shouted into the phone.

Taken aback by this, John apologized, "Sorry, it's just that I'm concerned for his safety; that's all."

"All you need to know is that he's safe, and that I won't harm him," she said before adding, "I could never hurt him."

She said all this in a calm voice and John knew she was telling the truth. He suddenly realized he was talking to Gerald's mother. But even this, he knew, didn't mean that the authorities shouldn't be notified of Gerald's whereabouts; after all, they had spent a large part of the day working under the assumption he'd been kidnapped. "You need to call the authorities," John said again. "I mean, I appreciate that you've called me, but they need to be told. And pronto fast so they can stop their search," he added.

"I can't," said Gerald's mother, "And you can't either. If either of us tell them, those two men may come after Gerald."

"What two men?" asked John. His frustration was back again and he knew it had come through in his voice. Calming himself down, he said, "I have no idea where you are, so I'm fairly confident that the two men you're concerned about don't either." Then he added, "Besides, I think you're his mother. Am I right?"

John's caller was quiet again and for the third time he grew afraid she was going to hang up. This time, however, there wasn't the customary pause. The first thing he heard was her sigh. "Yes, I'm his mother, but please, Mr. Calloway, please don't tell them I called you," she said and he could hear her crying.

"I have to," John replied. "They deserve to know more than that a woman called me to say he's all right. I have an obligation as Gerald's guardian *ad litem* to tell them where I think he is and with whom."

The woman began to say something, but the noise in the background got louder and John couldn't hear her. She must have realized this too, because she repeated herself in a louder voice.

"Pretty, what's that?" said John, perplexed upon hearing this word.

"Purdy, Mr. Calloway, that's where Gerald will be and I hope telling you don't make Gerald a target. If something happens to him there'll be no one for you to blame but yourself."

The phone then went dead. Holding onto the receiver he waited for Gerald's mother to call back, but she didn't and he soon hung up the phone.

John had heard of the town she mentioned but he couldn't remember where it was in southern Missouri. Opening one of his desk drawers, he took out a map of Missouri, one he had gotten somewhere for free, and opened it up. Purdy, he knew, was somewhere southeast of where he had grown up, but he wasn't quite sure after that. He first found Carthage and then began searching the southwest corner of the state before finding it in Barry County. It appeared to be about a hundred and seventy miles from Kansas City. Given the bad state of Missouri roads, John estimated the trip there would take about four hours. No wonder he had gotten such a late call from Gerald's mother.

Having found Purdy, John then shifted the map and looked for Noel, which was near where he was going camping on Friday. He located it about a quarter of an inch from the Arkansas state line. Satisfied with his exploration, he refolded the map and then called Anne.

He was barely able to contain his excitement when she answered. "If you aren't sitting down – you need to. I just had a very interesting call," he said and then went on to tell her about the conversation he had just had with Gerald's mother. Anne repeated several times that she couldn't believe it. When he was finished she asked if he was going to call the Sheriff's Department.

"Yes, I don't have a choice," John said. "You know, the old sworn to uphold the law thing. Besides, telling them may prevent Gerald from being harmed. Although I believe it was his mother I was talking to, it's always possible that it wasn't."

That possibility didn't make any sense to Anne. It had to be Gerald's mother who had called. In fact, her intuition had all along been that his mother had come and got him. Her main concern now was not that Gerald was with his mother, it was what his mother had said might happen to Gerald. "What about her concerns for Gerald's safety?" she asked.

"That bothers me too, but she didn't tell me any more about these two men. And honestly, he's so far from here – why would anyone go there to get at a ten year old?"

Anne didn't agree and urged him to tell the Sheriff's Department everything, even if he didn't think it was important. John listened and then admitted she could be right. They finished their conversation knowing that both of them had more to do tonight on the Walker case.

* * * * *

The call from Gerald Walker's GAL was transferred to a deputy who took down all of what John had to say, including his home and office numbers. Their conversation ended with the deputy saying that he'd pass on John's information and someone would call him back tonight.

Having given all his information, John, out of curiosity, asked Deputy Howard if he'd heard any other news about Gerald. The deputy's reply was that there was nothing he could tell him. "Departmental policy," he said. "Only the immediate family can be informed."

John started to say that as Gerald's Guardian *ad litem* he was immediate family. But he didn't, partially, because it was late and he wanted to go home and, partially, because even if he explained to the deputy what the role of a GAL was, he still wasn't going to get any information from him.

Their conversation over, John picked up his briefcase and left the office.

16

John drove home the back way. It took a few minutes longer and he used the time to think over the day – and what a day it had been. He stopped by the front door long enough to take the mail out of the box. The cat was waiting on the other side of the door - where she always was when he first got home. After looking through the mail he picked her up and rubbed her for a few minutes before he went to change his clothes.

Coming back into the living room he tried to watch a show on television, but was soon caught up in thinking about what had happened today. John concluded this time that maybe he was wrong; maybe the woman he'd talked to wasn't Gerald's mother. Maybe the phone call was a phony, designed to pass out false information. Maybe, in fact, what had really happened was that Harold Walker had finally gone over the edge and had taken Gerald to one of the Covenant compounds. If this were true, Gerald could be anywhere from Texas to Montana by now and with a new identity to boot.

This case, the Walker case, had always made John uncomfortable. Harold Walker was, in his opinion, a fanatic.

The Covenant cause didn't believe in the legitimacy of any government, federal, state or county or anyone who worked for them. Harold didn't like him, as John was a part of the system that was interfering in Harold's life. As a result, Mr. Walker was never pleasant and if it were possible, even less so since Gerald had been returned home by SRS in the middle of April.

Anne had said, more than once, that when she had first met with Gerald and his father at her SRS office that Mr. Walker had been so disruptive she was forced to call her supervisor to come sit with her so she could finish their meeting. After the same thing happened at their second meeting, Anne arranged to see the Walkers at Gerald's school. Mr. Walker, for some unknown reason, wasn't as disruptive at the school. He was still antagonistic but at least Anne was able to deal with him by herself.

John stopped himself from thinking any more about the case as he was getting depressed. He looked down at his watch and hurriedly got up off the sofa. It was time to get packed for his trip. Leaving the cat behind, John disappeared down into the basement to find his outdoor stove, ice chest, and two sleeping bags, including the one that had belonged to his ex. That was the easy part, the hard part was remembering where he had put the cooking utensils after the last time he'd used them. A ten-minute search for them ended with the depressing discovery of his wedding pictures. He looked at one or two of them before putting them back and starting out again to look for his missing cooking tools, but his anger momentarily took over and he turned and kicked the box where he'd found the pictures. His foot missed and he almost fell over. It was then that he remembered that the utensils were in the garage in a box behind his bicycle. He left them by the front door along with the equipment he had brought up from the basement.

It was now time to call Anne, as he'd done all the packing he could without talking to her. John knew she didn't like to get calls after ten, but this was different he said to himself, as he dialed her number.

Anne answered on the second ring and listened as John first apologized for calling so late before getting to the reason for the call. "We need to go over what each of us is bringing, you know, to make sure we're not doubling up on anything," he said.

Anne agreed that was a good idea and then finished the question that she had started to ask before John had cut her off to apologize. "What happened when you called the Sheriff's Office?"

"Nothing, the guy took down my information and said someone would get back to me tonight."

"That's it – with what you told them?" said Anne. "I can't believe it."

"How about you, did you make your call?" asked John as he had nothing to say in reply to her comments.

"No," said Anne. "After I talked to you, I felt it was too late to call anyone. I decided I'd tell my supervisor tomorrow."

With nothing more to say about the Walker case, they then went through a discussion of what each of them was taking. They decided that John's ex-wife's sleeping bag wasn't needed nor were two ice chests. Because it was bigger they decided to take John's. The rest of the duplicated items were minor and John quickly agreed to take Anne's instead of his. He knew, for a start, they were probably cleaner.

Having reached an agreement on what they were taking, they then confirmed that they would meet at Anne's at two p.m., load up her gray Honda and leave from there. It wasn't as though his car wasn't drivable, John had told her, after all they had gone to the Walker ranch in it today, but for the last week it had been making funny noises in the morning when he started it. That was enough for Anne to hear and she had insisted they take her car.

It was ten-thirty when they stopped talking and it was close to eleven when John finished packing. He then lay down on the couch to relax for a few minutes before going to bed. The last thing he remembered was the start of a movie.

* * * * *

The television was still on, but it was the cat moving around on his chest which had caused him to wake up. John pushed her off and got up to load his car. By the time that and his shower were done it was eight fifteen. Before leaving for the weekend he made sure Nutmeg had fresh water and a full bowl of food. Reluctantly, he scooped out her box and threw in some new litter. It was a job he never got used to but, over the years, he knew what would happen if he didn't keep the box clean. Nutmeg followed him to the door where he told her good by and that he would be home late Sunday night.

He then drove out to Olathe where parking at the courthouse was harder to find than usual. As a result John was five minutes late for his nine o'clock pretrial conference. That hearing was followed by two others - a half hour apart. After the last one John went down to the law library and used one of the phones to call Anne. She was away from her desk, but the person who answered her phone promised to give her the message that he had called and that he would be at his office at eleven.

Leaving the library John decided to go across the hall to the Sheriff's Department and speak to Deputy Howard. He was soon told by the person at the window that Deputy Howard wasn't due in until three. John then asked to speak to someone else. The sergeant who came out wouldn't tell him anything on how the search for Gerald Walker was going, not even when he told them he was Gerald's Guardian *ad litem*. He wouldn't even say why they hadn't contacted him yet. After he left John made up his mind to go see Judge Baker on Monday and ask him for help in getting information from the

Sheriff's Office. John wished he had time to go see the judge now, but knew he had to get back to his office.

* * * * *

The faint odor of ketchup from last night's dinner was still in the air when John opened his office door, but by the time he sat down it was gone. In the midst of reading his mail Jena interrupted him to say that Anne Hubert was on the phone. Anne hurriedly said she had only a minute to talk as a doctor she had been trying to reach all morning was on the other line. She started by saying she had no new news about Gerald, then listened as John briefly told her about his conversation at the Sheriff's office this morning. They both agreed that they needed to be kept more current on Gerald's case so Anne was glad John planned to see Judge Baker on Monday. Before hanging up she said they would still meet at her place at two.

The balance of the eleven o'clock hour passed quickly. John decided to work through lunch so that both he and his secretary could both leave early. The last letter he needed to go out she brought in at one twenty-five. Shortly after that, John locked up his desk and grabbed his sport coat. On his way out he told Jena to tell any of his clients who called that he had gone to a meeting which would last all afternoon. They both laughed at this – John never had any all afternoon meetings.

"Have a good weekend," she said as he opened the door to the hall.

"You too, Jena; see you Monday."

Staying on city streets John drove to Anne's apartment in the northern part of the county. He promptly violated the first rule of driving in Johnson County; never drive on Metcalf Avenue if any other route is available. The result was that it was almost twenty-five minutes later before he pulled into the parking lot of an older apartment complex off

Johnson Drive. Anne lived here on the ground floor of the two-story building.

John got there with three minutes to spare and parked next to her car. He left his empty ice chest in her kitchen before excusing himself and hurrying into her bathroom to change clothes. By the time he came out Anne had it filled and together they carried it back outside.

After several false starts in packing their gear, they managed to find room for everything in her car.

Anne went inside for one last look around her place to make sure they hadn't forgotten anything, while John did the same in his car. Before locking his car door, John grabbed his cell phone off the seat and they were soon on their way. Anne drove east on Johnson Drive and then south on State Line Road; she always liked this street because each side of the road was in a different state. Once on I-435 she drove east into Missouri before going south on U.S. 71.

"Well, the hard part of the driving is over," she said. "Once you're through the Grandview triangle it just naturally has to get better."

John laughed. "It's bad enough that three highways meet there, but it's Missouri - which means it will take forever to get corrected. Remember, it only took them twenty years to make 71 Highway a four-lane road from Carthage to Kansas City - twenty years," he repeated.

Conversation now turned to the weekend ahead. Anne began by saying, "I thought we had everything, but I just remembered we need milk. We'll get some when we get ice tomorrow to top off the cooler."

John nodded and looked over at Anne. She had great legs, but that wasn't all, she was really cute. Not beautiful, but very, very cute and his mind drifted into several reoccurring fantasies he had about her. Catching himself, he realized he had to tell her more about the area where they were going to float.

"Since you've never been down here," he began, "let me give you the short version of what to expect. Ok?"

"Sure, go ahead," said Anne.

"First, Southwest Missouri is very Republican – that means conservative Republican. It's also poor - the cost of living is 25 percent less than here. To make any money you either own your own business or are in a profession. Families have known each other since their great-great-grandfathers went to school together."

John stopped in case Anne had a response but she kept driving.

"Am I boring you?" he asked.

"No, go on and tell me about Carthage."

"Ok, but let me know if it gets to be too much. The town was founded in 1843 and burned down, I think five times, during the Civil War. Some of the guys I grew up with, their families have been there since the 1840's. My family arrived late, they didn't get there until 1867-1868, I forget exactly which year. The first Calloway was elected town marshal sometime after that and the rest, they say, is history. Oh, there's one thing I didn't tell you, there's a wagonload of gold hidden somewhere near the town."

Anne took her eyes off the road long enough to look at John to see if he was trying to make a joke. "Is that true?" she asked after deciding he was telling the truth.

"Oh, yea. A battle was fought there in 1861. The story goes that General Sterling Price, then a colonel, and the Missouri State militia on their movement south to join the Confederate forces in Arkansas, relieved several banks in the Union part of the state of the gold in their vaults. Union troops caught up with them near Carthage. The battle that followed lasted two days. The end result was a draw and the continued advance of the Missouri State militia toward Arkansas.

However, as the battle was raging on, General Price ordered the wagon with the gold on toward Arkansas. That was the last time anyone ever saw the gold. They did find the wagon - empty."

"Was any of the gold ever found?"

"No, that's what's interesting, none of it was ever found."

"What makes you think it's still there. Couldn't someone have found it by now and just not said anything?" she asked.

"They could have, --- except, and this is the kicker --- when they found the wagon it was alongside a creek, along with nineteen of the twenty soldiers who had left with it. One soldier was missing. And here it gets even better – they searched for him as they continued to retreat, but never found him.

Fast forward to 1869, eight years later. The town's growing and things are pretty much getting back to normal. My great, whatever grandfather, we'll say Grandfather just to keep it short, isn't town marshal yet, but he's working for the guy who is. It's late October and he sees a stranger hanging around the town square. At first he ignores him, but as the day wears on he runs into him at several places in town. He's not causing any problems, but something about him doesn't seem to be quite right.

Grandfather Calloway finally gets off work and starts walking for home. As he crosses Chestnut, one of the main streets now, but back then just a dirt path out of town, he sees the same stranger some distance off, holding onto the reins of his horse, while he's down on the ground looking for something.

This time Deputy Marshall Calloway decides to talk to him. Well, as Grandfather Calloway walks toward the man, he hollers out who he is and that he wants to talk. This, apparently, isn't what that man wanted to hear because he wheels around and fires three times at Grandfather. The bullets miss and he springs onto his horse and rides away.

Meanwhile, Grandfather has taken out his gun and tried to return the compliment, but his gun misfires and his hand is injured. By this time he's standing where the stranger has just been. To make a long story short, he sees something in the brush beside the road, a small grey bag, where the stranger had been looking. He picks it up and puts it in his pocket before going off to the doctor.

Nobody ever sees the stranger again in Carthage; that's important for what I'm about to tell you. Several days later Grandfather remembers the bag and takes it out to see what's in it. Inside he finds two twenty-dollar gold coins minted in 1857, one caked with mud and the other clean as a whistle, and a small but recognizable part of the original bronze seal belonging to the State of Missouri. Ready for this --- because this is the good part --- which seal was known to have been packed in the wagon with General Price's gold.

The Missouri Governor in 1861, Governor Jackson, who was pro-South, had taken it from the capitol in Jefferson City and carried it with him when he and Price retreated south after being driven out of northern Missouri. It too had mud on it. Now is that a great story or what!"

Anne was at a loss for words, the story was so fantastic. "What about the gold?" she finally asked.

"After Grandfather showed the sheriff the bag and what it had in it the hunt was on. Everywhere the stranger was known to or thought to have been was searched and researched. Nothing was ever found.

As a kid I even looked for General Price's gold on Saturdays for years. No one ever found so much as a scrap of wood, or anything else that could be connected with the boxes of Price's gold."

"So it's still there, waiting to be found?" asked Anne.

"It's supposed to be. But where, that's anyone's guess."

"Now that's fantastic. Why doesn't the town make a big deal about it and have a festival or something?" asked Anne.

John shrugged his shoulders and said, "Who knows. I haven't heard that much about the gold in the last few years, so people probably gave up looking for it – or worse - forgot about it."

The discussion about Price's gold over – they went on for several miles before John pointed out the Bates County Drainage Ditch as they passed Butler.

"There it is," he said pointing to a sign beside the road. "This is one of the reasons my ex said all the smart people have already left. Now this bridge covers what looks like a creek and this is the only name Bates County could find to name it," he said with a laugh.

Anne glanced at the sign and couldn't figure out what the big deal was; the sign was probably accurate. She told this to John and was treated to a short, but to her, boring monologue on the citizens of Bates County. When he finished she quickly changed the subject by offering to let John drive.

"Unless you're tired," he replied, "I'd just as soon wait until we get to Lamar." "It's an hour from here and a little over half way to where we're camping tonight."

This worked out, the subject changed to the weather. "I know it said Kansas City would be partly cloudy with a forty percent chance of rain and a high in the upper sixties or lower seventies," she said, and couldn't recall seeing anything about the weather in southwest Missouri.

"It'll be cooler down there," said John, "especially at night near the water. I hope you brought a heavy sweater."

"Yes, two in fact. You know me, I get cold easily," replied Anne.

South of Butler, the clouds began to thin enough for the sun to stay out for long periods of time. The interior of Anne's car heated up and John began to get sleepy. He tried to stay awake, but fell asleep just before Nevada. Anne decided to let him sleep and continued driving until she came to the first Lamar exit. John woke up as she slowed down to get off the highway.

"Turn at the bottom of the hill," he said trying to get the stiffness out of his neck by turning it from side to side. Anne came to a gas station and stopped beside one of the pumps.

"I saw a sign that said Harry Truman was born here," she said as she got out and began to cross the lot toward the station.

"He left before he was five, but we can go see the house if you want," said John. "It won't take long; it's about as big as a peanut." She disappeared inside without answering.

After filling the tank John started toward the station to pay for the gas and met Anne coming back out. "You want to go see his house?" he asked, unsure of whether she had heard him earlier.

"How much does it cost?" she asked.

"Nothing, the government operates it. It's close, about five minutes from here."

Anne thought for a moment then said, "Can we do it on the way back?"

"Sure, that's fine with me," said John.

When he came back to the car they traded places and John began driving south toward Carthage, which, according to a highway sign they saw, was thirty-three miles away.

"Ready to hear more about Carthage?" asked John.

"Will it be as entertaining as your last story?" said Anne as she looked out the window.

John laughed and, hearing him, Anne started laughing too.

"I swear the story's true," he said. "Anyway, I'm going to take that laugh as a 'yes' to more Carthage history, only this time it'll be about my family. My great-grandfather founded the family law firm in 1879. When I was growing up it consisted of my grandfather, two uncles and my dad. I thought about going back down there when I got out of law school, but it was too late. By that I mean I'd already been in Johnson County for several years.

To go back would have been a huge move. Besides, the ex told me she wouldn't move down there. That helped make up my mind. You know, 'how do you keep them down in Carthage, once they've seen KC?' I still love the area, but I can't live here."

When he finished she said, "I know what you mean. I grew up in Livingston, Texas. Wonderful town to grow up in, but I wanted more. My parents were really disappointed when I didn't come back after graduating from Rice."

Neither of them were now in a mood to talk and they both were soon lost in thought. The miles rolled by and they soon passed the exit for Jasper; that meant Carthage was eleven miles ahead. John began to rethink his decision to not stop and introduce Anne to his parents. "It just makes sense," he suddenly said out loud.

Anne jumped at hearing him and John quickly said, "I'm sorry, I was just thinking about when you asked me if we were going to see my parents. I still think granddad would be okay with meeting you, but mom and dad, no, now would not be the right time. Their meeting you on the way to our spending the night together; it would be too much for them."

"Well, I still want to meet them," said Anne.

"You will, just not this way. I don't want to poison the well."

The first Carthage exit came into view and, just as quickly, they passed by it and could see the next exit - Civil War Road. John pointed at the sign and said, "That apparently is the city's answer to the Battle of Carthage. Not Battle Line Road or Retreat Road, this is all you get—and no mention of the mystery of where the gold went. Oh, well so there it is."

They passed just as quickly by it and the other exits to the town; John hadn't seen anyone he knew on the highway, even though he looked in every car they passed. Still going south on U.S. 71 they passed under Interstate 44 whereupon the highway narrowed down to two lanes as they continued on toward the next town - Diamond.

"Diamond has a population of 800; you just saw the sign," said John going into what Anne knew would be another history lesson. "George Washington Carver was born near here."

"I think I've heard of him. Isn't he the peanut man?" asked Anne.

"Ten points," said John pretending to lick his finger and then pulling it down in the air. "This guy was born a slave and eventually went on to the Tuskegee Institute in Alabama where he did, in fact, develop a lot of uses for the peanut. You want to know something, I don't believe I have ever seen a peanut butter jar that's had anything on it about him. I've always wondered why. As a kid, I asked my mother why she thought that was true. Her answer was, 'they must be ashamed of that.'"

"Now that you mention it, I can't recall ever seeing anything about him on one either," said Anne.

"Anyway, where he was born is down that road a bit," he said pointing to a road as they passed by it.

Anne thought about what John had just told her and said, "Somebody ought to do something about that."

John didn't respond and Anne let it go, telling herself she would bring it up later.

The highway narrowed even more after Diamond and began to go up and down the hills that had become more frequent the further south they traveled.

The hills were even steeper and more frequent when John finally turned off U.S. 71 onto Missouri 59, and passed through Anderson. John slowed down on this road, as he wasn't sure how Anne's car would take the tight turns he knew lay ahead.

"It's fact time again," he said. "This time it's about Noel and the surrounding area. I don't know anything about

Anderson except there was once a governor of Kansas with that name." He then smiled at his own joke and went on, "Very small population - about twelve hundred. It has an obvious connection to Christmas. That's one of the town's two seasons; the other one is late spring and early summer when the Elk River runs high. Then the campgrounds in and near the town began to fill up Friday morning – sometimes Thursday. On Saturdays, starting early, the number of canoes begins to climb until, by one in the afternoon, there may be a hundred or more on the river at any one time. It's wall to wall people.

"The canoe rental place we're using, The Blue Eye, is one of only two that I know of who will take people far enough up the river so they can take a two day float. They'll bus us up about thirty miles to near Powell and drop us off. Then we'll float back to the city park in Noel.

Tonight we'll stay in the campground I called six weeks ago. I was the fourth person to call that morning for reservations for tonight. That's how busy it gets here."

John was on Highway 90 now and was still driving slowly. Signs announcing the location of their campground – Shallow Waters - were beginning to appear along the road. He saw the entrance just before one of the numerous bridges several miles outside of Noel. The campground got its name because the Elk and one of its feeder streams, Big Sugar, merged somewhere near here creating what was usually a wide, but shallow, river - except when it rained.

John turned off the highway and parked beside a small white building. Opposite it was a large building that held the camp toilets and showers. Anne got out and headed toward it while John went inside the office to register.

When he finished, John went back out to the car to wait for Anne. Upon her return he backed out and turned left to go about a quarter of a mile down a gravel road before turning right and parking the car facing the river.

The sun which had been out most of the day was now darting in and out of the clouds and casting shadows that disappeared across the river. At the same time, the air began to get cooler and they both put on a sweater.

This accomplished, they then discussed where to put up the green tent; eventually John's idea prevailed and they set it up beside the car with the opening facing the water.

While Anne continued unloading, John walked back to the office for firewood. Like most of these camps, it had a pile of wood scraps from one of the local sawmills. For four dollars, he bought a large grocery sack with which to carry back all the wood he could put in it.

It was a long walk back down the road under the weight of all the wood and John was glad to drop the sack beside the fire ring. Dragging the metal ring a little closer to their tent he then went to work building a fire. Behind him, on the west side of the camp, the constant sound of vehicles could be heard as they went back and forth over the nearby bridges.

While John was gone, Anne had turned the top of the ice chest into a kitchen counter and it was now covered with food and kitchen tools. She soon found herself traveling between the ice chest and the fire to fix dinner. They didn't have a table and John searched in the car trunk until he found his blue plastic tarp. He folded it in half and spread it out on the ground near the fire before sitting down to watch Anne as she finished fixing dinner.

After they had eaten, John began cleaning up. Anne offered to help, but he told her that it was only fair that he do his part. He always remembered that one of Janet's complaints about him, which she voiced several times during the divorce, was that he didn't help clean up after meals. John had vowed not to make that mistake again.

The last glow of sunlight disappeared over the ridge behind them when John finished cleaning and sat down next to Anne. She had her hands extended toward the fire and was rubbing them together to warm up. John threw on several more wood scraps which, as they began to burn, threw up sparks into the sky.

The added heat felt good to Anne. "It's wonderful here," she said.

"I know, just smell the air. It has a better smell than it does in the city," said John.

"I know and listen, the sound the water's making, it's so relaxing," she added.

"Did the wine help?" asked John.

Anne nodded. "And that didn't hurt either," she said.

They both fell silent. John looked around until he found the wine bottle and poured the last of it into their plastic cups. Anne held hers with both hands and continued to watch the patterns in the flames.

John decided there would never be a better time, so he leaned over and, after turning her face towards him, kissed her. They held their kiss until John slowly pulled away. "Thanks," he said taking hold of her left hand and gently squeezing it.

"My pleasure," she replied.

John continued to hold onto her hand as the fire began to burn out. "I'm tired," he said after watching it for a while.

"So am I," said Anne as she got up and walked towards the car. Before following her, John began to fold up the tarp. He knew from experience that if he didn't, it would be covered with dew in the morning and there would be no place to sit for breakfast. In the background John could hear Anne as she searched through her bag looking for something.

"I can't find it," she finally said.

"Can't find what?" he said turning around to see what she was doing.

"My flannel nightgown, I don't know where it is."

"Oh, too bad," John said, only half seriously.

"It is too bad," she said looking at the grin on his face. "Look, I get cold very easily."

John had finished folding the tarp and was now looking for a place in the trunk to store it until morning. Leaving it where it was he walked over to Anne and gently pulled her toward him. "I think I have the answer," he said, pulling her closer and looking into her eyes.

"You have a nightgown I can wear?" she said trying to keep a straight face.

They both began laughing and John leaned over and kissed her. "Wait here," he said as he disappeared into the tent.

Anne stood quietly against the side of the car waiting to see what he was going to do. Soon she heard noises that sounded to her like something being unzipped. Curiosity overcame her and she called out, "What's going on in there?"

"I'm putting our sleeping bags together," came back the muffled reply.

"That takes care of part of the problem," she said. "So, now, I'm going to go to the shower building; I'll be back shortly."

* * * * *

Anne didn't see John anywhere as she walked back toward their campsite. She did see that a gas lantern was now on the ground in front of their tent and, as she approached it, she could hear it hiss. Still unable to see John, she called out his name. His response came from inside the tent.

"John, I need to change clothes," she said.

"Come in here and we'll talk about it," replied John.

"Just a minute," she said, putting her makeup bag in the back seat of the car and closing the door. She then stood outside the tent long enough to take off one of her shoes.

Opening the tent flap with one hand and, holding that shoe in the other, Anne carefully stepped into the tent and sat down. She had just enough time to take off the other shoe and get in the sleeping bags before John reached out and turned off the gaslight.

Ignoring the sound of his heart, which he was sure Anne could hear, he moved his body over and up against hers. As he did, he began searching for her lips. They didn't take long to find.

* * * * *

It was nine fifty-five p.m. The noise from the highway had quieted down enough to have been replaced by that of the river, a sound which calmly filtered through the campground.

A white, four-door car with a Kansas license plate turned off the highway and came to a stop in front the camp office.

When she first saw the car Matty Brown had hoped that it was one of her friends coming by to tell her about a party somewhere. That two men proceeded to get out and walk toward the screen door instantly disappointed her. The driver was a fat man with a sunburned face who was wearing blue jeans and a T-shirt with a beer logo on the front. The other man was shorter by several inches, but equally as stocky – just not as fat.

Matty Brown greeted them from behind the counter as they entered the office. She hoped they wouldn't take long as it was almost time for her to get off work. In fact, she was just waiting for the other employee working with her to get back from checking on the bathrooms before they closed the office.

The first man nodded at her greeting and then said, "We're looking for two of our friends who said they were staying here tonight. Names are Calloway and Hubert."

Matty opened the registration book on the desk and began looking over the last couple of pages. "I don't see either of those names in here. Do you want to pay for them in case they're late? That happens more than you think," she said.

The fat man abruptly said, "Here?" then paused and in a more pleasant voice replied, "No, but thanks anyway." He started to leave but turned back and asked, "How many people from Kansas are here; you know they said they might come down with someone else."

Matty didn't need to look at the list again. "We don't have any," she said.

Roger Sumler thanked her again and walked outside. Once back in the car he said to Bill, "Now what? They could be anywhere tonight. For that matter they could already be on the river."

Bill had no idea what to do next and, instead of responding, asked a question of his own, "What time is it?"

Before Roger could respond Bill answered his own question. "It's a little after ten. How many more campgrounds are there?" he asked.

Roger shrugged his shoulders and said, "Your guess is as good as mine. We can go back inside and ask for the phone book."

"No, I've got a better idea. Let's go back to the motel. They'll be on the water tomorrow. We'll find them then."

"What makes you so sure?" asked Roger.

"What else is there to do down here?" replied Bill.

They both nodded in agreement, then after a moment Roger said, "Hubert's pretty good looking, I'm sure Calloway has found something else to do while he's here."

Bill laughed. "You got that right. So, we'll check the canoe rental places tomorrow and save ourselves the trouble of going to every camp."

Roger then pulled the car forward and began to turn around. As he did, his headlights shone down a gravel road revealing a green tent with a dark colored car behind it off in the distance.

* * * * *

John heard the sound of a car starting and it sounded to him like it was far off in the distance. Shortly afterwards the reflection of its lights illuminated the side of the tent. Just before falling back asleep, John prayed that whoever it was wouldn't park beside them.

* * * * *

Matty waited inside until the white car started to leave. Barry had not come back yet from checking the toilets, but it was now after closing time. She locked the front door and came back around the counter and, as was done every night, she turned over the last page in the registration book and put the clip back in place that held the next day's page. To her surprise across the top of the page was written "John Calloway, Overland Park, Kansas, two people."

Just then the white car passed by the office on its way out onto the highway. Matty ran to the door and had just managed to unlock it when she saw the car turn north on Highway 90. She stepped outside and half-heartedly waved her arms back and forth trying to get their attention, but it was no use, and she watched as the car disappeared off in the distance.

She went back inside long enough to turn off the lights. There was no reason she could think of to give the city any more free time; besides, between Barry and the strangers, she might never get out of here. She closed the door and went over to her pickup. On her way she saw Barry walking up from the restrooms and waved to him. If he wanted to give them some free time that was his business but, for her, the night was now her own.

17

John opened his eyes and slowly twisted his head from side to side hoping to reduce the stiffness in his neck. Sometime during the night he had lost his pillow and, without it, this is what usually happened when he slept on his stomach. He rolled over onto his back and started rubbing his eyes. The change in position made his neck feel better. "What a great-," he said out loud before putting his hand over his mouth. This was another thing that had driven Janet wild. She told him that his inconsiderate behavior was another of the many reasons she wanted a divorce.

Looking over, he hoped he hadn't awakened Anne. It was starting to get light and he could faintly make out the outline of her face as the sunlight filtered into the tent. She didn't say anything, but he saw that she had her eyes half open. He decided that he might as well own up to what he had started to say and spoke up again. "What a great night," he said.

"It certainly was, thank you," she said, closing her eyes again.

Feeling light-headed upon hearing this, John leaned over and kissed her before getting up and pulling on his jeans. "I'll start the fire and put on some water for coffee," he said, pushing aside the tent flap and stepping outside.

"Sounds great," said Anne as she stuck an arm out of the sleeping bags toward her bra which was lying in one corner of the tent.

John turned in time to watch as her arm disappeared back into the sleeping bags. "We need to be down at the canoe rental place by eight-thirty--- the bus leaves at nine," he said.

Anne was now noticeably twisting from side to side, which caused John to laugh. "What are you doing?" he asked.

"Putting on my clothes."

"Oh!" he said.

"Would you rather I not?" she said with a slight smile as she looked up at him.

John didn't reply, he couldn't help but notice her shoulders, they were so beautiful, and her face - she looked gorgeous. He thought about what Anne had just said, but not for long. Quickly stepping back inside he let go of the tent flap and crawled back into the sleeping bags. Lying beside her he began to gently rub one of his hands along her body.

"Hey, no fair, you've still got your pants on," she said gazing into his eyes.

"Not for long," he said. His words hung briefly in the air and quietly disappeared.

* * * * *

The coffee was ready when Anne got back from her shower. Her flip-flops alternately slapping her feet and then the ground had announced her approach despite the noise from the river.

"You ready to eat?" asked John as she walked past him toward the car.

"Starved," she said. "Thanks for fixing breakfast."

"Hey, it's okay. Besides, I'm a whiz at toasting bagels on a stick." And with that he handed her a paper plate with a bagel on it.

Once they finished eating the two of them began to pack the car. The first thing that went back in the trunk was the ice chest, closely followed by the tent. John left after that to go take his shower and when he got back Anne had put away the rest of their gear.

On the way out of the campground they agreed that, among other things, they needed another bag of ice to finish the trip. This decided, John waited until traffic cleared and then turned south on Highway 90 toward Noel.

"Ok, since I started the history tour of Southwest Missouri, I might as well go on with it," he said. "Noel is in McDonald County and about four or five miles from the Arkansas line. It's heavily dependent on the river for a large part of its money. As a result it has at least two grocery stores and there may be one other, I can't remember. Wilkins is on Howard, two blocks from the new bridge and Taylor's is one block to the east at the intersection of 4th and Grant Streets, next to the old post office."

They had decided earlier to stop at Wilkins - it was closer to where they were going to rent the canoe. Besides, John remembered, his experience was that Wilkins had a wider selection of beer and pretzels, two things he had forgotten to bring.

Going on, he said, "The County has a new river policy. No glass on the river. All beer has to be in cans now, no bottles anymore. If they see any glass in your canoe, the Sheriff's department will take it and give you, in return, a ticket that carries a minimum fifty-dollar fine. They even bought a johnboat and put an outboard motor on it to patrol the river. Why they didn't start this policy twenty years ago is anybody's' guess. You know what I mean?"

"I hear you," said Anne, "but since I'm not a beer drinker, it doesn't matter to me."

"Say, where's the other bottle of wine we brought with us?" asked John who had just realized it was somewhere in the car– and made of glass.

Anne had forgotten about it until now and with a worried tone in her voice said, "They won't search our canoe for it will they?"

"No way, not without some kind of probable cause. That pesky old Fourth Amendment, no unreasonable search and seizure, is still with us, even down here."

"Okay, well, let's hide it in one of the sleeping bags, just to be safe," she said.

John nodded as he pulled into the Wilkins parking lot and came to a stop near the front door. Once inside John began pushing a grocery cart toward the far west wall where he could see the start of a row of coolers. They turned down the aisle and came to the milk section.

"How much do we need?" asked John.

"A pint," said Anne. "Of 2%," she quickly added.

John put the small container in the basket and proceeded on down the aisle to the beer section. Here he took a six-pack of cans, that happened to be on sale, off the shelf. They were now at the back of the store looking for the pretzels that John wanted. They would then need only ice to be ready to go.

They were crossing the back of the store still looking for the pretzels and had just reached the cereal aisle when John stopped the cart so quickly that Anne ran into him. She started to apologize, but John cut her off. "Look!" he said pointing down the aisle.

Anne turned to see what was so important and saw a short, rather thin woman wearing jeans and a sweatshirt. Her brownish-red hair was pulled back into a ponytail. Beside her, though, was the person on whom her eyes quickly fell, it was Gerald Walker.

"Gerald--Gerald," called out John as he left the cart and hurried down the aisle.

The sound of John's voice startled the woman and she dropped the box she was holding and protectively put her arms around the boy. "What do you want?" she demanded of the two people who were now standing in front of her.

"Who are you?" demanded John.

They both continued staring at each other waiting for an answer to the question they each had asked.

Meanwhile, Gerald started struggling to get free of the woman's grasp. Finally, looking up at her, he exclaimed, "Let go, mamma, let go." When she did, Gerald sprang forward and threw his arms around the woman who was bent down in front of him. "Anne," he said pulling himself close to her.

"Gerald, are you okay?" she said as her eyes searched over him for any signs he had been mistreated.

"I'm okay," he said slowly letting go of her.

Gerald's mother relaxed upon seeing her son's actions and now said to Anne, "You're his social worker, aren't you?"

And then, without waiting for her answer, she turned toward John and said, "You're John Calloway. Well, thank the Lord; I thought at first you might be part of Harold's group. I'm Ralene Copley, Gerald's mom."

"Pleased to meet you," said John taking her outstretched hand.

Then looking down at Gerald he said, "You had us really worried. How long have you been down here?"

"Since Mamma came and got me."

Ralene added, "I came on Thursday, after Harold's Wednesday night call to come and get him."

"So you're the woman I talked to on the phone," said John. "You said you were Gerald's mother --- but I just wasn't sure. I thought you might be part of his group trying to throw me off in looking for Gerald."

Ralene listened and continued to nod as John finished talking.

It was now Anne's turn. "What are you two doing here?" she said to Ralene.

"We stopped here to get some cereal for Gerald," she replied. ""We've spent the last couple of days at his grandparents' in Gentry --- down in Arkansas. We're on our way back to Purdy because I go to work at three; I'm on second shift at the chicken processing plant."

It was now Anne who was nodding. When Ralene finished, Anne asked, "Why did Harold ask you to come get your son?"

Ralene waited until a woman pushed her cart by them and on around the end of the aisle. Then looking to make sure there was no one else around she whispered, "He said Gerald was in danger because he had heard and seen too much. That's all he said and, frankly, I didn't want to get into it with him as to what he meant."

"What's that mean, 'too much' - of what?" interjected John. The lawyer in him had taken over and was now back in the conversation, so much so that Anne put her hand on his arm. He quickly stopped talking.

Looking up and down the aisle again, Ralene continued, "Gerald was home with his cousin Wednesday night when two men came to the ranch. Go on Gerald, you tell them what happened next."

It was now Gerald's turn to tell them what had happened that night. He started with his cousin's arrival and quickly went into the chase through the field by the two men and their subsequent search for both him and his cousin in the woods and along the road. Gerald then went on to tell about what had happened Thursday morning before he left his house.

Nobody interrupted him until he had finished saying, "I was up in my room packing when I heard the loud voices. I could tell it was daddy downstairs; and then a man started shouting."

"What was he saying?' said Anne, her voice betraying her concern for the ten-year-old in front of her.

"All I heard was something like, 'We want to see the room."

Anne now said in a low voice, "What room?"

But, before Gerald could answer, John interrupted and asked, "Was it the same guys who chased after you the night before?"

Gerald turned to Anne and said, "I don't know which room."

"Was it one of the same guys, Gerald?" said John repeating his question, this time more firmly.

"I think so," he said. "He looked like one of them. And a white car, like the one I saw the night before, was parked out front of the house. When they took daddy away I saw it from the corner window."

Gerald finished and everyone was silent. John's eyes met Anne's and he knew she was in agreement that this was getting more serious the more they heard.

Anne now turned to Ralene and said, "We have to get Gerald back to Johnson County."

"Why?" she asked, putting her arm around him again. "I'm his mom, besides the divorce papers gave me rights to Gerald too."

"Ralene, Gerald's in Social Service's custody," said Anne firmly. "Besides the Sheriff's Department up there is still looking for him; he's a missing child."

John wasn't interested in where this conversation was now heading and broke in to ask the question he remembered he wanted to ask, "Gerald where did they say they were taking your dad; do you know?"

"No, but they said he was going to rest."

The answer didn't make any sense to Anne and it only added to her concern for Gerald.

"Ralene, we have to notify the Sheriff in Johnson County about Gerald," she said emphasizing Gerald's name.

"I know he's your child but he's in my care, and John's too, because a Kansas judge says so. We don't have a choice about telling."

"I'll leave and go back to Arkansas with him," she said.

"We'll just notify the authorities there," said John.

"But don't you see, Gerald's in danger up there," said Ralene.

"That may be true," said John, "but the Sheriff's Department up there will protect him. I don't know what's happened to your ex, but it's not as though he's led a monk's life."

"Don't you understand," she said, "there's more to this than what we've told you."

"So what else is there? Come on, get it out."

"Harold used their code. The one that he had taught Gerald."

"What code? Get to the point," said John impatiently.

"He called himself Gerald's father. He never called himself Gerald's father. It's always 'daddy this' or 'daddy that', never 'father.' Harold taught Gerald that if he used that word that something was wrong and Gerald needed to be quiet and go to his hiding place. Gerald heard him call himself that several times and he eventually hid, and it's a good thing too, because one of them came up to his room before they left."

Anne looked at John and said, "Now what?"

"Doesn't change my opinion of what needs to be done, how about yours?"

"No, not really, but I think I have a temporary solution. I'll call my supervisor and tell her about finding Gerald - that he's safe and with Ralene. She can keep him until we get off the river Sunday afternoon, as long she agrees to bring him to us, then we can take him back."

"I can live with that," said John. "I'll call the Sheriffs' Department and let them know what's happened down here and that Gerald will be back Sunday night." He turned to

Ralene and said, "How about it Ralene, will that work for you?"

"He'll be okay up there Ralene," said Anne. "You can hire a lawyer to get custody." Anne had put her hand on Ralene's arm to comfort her as she said this and could see the look of resignation on her face.

Searching for the right words Ralene finally said, "All right, I'll do it. Where do you want me to bring him?"

"The Blue Eye. You know, the canoe rental place," said John, who had decided to meet there even before Ralene had finished hearing Anne's offer. "At three o'clock," he added.

"Okay. But how do you know that I won't just disappear with Gerald?" asked Ralene.

Anne saw the sadness in her eyes and said, "Because you love him; you won't run."

"Because the law will fall on you like a ton of bricks and you'll be lucky to ever get him back," responded John in his best lawyer voice.

Ralene had nothing more to ask or say. Instead, she grabbed Gerald's hand and said, "Let's go," and hurried off toward the checkout counter.

Anne waved goodbye to Gerald, who kept looking back at her as his mother pulled him along. She stood at the end of the aisle and watched as the mother and son left the store. By the time John returned with the grocery cart she had told herself, several times, she would never let anything like this happen to a child of hers.

18

It was less than a two-minute drive from Wilkins to the Blue Eye parking lot. John left Anne with the car and went inside to pay for their canoe. While he was gone, she put the milk and beer in the cooler, but left the bag of ice on the pavement.

Finished, Anne then leaned up against the side of the car and waited for John to get back. Several people both went in and came back out before John emerged. He stopped as an old yellow school bus pulled in the lot and parked parallel to the street.

When he came back to the car Anne said, "I need to make the call to my supervisor on Gerald, but let's get the ice chest out of the car first. You can make your call when I get back."

"We need to get going," replied John upon hearing this. "It is 8:45 and that bus over there is leaving at nine. We need to get everything, including ourselves, on it before then."

"Maybe you want to wait to call," said Anne, raising her voice in response to his insensitive reply, "but I have a responsibility to let Sally know about Gerald." She then put her hand on one end of the cooler and said in a firm voice, "Let's get this out so I can go call." The tone in her voice was enough to get John over to the other side of the cooler without any further comments.

When they set it down, Anne left. John opened the drain and then started toward the bus with the two backpacks he had just taken out of the trunk. He left them on one of the back seats and went back to the car for the three plastic sacks filled with food. On the way back to the car for the next load he decided to leave the lantern and the gas stove – it would make it more difficult for them at night and at meals - but it would mean less weight they would have to carry. He took the tent and put it on the bus and then went back to get the ice chest ready to carry on board.

John was not alone in loading equipment on the bus. There were three other groups doing the same thing. Two of them were not going to spend the night on the river, so their main concern was getting their coolers on board. Once this had been accomplished they had found seats and paid no attention to him as he continued to get on and off the bus. The last people to get there, a young couple, had arrived late and were hastily bringing their gear on board.

While John continued to wait for Anne, he watched as two Blue Eye employees began loading canoes onto a metal trailer that was attached to the back of the bus. The bus driver stood and watched them for a while also, before wandering to the front of the bus and sitting down on the curb. His name was Mark and he had introduced himself to everyone as they first got on the bus. John thought he was in his late twenties. He wore a torn T-shirt with the name of a band that hadn't had a hit for at least five years and his tennis shoes were caked with mud. Between John's third and fourth trip he had reminded John to pick up enough paddles and life vests from the pile beside the office door for all the people who were going with him.

"State requires the vests, can't go no place without the paddles," he said.

John couldn't argue with that logic and stopped to comply with Mark's request. He had just gotten off the bus when Anne emerged from the office and motioned for him to come over to where she was standing.

"Sally's not happy, but she'll do it," she said. "When I told her we found Gerald and were going to bring him back tomorrow, she told me I should have taken him to the police immediately. I finally got her to listen to our reasons for handling it our way and she reluctantly agreed it would be the easiest way to get Gerald back."

After hearing this, John said, "It's my turn now," and headed toward the door. Calling back to her he added, "Wait by the car, you know we still have to load the cooler. Everything else is on the bus already."

"Wait, there's more," said Anne. "Sally also said she would take the responsibility of notifying the Sheriff's office."

"I really think I need to go ahead and call," John said, stopping to think about Sally's offer. "Well," he said finally, "do you think she'll do it?"

"That sounds more like the lawyer I know," said Anne. "Yes, she'll do it."

"I do have an obligation to Gerald."

"Go call then," she said.

The sound of the bus starting caught John's attention. Looking up he saw Mark in the driver's seat leaning out the side window to adjust his mirror. "Well, okay. I guess it'll be all right," he said.

Mark honked the horn and motioned for them to get on the bus. They quickly ran to get their cooler. It was John who got on the bus first and dragged the cooler down the aisle, toward the rest of their gear, while Anne followed behind him.

As she sat down, something caught Anne's eye and she looked over to her left where, several rows away, a couple in their early twenties was sitting. He was skinny and about John's size, but she was a couple of inches shorter than Anne and needed to lose at least twenty pounds. She wondered if they were married.

Anne looked at her left hand and wondered if she would ever get married again, then reminded herself that she was only dating John. It was way too soon to start thinking of marriage to a guy she had only been seeing for a couple of months.

* * * * *

Mark let out the clutch and the bus slowly moved out of the lot and onto Main Street. The stoplight ahead was red and he began to slow down. But as he did the light turned green so Mark pushed down on the gas pedal causing the bus to jerk forward. He quickly glanced in the rear view mirror to see what effect that had on his passengers. It appeared that no one had paid any attention, at least that he could tell.

He began to slow down again for the light at the end of the new bridge and this time he had to stop. From here to the furthest point on this trip was about thirty-five miles. Mark knew this because, after five summers of driving this bus six days a week, he could practically drive it in his sleep.

They were now at the place on his route where Mark always began his speech. Depending on how many groups he took in a given day he might make this speech as many as six times. "You-all need to listen up," he began. At sound of his voice the people inside the bus quieted down. The only sounds that could be heard were from the engine and the tires and, like always, they would periodically drown out parts of his talk.

"The first stop will be in twenty minutes, give or take and bit. Let's see, seven, yes seven, of you will get off there. For the rest of you, just so you won't fret, after this group gets on the water it will be thirty more minutes to your put-in point. Remember to wear your life vest. The Blue Eye and the state of Missouri both suggest you wear them while on the water. We all know they won't do you no good in the bottom of the canoe if you tip over.

Which brings me to the next thing. At least one deputy sheriff will be on the river today. He may be where you are, so listen up here, no, I mean no bottles are to go on the river.

Next, if you plan on fishing you must have a license --- a Missouri fishing license. And no, your Arkansas, Oklahoma or Kansas license is not good here, this is Missouri. McDonald County is not, as a man tried to convince a deputy last week, in Arkansas."

Some of the people laughed at this and Mark waited a moment before he continued. "Remember, whatever you take on the water take it off with you at the end. This means no cans, paper or plastic should be left at any campsite, gravel bar or stopping place or thrown in the water.

And lastly, the Elk is an easy moving river with many places to stop. But now, don't let that fool you into thinking you can climb on everybody's land. Some people don't care, but there's those who do not take kindly to strangers on their land. That's it, did I make myself clear enough?"

The people on the bus clapped. John then looked at Anne and said in a low voice, "He's having his fifteen minutes of fame."

Anne smiled and nodded in agreement.

For some reason, Mark decided he needed to repeat part of his speech again. "People, I have to repeat this last point. Some people along the river will get very unhappy if they happen to find you on their land. They have been known to get physical, so stay on the gravel bars and off the bluffs and out of any fields." After again asking if there were any questions and getting none, Mark turned his attention back to the road.

* * * * *

John went back to looking out his window. It was now sunny, but a slight chill still hung in the air. The trees were fully out down here and the grass along the side of the road was green and starting to get thick. Here and there dandelions showed off their yellow color and sometimes, as the road twisted and turned, sunlight would spill into the bus and he could feel its heat.

Anne sat cross-legged on the seat and began her breathing exercises. It was, she reminded herself, going to be wonderful with John on the river even if she had to wait until tomorrow night to take a shower. The thought of smelling dirty made her shudder and she quickly focused back on her breathing.

The first stop was actually under the U.S. 71 Highway bridge. To get there Mark had to first go over the bridge and then turn onto a side road about a quarter of a mile past it and then immediately onto a narrower road which led down to the river. He carefully turned the bus around in the rocky area near the base of the bridge and stopped with the canoe carrier close to the water. With help from the two departing groups, he took off three canoes. He watched while the people loaded them with whatever they had decided to bring and then waved to each canoe as it was shoved off the bank and into the current.

Once back on the highway, Mark continued driving north toward the Bethpage exit. Turning on the radio he settled on a station in Tulsa whose sound carried back through the bus to the two remaining couples. John didn't care for country music and concentrated on looking at the passing scenery trying to ignore it. For her part, Anne went back to her breathing exercises and quickly blocked out the sound.

The bus eventually turned off onto County Road AA and headed east toward the AA Bridge.

Mark soon saw the place he was driving to up ahead. Just before, it, on the right hand side of the road, was a piece of land that looked to be wide enough for the bus and the canoe trailer to turn around. It was here that Mark pulled off the road and, with the skill born of five years of experience, turned in such a way that, like the last stop, the trailer stopped next to the river. After shutting off the engine, Mark asked the two remaining men to help him unload the canoes. The two women spent their time unloading what they could of their belongings, but both of them had to wait for help to get their ice chests off the bus and into their canoes.

It was starting to warm up, taking away what was left of the morning chill. John took off his Missouri sweatshirt and tied it around his waist. He wore it a lot and it showed – a seam on one side was torn and both cuffs and the neck were frayed. It was time, he knew, to get a new one, but John liked this one because it was perfect for trips like this.

Anne was the first into the canoe. Holding onto both sides she carefully walked herself up to the bow and sat down using her life jacket as a cushion. John waited until she was holding her paddle before he pushed the canoe off the bank. At the last possible moment he hopped in the back and, taking up his paddle, turned the canoe into the brown current. Then both he and Anne waved goodbye to Mark as the AA bridge slowly disappeared behind them.

The next time he looked back John saw that the last canoe was finally in the water. That couple had been slow to leave because she couldn't find her sunglasses. He couldn't tell if she had found them, but for her sake he hoped she had, as the sun bouncing off the water could be blinding this time of year. For his sake, he hoped it got cloudy - and stayed that way - for her search had reminded John that his sunglasses were in the center console of Anne's car.

John began to watch the river. There was something about being on the water that was soothing to him. Maybe it was because it was so different from his usual surroundings or maybe it was just that there was nothing else to do on the river - except play.

He began to hear the crickets hidden in the deep shadows of the riverbank and somewhere, out of sight, a crow would caw now and then only to be answered back ever so faintly. The trees lining the sides of the river blocked out much of the sun and kept John in the middle where he could see ahead better. It had rained earlier in the week and so much dirt had been flushed into the river that its color had changed. That also meant that downed tree limbs and rocks were harder to spot. Although the water was now brown it would sometimes change back to its usual dark green as they glided through the deeper pools.

Anne had laid her paddle down and was spending her time enjoying the passing scenery. Earlier she had asked John to keep in the sun as much as possible saying that she had been cold all morning. He had done just that. Now, feeling warmer, it was her turn to take off a sweatshirt.

Their canoe continued to drift along in the current. After a while John broke the silence and asked, "Do you think she called?"

"Who?" said Anne as she finished with the suntan lotion and put it in her backpack.

"Your supervisor, do you think she called the sheriff?"

"Yes, she does what she says," replied Anne.

"That's good. I've started to feel guilty because I didn't call."

Anne was still calm from her breathing exercises, but could feel the tension in John's voice.

She quietly said, "Why does it matter who called? You found Gerald; you did your job."

Anne's words made sense and John began to relax. His mother, and even his ex, had both told him he needed to be more trusting. Maybe, he thought, now was the time to start. "You sound like Janet," he said and immediately wished he could take the words back.

"I am not your ex-wife," came the predictable, but remarkably calm reply.

"I know, I know," he quickly said. "What I really meant to say is that's what she would have said, to me, but not in such a nice way --- like you just did." "Thank god," he said to himself, for at least he hadn't added that his mother would have said it too, that might have killed the weekend.

Turning around to see the expression on his face, Anne said, "If this is not too inappropriate, you just sounded like my ex-husband."

Breaking out in a smile that was partly an expression of relief, John replied, "Say, how many people are in this canoe? Looks like four to me."

"Do we have enough food for all of us? I know we have enough baggage," said Anne.

Their laughter bounced off the water and then disappeared into the thick stands of trees that still spread out over the river's edge. It sounded, to John, like at least four people laughing.

* * * * *

They had been floating for an hour when John guided the canoe toward a narrow gravel bar on the left side of the river. As the front of the canoe began to slide up the rocky bank, John jumped out and pulled it forward until half of it was out of the river.

Careful not to get her feet wet as she got out, Anne ran back behind some tall weeds, quickly disappearing from John's view. And although he looked, he couldn't see what she was doing but, when she came back out, Anne had a pinched look on her face.

"You forgot the toilet paper," said John, guessing at the reason for her look.

Anne nodded. "There weren't any leaves either," she added with disgust.

The water moving through the shallows gave off a soothing murmur that was occasionally interrupted by several blue jays calling back and forth to each other. Anne looked up to see if she could find them and caught sight of a hawk lazily circling overhead. "This is heaven," she said before leaning over and giving John a kiss on his cheek.

All John could manage to do was to stammer out, "I know." He wanted to add "I love you," but couldn't get the words out.

He was building up his courage to tell her this when the sight of a canoe coming down the river broke the magic of the moment. It was the other couple who had been on the bus with them. The woman was sitting in front and no longer wearing her T-shirt. In one hand she held what looked to be a can of beer.

Her companion had removed his T-shirt and John could see he had a big tattoo of something on one side of his chest. He too was drinking, but, unlike her, he finished whatever it was and dropped the can in the boat.

They beached their canoe on the gravel bar while Anne and John stood and watched. The man, whose name John thought was Mac, said, "Hi" and moved off toward the same bushes Anne had ducked behind. The woman, whose name was Tanya, took out her suntan lotion and was using the time to apply it to her face and legs.

John looked at Anne and they began to push their canoe back out into the current. He held onto its side while Anne waded out and got in, after which John climbed in the back and started paddling. He really didn't need to as the current here was fairly swift, but he was in a hurry to find the magic again. On the gravel bar he had felt better than he had in a long time and John wanted to chase that feeling on down the river until he caught it again.

The sun was now high enough in the sky that the sunlight bouncing off the bottom of the canoe was starting to bother John's eyes. He tried squinting for a while and even moved his head around hoping to find an angle where the sun wouldn't bother him. Finally, when none of this worked, he reached to untie his sweatshirt from around his waist to lay on the bottom of the canoe to block the sun. It wasn't there. He looked around to see if he had laid it down somewhere else, but it was gone.

"Anne, have you seen my Missouri sweatshirt?" he finally asked.

"No, but you had it on the gravel bar. That's the last time I saw it," she said.

John looked back up the river, but knew it was too late. The gravel bar, like the couple they had paddled quickly away from, was far back upstream. "It must have come undone back there when we stopped," he said, resigning himself to having lost it. "I don't know what else could have happened to it."

"Turn around and let's go back and get it," said Anne.

"No, it's not that big a deal."

Anne didn't believe him. "That sure doesn't sound convincing to me," she said.

"We'll, okay, it was my favorite sweatshirt --- but it was starting to wear out."

"So let's turn around and go back and get it," she said, again and began pushing her paddle forward in the water to slow the canoe down.

John quickly used his paddle to counter her stroke. "It's okay Anne," he said. "I need a new one anyway, I can live without it."

"Maybe you wanted to lose it," she said. Swallowing hard she waited for John to comment on this while she continued fighting the battle raging on in her head. However, the thoughts kept coming, "What are you doing? That was a dumb thing to say, he's not your ex. What did he tell you, and just about everybody else, about your mouth?" That is, until Anne forced herself to think of something positive about herself.

John looked at the back of her head and said, "Maybe you're right. Anyway we're not going back. It would take too long and would be very hard work to go back against the current."

The river had now started curving to the left and the trees on the right bank gradually receded away and were replaced by fields. Anne and John were quiet now; both of them having lapsed into their own thoughts, as the canoe slowly drifted down the river.

Anne was soon through what her therapist called a "periodic situational anxiety episode." This time, though, she had been able to center herself in a shorter than usual time and she now began to talk again. First it was about dinner, then about Gerald Walker and so on, until finally she was ready to venture into new territory. She had watched as the river widened out and began to get shallower. Behind her she could hear John's paddle as it rhythmically went in and out of the water. "I liked it back on the gravel bar," she began.

"So did I."

She hesitated and then said, "It was because I felt safe with you, John. It was like there was only me and you and no one else in the world."

John thought about this for a moment and then said, "I felt close to you too, closer than I've felt to anyone for a long time."

"I'm glad," said Anne.

John strained to hear her but her voice was so low John asked her to repeat herself.

This time in a louder voice she said, "I think I love you."

John's back stiffened. He couldn't think of anything to say and so he continued paddling. "It's been a long time since I've heard those words," he finally said as he realized what he had just heard.

Anne smiled but didn't have the courage to look back. She had wanted to say that to him last night, just after, well, just after last night. She had felt the love in her heart for him for at least a week but somehow, for whatever reason, she didn't think last night was the right time to tell John.

It was when they were on the gravel bar that Anne had decided there was never going to be a right time. And it was then she had promised herself to tell him she loved him before the day was over. It had taken everything she had to say it. Hearing his answer made her feel stronger and Anne summoned up enough of her newfound strength to turn around and smile at him. She realized she had always appreciated the way he treated her, even if he had cheesily looked her up and down at court hearings.

John's forearms had started to tingle when Anne said she loved him and they hadn't stopped yet. He managed, not without some effort, to now say, "Thank you." His face felt hot after saying that and he hoped she didn't turn around again and see him. The hypnotic effect of the river now took hold of John again and he was soon lost in thought. He wondered if she knew how shy he really was and how hard it had been for him to say as much as he had.

* * * * *

They had been traveling for another hour when, ahead of them, a large island slowly appeared, an island that seemed to fill up the middle of the river. While not perfect, it looked to be a good place to stop for lunch. As they drew closer they could see it was covered with debris that had washed onto it from the high water coming down the river after the recent rains.

John began to steer their canoe into the main channel while trying to keep it as close as possible to the island; while, for her part, Anne kept looking for a way to get on shore without getting her shoes any wetter - now that they had started to dry. Finding nothing that was promising she gave up and jumped out. Landing in the shallow water she scrambled onto the rocky beach and shook her feet, one at a time, trying to get the water out of her shoes.

Anne's jump had caused the canoe to dip and for a moment it acted like it might capsize. However, John quickly leaned the opposite way and kept it upright but, it had dipped far enough over to take on some water - but not much. He then turned the canoe in toward the shore and grounded it. Climbing out into the water he pushed the canoe up the narrow bank until it stopped moving.

Anne and John then sat down and ate in the shade of several big trees that were beside their canoe. They talked about nothing in particular as they watched the river go by. Anne stopped long enough to put more sunscreen on her face and roll down the sleeves of the blue cotton work-shirt she was wearing. No skin cancer for her, she said to herself.

Sitting in the cool shade after eating, John began to get sleepy and he slowly closed his eyes. The last thing he remembered, before falling asleep, was the sound of a car backfiring several times way, way off in the distance.

What exactly it was that woke him up, John never knew but, whatever it was, it caused him to look up river where he watched as a canoe slowly came around the far bend. John was almost positive it was the same couple who had been on the bus, the people they had left behind at the gravel bar, coming their way again. Squinting in the hope of seeing better, since he didn't have his sunglasses, he saw that a woman who looked about Tanya's size was seated up front and appeared to be leaning forward as though she had fallen asleep. The man – who must be Mac - was still in the back, but was now wearing a jacket or something that was black with dark letters on it. However, it was not his clothing that got John's attention. It was the way he was paddling. He was paddling very awkwardly, as though he was having trouble keeping the canoe going in a straight line. While keeping one eye on them John looked over and kept nudging Anne until finally she opened her eyes to see what he wanted.

After looking at the canoe, Anne agreed that it looked a lot like the same couple, but she wasn't positive.

"It has to be them," said John, "because so few people do this long float. But let's go before they get here." Pausing briefly, he then added, "They were drinking up a storm earlier. There's no telling what shape they're in now, but they look like they've gotten worse."

Anne said, "Okay by me, I'm ready to go."

They got up and went down to the edge of the water. Anne waited until John dragged the canoe back out into the shallows. Taking a last look around, to make sure they hadn't forgotten anything this time, she then waded out and climbed in the front. Once she was seated John climbed in the back, took up his paddle and pushed off the bank and back out into the current.

As they began to pick up speed John turned and noticed that the other canoe was moving even more slowly. The man in back - who he was almost certain was Mac - appeared to be very drunk and, for some reason, this really annoyed John. He told Anne in a voice filled with disgust that he found it hard to believe that people would miss such beautiful scenery, not to mention put themselves at risk, by getting so drunk this early in the day.

Anne nodded and said she wondered why, too. After her earlier questioning of John's motives when he lost his sweatshirt, she decided not to offer her professional opinion on their apparent behavior. Maybe she would tell him later, maybe she wouldn't.

Their canoe began to pick up speed as it approached the end of the island where the river narrowed. Here the banks of the river were now steeper and tree limbs hung in the water where its leaves would bob up and down with the current.

The canoe glided on through deep pools of water aided occasionally by John's paddle strokes. Now and then they startled a cow on the riverbank that would look up at them and, just as quickly, go back to drinking at the water's edge.

They saw no one else after they floated away from the couple behind them. Mark, the bus driver, had said that the chances of seeing other people along this stretch of the river were slim. Much of the land was forested and few people lived near the water. Besides, he had added, most people only floated for a day and that meant they got on the river at the first stop - under the U.S. 71 bridge.

This time they had been floating for over an hour when John noticed that the sun was beginning to disappear behind a bank of clouds that was building up ahead of them. He had long ago stopped thinking about who else was on the river; Anne was enough for him.

19

John was still watching the clouds; indeed, they had periodically pulled him out of the trance he was in - a trance he seemed to experience every time he was on the river for a while. Looking at his watch and saw it was now five-fifteen. The last time he had checked it had been four-thirty. He thought then that he had put on enough sunscreen, but in checking the time now he could see the outline of his watch on his skin. "Oh well," he said to himself, knowing there was nothing he could do about it now.

The canoe was now floating toward the bridge where the Blue Eye bus had made its first stop. John saw that no one was there, which gave the place a strangely empty look. Above them, in the distance, cars and trucks could first be seen and then heard as they went across the bridge.

"Anne, we need to find a place to camp for the night," said John glancing up at the figure sitting in front of him.

"Here?" she asked pointing toward the bridge.

"No, not here," said John. "It wouldn't be good here. Too much noise and no privacy. Besides, near a highway, who knows who might pull off the road at the sight of our camp. Let's go on until at least until six; there are better places ahead."

With that John continued on with the steady stroke he had developed over the last several miles. The people in the canoe behind them hadn't been seen for hours and John guessed they had already stopped for the night, given the way they had been drinking.

Remarkably, he wasn't tired. The exercise he'd been doing every other night for the past month was paying off. The agony of the sit-ups and push-ups had been worth it. Nothing, he thought, could have been worse than having to get off the river because he was too out of shape to keep going. Well, one thing could have been worse, he decided - Anne having to take over the paddling.

The noise from the bridge traffic slowly faded as they continued on down the river. The clouds that had been forming off to the west around three o'clock were now bunching up and climbing higher in the sky. As they did, they began to block out the sun and drop the temperature. John had continued to hope that they would blow over. When it became apparent that wasn't going to happen, he grew concerned.

"It looks like it's going to rain," he said, "whether we want it to or not."

"It better not." said Anne. "After such a perfect day, I want a perfect night."

"It may be perfect all right, perfectly awful," said John with a laugh.

Anne caught sight of his grin and said, "You know what I mean."

Another half-hour passed by before they heard the first sounds of thunder. The sun was now totally hidden behind grayish-black clouds. John couldn't tell from what direction the thunder had come, but knew it didn't matter, it was time to stop and set up camp. "Anne, we need to get off the river," he said, a worried tone in his voice.

"I know. It's dangerous to be on water when there's thunder about." she said.

"Well," said John, "if lightning ever struck the water near us, we'd be toast." He continued to scan sides of the river for a place to pull in, but there didn't seem to be any good spots.

They had floated on for several minutes more down a narrow valley, the sides of which almost came down to the river's edge. Coming around yet another turn, John spied a small clearing on the right. The ground still rose steeply up from the river but at least it managed to flatten out near the top of the bank. He began to guide the canoe toward the spot he had picked. "Over there Anne, do you see that clearing?" he said pointing toward it.

"Yes," she said without knowing which direction he was pointing – because all she could see were trees.

"That's where we'll camp. It's high enough up that, if the river rises, we won't be washed away. And we can use wood from that dead tree on the left for firewood," he said.

It was then that Anne saw the place he was talking about. "Looks good to me," she said. "Do you think there'll be enough time to dry out our clothes before the weather breaks?"

John looked overhead. "Maybe, this may not turn out to be as bad as it looks." he said. "It could just blow over; it's too hard to tell."

When the canoe grounded against the bank they both jumped out and John took the guide rope and tied it around the stump of a tree. They both began unloading and carrying the equipment up the sloping bank to the clearing. The last item they took was the ice chest. It took both of them to get it out of the canoe and then to drag it up the bank. The effort quickly tired them out and they had to stop to rest.

The empty the canoe now posed a dilemma. John knew it needed to be out of the water and far up the incline just in case the water level rose during the night. With much effort, he and Anne managed to pull the front end out of the water and then drag the entire boat about two thirds of the way up the incline before they turned it on its side to keep out as much rain as possible. John knew if the river rose that high they could kiss themselves goodbye, as the rain needed to accomplish this feat would be of biblical proportions.

Anne now went back to setting up the tent. She was able to lay it out flat, but hammering the stakes in the ground did not go according to plan. Two of them wouldn't go in the ground no matter how hard she hit them. John came over to try his luck, but it took moving the tent before he could get four stakes in the ground. Once it was up, Anne quickly began putting their gear inside. The sky continued to darken and she didn't want spend the night in a wet bed or, worse, have to get up and put on wet clothes.

Meanwhile, John had begun breaking branches off the dead tree and tossing them into a makeshift pile. After several minutes he stopped and gathered up an armload of wood and carried it to a spot closer to the tent where the wind was partially blocked by the trees and the hill behind them.

The sunlight was almost gone by now. Smoke from the fire John had just built was being pulled upward in a thick swirl toward the black clouds moving across the sky. As the first pieces of wood began to burn down John started placing thicker ones on the flames. The temperature was still falling and the heat felt good to him.

Anne now emerged from the tent wearing a sweater and carrying a paper bag and a small box of aluminum foil. She stopped long enough to remove several items from one of the plastic bags holding their food before coming over to the fire. Once there, she proceeded to wrap a large and a small potato, along with several carrots, in foil. Kneeling down she found a stick on the ground and used it to dig a small trench in the embers before dropping in the foil-covered food and covering them with embers. Satisfied with her work she sat down and began to watch the fire. Occasionally, she would lean over and push more embers over any foil that managed to become exposed.

It was John's job to cook the steak. He had barely started when the first drops of rain hit the fire, exploding into puffs of steam. "I hope you like your steak raw," he said upon seeing this happen a second time.

"Not particularly," replied Anne. "I hope you like eating alone, because if anymore rain hits me, I'm going into the tent."

John laughed and wondered where she got her quick comebacks. That was something Janet could never do.

Anne didn't have long to wait. The rain continued and she got up and ran to the tent, disappearing inside and leaving John to finish the meat. He pulled up the hood on his poncho and waited for the steak to cook as the rain began to come down ever harder. When the meat was done he hastily pulled it off the fire and threw it onto a paper plate before handing it through the tent opening to Anne. He then quickly dug the vegetables out of the coals and threw them on another plate. Handing it to Anne, he ducked inside the tent where they sat and ate as they watched the rain come down.

By the time they finished eating the rain had noticeably increased. John dashed out long enough to throw their paper plates on the fire before jumping over several puddles that had appeared on his way to the pile of firewood. Once there he began throwing pieces of wood under a nearby tree, hoping they would be dry enough to use later.

When he finally got back in the tent he looked at his watch. It was nearly eight o'clock. Dinner had taken longer than he had thought. The fire had started to drown under the constant pounding from the rain and he could barely see Anne in its fading light. Reluctantly he zipped the tent flaps together to keep both the rain and the increasing chill out.

Reluctantly, that is, because he could feel the first pangs of his claustrophobia coming on. "Damn Cusco," he said, "and that room. If it hadn't been so cold there."

Anne had heard what had happened to him in Peru and she didn't say anything. She'd heard the story enough times. John couldn't take it anymore and reached over and unzipped and opened the flaps about a third of the way before sitting back down on his sleeping bag.

"What do you want to do?" he asked as he took off his shoes and then looked around in the near total darkness for his towel to wipe the rain off his face. He could feel his claustrophobia easing up now that the tent wasn't all closed up. John even felt sure he wasn't going to throw up. He just couldn't do that, not with Anne here, that would be the ultimate in embarrassment. However, both of them, he knew, were doomed to working with his problem tonight.

"I don't know. Right now I wonder if I ate too much," said Anne.

"I don't think so; a small potato, two carrots plus half as much steak as I ate doesn't strike me as too much."

"Well, I don't want to get fat."

"Don't worry, you're not fat."

"You don't think so?"

John paused for a moment then said, "Do I really want to say this to you?"

"Say what?" she asked.

"Say what I'm thinking," he replied.

"Oh, come on, tell me," said Anne.

"Okay. Well don't get mad at me. Remember, you asked for this," said John feeling, again, the wine they had been drinking. He first took a deep breath and then said, "Anne, you have a great body. You're definitely not fat." When he finished talking he could feel his face getting red.

There was no response from Anne and John couldn't see in the dark to tell if she was shocked, offended or just didn't care what he had said. When the inside of the tent suddenly lit up from one of the lightning flashes he was still unable to tell from her face what she was thinking. Finally, because she was still so quiet, he nervously said, "Anne – Anne did I offend you?"

She still didn't answer.

John was now really concerned. Maybe, he thought to himself, honesty wasn't the best policy. Maybe this was it; his big mouth had just caused him to lose another relationship. Worried, he leaned over closer to where he had last seen Anne. He hesitantly touched her shoulder to get her attention and almost instantly felt her arms take hold of him and pull him gently down. Neither of them said anything more.

* * * * *

The rain had been coming down for several hours when the lightning struck. John sat up immediately. He knew it must have hit close by, very close by, as he had felt the ground shake. Anne started screaming and had, unsuccessfully, tried to get out of the tent for she was certain that a tree was going to fall on them. Light from the next burst of lightning helped John find the zipper holding the tent flaps together. He quickly unzipped them, pulled one side back, and looked out into the night.

Across the river was a tree that had been hit by lightning, causing most of it to fall in the water. Its base was glowing deep red and little yellow flames were beginning to shoot up toward the sky. Soon he smelled rain-dampened smoke as it drifted around the tent. He let go of the flap and felt around inside until he located his jeans, which he hurriedly pulled on before sticking his head outside again. He felt the rain as he stared out into the night.

"I can't believe it," said Anne who was now holding the other flap open and looking across the river.

"Have you ever heard anything that loud before?" said John pulling his wet head back inside the tent.

"Never. This is really unbelievable."

"That scared me almost as much as, well, you know the story. It was really close," said John.

"Really close," said Anne. "What time is it, anyway?"

John looked around until he felt his shoes then fumbled with them until he found the one containing his watch. Taking it out he held it close to his face, but he wasn't able to read the dial until the next lightning flash occurred. "Three fifteen," he said.

"Three fifteen!" said Anne in disbelief. "It's too early."

John agreed and then began looking for their canoe. Scanning the riverbank in the disappearing light from the latest lightning flash, he was relieved to see its outline just where it should be. The river had risen, he could tell that, but it was no where near their canoe. It was safe for now; still, it would be a good idea to drag it higher up the bank, just in case.

"What's that?" said Anne suddenly sticking her arm out into the rain and pointing to a dark object floating toward the newly fallen tree.

"I can't tell," said John staring at where she had pointed. He wiped the rain out of his eyes, but still couldn't see anything – he would have to wait for the next bolt of lightning. He didn't have to wait long. A flash of light went off in the distance and, by habit, John began counting out loud by thousands to see how far away it was from them.

He stopped counting at seven one thousands when Anne exclaimed, "It's another canoe!"

John could barely make out its form as the last of the lightning faded away. Something, he was never able to say what, made John spring out of the tent and run down to the river's edge. From where he stood John couldn't tell if anyone was in the canoe or not. What he could tell was that the river had risen at least five or six inches since dinner and was still rising. This meant the current had picked up, making the water dangerous. If there was anyone in the canoe, they were in real trouble.

Standing in the darkness John thought he heard, over the noise of the rain and water, what sounded like the canoe running into the branches of the newly fallen tree. He then saw its outline again, this time faintly silhouetted against the glowing base of the downed tree. Because he still couldn't see if there was anyone in the canoe, John strained to hear any sound that might indicate that someone needed help.

With the next flash of light he looked at it again and thought he saw someone in the back. But part of him was convinced that it could be the leaves and branches of the downed tree that were making the shape. No one, in his way of thinking, would be foolish enough to be moving on the river at night and, especially, in this type of weather. More likely, John thought, the river had risen unexpectedly, pulling the canoe away from where it had been left for the night. While it was the only explanation that made any sense, he still wasn't positive someone wasn't over there.

He quickly dismissed the idea of leaving the canoe where it was until morning, because he knew it wouldn't be there in the morning. Something else floating in the water would either hit and sink it or it would somehow break free and receive an equally bad fate further on down the river. But if someone was in the canoe, and he reminded himself he wasn't sure of that, he knew that morally, forget everything else, he had to go check on them.

Still he hesitated. Every experienced canoer, he knew, knows it is never wise to get on a river during a storm, let alone at night and in the dark. But this canoe was over there, just on the other side of the river, maybe thirty some feet away, and to John that wasn't so far away. Even with the rising water John believed he could get over there and back without too much effort. At least, he would know for sure if someone were in it or not. After all, he could never forgive himself if it were later discovered that there had been someone in the canoe and he, John Calloway, had done nothing to help them. This resolved his conflict and, before he could change his mind, he waded out into the current.

Behind him he heard Anne yelling something. He was unsure of what she was saying, but hoped it was positive. When the water reached to his knees, John leaned forward and plunged into the dark liquid. Half swimming, half wading he forced his way across the river. The current was stronger than he expected and as he got closer to where he hoped the canoe was still lodged he struggled to keep his balance.

Reaching out he grabbed onto the side of the canoe with his left hand. He still couldn't tell if there was anyone in it so he took his right hand and reached in hoping to find the tie-up rope that should be there. His hand grabbed onto something that felt like a pile of very thin spaghetti. Some-thing about it didn't feel right and John quickly pulled his hand back. And as he did, he lost his grip, fell backwards and plunged completely under water.

Gasping for air, John fought his way back to the surface and began spitting up the water he had just swallowed. Finding the side of the canoe again, he seized onto it with both hands while he caught his breath. As he regained his composure he began to smell something on his right hand – the one that had been in the canoe. The odor was familiar but, right now, he couldn't remember where he had encountered it before. One thing he did know, he would never find out by clinging to the side of this canoe. With that, he began pulling himself out of the water. This caused the canoe to tilt precariously and it was only by kicking hard with his feet that he kept it from turning over.

John was now half way out of the water and starting to fall forward when a new burst of lightning sliced across the sky. As it did he looked down into the canoe and then, desperately, began trying to stop himself from going forward. It was too late and he fell on the body. Screaming, he quickly pushed himself off the motionless figure and back into the river. The force of this action rocked the canoe enough that it took on water. It also caused an arm to momentarily splash into the river before disappearing back into the canoe.

This time John kept from going completely under water by grabbing onto several branches of the downed tree as he fell. Struggling to keep his balance he climbed onto a submerged limb - and immediately took his left hand and tried to clean off his clothes where they had come in contact with the body. He also started to gag. Unable to throw up, he then let out a loud sigh and realized he was up to his chest, again, in a current that seemed to be getting faster.

Over all this confusion John thought he heard Anne calling out his name. By concentrating he was able to block out enough of the sounds of the rain and the river long enough to hear her asking if he was all right.

"I'm okay, I'm okay," he yelled out in the direction where he heard her voice. The rising water was now pushing harder against him, forcing him to grip tighter to the branches of the downed tree. John took a deep breath and then shouted, "Stay back, it's too fast - don't come in." He strained to hear her reply and, when none came, he tilted his head back and yelled out, "There's a body in the canoe!" hoping this would discourage her from trying to join him.

He tried once more to hear her response and thought he heard her say she was coming over to help him. He knew he had to have heard wrong, as only he could be foolish enough to have gotten in this position. No, Anne was smarter than that, and he was sure she had said something else. But, just in case, John called out, "Don't come, don't come. It's too dangerous." Straining to hear her reply, he heard nothing.

It was past time, he knew, to get out of the water. He was getting colder by the minute. Even more importantly, to be in the river now was an invitation to be struck by floating debris or worse - he might be bitten by a snake. That thought caused him to shudder even more than the cold.

Grimacing, John forced himself put a hand back in the canoe to find the rope that every canoe in the world but this one, apparently, had attached to it to secure it when it was beached. This time he found it and without much effort managed to wrap it around his right hand. At least something good, he thought, had come from the canoe almost tipping over.

John knew he had no more time to waste; he either had to tie the rope to some object or start moving the canoe toward shore. But whatever he was going to do, it had to be decided on quickly, because the constant rain meant even rising water and already it wasn't safe to be out in the current. The rope was now tugging on his hand and so he wrapped it several more times around it.

Tightening his grip on the branch he had braced himself against, John began pulling the canoe back out of the tangled mass of leaves and sticks. With great effort he was able to get it about a third of the way out before the river suddenly surged higher. The rise was so quick that John was forced to start treading water with the result that the canoe wedged itself back in the branches.

John took another in his endless series of deep breaths and began to use his feet to locate the limb on which he had just been standing. Once he found it he started walking back against the current pulling on the canoe.

Suddenly, he felt something crawling on his shoulder. He shouted for help as he let go of the branch he was pulling himself along and started slapping at his shoulder with his newly free hand. At the same time he tried to shake off the rope that was still twisted around his right hand. While doing all this he realized that, whatever it was, it had now began to move rapidly up his bare arm.

In a near panic, John reached out to dislodge whatever was there. Worst fear or not, no snake was going to attack him without a fight. His hand clutched tightly onto - a piece of clothing. Turning, John found Anne in the water next to him.

"Why are you here? I told you not to come," he screamed, grabbing back onto the safety of his branch. Anne had scared him so much his heart felt like it was going to pound its way out of his chest. He hoped he wasn't having a heart attack and that thought made him angry. "You scared me," he yelled at her.

Anne ignored him and shouted back, "Push it through. Push it through the limbs." That's not what she wanted to say to this irritating clod. What she had wanted to say was, "Why do you think I'm here; I've risked my life to get out here and all the thanks I get is to be yelled at" - but she didn't. That, she knew, wouldn't be helpful now, at least that's what the social worker in her was saying. However, for just a moment, a wonderful moment, another part of her thought about just telling him off, then swimming back across the river and going back to their tent. But before she could savor this thought for any length of time, a voice caught her attention.

"Why did you grab me like that? Why?"

John's screaming caught her off guard and all she could think of to say was, "I'm sorry," and hope he could hear her over the noise both he and the river were making. That all depended, she decided, on if he was calm enough to listen. "Push it through the branches," she said again when there was no reply to her apology.

"It won't go," he said.

Anne could tell by the tone in his voice that John was still angry. She continued to ignore his anger and said, "Yes - it will. Now come on, help me."

With that she grabbed the back of the canoe and began pushing it forward. Hopefully, she thought, by staying with the facts and not getting emotional, John would snap out of acting like a jerk and start behaving like an adult. If this didn't work she was going to be even more concerned, for it was possible he'd been in the water too long and was starting to deteriorate from the cold.

John did as he was asked and soon the canoe moved ever so slightly. He still wanted to ask Anne why she had grabbed him, but for now he decided it was better to get the canoe out of the tree.

The moving canoe was now pulling hard on the rope that was still wound around his right hand. John tightened his grip on it and strained to see what was ahead in the darkness. All he could see was a massive blotch. He could feel Anne pushing on the canoe and thought he heard her kicking at the water with her feet. He wondered if the cold water was affecting her as it was getting to be almost unbearable for him.

Anne's efforts, plus the faster moving current, began to steadily move the canoe through the downed tree's branches. John had taken to pushing with all the strength he had left. Suddenly his feet slipped off the limb he had been walking along, causing one of its branches to flip out of the water and strike him in the face. He ignored the pain because, at the same time, the canoe broke free and began sliding through the last of the downed tree. As it passed out of the remaining branches, both John and the canoe were grabbed by the current. Behind him Anne was shouting that she had let go because she was being dragged into a tangle of branches.

Holding tightly onto the rope with one hand and the side of the canoe with the other, John began kicking at the water to guide the canoe toward a shore he saw during the flashes of lightning. Soon his feet began to bounce off the river bottom while he continued to struggle to keep the canoe from being pulled further on down the river. Slowly John's feet found the bottom of the river consistently and, after what seemed like forever, he managed to push the front of the canoe onto land. Then he immediately let go of the side and grabbed the back end. Standing in the river he kept pushing until most of the canoe was up on the shore. Exhausted, he bent over to catch his breath and began looking for the smoldering tree. John spotted it back up the river on the opposite bank. Oriented as to where he was, John then searched for their campsite. Instead, a fading flash of lightning showed him that their canoe was about thirty yards upstream. "Thank God," he muttered and flung himself down on the ground.

* * * * *

John gradually felt a stabbing pain in his right hand and he realized the towrope was still tightly wound around it. Unwrapping it he let it fall to the ground.

Suddenly he remembered Anne. The last he remembered was her shouting out that she was caught in some branches. He sat up and began looking for her in the water and on both banks of the river, using the light from the passing flashes of lightning.

Unable to see her, John started calling out her name. After each time he strained to hear her voice, and each time he heard nothing but the roar of the current. His anxiety rose with each passing moment. Then it hit him; she had to be back at camp. Of course, that's where she was, but he wanted, no needed, to run back to be sure. But first he had to do the right thing and that meant getting all of this canoe on land. To leave it partially in the water was to invite the river to take it back. And after all that he had just been through the river wasn't going to win.

Summoning up energy he knew he couldn't come up with again, John took hold of the front of the canoe with both hands and started to drag it forward. It was beginning to move when he lost his grip and fell backwards. Pain instantly shot up his back when he hit the ground and John knew that was the end for him, he had nothing else to give. He now lay where he had fallen and closed his eyes. Thoughts of being dry - and warm –filled his mind. That is, until he remembered Anne again. Where had she gone?

He began calling out her name over and over as he lay on his back. He needed her; he needed her to help him get up so they could go back to their tent. John closed his eyes and felt the rain on his face. Gradually it began tapering off, a fact which made him happy, as it was time, he said to himself, to be happy.

Lying there, he began to hear something moving off to his right. Turning his head, he opened his eyes in time to see a shape coming toward him in the darkness. It was bent over and getting ready to spring. In anticipation of the coming attack, John forced himself to roll on his side and began to get up. If he were going to be attacked he wanted to at least put up a fight.

The shape continued to advance on him. Just then came a new burst of lightning and with that light he saw it was Anne. A huge feeling of relief swept over him and John started crying. Collapsing back down on the ground he felt her drop down beside him. One, two, three minutes passed before their breathing began to slow down enough to talk.

John was unable to get the taste of river water out of his mouth so, before he could say anything he turned his head away from Anne and spit. Turning back toward her he called out her name.

"Yes," she replied.

"I was afraid something had happened to you," he said.

"Something almost did," she said matter-of-factly.

"Anne."

"Yes."

"There's a body in this canoe." And as he told her this, John still couldn't believe it was true.

"No, John, there's two bodies in there."

Her answer stunned him and he said, "Don't tell me that, one's all I can deal with right now."

"I'm not lying. If you don't believe me, what am I doing here? I'm wet, cold, tired and I've almost drowned twice. Plus, I plunged into that stupid river to help you retrieve someone else's boat - after telling you it wasn't safe."

John thought over what she had just said and then replied, "Would you help me pull it further up the bank?"

Anne didn't say anything.

John forced himself to wait for her answer. He had already decided not to antagonize her any further by demanding one immediately - although he wanted one now.

Finally she said, "Okay, but that's it. After that - I'm going back to the tent."

John couldn't keep himself from then saying, "What about the bodies?"

Hearing this, Anne used her elbow to hit him in the side as she shouted, "I said I'm going back to the tent. They don't care if they get any wetter, but I do. I've been out in this nightmare for at least twenty minutes and I'm starting to freeze." With that she sat up, wrapped her arms around her legs and waited to see what, if anything, John had learned about how to be considerate.

"Okay, okay," he said. "Let's pull the canoe up and we'll leave the people here until morning." Then he added, "I still can't believe their canoe was able to float this far down the river."

Anne was now on her feet. "How do you know it did?" she said as she walked over to the end of canoe that was out of the river. Whereupon she stopped and waited for John to join her. When he did, with great effort, they managed to drag it to a spot where it would be safe from the rising waters. As John let go he looked down at the two people and said, "I hope they'll stay there."

"They're dead," said Anne back over her shoulder as she ran off toward their tent. "If they move on their own, we'll be witnesses to one of history's greatest events."

John hadn't moved since dropping the canoe. It was still lightning, but the storm was moving off in the distance, and when the sky next lit up, he saw that Anne was at the top of the riverbank. "Thanks for everything," he shouted toward her. It was then he realized he was alone in the woods, at night, with two bodies and he began slowly moving toward the campsite.

Once outside their tent, he undressed and dropped his clothes in the mud beside Anne's. Pulling back the tent flaps he stepped into what he thought must be the only dry spot on earth and immediately stumbled over his backpack. It hadn't been there when he left earlier, but he wasn't going to ask how it got to be there now. He dropped down and began searching through it until he found his towel. Drying himself off, he put on his spare clothes before crawling into the sleeping bag. The last thing he heard was Anne moving around on the other side of the tent.

20

Anne opened her eyes and gazed up at the roof of the tent. In the background, she could hear the sound of the river rushing by their camp. She wasn't ready to get up just yet and so she lay there and spent her time going over what had happened last night. She then looked over to see where "Mr. Maturity" was and in the gray early morning light saw that he was still asleep. Still, despite his faults, John was cute and certainly what had occurred was unusual by anyone's standards. So maybe there was still hope for him. This thought made her feel better and she got up and unzipped the tent flaps.

The river had continued to rise during the night and she saw that the water level was up to within a few feet of the back of their canoe. Looking to her right she was able to make out the shape of the other canoe, but there the water was almost to its backend. Looking more closely she made out what she thought were the shapes of the two dead people. "So that wasn't a dream," she said to herself. It had really happened, just as she had remembered it when she woke up.

Anne sat back down on her sleeping bag and reached over and shook John's shoulder. "Time to get up," she said. His body stiffened and he let out a gasp. Anne waited for a further response and when there was none, she shook his shoulder again. This time John rubbed his eyes with his hands and began groping for his backpack.

"Yes, yes. What is it?" he asked as he looked at the face of the watch he was now holding up in front of him.

"Time to get up," Anne said again.

John rolled over, looked at Anne, but didn't say anything more. Instead he sat up and pulled back a tent flap. Sticking his head out he looked over at the rescued canoe. "They're still there," he said.

"I know," said Anne. "Are they the couple that was on the bus with us?"

"I think so, but I'll have to look at them again to be sure. That is, if I can stomach it," he said. And with that John began looking outside the tent for his shoes. He could tell they were wet so he didn't bother to pick them up. Instead, he found his towel and wiped them off as best he could. Satisfied they were dry enough to wear, he put them on and started down toward the other canoe.

Anne finished tying her shoes and ran after him. "I wish you'd said something before just leaving like that," she said when she caught up to him. She could tell she was still angry with his continued insensitivity. She was now of the opinion that it must be genetic, for what else could explain it.

John apologized and she decided to drop it for now, but knew that sooner or later they were going to have a big talk about the way he'd been treating her ever since the first lightning strikes last night.

Together they warily approached the end of the canoe nearest the water. The body of a woman lay slumped to one side in several inches of a cranberry colored liquid. Her swimming suit appeared to be smaller than John remembered it from yesterday and the lower half of her body was a deep purple. John gulped several times to keep from throwing up when it dawned on him she had started to swell.

Her most noticeable other feature was a small hole on the left side of her back. Anne fell to her knees at the sight and it took a major effort on her part to keep from throwing up, effort that forced her to stay where she was and close her eyes to blot out what she had just seen.

John had watched her drop to the ground. When she did, he asked if she was okay. She said she was, so he left her alone and looked back at the dead woman. She both fascinated and repulsed him at the same time. Unsure about what to do next, John finally decided to reach out and touch her just to make sure she was really dead.

As his hand came close to her, another one came out of nowhere and slapped his away. "Don't do that. Haven't you heard of disease?" said Anne in a panicked voice.

John hadn't thought about disease but, upon hearing the word, quickly pulled his hand back. Pointing at the body, this time he exclaimed, "Look at the size of that hole in her chest. Only a large caliber gun could have done that kind of damage."

Anne had started trembling after hitting John's hand and, at the moment, couldn't think of anything to say. Neither could John, who proceeded to reach over and pull her to her feet. He then led her to the other end of the canoe where, laying face up in the same cranberry juice was the other half of the couple. It was readily apparent that he, too, had begun to swell. His face was all puffed out and he stared up at them with open, bulging eyes.

Motioning toward him, John said in astonishment, "He's wearing my Missouri sweatshirt!"

Anne had already closed her eyes when she felt the urge to throw up return. Hearing John's comment, she swallowed hard and prayed for strength before forcing herself to open her eyes - it was true. She also saw a large dark red stain on the front of the sweatshirt and a small tear in one of the S's. Horrified at what she had just seen, Anne threw up.

John quickly turned and saw Anne standing beside him with her mouth open. On the ground around him and on the side of his leg was a frothy liquid. He ignored it and reached out to hug her.

That was the last thing on Anne's mind and she stuck her hand out to stop him. "Not now, I don't feel like it," she said. She was now aware of the odor, the odor of sweet perfume, which she had first noticed near the dead woman. The smell made her throw up again. Just in case John had any other plans to be helpful, she kept her hand up and glared at him while she tried to wipe off her mouth.

Seeing her outstretched hand, John kept his distance and said, "Why would anyone want to shoot these people?"

Anne began to feel better and now walked over to the river's edge to wash herself off. "Drugs, maybe," she said. "I imagine there are plenty of deals that go bad down here, just like in the city," she added, wiping her hands on her jeans. Something made Anne want to throw up again and she started one of her breathing exercises.

"Maybe someone's not with their spouse," said John.

"Could be," she said and slowly released her breath.

John had begun looking in the canoe for anything that looked suspicious. "I hate to say this, but it could be me, or us, they were after - he's got my sweatshirt on, you know."

This thought had crossed Anne's mind but, unlike John, at its first appearance she had told herself not to go down that road. For if she did she knew there were many scary stops. Now hearing John say the same thing, she quickly looked up and down the river for anyone or anything suspicious. Reassured there was nothing that looked out of the ordinary, she gazed back at the people in the canoe again and said, "I want to get out of here - Suppose you're right and whoever did this is now looking for us."

Anne couldn't bring herself to say anymore and she looked up and down the river again to see if anything had changed since her last check. Relieved to see it hadn't, she glanced at John to see what effect her words had had on him, but she couldn't read the look on his face. Maybe she really was unable to make good choices in men, just as her sister had told her when she was sixteen.

"We'll have to bring them with us," John said as he hit his hand against the side of the canoe.

"I refuse to be in the same canoe with them," said Anne. Her sister might have been right back then, but that was the old Anne.

"Well, don't worry about that. I was planning on tying the two canoes together, at least to start," said John unaware of the battle going on near him.

"For now, however, I want to know who they are," said John, reaching over and picking up a backpack that was in the middle of the canoe.

"Look, don't do that. Think of the diseases you could get off that thing," exclaimed Anne, "It's been sitting in blood for hours. And besides, suppose it's filled with drugs or worse."

John could tell Anne was on the edge, maybe even over it because she had started shaking again, but this didn't mean he had to do what she said, even if she was right. He dropped the backpack and crossed his arms over his chest.

Changing the conversation, he said, "I don't think he died instantly. Remember when I told you how funny he was paddling yesterday."

Anne's started crying. "We-could-have-saved-them," she sobbed. "We could have, if we hadn't been in such a hurry to leave."

John couldn't believe what he was hearing and harshly said, "Stop it; that's enough. Who knows when they were shot, it could have been anytime yesterday. And just because

I said he was acting funny, that doesn't mean it was because he had been shot."

Anne continued crying and John started to wonder how the two of them were going to make it down the river if she didn't pull herself together pretty soon.

"Can't we go back to that bridge where we first stopped yesterday?" she finally managed to get out.

"You mean on 71?" asked John. "No, the current's too swift."

Her crying now slowed down to sniffles, which she managed to stop long enough to say, "We can walk back. We could get help on the highway. Look, the longer we stay here the more unsafe it gets."

John thought this over, then said, "Okay – I'll go up the hill and see if we can get back to the bridge," and with that, he turned and disappeared into the dense brush. After a hard ten minutes' climb he arrived at the crest of the hill. From where he stood John could see that the land to the east was densely forested and he was unable to see the bridge. The distance and difficulty of getting to the bridge could only be based on speculation. Looking around in all directions, John became convinced that the best and safest way to get out of here was to continue on down the river. On his way back down the hill he wondered how Anne would take the news.

He stopped at the canoe long enough to check up on the people again. Either from being tired or the smell, he leaned over and threw up.

* * * * *

While John was looking for a way out, Anne had walked back to camp and, with some reluctance, taken out the small mirror she had brought with her. Seeing how she looked embarrassed her so much that she wanted to hide. Her hair was so tangled she was afraid to use a comb on it and the bags under her eyes looked huge. She decided to pull her hair back into a ponytail and put on John's baseball hat. Then holding the mirror in one hand she did what she could using the makeup she had brought with her. Thankfully, she hadn't left it all back at the car. She put it away when she had finished and began taking everything out of the tent.

She was still packing when she noticed John slowly coming in her direction, altogether wetter and dirtier than when he had left. How romantic this trip was turning out to be she thought. As he came closer she gathered, from the way he was walking, that his trip up the hill had not been successful. "No luck, huh?" she asked.

"No. The bridge's too far away to see - too many hills – too many trees - in the way. I stopped by the canoe and the only thing I saw there was the contents of my stomach. I don't know what possessed me to go after that canoe," he said sheepishly.

"So you threw up too," she said with a feeling of satisfaction.

"Yea, I threw up."

Anne was beginning to feel queasy again and changed the topic. "We need to eat something; at least I do, and get out of here. I guess you're telling me we have to go down the river."

"Yes," said John dejectedly.

Anne continued talking as she opened the cooler, "Do you think whoever did this is out searching for them - or us?" Taking out the carton of yogurt she opened it and waited for John's answer.

"The spoons are over there," said John pointing to a plastic bag when he noticed her looking around.

"Thanks," she said. "How about an answer to my question, just give me your best guess." She found a spoon and started eating. If he wanted some, he could ask and she'd share, but for now she needed to eat.

John sat down on the cooler and stuck out his hand. "Can I borrow your spoon?" he said.

"Answer please," said Anne handing the open carton to him.

"I don't know. Anything's possible," he said. Finishing a second spoonful he handed the spoon back to her and set the carton down beside him.

Anne started to say something about his lack of manners, but decided against it. They were in enough trouble without going after each other about everything. She decided instead to wipe off what she could of the water puddled on the cooler and sit down next to him. She finished eating the rest of the yogurt while speculating on what might happen on the rest of the trip. This began to depress her and she made herself quit thinking about it.

John appeared to be lost in thought and had said nothing while she ate. Finally, when she was almost finished he said, "It's time to get going."

Anne responded by shaking her head in agreement and handing him the empty yogurt carton, with the spoon still in it, before getting up and going back to work. It was almost seven o'clock.

She didn't pay any more attention to what John was doing until she saw him going toward their canoe. She watched as he turned it over and dragged it down to the water's edge before pushing it partially into the river.

Coming back to the camp John began taking their gear down to the canoe. Bringing the last of the camp items with her, Anne walked down to where John was standing and handed them to him. Finished at last, she picked up her lifejacket and stood waiting to go.

There had been no conversation between them as they packed the canoe and got ready to leave. Anne had checked up and down the river frequently, each time afraid she would see someone or something suspicious.

John had spent some of the time thinking about how best to bring the other canoe with them. He had considered putting Anne in charge of their canoe while he paddled the other one, but abandoned that idea after reflecting on the way she had been acting. Tying it behind theirs was also quickly rejected because of the problem of controlling its movement in this current. After going through all the possibilities he could think of, John came to the same decision he had made earlier--he would tie the two canoes together and hope for the best. Leaving it just wasn't an option. He and Anne had discussed it, but neither of them felt they could just leave the bodies to the elements or worse - a wild animal.

Putting away the last of the camping gear, John looked up one last time at what had been their campsite before putting on his life vest and wading into water. Carefully bracing himself against the current, he pulled the rest of their canoe into the river and then walked it down the river toward the other one as Anne followed along the bank. When he got there he pushed it up on the gravel shore.

Standing in the water he searched through their belongings until he found a small skillet. Carrying it over to the other canoe he began to bail out the bloody water. He was able to get three scoops out before the smell made him throw up. Out of the corner of his eye he caught Anne taking her fingers out of her ears. "I'm sorry," he said as he went over to the river to clean up for the second time that morning.

"I know, I can smell them from here," she said.

"But I have to do this," he said.

"I know."

There were two more trips to the river's edge before John got the water level down to where the bottom of the canoe was clearly visible. He then stopped and found a beer in the cooler. Drinking it, he threw the empty can into his canoe.

He then motioned for Anne to go to the front of the canoe and push it back toward the water. Together they managed to get it out into the current. Once there, Anne held it, while John brought their canoe along side and tied the two together.

As usual, Anne got in their canoe first before John climbed into the back. As he positioned himself to paddle, the canoes began to pick up speed. "We're off," he said. "You ready?"

"Ready as I'll ever be," Anne shouted back.

"From here on I'll need you to tell me about anything you spot in the water –anything - submerged limbs, turbulent water, rapids, anything," said John.

"Okay, okay, I've got it," she snapped.

Detecting the irritation in her voice, John said, "Anne, I know it's been tough on you."

She wondered what the "it" was that had been tough on her. All she knew was that, for the most part, "he" had managed to make a bad situation worse because of his mouth. They were still going to have that "now or later" conversation, the one about his insensitivity, but for the moment it was important to keep things as calm as possible. "Thank you for saying that," was the only honest thing she could think of to say. And with that she began watching the river in front of her.

21

The rains had swollen the Elk River to where it was running high and fast. So it was with effort that John guided the two canoes through the current.

Anne stayed busy watching the water ahead. Occasionally she would glance over at the other canoe, but could only do that when she told herself the two forms were not people. Even with that deception she had a hard time keeping herself from throwing up. Still, after each glance, it was a little harder to get her stomach calm again. For some reason the bodies both fascinated and repulsed her and on her fourth look she lost her battle.

Startled by the noise John looked up to see Anne leaning over the left side of the canoe. "You okay?" he said when she had stopped gagging.

"Drink, get me something to drink," she said.

John put his paddle sideways on the canoe and searched in the cooler until he found a can of pop. Placing it on the blade he then extended the paddle toward her.

"I can't believe it," she said after taking several sips from the can.

"Believe what?"

"I threw up my pill."

"You did, you mean 'the pill'?" asked John. "That's not good." The last sentence had barely gone out and he knew those were not the words to have said.

Restraining herself again, Anne said, "You're right, that's not good."

John's mind started racing ahead after he heard this and he was at the altar when he heard Anne saying something that ended with "… anymore."

"What?" he asked.

"I said, I can't bear to look or smell them anymore, it's too hard on me."

John wanted to talk some more about the pill, but decided against it. Sometimes, he knew, the less said the better and he began concentrating on finding a place to stop where he could cover the bodies. Anne was right on one thing; they were starting to smell more.

The river's rise overnight had covered many of the gravel bars and small islands that would normally have been ideal places to go ashore. The sun had come up over the hills behind them and the chill in the morning air was almost gone. Overhead, the sky was dotted with puffy clouds. The beauty of the morning sharply contrasted with the contents of one of the canoes now moving down the river.

"What about them?" asked Anne pointing at the other canoe. She had waited long enough for John to solve the problem; it was time for her to make it happen. After having thrown up, Anne was no longer able to look to her right. She had taken John's baseball cap and turned it sideways, pulling the bill down until it blocked her right eye. This way she could look ahead without seeing the dead woman across from her. That took care of one problem, but did nothing about the smell. Temporarily, by continuing to do one of her breathing exercises, Anne was able to block the smell out. That worked until the wind shifted and the full force of the odor was blown directly into her face.

John, too, was having the same difficulty. The wind shift and Anne's last question had made it time to do something, even if there wasn't a safe place to land. "Keep watching the river," he said, "I think I have the solution - I'll use the tent."

With that, John began to move forward. The other canoe provided enough balance that he was able to ignore his usual concern about tipping over. Part of him, though, wished both canoes would tip over and get rid of the bodies. It would be, he imagined, like a burial at sea. Reluctantly he let that idea go and sat down on the ice chest to untie the tent, then opened it as he stood up.

He then threw it over the other canoe with as much care as he could manage. Reaching back he grabbed his paddle and began pushing the sides of the tent down around the two people as best he could. The sickly sweet smell immediately became much less noticeable. When she was sure he had finished, Anne took a deep breath for the first time in quite a while and then straightened the ball cap on her head.

Satisfied with his work, John moved to the back of the canoe and sat down. He turned his attention to the river ahead and using a few strokes of the paddle straightened out their course. Glancing at Anne's hair he thought back to before the storm. It had all been different then, for one thing he hadn't been as much of a jerk. Janet, his ex, would have said that after the storm he had finally revealed his true self. He'd heard that enough times in marriage counseling, "He's so immature, doctor." Good riddance to her, he thought, but Anne, she was different. He knew he was going to have to apologize to her again. Not the usual, "I'm sorry", he'd already done that; no this would have to be a big time apology. An adult apology. For now, though, all he could think of to say was, "This is easier to take."

"Much, much, better. Thank you for doing it," said Anne, starting to cry.

"I'm sorry. I didn't mean to upset you so much," replied John.

"It's nothing you did," she said. "Here I'm worried about having lost my birth control pill and that girl – woman - will never worry about anything else again." Still crying she turned around to look for her backpack. Finding it, she placed it on her lap and opened it up. Taking her purse out of the plastic bag that she had covered it with, Anne searched through it until she found John's cell phone.

"The phone!" exclaimed John when he saw her holding it. "I bet it would have worked back there on the hill. I wish I'd remembered it," he added with a sigh of remorse.

Well, let's see if it'll work here," Anne said turning it on. She then entered a number and punched the talk button. Nothing happened. Anne looked at the phone and could see from the display that it wasn't working.

"Probably too many hills in the way or, what's more probable, they don't have a cell tower down here," said John with a laugh. "It's practically wilderness, you know."

"Whatever," said Anne as she tried the number again. The phone still didn't work. She reluctantly put it back in her purse and resealed the plastic bag. "I'll try again later," she said closing her backpack and placing it behind her.

Up ahead John saw that they were rapidly approaching a narrow bend in the river. In quick succession he maneuvered both of the canoes around two partially submerged logs. That was followed by some hard paddling to avoid the brush piled up against the main channel side of the riverbank. Once they had managed to get around the bend, John saw a road off on their right. He pointed it out to Anne, who was so encouraged by the sight of it that she took the cell phone out again and tried, again without success, to make a call.

As she was attempting to do this John suddenly remembered the map the rental place had given him. He put down his paddle and searched the outer pockets of his backpack until he found it. Although he had a general idea of where they were on the river, he had no idea of their actual location. He couldn't find the exact location of the road on the right or the bend in the river they had just negotiated; for this map showed several places where a road was near the river and there were lots of bends in the Elk River.

The best John could determine was that somewhere up ahead was the low water bridge with a dam on the far side of it. It was probably, he finally decided, the place where he normally put in his canoe. How far it was up ahead he didn't know, it could be as little as a half a mile or as much as two miles away. There would then be another question to answer once they came upon the bridge - one that couldn't be answered from the map. Because of the rain, how much room would be for their canoes to pass under it?

John hesitated to do so, but ultimately decided to tell Anne about his concerns. After hearing him out, she promptly suggested they beach the canoes now and leave the river to find help. The road, she pointed out several times, was a sign of civilization.

John told her he was uneasy about her idea for several reasons, the first of which was because he couldn't tell how far they were from any real help. In frustration he now admitted to her, "I haven't seen that road for a while. Even if we find it again, there's no telling how far we'll have to go to find a house."

John also had another reason for not wanting to get off the water here. For some time, maybe the twenty or thirty minutes since they had last seen the road, he had begun to sense that they were not alone. It wasn't like he hadn't looked behind them. He had done that off and on since they had left the campground and never seen anyone. That is, except once, when, after going through a long stretch of the river, he turned around and thought he caught a glimpse of a canoe way back up the river. Before he was sure, another submerged log forced him to turn his attention back to the river, and, when he looked back again, it was gone. He didn't tell Anne about it for fear she would get upset all over again.

"Please give me the map," said Anne wanting to see for herself if she could find out where they were. Studying it for a few minutes, she decided that John was correct; there was a bridge up ahead, but where was anybody's guess. She then folded up the map and gave it back to him before resuming her job of watching the river ahead of them.

Anne hadn't yet given up the idea of pulling over when, off in the distance, she saw the outline of what could only be - the low water bridge. From where they were now Anne couldn't tell how much space was between the bridge and the water, but it didn't look like much.

Until now the river had belonged to just them, but John knew from experience that beyond this bridge and on the far side of the dam was a put-in point. There had been times in the past that as far as John could see ahead there were canoes along this next stretch of river. It was on those hot sunny days that the river became a liquid highway and, like a Sunday driver, John enjoyed looking at the other canoes and the people in them.

Especially the women; he never ceased being amazed at the number of women with tattoos on the Elk. Yesterday, when they had first gotten on the river, he told Anne to watch for them. It was, he said with a laugh, his opinion that they were "the trailer Graces of the Ozarks." She had no idea what he was talking about, but laughed anyway. Later she asked him what he had meant by that. "Greek mythology," he replied. "One semester at Missouri, passing grade. They are an integral part of the Elk River experience, daughters of the Sun, and they add charm to the experience."

"That's interesting," said Anne, still confused by his answer.

That conversation was all in the past; what was important now was that the two canoes were rapidly approaching the bridge. John quickly decided that if both canoes were kept toward the center of the river, and he and Anne knelt or bent down in their canoe, everybody would pass under the center span of the bridge with a few inches to spare. But that was just the start. They would then have just a few seconds after the canoes emerged from under the bridge before they went over the top of the dam. Normally a three-foot drop, with the rain it had to be less, but how much less - he had no way of telling.

In good weather, it was fun to put in above the dam and hang onto the back of the canoe as it went over the dam. John knew this would be a bad idea today, what with last night's rain and the fact that they had two canoes tied together.

The current swiftly pulled them toward the bridge and John hastily dropped his paddle in the canoe and bent forward as far as he could. They were now almost at the bridge and John didn't have time to see what Anne was doing as his face was as near the layer of water covering the bottom of the boat as he could get it. It smelled bad, like river water always did, and he realized he had never gotten used to the smell. He decided to hold his breath and as he did the canoes passed under the bridge and emerged on the other side. Quickly sitting back up John had just enough time to see the bow of his canoe go straight out into the air as it went over the top of the dam. Almost as quickly, the back end followed and the canoe hit the water below with a loud bang, the force of which lifted him out of his seat. The water ahead glistened in the sunlight as the two canoes continued moving swiftly forward.

"I don't know if it was a good thing or not that we didn't stop, but it was the safe thing. I've never seen the current so fast there," said John hoping Anne was listening.

Anne turned and glanced back up the river before grabbing her backpack again. Retrieving the cell phone from the plastic bag she pushed the redial key and held it to her ear. "911 still doesn't work," she said putting the phone back. "EEEEEEE, that's all I hear. There still must be no cell tower around." She was sealing the bag when she reopened it and said, "Okay, let's try it one more time." And with that she hit the "O" button on the phone. Almost instantly, she turned and smiled back at John.

"Yes, the number for the Sheriff's Department, please." Anne repeated the number back aloud and quickly dialing the number began talking to the person who answered the phone. The response was not what she anticipated and Anne hollered into the phone, "Didn't you hear me, what should we do?"

Holding the phone out for John to hear the answer they both heard the voice on the other end say, "You'll have to keep coming on. There's no place to stop 'til you get to the campgrounds."

Anne nodded and continued holding out the phone and looking at John. He kept his eyes on the river while trying to hear the conversation, but the rush of the water was drowning out most of what was being said by the person at the Sheriff's Department.

Anne could tell John wasn't hearing everything, so she began loudly repeating what the dispatcher was saying. "There's a campground about six miles from where you're at," the dispatcher said. "But that's by car. It's further by boat, but with the current you should be there in an hour - or less."

Anne said out loud, "Oh."

"There's no place to meet you before then. The road was closest at the low water bridge – but you've passed there. Every place else has turned to mud by now." The dispatcher finished by saying that this was the best he could do for her. Anne had repeated all that she had heard and now looked at John for his response. All she got was a shrug of his shoulders.

Anne shook her head, thanked the dispatcher, and then hung up. "No ambulance for them," she said, pointing at the other canoe, "the county's too small, they'll call for one when we get to the campground. The most he'd guarantee was a car to meet us."

After some discussion they both agreed that the most important thing now was to find the campground. To get there more quickly they decided not to stop, not even for lunch, but to continue on down the river as fast as they could go.

John and Anne were now in the heart of every float that took place on the Elk River. Today there were not as many canoes as John had seen in the past, but they began appearing on the river in increasing numbers. The Elk had widened out past the dam and consequently the current had slowed just enough that John had to keep a regular stroke with his paddle to keep them moving as fast as before. Time seemed to slow down and he began to see himself as a French voyager from the 1700's as depicted in some of the old black and white movies. And just like the men in those movies, John kept repeating the same paddle stroke over and over again.

Anne sat motionless in the front of the canoe, her paddle lying across the gunnels. Now that the smell coming from next to her was almost undetectable, she would periodically take in a deep breath of air. She soon realized how much she loved the smell, feel, sound and look of the river.

Partial conversations came and went as they floated by the different canoes. Some people would holler and yell, but most were quietly talking to each other. The tone in their voices seemed to echo her own enjoyment of the warmth of the sun and her time on the river.

Time and the landscape passed so quickly that, after a while, Anne decided that if they didn't see the campground and the patrol car soon, she was going to call the Sheriff's office again. They had been on this leg of the river for almost an hour and according to the dispatcher it was close to time to stop. The joy she had felt from the sunshine as it increased had quickly faded as the heat brought back the smell again. Anne was finished with them— the people in the other canoe.

The dead could be someone else's responsibility, just so long as it wasn't hers.

In spite of John's best intentions he had been forced to pull over so Anne could go to the bathroom. And since they were already stopped, they decided to go ahead and eat. The break, they had both agreed, would be good for them. Most of their lunch conversation had been small talk, that is until they were about ready to leave. It was then John tried to explain his behavior after the lightning strike. He started but couldn't find the right words, so he stopped and then simply apologized.

Anne listened and when he was finished, said very little. She told herself that it was a good start on John's part, but now was not the time to do anymore than accept John's apology, which she did.

Back on the river they each filled the time with thoughts of what had happened over the last twenty-four hours – the good and the awful. The awful was more than either of them had ever wanted to experience. As a result they said very little to each other for a long time.

John was the first to spot the Sheriff's car and he hurriedly shouted out its location to Anne. Unmarked, it was parked out on a gravel bar close to the river. A casually dressed man could be seen leaning up against the driver's door looking in their direction. When he saw their canoes, he straightened up and waved as he began walking toward the water's edge.

Both John and Anne waved back and John started guiding the canoes in his direction. As the river became shallower, Anne leaped out in to the water and started pulling her canoe toward the gravel shore. As she got closer, the deputy waded out, grabbed the bow of the other canoe and began pulling it toward land. The two of them managed to get both canoes fairly close to the shore by the time John climbed into the river and started pushing on the back of his boat.

Their combined efforts got most of both canoes up out of the water and onto the beach.

"This them," said the deputy looking down at the tent covering one of the canoes.

"Yes," replied Anne.

"Terrible tragedy – but I'm sorry, I didn't introduce myself. I'm Deputy Sumler," he said as he stood upright and wiping both hands on his pants before extending one of them toward her. He then waited for John to come out of the water and did the same thing with him before adding, "It's good to see you both. Tough trip, huh."

"Very," said John.

"Well, I know you're ready to go to Pineville and headquarters, but we have to wait for someone."

"Who?" said Anne skeptically, "I thought there was only going to be one of you."

The deputy frowned and gave her a dirty look as he said, "Orders, you know how that is, they change things all the time."

Anne wasn't satisfied with the answer and started to ask another question but John cut her off by asking one first. "How long do we have to wait?"

"Don't know, not long," said the deputy.

"How about the ambulance for them?" said Anne, pointing at the covered canoe. "I thought you were to call for one when we got here."

"Yea, well I'm going to do that shortly," said the deputy, this time looking at her with a smile on his face. "But we still need to wait. Would either of you like to wait in the car until he gets here?" he asked.

"Sounds great to me, I'm exhausted," said John.

"So am I," echoed Anne.

They left the river behind and slowly walked toward the deputy's car. John opened the rear door for Anne and then went around to the other side and got in the back seat on the passenger side. The seat felt good and he let out a sigh of relief.

Anne had settled back in the seat and closed her eyes. "I can hardly wait to take a bath," she said.

John agreed and then sat up. He stuck his head out the door and called toward the deputy, "Can you let me use your radio to- -"

"Blue Eye Canoe Rental," said Anne.

"Sorry, can you let me call Blue Eye Canoe Rentals and tell them where their canoe is?"

Roger Sumler cupped a hand over one ear trying to hear what John was saying. Unable to tell over the noise of the river and from the passing canoes, he walked back to the front bumper of his car and asked John to repeat what he had just said. He then thought about John's request before replying, "Sure, if you'll just wait a bit, I'll take care of you." And with that he turned and walked back to the river.

"That's odd," said John.

Anne didn't want to get involved in any conversation, so it was with some effort she made herself say, "What's odd?" hoping that would be the end of it.

"He keeps looking up river. That doesn't make sense, why would he do that?"

"This whole trip is odd," said Anne. "Don't take this the wrong way, but I am so ready for this to all be over. Thankfully we're safe and off the river. So if he wants to look up the river or down the river, it's okay with me."

John didn't say anything more. He had spent enough time with Anne to tell from the tone in her voice that she wanted to be left alone. But after she finished talking, though, she had reached out and touched his arm. The feel of her hand on his arm had sent shivers through John and his arm continued to tingle even after she took her hand away.

"I still think it's odd the way he's acting," he said a few minutes later. "And where's his uniform?" John looked over at Anne for an answer and saw she was asleep.

Turning back toward the river, he noticed that the deputy had moved closer to the water's edge and was waiving to someone. John couldn't tell which of the canoes coming toward them he was waving to until he saw someone raise and lower his paddle.

"There he is," said John. "The other half of the duo." He hoped Anne was listening this time.

John watched the lone occupant of the oncoming canoe glide past several groups on his way toward shore. He was younger than Deputy Sumler and, for some reason, looked familiar. John watched as the deputy waded out into the river, took hold of the bow of the new canoe, and began pulling it onto the beach next to the others.

Deputy Sumler then stood and waited for the other man to wade up to him whereupon they had a brief discussion before both of them started toward the car. They split near the front bumper with Deputy Sumler walking along John's side. He walked around the open car door and, putting both hands on the roof, proceeded to peer into the back seat of the car.

"What's next?" said John. "Can I make that call now?" asked John, who then waited for an answer. The uneasiness he had felt earlier had increased and he didn't like the way the deputy was looking at him. Out of the corner of his eye John could see that the younger deputy was opening Anne's door. John was certain he'd seen that one somewhere before - it was either him or someone who looked a lot like him.

Anne didn't wake up as her door was opened and with a nervous laugh John said, "Be careful, she bites if disturbed." Neither deputy laughed at his joke.

"We need to talk," said Deputy Sumler leaning further into the car. His size and nearness to him made John feel uneasy and he felt like throwing up. The deputy had looked to either side of where he was standing before he stopped and without warning hit the side of John's face with his fist. The blow jerked John's head sideways and he fell over onto Anne who, unexpectedly, made no sound.

As he lay sprawled on top of her a nearby voice said in a loud whisper, "Listen up. If you want him to live, do exactly as you're told. Now nod if you understand." It was then that John saw the gun in her side and the hand that was over her mouth.

It had all happened so fast. One minute Anne had been asleep and the next she was awake and being told how to save John's life. What had happened? Who was this guy? She had no answers to these questions. But that didn't stop her from feeling the gun dig deeper into her side.

"I'm waiting," whispered the voice, this time louder than before. Anne summoned up a nod.

"Where are the papers? Tell me, where are the papers that you found at the Walker house?" said the voice next. "Do you understand? Nod if you do." He hadn't taken his hand off her mouth and her lips were hurting from the pressure, but she managed to do as he asked a second time.

"Now when I take my hand away from your mouth, I want you to tell me, in a very low voice, where they are," continued the man, still keeping his grip tight against her mouth. Almost as an afterthought he added, "Do you understand?"

Needing no further instructions, Anne again shook her head up and down. With that he took his hand away from her mouth, but she could still feel the gun against her side. It had just dawned on her that these men were from Johnson County. The implications from this knowledge made her whole body feel weak and she started coughing.

While this question and answer session was going on, John had managed to get himself up enough in the seat to where he could massage the side of his face to ease the pain. There wasn't any way for him to look to be sure but, judging from the way it hurt, he knew he was badly bruised.

Anne turned and, looking into the eyes of the man standing next to her, said, "I don't know what you're talking about."

"Don't play stupid, I'm way past wanting to deal with that," he said. Pushing on the gun he went on, "I know how to use this in a way that'll result in the most pain."

"Like you did with them?" said Anne looking toward the beached canoes.

"You go to hell," he snapped jabbing the gun forward, causing her to cry out in pain.

Roger Sumler had heard all he wanted to and now reached in and grabbed John by his T-shirt. "How about you counselor, you want to tell me where to find the papers?"

John tried to pull himself away but Roger tightened his grip, "I'm growing short on patience", said Roger, "Tell me where they are."

The pain he felt in his jaw made it hard for John to speak. He tried yawning to reduce the ache, but he could only open his mouth half way before it started hurting again. Turning his head away from the open car door, he prayed the answer he was about to give wouldn't result in his being hit again. Finally, he blurted out, "We don't have what you're lookin' for," and quickly covered the right side of his face with his hand.

The two men were now almost in the car. Looking across the back seat they frowned at each other. The one on Anne's side, the canoeist, said, "It appears our friends don't take us seriously enough, Roger."

"So I see," replied Roger. "We'll, I suggest a ride in the country. Fresh air has been known to restore memory."

John knew that if this happened, it wouldn't be good news for them and he began scanning the canoes going by. No one was paying the slightest bit of attention to what was going on in the car. He thought about yelling for help. That would certainly get someone's attention but, he knew, by the time they got to a phone to call for help he and Anne would most likely be dead. He quickly gave up that idea and almost off-handedly said, "Okay, okay, I'll tell you where they are."

"It's about time smart mouth," said Roger releasing his hold on John's T-shirt. "So where are they?"

"In our car, back in Noel, in the trunk," said John with an air of resignation.

The two detectives now looked across the back seat at each other and, this time, they both managed a smile.

"Think we should believe him?" asked Roger.

"If it's not true, I'd hate to be him and have on my conscience what would happen to her," said Bill, moving his gun up and down Anne's side. She started shivering and felt sweat rolling down her underarms.

John looked over at where Anne was seated, but she wouldn't make eye contact with him, and he knew she was aware of how serious his lie had been.

"Cuff them," said one of the men. John wasn't sure which one had said this as he had been thinking about what would happen to them when they found out he didn't have the papers. The two captives in the back seat were soon cuffed with their hands behind their backs. When Roger finished, he put his face directly in front of John's. Not an inch separated the two of them and John smelled the heavy odor of cigarettes on Roger's breath. The smell made him turn his head.

"One sound, one wrong move, one inappropriate act on your part and you'll be a quadriplegic," said Roger, grabbing John's face and pulling it back toward him. "I won't kill you, but you'll wish you were dead. Do I make myself clear?" He was almost shouting at John when he finished and Bill nervously looked at the canoes on the river to see if anyone was watching.

John stared directly back at him and made himself nod.

"How about you?" said Roger, now looking over at Anne.

She also nodded and this time felt goose pimples on her arms. She had always thought she only got those when she was cold; now she realized she also got them when she was very scared.

Satisfied with their responses, Roger closed the car door and walked around to the other side of the car and got in the driver's seat. Bill followed suit and got in the front passenger seat.

As he watched Bill get in the car, John remembered where he knew him from and he began to wrestle with what to do with the information. Part of him said to say nothing - the less those two knew the better it was for his and Anne's chances to survive. That the word "survive" had come to mind was a more immediate shock to him, but John knew it was true. What reason did they have to keep Anne and him alive, once they got what they wanted? And since John didn't have "the papers", whatever they were, he didn't want to think about what would happen when they found out he had been lying. But John also wondered that if he said something, anything, about his knowing who Bill Stewart was; maybe, just maybe, he would hesitate before doing anything extreme. Having run through all these arguments, John still couldn't decide what to do and so he sat in silence.

"Can you get us back to town?" said Bill to Roger.

"Yea, do I ever forget directions? Now be honest," answered Roger.

"No. No you don't." Then Bill added, "Do you think anybody saw us?"

Roger looked out at the canoes passing by on the river and said, "If they did, who cares. They've already gone further on down the river and we're leaving."

The tone in Roger's voice made John rethink his decision not to speak up. Kicking the seat behind Bill several times, John waited until he turned around before saying, "I know you. The Quinton case, it was my job to represent their kids. That was two-three years ago. You were the ..."

"You have a good memory counselor," interrupted Bill. "I hope it's that good when we get to your car." The look on his face scared John, but it was too late to take back what he had just said.

Anne had remained quiet while John talked. It was taking all her energy to understand what was happening to them but, she had already decided, it would be nothing good. For no matter how optimistically she looked at their situation, she could only foresee a bleak and dark ending.

Keeping her eyes on the two men in the front seat, Anne slowly leaned toward John and nudged him with her elbow. John responded by turning his head slightly and looking across the seat at her. She tried to silently mouth her question but halfway through it the engine started and Roger turned his head to see behind the car. Fearing she would be discovered, Anne turned her head the other way and looked out the window.

One of the two men had turned on the car's police radio, only to have static crackle out from the channel on which it was set. Bill quickly leaned over and made some adjustments to it, but the end result was still only the spit and snap of the static. "Nobody has told them anything," he said to Roger.

"Seems that way," said Roger only to be cut off by a voice on the radio requesting a status check. This was shortly followed by a different voice, which said, "I don't see 'em yet." Then the static began again.

During all this Roger had put the car in reverse and backed away from the beach. On his way toward the exit he passed two trucks with camper shells parked next to each other. They were the only other vehicles in the campground. The music coming from one of them almost drowned out the crunch of the police car's tires on the stones that covered the road. It was country music and John reminded himself that he'd have to get used to it if he ever came back down here again - that is if he lived past today.

The car soon approached a signpost by the exit that read 'Rocky Point Park & Camp' but a chain was stretched across the actual exit, blocking their way out. Roger ignored it and followed the worn path that went around one side of the post - then turned left onto the highway. John looked back and saw a sign hanging from the middle of the chain that read "Closed".

They had gone about a mile down the highway when they saw a marked sheriff's car off on their left, parked down near the river's edge.

Bill smiled and said in a sarcastic voice, "It pays to listen to radio."

Without taking his eyes off the road, Roger managed a short laugh before adding, "It also pays to ignore signs down here."

It was now Bill's turn to laugh. Turning around and looking back at John he proceeded to say, "These two were kind enough to tell us where they were going. Thanks to all the searching we did for you down here we also knew about Rocky Point. Not that we hadn't taken alternative measures, you must have guessed that from our having the canoe. Had you not had such a head start on me this morning, we could have had a quiet and, no doubt, productive talk on the river."

"You wouldn't have gotten away with anything on the river," retorted John, still feeling the pain in his jaw as he spoke.

"You underestimate me, counselor," said Bill looking directly into John's eyes. "I believe you would have willingly told me everything," he said before shifting his gaze over to Anne. "Maybe, sometime, I'll tell you the story of my first day on the Elk."

"I can hardly wait," said John. Tired of hearing the constant threats, he changed the subject. "Okay, so what's to happen to us once we give you the papers?" he asked.

"We'll let you go, but first we'll need a head start," said Bill.

"A long head start," interjected Roger.

"What's that mean?" asked John, becoming uneasy at the way they were talking. He knew they were lying.

"It means we don't want anyone to find you until after we're gone," said Bill.

"You going to hurt us?" asked John apprehensively.

"No, and you ask too many questions, counselor," said Bill in a voice that sounded like a threat, so much like a threat that John decided to stop talking and began looking out the window. He knew the guy was right, he was asking too many questions. John also knew this wasn't the way he had planned to die - young and trying to start a new relationship. Well, maybe not that young, but at least the relationship part was true. And Anne, what had he done to her but manage to get her mixed up in all this - so how was he going to tell her this was the end?

Looking over at her he could see she was deep into her own thoughts. It hurt him to think about what was going to happen to her and he bit his lip to keep from crying. In a short while, he was absolutely sure, she wouldn't have to worry anymore about losing her birth control pill.

22

Sally Anthony was surprised to hear Anne Hubert's voice on the phone. She hadn't put her watch on yet and guessed that her call had come in around 8:45 a.m. As Anne's supervisor, she was well acquainted with the Walker case. Gerald's disappearance was one more twist in this sad, but all too typical situation. Typical, except for the father's involvement with a militia group.

The father, however, was not Sally's concern. Gerald was Sally's concern. His having been found with his mother was much better than his ending up in an armed compound somewhere. These were dangerous places where the men were always carrying guns and the women, apparently, were always pregnant. She had been pregnant twice and that was enough. She patiently listened as Anne relayed to her the story of how they had come upon Gerald in the store. When it was here turn she said, "I'm glad you found him."

"So am I," responded Anne before going on. "The main thing is he's safe and is being cared for by his mom. We told her to keep him until Sunday afternoon when we'll bring him back with us to Juvenile Intake in Olathe."

"Have you notified the authorities down there yet?" asked Sally.

"No, you're the first to know. As I said, this all just happened. Besides, I really don't want to tell anyone down here. If they get involved, it could delay his getting back to Johnson County and I want him back as soon as possible. And Sally - I also have a selfish reason not to do it, I don't want to ruin my weekend."

Sally had smiled when she heard Anne was with John Calloway. First telling herself she never would have guessed, Sally then quickly reminded herself that she was Anne's supervisor, not her dating counselor, and said, "The authorities still need to be notified, Anne."

"I haven't got time to call anyone else Sally - that's why I called you first. Would you call the sheriff's office up there for me and, please, don't call anyone down here, you know why." Anne had been watching out the window as she waited for Sally's answer. But when she saw the bus driver start climbing the steps into the bus she said, "I have to go Sally. Please call for me, will you? We'll be back in town Sunday night by eight - at the latest. I promise I'll take Gerald directly to Juvenile Intake myself."

Sally hesitated then said, "Well, all right then, I'll call and tell them. Take care of yourself Anne."

"I will, thanks Sally - bye." And with that Anne quickly hung up the phone before Sally could change her mind.

* * * * *

Sally continued to hold the receiver in her hand as she replayed the just ended conversation. Without a doubt SRS procedure was not being followed. However, she knew Anne Hubert was an excellent social worker with good judgment. Sally had not yet satisfied herself that she had made the right decision when the phone started making a buzzing sound. She quietly hung up the receiver, then picked it up again and dialed the Johnson County Sheriff's Office. "I want to talk to a detective about the Gerald Walker case," she said. She was put on hold until the phone was answered by a woman who said, "Detective Carpenter. Can I help you?"

Sally Anthony began talking. When she was finished, Jill Carpenter knew everything that Sally had said to Anne Hubert. The detective ended their conversation by thanking Sally and promising to pass on the information immediately. Just before hanging up, Jill remembered she had one last question. "Are you going to be home for a while, in case we need to talk to you some more?" she asked.

"For the next half hour," replied Sally, "but then we have to run errands - it's Saturday, you know. But we'll be back around lunch."

Thirty minutes later, as Sally was putting on her jacket to leave, the phone rang. Reluctantly, she lifted up the receiver and heard a voice ask for her. "This is me," she said.

"Mrs. Anthony, my name is Phil Batson; I'm a Lieutenant with the KBI, the Kansas Bureau of Investigation, in Topeka. I'm glad I caught you before you left. I promise not to keep you too long, but can you tell me what you told Detective Carpenter?"

"Well, all right, but my family's already in the car," said Sally.

"I'm sorry to ask you do this twice, but it's very important I know exactly what you were told by your social worker," said the Lieutenant with a forceful tone in his voice.

A horn honked in the background and Sally opened the back door and held up the phone for her husband to see. She heard the motor being turned off and saw him say something to the kids. That accomplished, she closed the door, took off her coat, and then proceeded to go back through her conversation with Anne, step by step. When she had finished, the Lieutenant began asking questions about Anne, date of birth, address, a recent picture, and the type of car she drove. But these were questions that Sally couldn't answer off the top of her head.

"Is there a personnel file on her?" he asked after the fourth "I don't know".

"Yes, but I don't have any way to get in that office. I might have some of what you want in the Walker file, but it's in my file cabinet at work."

"Will you go to the office and call me back?" asked the Lieutenant.

The question was so unexpected, Sally immediately felt herself getting defensive. Didn't he know her family had been waiting in the car for her for at least ten minutes? "How important is this?" she asked. "I mean, isn't there someone else you can call?"

"There probably is, Sally, but that'll take too much time - and we don't have much of that. Mrs. Anthony, Sally, I need that information as quickly as possible."

"Is Anne in some danger? Is that what you're telling me?" asked Sally apprehensive of the answer she was sure she was about to hear.

"Yes."

"How much? Tell me – how much?" she now asked, almost panic-stricken to get a response.

"I'm not at liberty to say, Mrs. Anthony. All I can say is I need your help. Now, will you please go to your office and call me."

Crestfallen by his response, Sally reluctantly agreed and wrote down the number he gave her. As she put her coat back on and headed out to the car again, Sally debated about how much she could tell her family. She finally concluded it didn't matter; she would do anything to help Anne. Her family would just have to deal with whatever she told them. As for John Calloway, she had told the lieutenant, when he asked about him, she would see what information she could find in the Walker file about him, but it wouldn't be much.

"One final question, Mrs. Anthony," said the lieutenant before she hung up. "Did Anne ever mention anything about seeing a white car with a Kansas government tag when she was talking to you?"

"Down there, a state car - down there?"

"Down there, up here; anytime really."

Sally again thought back through what Anne had said to her, then answered, "No, she never said anything like that. So do you have someone down there?" And without waiting for his reply added, "What a relief."

* * * * *

Lieutenant Batson finished his conversation with Sally Anthony and then turned to the people in his office. "Stewart and Sumler are still looking for them, or at least they were as of nine o'clock this morning. We still have time. Ms. Anthony's going to call me from her office with more information on the woman - Hubert. I'll have her fax a copy of any picture she might have. As for the lawyer – she'll check the Walker file and give us what she has, but it won't be much."

The officer sitting next to him waited spoke up when Phil had finished and said, "I checked on your question. There's an airport at Pineville, the county seat, which is about 180 air miles away. Flight time will be one hour, maybe a little longer from here."

* * * * *

Phil Batson had been called early Friday morning by the Johnson County Sheriff's Department. They wanted the KBI's help in finding Ralene Copley, the missing boy's mother. They reportedly had received information about her whereabouts from an attorney, John Calloway, as a result of his Thursday night telephone call to their office.

In another call, later that morning, the Sheriff's Department informed him of the discovery of the body of Lonnie Gilley. Lt. Batson was then told of the growing focus on two Bowers Mill detectives and their possible participation in what was now unfolding. These concerns had originated from an interview with Gerald Walker's cousin, Robin Brown, on Thursday evening. In her interview she told the detective, Jill Carpenter, about what had happened when she went back to the Walker house on Thursday morning to retrieve the backpack that she had left there the night before. Turning into the lane, she had stopped immediately when she saw a car that looked exactly like the one that she had seen the night before – parked in front of the house again. Unwilling to find out if she was right, Robin backed up and left with the intention of getting her backpack later on that Thursday morning.

However, at three when she came back by, she found all the doors to the house locked, which they never were, and grew concerned. She went home and waited for her mother to come home from work later in the afternoon. After listening to what her daughter was telling her, Trisha Michaels called the sheriff's office.

At about the same time as her call, a rancher reported that a car had been parked all day at an abandoned house near his place. The officer who was sent to investigate discovered that it was registered to Lonnie Gilley. That prompted a search of the area, which led to the discovery of his body, complete with handcuffs. The tire tracks found in the driveway from a second vehicle were matched by the crime lab early Friday afternoon to a brand only sold to police departments. Only Bowers Mill and two other cities in the area were currently using that brand. A hastily organized check by those police departments located all the cars equipped with the tires, except one. The detective assigned to it, Roger Sumler, had the weekend off. A call to his family by his police department revealed that Thursday night he had rather unexpectedly told them that he and another detective, Bill Stewart, were going fishing for the weekend and that the car was going to the police garage to be worked on. The two often went fishing at this time of the year so the Sumler family was not surprised by his announcement. Further checking, though, failed to locate the police car at the garage.

Neither detective had been found by the time Lieutenant Batson made his Saturday morning call to his Missouri Highway Patrol counterpart, Lieutenant Tom Graham. Quickly updating Lt. Graham on the missing boy since their last conversation on Friday, Phil Batson then went on to say, "Tom, we're almost certain the two Bowers Mill detectives are down in McDonald County. We plan on being in Pineville by noon. You still think you can you meet us then?"

Tom Graham again didn't hesitate in agreeing to meet them. He was still curious, however, as to why the two detectives would be in far southwestern Missouri, especially since the child had been found unharmed. Phil didn't have an answer to this question.

Tom Graham had now shifted the conversation to his agency's successful effort to locate the mother of Gerald Walker, Ralene Copley. "Purdy, the town she lives in, is approximately thirty miles from Noel. She works the second shift at a nearby chicken processing plant. I sent a trooper out to check her house after we talked yesterday, but she wasn't there. A call to her work, as I told you yesterday, revealed that she had called in sick Thursday and Friday. In her Friday call she said she was better, but not enough to come in to work. Nobody knows where she could be, although one person we checked with thought she had family in Arkansas, but couldn't remember where. I'll call Troop D down in Carthage and ask them to send two troopers to her house. If she's there or if she shows up, we'll take both her and the boy into protective custody."

Phil agreed with this plan, but had one concern, the same one he had voiced to Tom several times yesterday. "I would appreciate it if your people don't use their car radios. If they're down there they have the ability to monitor your radio bands with the equipment their car carries."

"I know, I've told them, but I'll tell them again to use their cell phones for anything connected with this case."

Agreeing again to meet at noon in Pineville, Lieutenant Batson hung up and hoped Sally Anthony would call before he had to leave.

23

Tom Graham was late. Phil Batson and the two KBI agents he brought with him had landed at the Pineville airport just as they had promised – at twelve. After several phone calls that went frustratingly unanswered, they stood around their plane and waited.

Twenty minutes had passed by when they saw the Missouri Highway Patrol car coming slowly toward the hanger where the KBI plane had taxied to a stop. The lone trooper who emerged from the car relayed Lieutenant Graham's message that he could not be there until four. The trooper then said, "We have the Walker kid and his mother. They were found at the mother's house about 10:00 o'clock and were immediately taken up to Troop D headquarters south of Carthage. We did get something from the boy, an envelope he found taped under a dresser at his house."

"What was in it?" asked Lt. Batson, hoping this would provide a reason for what had been happening for the last three days.

"A bunch of court papers-papers relating to the dead victim Gilley. They were all court papers - that's all we know."

Phil Batson shook his head. Why would Gilley hide these papers, court papers were public records, and was this what the missing detectives might be after? It didn't make any sense, but then again, nothing in this case was making sense.

The trooper finished by saying, "I'm here to take you to the sheriff's office in town. The search for the two officers and the couple is being coordinated from there, but, unfortunately, there's still no sign of any of them as yet."

* * * * *

Deputy Grovner Erdman sat in his patrol car and watched canoes going down the Elk River. Sunday was supposed to be his day off. But not this Sunday. Wayne Green never called unless it was important. The sheriff had asked him to take his car and go out to the Millstone campground and watch for two canoes tied together coming down the river. One of them would look empty and have a cover spread over it. When he saw them, he was to quickly get them to shore and then call dispatch - but only on a regular phone.

Grovner had remained quiet as he heard this but, when the Sheriff finished, he immediately began to ask questions, only to be stopped and told to get over to the river - that he'd learn more later. It was eleven when Deputy Erdman drove into the campground and parked. Another deputy, Jack Tidnish, joined him a half-hour later. He didn't know much more than Grovner, but did tell him that the covered canoe reportedly had two bodies in it.

It was around twelve-thirty when the river began to file up with canoes. Before then canoes had drifted by the two parked sheriff's cars one or two at a time. They saw this scene every weekend starting from the middle of April to the end of September – sometimes longer. Periodically, people would wave and more than once a hand holding a can went down below the gunnel when the two sheriff's cars were spotted by the canoe's occupants. "Underage drinkers," the deputies said to each other whenever it happened and always with a laugh.

They soon became bored with the parade of canoes and started talking on their usual topic, fishing. This was just after they had failed to remember the last time anyone had died on the river. They finally decided it had been at least ten years ago. That was one reason the call from the woman on the river had put the department into such a state of turmoil.

Sheriff Green pulled in at one o'clock and parked behind the two cars. He had been the Sheriff of McDonald County for many years, which some said was too many. For the eight years before this he had been a sergeant in the Kansas City Missouri Police Department. He had been forced to quit and come back home after his dad had suffered his first heart attack.

Once back, Wayne sold his dad's farm and moved both of them ten miles up the road to a small house in Pineville. Because he was quickly running out of money, Wayne applied for and got hired as a deputy sheriff. He had been on the job for three weeks when Sheriff Lawrence suffered a stroke which eventually forced him to retire. In a special election called to replace him, Wayne Green ran for sheriff and was elected. He had continued to be elected every four years since. Within the budget constrains of a poor rural county, Sheriff Green had managed to build what was regarded as a good and honest sheriff's department. He was well liked and considered fair by most people. Personally, Sheriff Green had always been proud of the fact that, to his knowledge, his was the first department in the four-state area to hire women to be deputies.

"Sheriff," said Grovner nodding as Wayne walked up beside his open patrol car door.

"Grovner," replied Wayne, ignoring the usual pleasantries and getting directly to the reason for his being there, "We've got a big problem on our hands. The state boys are coming down from Jefferson City along with several from the Kansas side. If you haven't heard, we're looking for a couple of bad cops that came down here Friday."

"That's not good Sheriff," said Jack closing the door on the passenger side of Grovner's car and coming around to where the other two men were standing.

"Yea, but it gets worse - they may have been listening in on our radio conversations since they got here. That's why I told you earlier not to use your car radios. So here's why I'm here. Grovner, stay here and watch for the canoes. Start asking people if they've seen them. Jack, go back up along the road and start scanning the river for them from the highway. Now don't go and get too excited, I don't want to start a panic on the river. That goes for the both of you," he said looking from Jack to Grovner.

The Sheriff's eyes then wandered out to a canoe that was floating by carrying a young redhead with a small bikini top. Times never changed, he thought, before he caught himself and went on, "Again, just the standard stuff if you need to use your car radio. With these guys most likely monitoring us, I don't want to clue them in to what we're doing. Use a regular phone if you have anything important to report. Understand? Good. I'm going back to the office now. Both of you know what you're to do – so let's get going."

Grovner Erdman stood by his car and watched as the two sheriff's cars left the campground. He then turned back to the river and resumed looking for the mystery canoes. As he did he noticed that the weather was changing again. Shadows fell off the trees and sprang across the water only to disappear, then reappear, on the bank on the far side as the sun went in and out of the clouds. Canoes still continued to pass, but in greater numbers than before and Grovner heard pieces of conversations coming from them until they drifted out of range of his hearing.

After a while he grew tired of standing and sat back down in his car. The faint sounds of passing conversation coupled with the rush of the water soon made him sleepy. A look at his watch showed the time as one-thirty; barely twenty minutes since the Sheriff had left. However, unless he got out of his car again, Deputy Erdman knew he was in danger of falling asleep. While in the process of doing just that he heard his name being called. Looking up, he saw his neighbor's youngest boy paddling a canoe toward him.

"Hello, Mr. Erdman," he hollered out again.

The deputy walked to the water's edge and stood on the gravel bank as the canoe slid up on the rocks beside him. Holding onto the canoe, Grovner waited until the boy in the front got out and, together, they pulled it up further on shore. When that was done Grovner turned and said, "Josh, how you doin'? How's the river?"

"Great, it's rough and fast, just the way we like it."

"Any fish?"

"Nah, too fast even where the pools are."

"That'd be true", said Grovner. Remembering his reason for being there he then asked, "Say, have either of you see a couple, older, in their thirties, in two canoes – one has a tarp covering it."

Josh Ferguson looked back at his friend still seated in the canoe and said, "Duayne, the two we passed just back there, wasn't their canoes tied together and one of them have a cover on it?"

"You mean the ones by the closed campground?"

"That's it, back at Rocky Point."

"Yea, I'm the one that pointed them out to you. They were near the white car, the one I told you looked like a sheriff's car."

Deputy Erdman remembered what the Sheriff had said about not spreading panic on the river and cautiously asked, "Was it a man and a woman? The woman about five four, dark hair, thin. The guy about six feet and thin, too."

Duayne spoke up first, "I think that's about right," he said. "They were on their way up towards that car, so it was kinda hard to tell."

"How long back?" asked the deputy.

"Fifteen, twenty minutes ago."

"You're sure it was the campground where the owner died last February. You know the Oklahoma guy?" said Grovner just to make sure they were talking about the same place.

"That's it, is something wrong, Mr. Erdman?"

"No, not really, I just need to tell them about their car."

"What happened?" said Josh.

"Someone hit it last night."

"Much damage?"

"No, but they ain't goin' to be happy."

They all laughed and then said their goodbyes. Grovner excused himself and with a deliberate pace walked up to the campground office and hurriedly got on the outside pay phone and called the sheriff's department. "Terry, give me the Sheriff, this is Erdman; I've got news for him," he said recognizing the voice of the dispatcher on duty.

"He's with some people," said Terry Malden, who had just been told not to give the Sheriff any calls, "and doesn't want to be disturbed."

"Give me the Sheriff, he'll want to talk to me," said Grovner angrily, mad that he had to beg to talk to the Sheriff when he had just found out this important news. The dispatcher's response was to put him on hold.

Grovner was about to hang up and call again when a familiar voice came on the line. "Grovner, what is it, you got them?" asked Sheriff Green.

"No Sheriff, but I know where they are - Rocky Point. At least they were about twenty minutes ago. And Sheriff, I think our friends are with them; they were walking toward a car that I was told looked like one of ours."

"Hold on," Wayne Green said and putting his hand over the end of the phone held a conversation with the men in his office. When he finished, he took his hand off the end of the receiver and said, "Grovner, go back to your car and stay there for now. Don't leave or use your radio until you hear from me again. Understood?"

"Understood, Sheriff."

"And be careful, these guys are dangerous. I've been told they have killed at least one person already."

"I got you Sheriff."

The conversation over, Grovner hurried back to his car. As he did he looked around for any potential hiding places from which someone could spring out at him. There were none and he laughed to himself. As a precaution, though, he unsnapped the strap over his gun and put his hand on the grip as he resumed watching the river. Now and then he would look around to make sure no white cars were pulling in anywhere near him. Grovner Erdman was no longer sleepy.

24

"We've lost the race," said Sheriff Green after hanging up the phone. "They've got them, probably twenty minutes or so ago."

"What time did you say?" said Phil Batson, looking at his watch and realizing it was going to be another couple of hours before his counter part would arrive from Jefferson City. He hoped he could remain civil to this ex-KCMO sergeant-now playing sheriff. To put two civilians at such risk, by not getting them off the river immediately, was to him inexcusable. Hillbillies, that's who ran this county, no wonder he'd never been here before. And he'd make sure that after this was over, he would never come back. Especially after hearing the long-winded sermon on how the deputies here were set to save these people. Now, however, the two Bowers Mill cops had a pair of hostages. What clowns, Phil wondered, did they find to put in uniforms down here?

"At least we still have the element of surprise," said Wayne.

"I hope so for the sake of the two civilians," replied Phil. He hadn't hid the disgust in his voice and he wondered how the Sheriff would react to hearing it – that is if he even knew what disgust meant. Hopefully the county had at least one dictionary in case he needed to look it up.

"Not all plans work", replied Wayne. "But I know where they're going and I'll get them. You don't have to worry, I'll get them," he said repeating himself. He then resumed studying the map on the wall behind his desk. It was old and yellowed and in several places there were tears that had been patched with tape that was also yellow. In the lower right corner the words 'McDonald County' stood several inches high.

Poking at it several times to emphasize a point here and there, Wayne went on, "They only have two ways to go on 59. North or south. North would take them out of the area and since they don't know we've found out about them - that doesn't seem to be logical. No, based on what I know, they're still looking for whatever it is they want. My guess is, they think those people, the social worker and the lawyer, have it or know where it is. No, they're going south - into Noel. That's where the other car and what they want is probably located. Now with that decided ..."

"Wait a minute, who's decided? You have, I haven't. I think we need to talk more about this before going off in that direction." said Phil not caring anymore whether he offended the Sheriff or not.

Wayne Green had forgotten how much he disliked Kansas cops, no matter where they worked, but this highway patrolman, or whatever he was, was helping him to remember. In his former life in Kansas City, the guys on the force referred to the Kansas side as "The Bush", since there never was any action over there and Kansas cops as "Bushriders." From his experience it appeared most of their training had been gained from watching television. He started to say something back, then didn't. He was the Sheriff and this was his county, so it didn't matter what this guy said.

Wayne regained his composure and said, "We'll get them, I know just the place. I'll arrange to stop or at least slow down traffic while we get in place." He then looked across the room to see what effect what he had said had on the Kansas lieutenant.

Phil shook his head slowly and could tell by the way the Sheriff had emphasized the word 'I' earlier that anything he had to say would be politely ignored from here on out. He had no authority here and they both knew it.

"These, these two city men - I can't use the word policemen, as they sully the honor of anyone in a uniform; they think like we do in this room. So I'll use that to my advantage and, with luck, we can catch them off guard before they even know what hit them."

Wayne didn't wait this time for any comments on what he had said and immediately picked up the phone to call the Arrow Rock Campground office.

J.P. Blaise picked up the phone and heard the familiar voice of his grade school friend say, "J.P. this is Wayne, how you doin'?"

Wayne then paused and politely listened to J.P.'s response. When J.P. had finished he went on to say, "Fine, fine, J.P. Yes, she's planning on you and Sherye tonight. Six thirty's good. Now J.P., I need your help." The tone in the Sheriff's voice had changed and he was now looking back at the map on the wall. "I need you to drive your old pickup; you did take it today – good – and drive it off into the ditch about a half mile up the road toward town. You know where I mean – that's right – there at the start of the curve. But leave half of it on the road," he added as an afterthought.

Wayne then stopped talking, again, and listened as the voice on the other end expressed his disbelief at this request. The Sheriff listened for a moment before interrupting him to say, "J.P., this is no joke, you know me better than that. Have

I ever joked with you about business - ever? Now, people's lives are at stake here. I need you to stop talkin' and start doing what I'm asking – now. I'll tell you more later; so stop asking questions, you hear."

There was a silence on the phone before J.P. agreed to do what he had been asked by his lifelong friend.

Wayne quickly thanked him and then before hanging up added, "One more thing, J.P. I want you to throw some liquor on your clothes and take a couple of swallows before you leave. Use the bottle you keep in the cabinet drawer."

* * * * *

J.P. hung up the phone and got ready to leave. He had a fleeting thought that Wayne was pulling a trick on him, but dismissed it knowing that if he was – he couldn't think of what he'd do to him – he just knew he'd pay him back. Following all the instructions he'd been given, except one, he got in and started up his truck. He'd ignored Wayne's command to take a couple of drinks before leaving; he knew he'd had enough today already.

At the entrance to the highway, J.P. turned his brown and rust colored pick-up north on 59. The road was crowded, as it always was this time of year. The spot where Wayne wanted him to run off into the ditch was at the narrowest part of this stretch of road. He was also, he realized, going in the wrong direction. Shaking his head, J.P. hit his brakes and pulled off at the entrance to the neighboring campground and stopped. He waited for traffic to clear before pulling back on the highway in directly front of a slow moving cattle truck and heading south, back the way he had come.

This time he found the place where Wayne wanted him to go off the road. Checking in his rearview mirror to see where the traffic behind him was, J.P. then slowed down, swallowed hard, and forced himself to steer his truck toward the narrow ditch beside the highway. He stiffened and braced himself as the truck bounced off the highway onto the shoulder and on toward the ditch into which, seemingly without warning, the front of the truck dropped.

J.P.'s head hit the steering wheel as the truck abruptly stopped. He cried out in pain as he fumbled to find the ignition key and throw it under the seat. The knot he felt with his other hand was not supposed to be part of this deal. He'd show this to Wayne and, if he found out all this was a joke, he vowed revenge again, this time of the foulest kind, because now he was hurt.

A northbound car quickly came to a stop by the side of the highway when its driver saw the accident. He ran over to the truck see if anyone was hurt and was relieved to find that the driver was only shaken up. But, smelling alcohol, he excused himself and, using his cell phone, called the Sheriff's department to report a drunk driver who had just been in an accident. The dispatcher asked for the truck's license plate number and, upon hearing it, requested that the salesman stay at the scene, and keep an eye on the driver telling him he was a repeat offender who might try to drive off. Momentarily puzzled by this, the salesman finally agreed to stay, but told the dispatcher that to do so meant his car would be blocking traffic on the highway. The dispatcher understood his concern, but repeated that it was more important to keep the truck's driver from leaving until someone from the sheriff's department arrived to arrest him and if that meant a traffic jam, it meant a traffic jam.

Coming west out of Pineville, Wayne Green heard the initial dispatch of two vehicles to the accident scene. He glanced over at the Kansas lieutenant who was in the passenger seat of his car and said, "They're going nowhere now. In five minutes traffic will be backed up for a mile or more in either direction, if it isn't already." Phil Batson didn't say anything; he only nodded and kept his opinions about the Sheriff's plan to himself.

* * * * *

Subsequent calls to the dispatcher from concerned, and sometimes irate, citizens began to tell of long lines of traffic that were barely moving. As the Sheriff had also told him to do, the dispatcher waited ten minutes before announcing he was dispatching two additional units to help clear the backup. The four deputies were well on their way to the wreck when they were officially notified to head there. This would put six sheriff's department cars at or near the accident scene. Fifteen men should be enough, felt Wayne Green, to handle this matter since he had the element of surprise.

25

John continually felt the tightness of the handcuff on his right wrist. Even intensely concentrating on making the pain go away only helped a little. He glanced over at Anne, hoping that this time she would look at him and say something. Ever since the car had turned onto the highway she had spent her time staring out the window. John gently kicked her right leg again. This time she looked at him and their eyes met. He could tell she had decided the same thing he had; they would have to try and escape. Anne then turned her head and went back to looking out the window again.

The two men in the front seat had not seen what had just happened as they were too busy watching the road ahead and listening to the police radio. They had just rounded another turn when they heard the Sheriff's dispatcher call for two additional units to respond to a wreck that had happened some time ago. From the location given out, they believed the accident was several miles up ahead of them and on their side of the highway.

"There's drunks everywhere," said Bill.

"If I lived here, I'd be drunk by this time in the afternoon, too," said Roger.

John had quit working to relieve the pain in his wrist and had turned his attention to the traffic up ahead. He knew that on an old two-lane highway like this, an accident - any accident - could bring traffic to a halt. Call it what you will, divine intervention, luck, or fate; this, John knew, might just give them their chance to escape. He immediately began to notice a number of semi-trailer trucks coming north out of Arkansas. There were also a lot of cars, but they at least were going in both directions. Probably, he thought, filled with people either headed home from a weekend on the river or just out for a ride.

It was not yet possible to see the accident, but John and the others could tell they were getting closer to it because the traffic in front of them began to slow down. As it slowed again John looked up at the dashboard and saw that their car was going only thirty miles an hour. The next time he checked it was going twenty miles an hour. After that, the car went slower and slower until finally it came to a complete stop.

As Bill Stewart looked nervously at his watch, Roger Sumler started moving the car into the northbound lane. But just as quickly he steered it back into his lane as one then another semi passed by him going the other way. Traffic in the southbound lane then began to creep slowly forward - only to stop after a short distance. After what seemed like several minutes, the line began to move forward only to stop again several feet later.

By now Bill had put his window down and stuck his head out in the hope of seeing what was going on up ahead. When he didn't, he turned to Roger and said, "See anything on your side?"

"No, and I can't get around these cars because of the trucks, there're too many of them going by." And as if to emphasize his point he threw out the butt of his latest cigarette and watched as the last of the smoke he had just exhaled was forced out of the car by a passing truck.

John ignored what was going on in the front seat because the pain in his wrist had returned, this time to the point where his wrist was now throbbing constantly – and no amount of concentration was reducing it. Because his hands were still behind his back John couldn't see if the circulation was cut off, but it felt like it had been. John kicked Anne again, harder this time than before. As he did he leaned forward and jingled his handcuffs. Anne looked down to see where the sound was coming from, but still didn't say anything.

Bill Stewart had heard John moving around followed shortly thereafter by the sound of his handcuffs being shaken. He looked back and said, "What're you doing? Get back in your seat - now." And having said that he reached over the seat and put his hand against John's chest.

"These things, they're too tight. Especially the right one, I think its cutting off my circulation," exclaimed John, leaning his body into Bill's hand.

Grabbing him by the shoulder, Bill roughly turned him sideways and reached over the seat to feel around the two cuffs. Satisfied with the results he then said, "You're okay. The circulation's not cut off. Stop pressing your weight against them and they won't hurt as much – now sit back."

John did as he was told and his wrist stopped throbbing as much as it had. "Thanks," he managed to say as the pain subsided even more.

"Glad to help," replied the detective over his shoulder as he turned around and resumed looking for the wreck up ahead.

Their car had stopped completely and John, now that the pain had lessened, began thinking about escape again. He could see the door locks were at such a height that he couldn't reach them, not with his hands behind his back. And even if he could manage to unlock his door, he would have just a few seconds to open it before one or possibly both detectives would reach over the seat to try and grab him.

John next thought about turning toward the door and kicking it open. He guessed he could get in two kicks at most before Detective Stewart would stop him. And even if by some miracle he was able to get the door open and out of the car, what would happen to Anne? He couldn't leave her there but, if he got the door open, what other choice would he have? John finally came to the conclusion that, no matter what happened today, even if it meant his death, he would stay with Anne. Having made up his mind, he now wondered what time it was, so he asked his question out loud.

Bill looked at his watch and said, "Ten after two." Then sarcastically added, "You in a hurry to get somewhere?"

The two men in the front seat started laughing at this comment. John didn't and out of the corner of his eye caught Anne looking over at him. From the expression on her face he could tell she didn't think it was funny either.

Roger hadn't tried to pull out into the northbound lane for some time and while he'd been laughing at Bill's "joke", he had let the traffic move far enough ahead that there was now a three car length distance between him and the car in front of him. He adjusted his rearview mirror while looking back at the car behind him and then slowly turned his car into the other lane. But, just as before, he quickly pulled back in as a trio of cars sped by. However, not all was lost as he had managed to see flashing lights up ahead. "I can see a police car," he said. "My guess is that if traffic keeps moving as it is, we should be by the accident in fifteen minutes – tops."

Hearing this, Bill turned to the people in the back seat. "Look at me, you two," he said with eyes narrowed. "When we tell you to sit back - sit back - and act natural. If there's any funny stuff, you'll regret it."

John wanted to ask how could they act natural with handcuffs on in a car with two murderers, but he didn't. Instead he nodded. He didn't know what Anne had done, but it must have been the same thing, because Bill then turned back around and started talking to Roger. "This radio's been mighty quiet for such bad accident. Not much chatter," he said.

Roger nodded his head in agreement and then pointed to a sheriff's car that was just then passing by them heading north. "That's unusual, no call about where he's going. And after he just passed such a big accident, too. What kind of sheriff's department do they run down here?" he asked. Then answering his own question as he threw out yet another cigarette butt he said, "Not very good."

John ignored the front seat conversation and softly called out, "Anne, Anne." She turned away from the window when she heard her name being called and looked over at him.

"How you doing?" he asked glumly.

"What do you think?" she shot back.

"Not the weekend we planned," he said ignoring the sarcasm in her voice.

"Well, it's beyond any I've ever had happen," she said, this time softening her tone.

"Quiet back there," said Roger interrupting John before he could say anything more.

"Why can't we talk? We're not hurting anyone," said John angrily. He'd had enough and decided he wasn't going to take anymore from them.

"Because I don't want to hear your blabbering, that's why," and with that Roger tried to push him back in his seat. Seeing his hand coming over the seat, John slid back and watched as Roger's hand missed his shirt. "Keep your mouth shut," said Roger before quickly turning back to watch the road.

Anne said nothing. After Roger's warning she went silently back to looking out the window. John thought about saying that, as far as he could remember, he still had the right to free speech and that as a police officer Roger should know that. After about a minute of considering this, John realized what a stupid mistake that would be; as these were not regular officers - they were criminals with badges. And playing lawyer with them wouldn't work; it would only be a ticket to quicker misery.

Their car continued to make slow, but steady, progress toward the accident. After all Roger's and Bill's comments on the lack of radio traffic, conversations had now become more frequent. The detectives were quick to remark on the return to what they considered was a normal pattern of calls involving this wreck. A tow truck had evidently arrived, followed by an ambulance whose personnel were now in the process of checking out the driver of the pick-up for injuries.

All the while cars and trucks were passing by, picking up speed as they headed north on Highway 59. The trucks slowly lumbered forward, frequently shifting gears and making much more noise than the cars as they went by.

The closer their car got to the wreck the slower the speed of the vehicles that went by them. Roger had been watching their speed as this had become his gauge of the distance to the wreck. Suddenly the car in front of him pulled out into the northbound lane. Startled, Roger slammed on the brakes as the car hurriedly retreated back into its lane with barely enough time to avoid being hit by another oncoming car. "We're about there," announced Roger. "That is if we don't get killed by the guy in front of us."

A semi carrying new cars was in front of the three cars ahead of them. Its size was one of the reasons why it was hard for anyone behind it to see what was further on up the road. John, for some reason, had been looking at the cars it carried, knew he'd seen them in an ad, but couldn't get their name to come to mind. Realizing it wasn't going to come to him, he asked if anyone knew.

"Shut up back there," said Roger. "Didn't you hear what I told you earlier?"

"I heard - what kind of cars are on the truck? I still want to know," and having said that, John made sure he was back as far as he could go in his seat.

"I'll take care of this," said Bill in a loud voice, "I think they're Chevys. Now shut up."

"No," said Roger. "They're Fords. And what difference does it make anyway; they all look alike anymore. Now both of you shut up, I need to focus on what's going on ahead."

John put his face up near his closed window and watched as two sheriff's cars came slowly into view. He could see them at the far end of a big turn that went to the right up ahead. One car was parked in the southbound lane facing north. In front of it stood a deputy who was regularly directing the oncoming vehicles into the northbound lane. About fifty yards beyond him was another sheriff's car, this one parked in northbound lane facing the opposite direction. Behind it stood a deputy who was just barely visible. It was now apparent to John why traffic had been backing up so much. Vehicles going in both directions were being directed around the wreck one at a time.

"We're almost there, no thanks to the way traffic is being directed. You'd think they never had any accidents down here," said Bill disgusted with the same scene John was watching.

"I can hardly wait," said Roger in a voice filled with frustration.

The tractor-trailer carrying the new cars now began to pull into the northbound lane. As it did it abruptly came to a stop. Neither Roger nor Bill could see any reason for this and both of them began to get increasingly more uncomfortable.

"See anything?" said Bill for the third time as the truck slowly moved further into the other lane. Both lines of traffic were completely stopped as the big truck inched its way forward.

A strange quiet filled the air and John realized he could hear the Elk River, off to his left, as he saw the tractor-trailer finally finish moving into the northbound lane. He was now able to see a county deputy standing by the ambulance who was, it seemed, staring directly at their car.

John glanced at Anne to see if she had also noticed this, but her head was bowed and her eyes were still closed, which was the same position she had been in for the past several minutes. He decided not to interrupt her and went back to watching the scene in front of him.

Two new deputies now appeared out on the road up ahead. One of them began to walk away from the wrecked pick-up and toward their car as the other one stood holding one end of a tape measure. They both began a conversation with a highway patrolman, who was now standing in front of the parked sheriff's car, directing southbound traffic.

During all this the tractor-trailer had managed to get around the wreck and was now pulling back into the southbound lane. Both the sound and the size of it were fading off into the distance, but nothing was moving - in either lane. The highway patrolman turned toward the one deputy standing by the pick-up truck and said something. As a result, that deputy then bent over and put his end of the tape measure down on the highway. He then hollered something to the deputy holding the other end before quickly moving in front of the parked sheriff's car and raising his hand to prevent the next car in line from moving forward.

That accomplished, the highway patrolman crossed over to the other side of the highway and began walking along the shoulder of the road in the direction of their car. Left by himself in front of the sheriff's car, the new deputy finally lowered his hand and motioned for the next car in line to go into the northbound lane.

Bill Stewart had been watching all this with an increasing air of suspicion. Suddenly he saw the new deputy began pointing at the deputy holding the tape measure.

Looking down at the pavement, Bill could see that the tape wasn't unwinding and was just being dragged along as that deputy continued walking toward their car. Bill then heard the new deputy call out for the other one to stop and wait until he could come up and get his end of the tape again so they could continue on with their measurements.

"I don't like this, something's wrong here," said Bill. "This tape measure thing – it's not making sense. And all along they'd been letting cars go by this wreck in groups – then, as we show up, they only let one at a time go around. I don't like it."

"I'm with you – something's not right," said Roger sitting up straight in his seat. Reaching into his windbreaker he pulled out his gun and laid it on the seat beside him.

The deputy who had started directing traffic now motioned for the second car ahead of them to go into the opposite lane. Meanwhile, the highway patrolman had stopped walking. Ahead of them, the deputy holding the tape measure had stopped and was beginning to go back toward the wreck.

The second car slowly went by the line of emergency vehicles and the passenger could be seen leaning out the window eyeing the truck that was still in the ditch. As that car moved into the northbound lane the deputy directing southbound traffic raised his hand again, this time to stop the car just in front of them. Finally he motioned for the car to move forward. He kept moving his hand around in the air as that car slowly moved half way into the northbound lane and stopped. With a disgusted look at the driver, the deputy frantically signaled for it to come on again. As it passed by him he could be seen saying something to the car's driver.

The deputy now turned toward their car and raised his hand for them to stop. Two deputies stood on the side of the road about ten feet from the front bumper of the parked sheriff's car. They were talking to each other and occasionally looking up at Roger's car as he drove toward them.

The closer their car got to the wreck, the closer Bill watched the two deputies and the highway patrolman on the opposite side of the road. The new deputy still held his hand in the air as he waited for the last car to slowly finish its journey back to its proper lane. The air was still again, the only sounds this time were coming from the river - and the receding car.

Suddenly Bill screamed out, "Turn around – it's a trap. Get out – get out of here - now." And with that he swung his gun up and pointed it at the nearest deputy and began firing. As his words faded nothing seemed to happen, it was if time had stopped. The calm was quickly broken by the roar of an engine as Roger turned the car sharply and drove directly toward the highway patrolman on the opposite side of the road. This and the squeal of the car's tires drowned out Anne's screams as the car jerked violently to the left. Just as quickly it lurched to the right, when Roger slammed on the brakes and threw the transmission into reverse, forcing the car backwards as noisily and violently as it had moved forward.

John had managed a quick look out his window before he was tossed around again. The two deputies had fallen to the ground and lay there with their guns drawn, but had made no effort to use them. The highway patrolman was nowhere to be seen. Anne screamed again and Bill, in one fluid movement turned, leaned over the seat and placed the barrel of his gun on Anne's chest. At the top of his voice he told her to shut up.

Roger now crammed the transmission lever back into drive and jammed down on the gas petal. The tires made an incredible noise and smoke poured out from under the car. As they raced rapidly away from the deputies, Bill fired one more shot in their direction, then watched as they quickly disappeared behind him.

"I should have known," yelled Bill as he stared intently into his side mirror. "No back in service call, the slow down to let only one car at a time by the accident – just as we got there. That sheriff's car going by us earlier – he was looking to see where we were. Hicks – these hicks almost outsmarted me. If it hadn't been for the one holding the tape, I – I would have fallen for it. How stupid – stupid – stupid," he said, pounding on his seat with his free hand.

Roger rapidly shifted his gaze between the rearview mirror and the road. "We've got company coming," he said jerking his thumb backwards.

Bill and John both turned and saw the flashing red lights off in the distance. Lights that were not gaining on them, but neither were they falling further behind.

"Where now?" shouted Roger over the noise.

"Take 90," said Bill without hesitation.

"90?"

"Yes – 90 – Highway 90, it goes west. We're close to both the Oklahoma and Arkansas state lines, we'll lose them by crossing into one or the other," said Bill pointing behind him. "Or both," he added.

They had now sped past the last of the southbound traffic that was waiting to get around the wreck. John immediately noticed there weren't any cars ahead of them in either lane of the road. And the police radio was silent again. Bill had also noticed this and had begun moving the dial back and forth searching for the frequency being used by their pursuers. He tried the entire dial twice and then in exasperation screamed out, "Where're the calls?"

"This isn't good," replied Roger. "They must have a road block up ahead. How did they find out about us – or our plan? There was no way it for it to fail."

"I'm currently busy and fresh out of answers," said Bill as he tried to unfold and search the road map he had scooped off the seat beside him.

"Okay – okay, just give me the directions – and tell me when to turn," said Roger as he continued alternately looking between the rearview mirror and the road. "Hurry, I think they're starting to catch up."

"Stop talking – let me think," said Bill, frantically searching one side of the map.

Roger had tried to speed up but because the road was becoming hillier and with more frequent curves, he constantly had to brake to safely make it around them.

Suddenly, in a burst of frustration, Bill ripped the map in half and threw the half he didn't want out the window. "It's no more than a mile ahead," he said. "The sign should be coming up on the right – anytime."

"There it is," shouted Roger pointing to a sign on the side of the road. He quickly pumped on the brakes and prepared to make the turn, a turn that was fast coming up on his left. Ahead a red pickup had slowed at the intersection and then continued out onto the highway.

Roger continued to pump his brakes. The distance between the two vehicles was closing rapidly and Bill screamed out, "We're going to crash unless you turn now, turn –."

"Watch me," shot back Roger as he gripped the steering wheel.

John flung himself down in the seat and braced for the coming collision. He heard the sharp squeal of the tires and quickly felt the car slid sideways, and then fishtail back and forth until Roger was able to bring it back under control. Once it was, Roger quickly jammed his foot on the accelerator and the car jumped forward again.

John could still hear the sound of sirens behind them, but they were further back than before the turn. He wanted to sit up and see where they were but Anne was lying on top of him. The speed and the sharpness of the turn had tumbled her onto him and, in turn, they both had fallen onto the floor. Anne struggled up onto her side of the seat never once saying anything. John managed to get back up in the seat, but not before an unsuccessful attempt to see if there were any cars behind them.

"Get me out of these! Get me out of them!" The sound of Anne's voice filled the car and Bill turned to see what was wrong. "Take these off," said Anne hysterically as she tried to pull her handcuffs apart. Tears were running down her cheeks as she spun herself sideways and held out her arms toward Bill. "I don't want to die like this," she cried out several times.

Bill pushed her hands down and slapped the back of her head all in one motion. "Shut up and get back over there," he said shoving her away from him.

Anne turned and her head fell back against the seat as she continued to cry. Bill stared at her for a few seconds before picking up the remaining part of his map and studying it again.

John tried to ignore the incident as he continued to search his mind for a new plan of escape. As a lawyer he knew he was suppose to see as many possibilities as he could in any situation but, so far, nothing was coming to mind. Except that he felt angry with Anne for what she had just done as it had taken away some of his concentration.

The first problem, John knew, were the handcuffs; Anne's quest had been sound even if her path wasn't. If he could only get free of them, plenty of opportunities would open up for escape. John decided it was his turn to ask to have his removed. "Please let me out of these cuffs, it's the only way I can calm her down," he said in a loud voice. And to further emphasize his point he kicked the back of the seat in front of him as hard as he could.

Bill didn't look up from reading the map and Roger said nothing. John asked again, this time in an even louder voice. Bill continued to ignore him and turned to look out the back window. His movement caused John to look to one side, whereupon he saw two cars with flashing red lights about one hundred yards behind them. Before screaming, "They're gaining," Bill stuck his gun out the window and fired twice at the lead car.

John immediately saw the cars fall further back.

"I see – I see them," shrieked Roger. "You have the map; now tell me how to lose them."

The noise of the racing engine was the only sound as Bill didn't respond. The police radio began to spew out orders at an alarming pace – orders setting up roadblocks at locations Bill couldn't find on the map or at least the half he held in his hand. In disgust, he threw it down on the seat beside him and began to scan the road that was flashing by.

"Find someplace for me to go," demanded Roger, taking his right hand off the steering wheel long enough to grab the map off the seat and throw it towards Bill.

Bill made no effort to catch it and it fell to the floor; instead he continued to search up ahead for a way off this road. He then realized no cars were coming in the opposite direction and said, "They've probably diverted all traffic off this road by now; there's nothing moving except us."

Their car was coming upon curves more frequently, forcing Roger to constantly move his foot back and forth between the brake and the accelerator, which had the effect of throwing the occupants of the car back and forth.

John gave up asking to get out of the handcuffs and now, having turned himself sideways in the seat again, saw that the police cars were still keeping their distance. They must know something is about to happen up ahead, he thought.

The fleeing car had just gone through another sharp S curve when Roger spotted a dirt road on his left about a quarter of a mile up ahead. "There's our road!" he yelled out.

"Take it, take it," hollered back Bill.

Roger jammed his foot on the brake and continued pushing down on it as hard as he could. The smell of burning rubber filled the car as it rapidly slowed down. Roger's left turn was every bit as abrupt as the one off Highway 59, only this time John didn't have time to throw himself down in the seat. Anne rolled into him and together the two of them hit his door. The car fish-tailed wildly and it took Roger longer to get the car back under control this time even though they were going slower.

The occupants in the back seat managed to untangled themselves and John had just begun sliding back to his side of the seat when up ahead he saw the farm tractor in the middle of the road. Instantly, he knew they were not going to be able to stop in time and were only moments away from ramming into the back of it. "Look out," he yelled at the top of his voice and threw himself down in the seat for the third time.

Bill let forth with a string of abuse and threw his hands up to protect his face. He managed to exclaim, "Watch out, you're going to hit that –" before he stopped, closed his eyes and braced himself for what he knew was inevitable; leaving Roger to work a miracle without his help.

Jerking the steering wheel hard to his left, Roger barely avoided colliding with the tractor. He followed this by immediately turning the wheel back to the right in an attempt to steer around it. His quick motions, however, had started the car sliding toward the edge of the road and all his attempts to get it back under control were failing. Roger watched helplessly as the car kept drifting toward the edge of the road. "I can't stop it," he said with just a hint of impending doom in his voice.

Roger's apparent calmness led Bill to open his eyes, that is until he saw their car rapidly approaching the edge of the road. "Hit the brakes," was all he could get out before quickly closing his eyes again.

"I'm trying," retorted Roger, who had given up any hope of accelerating the car around the tractor and away from the edge of the road and was now rapidly pumping the brakes with both feet.

The rear wheel was the first to drop off the edge and once it did the car began bouncing up and down as it ran over the uneven ground. This continued for a few seconds until the front wheel also dropped off. Roger continued to fight with the steering wheel, trying to keep it turned to the right in the hope of getting both tires back on the road again when, without warning, the car plunged sideways into a shallow ditch before hitting the edge of a corrugated metal drainpipe. The force of the impact blew out the front tire, deployed the car's airbags and caused the car to roll onto its side and then over on its top. It then slid up and out of the far side of the ditch and tore through a barbed wire fence pulling out several wooden posts as it continued moving forward until it came to a stop.

Quiet descended over the upturned car. John quickly opened his eyes and found himself lying on the headliner. He listened to the sound of birds chirping somewhere nearby until the increasing sound of sirens drew him back to why he was here. This sound was soon replaced by groaning; groaning that was coming from somewhere behind him. John wanted to find out where and who the sound was coming from, but first he turned his head slowly back and forth to make sure his neck wasn't broken. That's when he noticed that the car's rear window had been completely blown out by the force of the accident. Through the open window he could trace the path the car had taken across this field to where it was now.

Satisfied his neck wasn't broken, John next moved his hands and arms before going on to his feet and legs. When he was sure he didn't have any broken bones, he knew the pain he felt was from his muscles starting to tighten up. If he was alive tomorrow, he knew he was going to be very sore.

In the course of checking his body, John had felt someone up against him. Confident he wasn't seriously hurt, John then rolled over and saw it was Anne. She was lying crumpled up facing him –and wasn't moving. John pushed himself over next to her and nudged her with his head several times before stopping to look for a response. When he didn't get one, he pushed her again. Slowly one eye opened and looked at John. However, she didn't say anything. Now fresh groans, each of which was more intense than the last, could be heard. John ignored them and called out Anne's name.

After a long pause, Anne managed to get out, "Yes," before proceeding to spit several times.

The voice didn't sound like her and John quickly asked, "You okay?"

"I don't know," she answered in a barely audible voice. "But I think so."

John had managed to get next to her ear where he now whispered, "Anne, go out the back window, it's gone. Do it now - don't ask questions - go." From behind him he could hear one of the detectives starting to move around. John finished by saying, "I'll be right behind you."

Feeling more than hearing the urgency in his voice, Anne slowly began to pull her body forward. Little by little she labored toward the back of the car. Broken window glass littered the path and she had no choice but to half slide-half crawl over the pieces. The sting from the cuts that came from moving across the sharp edges forced her to bite her tongue.

As Anne began moving toward the window John continued to lay on his side, blocking any view from behind him of what she was doing. He lay there motionless and watched as, at last, she reached the rear window and then crawled on out into the field.

Once on the damp ground Anne began rolling herself out from under the car until she felt it was okay to stand up. She struggled to her knees only to fall back down when a wave of lightheadedness overcame her. Immediately getting back on her knees again, she managed this time to catch her balance as the wave came again and then stagger to her feet as it passed. She looked around long enough to see which way to run before heading back toward the opening in the fence and the safety of the police cars that were stopped on the road beyond it.

Anne ran as fast as she could. All her energy was focused on narrowing the distance between herself and the fence. But, as she continued to run, she felt the pain increasing all over her body, and especially from one corner of her chest. Instead of stopping to see why she was hurting so much, Anne began telling herself that, just ahead, just beyond that fence, was the help she needed. Coming to the narrow ditch that separated the fence from the road, she tried to jump it, but her foot landed on a rock and she fell to the ground. Crying out in pain, she knew she couldn't get up.

Suddenly, from out of nowhere a uniformed figure pulled her up on her feet and dragged her behind a nearby car. The officer then grabbed her muddy wrists one at a time and removed the handcuffs. As he worked to free her, he kept asking questions about the car, who was still in it, and whether they were hurt or not.

Anne answered every question until she couldn't hold back her tears anymore and began to cry. The deputy sheriff, who said his name was Jack, apologized and stopped asking questions. It was then the turn of a medic who came and sat down beside her to ask more questions, all of which Anne answered before, just as suddenly as he had come, he disappeared.

Now alone, Anne wiped at her eyes and began looking for John. She didn't see him behind any of the cars and finally said to Jack, "Where's John?"

Jack Tidnish pointed out toward the field and the upturned car.

Anne was so stunned she couldn't say anything for a moment. Suddenly, she felt very angry with John for lying to her - as he had promised to be right behind her.

She grabbed the deputy by the arm and demanded, "Why didn't he come with me?"

Looking down at the muddy mark her hand had left on his sleeve, he calmly said, "I don't know."

"Well find out," she said indignantly.

Deputy Tidnish didn't say anything more. Instead he waved to a female deputy and motioned for her to come over.

Anne had turned to look back at the field when the woman deputy suddenly knelt down beside her. "You need to come with me, Miss," she said without introducing herself.

The name, "Miss", sounded funny to Anne, but she didn't laugh.

"Miss, you need to go with me, the Sheriff wants to talk to you," said the deputy. She didn't wait for an answer, but took hold of Anne and led her toward the back of the car.

From there they ran behind several cars until they stopped beside three men. One of them extended his hand out toward Anne and said, "I'm Wayne Green."

Anne took his hand and said in a dull voice, "Anne Hubert."

"Phil Batson," said the man next to him. "We're sorry, Ms. Hubert, we tried to get to you back where the truck wrecked."

She wearily nodded and suddenly felt a jolt of pain in her back.

"You okay?" asked Phil.

"I don't know," she said, "the pain's now in my back."

"You need to be checked out by the paramedics," said Wayne pointing to an ambulance parked further back up the road. It looked to Anne like the same one she had seen at the wreck.

"I was just checked, thank you. Besides, I'm not ready to do anything until I know John is safe," she said with tears in her eyes.

"That could be awhile," said Phil.

"I don't care; I can't go off and just leave him there. After all, he's the reason I'm safe now."

Phil's smile quickly faded. "I understand," he said, "but at least you could go and have them look at you. You sound like you're in a lot of pain."

Anne knew whoever was in charge here could order her to leave and, if she didn't go, could have her forcibly removed. But these men were trying to be nice to her. "Okay," she said and touching Phil's sleeve added, "please try and see that he isn't hurt."

Looking down the road at the line of police cars with their lights flashing and then over at the upturned car, Phil then turned to Anne and said, "We'll do everything in our power to get him out of this alive." And having said this Phil turned and began talking in a low voice to the other two men.

With nothing else to say or do, Anne let the woman deputy lead her away again, this time over to a waiting ambulance and the same medic she had seen before.

26

John watched as Anne turned and twisted her way back toward the destroyed rear window. Her body would occasionally shudder as she moved over the broken glass along her path and he could imagine the painful cuts she was enduring. Behind him he could hear constant moaning, moaning which had been continuous almost since the car had come to a halt. There was nothing John wanted to do about it; whoever it was deserved his pain and more and, besides, he was going to follow Anne.

Starting forward, John followed Anne's path over the broken glass. The groaning behind him intensified and this caused him to look around and see who was in so much pain. The first thing to catch his eye was the deflated airbags hanging limply down from the dashboard. Next he saw that the former occupants of the front seat were now bunched up together under the steering wheel. It was from there that the groaning was coming. "They both deserve it," he muttered to himself, unable to readily tell which of the two was suffering so much.

Turning back around John began again to crawl forward. Looking out the back window he saw that Anne was no longer in the car – in fact she was on the ground outside trying to get up. Continuing on toward the back window grew increasingly painful as small pieces of glass relentlessly nicked his body. The window opening was now directly in front of him and John steadied himself for the drop onto the muddy ground just beyond it.

It was then that, without any warning, a hand grabbed his left ankle and held on fast. "Not so fast counselor," said a voice behind him.

John pulled his free leg up in anticipation of kicking himself loose but, before he could do so, another hand grabbed the chain between his handcuffs and jerked him backwards. The pain in his shoulders was so intense that it caused him to cry out.

"Counselor, it's not time to leave yet," said the same voice. This time John recognized Detective Stewart, who had let go of his ankle as he continued to pull harder on the chain. "Come back inside, won't you. I need your help," he said in a sarcastic voice.

Looking back out beyond the car, John saw that Anne was almost to safety. "Okay, I'm coming," he said. Then he added, "Just don't pull so hard, it hurts my shoulders."

Bill Stewart ignored John's request and continued pulling on the handcuff chain. John was being dragged back toward the front of the car over the same glass that he had so painfully crossed only moments before. And, again, John felt the stings from the glass as it gave him more cuts.

Bill finally stopped and told John to turn himself around. "Now counselor," he said when John had finished doing as he was told, "we need your help. We're," he said, pointing a finger at John, "we're going to pull him out of the car – then head for that line of trees over there." As he said this, Bill motioned toward Roger Sumler who continued to lay motionless under the steering wheel. And as if to emphasize

Bill's point, a loud groan escaped from that corner of the upturned car.

John had turned on his side and was now facing the crumpled body of the other detective, which still had not moved. "That man's hurt," John said, angered by what he saw before him. "You need to get him some medical help - not have the two of us drag him across a muddy field."

Bill was sitting up now. From his new position he looked down at John and then across the field at the collection of vehicles gathered on the distant road. He thought about what John had said before replying, "Roger doesn't want to go over there. That would be letting those people win. And we can't do that - it's us who win – every time."

"Win what?" asked John, bewildered by this comment.

The detective looked directly at John. "Nothing, forget it," he said. "You'll push after I get him pulled out of there."

"That's crazy," said John. "My hands are still cuffed. Besides, you don't know how badly hurt he is; it'll probably make things worse." And jerking his head in the direction of the road, John said, "He needs to be over there where that ambulance is parked."

Bill snorted at this suggestion. "I may be crazy, but given a choice between helping me or dying now, you'll help," he said sticking his hand in the pocket of his jacket as he finished talking.

John had said all he was going to say as his eyes intently watched Bill's hand, expecting momentarily to see a gun appear.

"Right counselor?" Bill's voice interrupted John's thoughts and he looked around for the detective who, when he found him, had managed to work his way out of the driver's side window which had been shattered by the wreck. From out on the ground Bill reached back into the car, grabbed Roger's legs, and began to pull him through the window. "Start pushing," he barked at John.

John responded by muttering something under his breath before moving into the corner, laying his shoulder up against Roger and pushing, but having his hands cuffed behind his back wasn't making it easy.

"This isn't right," shouted John as Roger began moaning more loudly.

"Push," said Bill showing no sign of changing his plan.

Reluctantly, John began anew to push and, again, this caused Roger to groan. Roger's groans made John wince.

"Don't – do – that – it hurts." The words were barely audible and caught John by surprise. He stopped what he was doing and waited for Roger to say something else.

"I told you to push," said Bill in an irritated voice when he felt John back away from Roger.

"Didn't you hear him," retorted John. "He said it hurts and he doesn't want to be moved."

Bill hadn't heard anything. He had been focused on getting his partner out of the upturned car as well as watching the people on the far side of the field. He now crawled back inside the car, and stopping near the other detective asked, "Roger, Roger, can – can you hear me?"

The same barely audible voice said, "It's – it's okay, nothing broken. Help me out."

John heard this and didn't believe a word of it. Bill turned to John and said icily. "When I get back out, start pushing again - understand?"

John nodded. He no longer had any desire to take up for the injured detective or object to the commands issued by his partner. Having decided neither one was going to listen to him, John was now content to concentrate his efforts on getting Roger out of the car. Roger, with a final push from John, soon slid out the window and fell on his back into the mud.

It was now John's turn to wiggle out the window and he, too, landed in the mud. Almost instantly water began soaking through his jeans.

"Now- what?" asked Roger gasping to get his question out in the same faint voice.

Bill worked on shaking a cramp out of his left arm. "We're going to those trees over there," he said. "It'll be safe there 'til we decide what to do next."

Roger saw the distant line of trees and attempted to raise himself up, but he slowly slid back down. The two men with him watched and did nothing until he was lying on his back again. Bill then motioned for John to get on the other side of Roger.

"I can't do any more good unless you get me out of these," John said, rolling on his side and holding his cuffed hands out toward Bill.

"Forget it; do as I told you," came the expected reply.

"It doesn't make sense," said John ignoring what he had just heard. "I can't carry him with my hands like this. Look at him, he weighs too much. I'll need both hands for this to work."

"Try anyway," said Bill putting his hand on the gun that was now in his waistband.

John gave up and inched himself over to the far side of Roger, who was still sprawled out on his back. Bill pushed him up enough to place Roger's arm over John's shoulder and the two of them then got Roger up into a sitting position. At the sound of 'lift' the three men tried, but without success, to get up at the same time. All they accomplished was to stumble and fall back down again.

"You're going to have to uncuff me," said John as he tried to wipe his face on the back of Roger's shirt.

Bill started to say something, but was interrupted by Roger.

"Uncuff – him," he said.

John could plainly hear the pain in his voice.

"No," said Bill firmly.

"Uncuff him – or – leave – me – here; you – choose," said Roger in his strongest voice yet.

John could hear the effort it took for Roger to speak each word.

Bill looked down at his friend and shook his head. "I can't do it," he said. "It makes no sense – you know that - not with those people over there," he said, pointing toward the far side of the upturned car and the road beyond it.

"Do – it," said Roger. The pain in his voice had noticeably increased.

This time Bill didn't say anything; but instead reached into his pocket and pulled out a key. Crawling around his friend he told John to turn toward him. As John complied, Bill grabbed one of his arms and roughly turned him on his side. "Nothing funny friend; remember I'll be watching," he said as he unlocked the left cuff and put it through the back belt loop of John's jeans and then relocked it.

"Why just one?" said John rolling his shoulder as he waited for an answer.

"Don't ask stupid questions," came the brusque reply.

"I still need the other one free," said John.

"That's all you're getting," said Bill, adding, "I wouldn't trust you with both hands free."

"What do you mean you don't trust me?" said John looking at Bill. "I've more than proved my trust." He had started to raise his voice, but the sight of a gun pointing at him changed his mind and he stopped.

"She's over there," said Bill, pointing his gun toward the road. "That's how you showed your trust. Now, shut up and help me get him up."

John quietly got back on his knees. Again the injured detective's arm was placed over John's right shoulder but this time John grabbed his wrist with his newly freed hand. Slowly the three of them got up, leaning against each other like drunks.

"That way," said Bill motioning with his gun toward the trees. Abruptly, however, he added, "Wait a second."

John and Roger had begun moving after the first command. The order to stop had thrown Roger into John and they now fought against gravity to stay upright. John could hear Roger's labored breathing and felt him shaking with pain as they undertook to stand there.

"What now?" asked John. He watched as Bill's hand disappeared and then reappeared holding a gun which he then placed in Roger's free hand.

"Here you might need this," Bill said, closing Roger's hand around it. Then looking over at John he said, "Now you can go."

The group slowly began marching toward the trees. The weight on John's right shoulder seemed to intensify with each step and he went back to wondering just how badly Roger was hurt. He hadn't seen a lot of blood on either of the detectives, but if they were anything like him, they had to be aching all over. And with each step, John could feel the need to come up with more strength as Roger began to weigh more and more.

John looked over at Bill to make sure he wasn't letting him take all the injured man's weight. What he saw was him looking back over his shoulder at the road. It was then John realized that Bill had managed to put himself on the side of Roger farthest from the road. This meant that he, John, was fully exposed to any trigger-happy cops who might not know who was a good guy and who wasn't.

"Why don't you give up?" John said between the large swallows of air he was forced to take to keep walking. "I'm tellin' you this guy's hurt bad."

And as if on cue, Roger let out a loud groan as he tried to take a new step.

Bill didn't respond and John went back to concentrating on each step he was taking. To do otherwise was to invite a spill into the mud and the ensuing messy effort to get himself and Roger back up on their feet again. John had slowly and laboriously finished counting out ten more steps when Roger suddenly dropped to his knees taking the other two men down with him. Bill let go of Roger to keep from completely falling to the ground. He then put himself in front of Roger and asked, "Can you make it?"

What seemed to John like a full minute went by, a long minute punctuated with occasional gasps and wheezes, before Roger spoke up. He seemed to flinch in pain with every word. "Yea – I can, but – help me – on – both – sides," he said in a voice weaker than before.

John thought he heard Bill crying. But before he could look to make sure, Bill said in a loud voice, one that John felt could be heard across the ditch behind them, "Hold on, we're no more than fifty feet from safety."

Turning back to John he said more quietly, "Come around to this side and lift over here," as he reached down and picked up the gun Roger had dropped when he fell and stuffed it in his belt.

Nothing happened. Bill glanced over at the road and waited for John.

"I need you to take off the other handcuff," said John standing in the same spot and not moving.

"What?" said Bill, surprised by this statement.

"I said you need to uncuff me so I can get a better grip on him," said John pulling on his remaining cuffed hand to show Bill it was still attached to his belt loop.

"Don't start that again, I've about had it with you."

"Uncuff – him," said the low, but firm, voice that came from between the two men. "Uncuff 'im, I n'ed his 'elp."

Bill's response was a glance toward John that caused him to shiver. Then, without further comment, he took out his key again and unlocked the other cuff. John rubbed his now free right hand and quickly moved to Roger's other side and placed his left shoulder under Roger's right arm. As he slowly took on Roger's weight, John felt a rush of pain in his back and he grimaced with every new step toward the trees. He no longer wondered why Bill had him change for he saw that they all were now fully exposed to the people on the road. He was fairly certain that each held a gun which was pointed at one of the three of them. John prayed that Anne could still point out which of the three was him.

It was not something John planned as a way to escape – or end – what was going on, but after Bill tucked Roger's gun in his belt John began to think of ways to get hold of it. He thought about quickly reaching across Roger and grabbing it. In anticipation of possibly doing this John had looked for the gun's safety. His first problem was - he didn't know what he was looking for - and, if he solved that one, there was a second problem; he hadn't fired a gun in ten years. John guessed he would have between five and seven seconds to get to the gun and release the safety before Bill had time to react. It dawned on him he could gain more time, maybe just enough more, if he pushed Roger into Bill. If everything went according to plan, Bill could be quickly disarmed and this nightmare would be all over.

But John also knew that if he guessed wrong, he would probably get shot, most likely by Bill, but there was also this to consider - were he successful in getting to the gun - how would whoever came charging across the field know he wasn't one of the bad guys?

With each step toward the trees, no matter how slow or fast he went, he knew his chances of ending this madness were decreasing. He reminded himself that these two guys had shown no mercy to the couple he found dead in the canoe last night. They had meant for it to have been his death and Anne's too, for that matter, although he wasn't as interested in her well-being at the moment as he was his own. The image of the dead couple this morning reinforced John's need to act. He decided they served as a warning that his value was almost up the closer they got to the trees.

They had now fallen into a rhythm of sorts. Each of the men on the outside pulled together while the man in the middle, for his part, moved less and less. They were now to the point of virtually dragging Roger.

John guessed the distance to the nearest tree was now less than twenty feet. He stopped and tried to straighten himself up enough to give his back some relief. "My back hurts," he said when Bill asked why he had stopped. "I've got to rest for a moment."

"Keep going, we're almost there," said Bill struggling to keep on his feet after John left him with Roger's entire weight.

John ignored him, took in another deep breath, and coughed several times. As he started out again, he could feel Bill trying to pull Roger forward by himself and this made his back feel better. John looked at the trees in front of him and then up at the sky. The sun felt good on his face. It was easier now, with more of the weight on Bill, for him to look back toward the road. All the cars looked like they had been assigned a parking space, but what he noticed most was how clean they all were. He had never thought, until now, just how clean policemen kept their cars.

John shook his head and bit hard on his lip to free himself of these odd thoughts. He used the pain this caused to focus himself just before he shoved Roger as hard as he could with one hand while quickly seizing the gun in Bill's belt with the other. The two detectives fell to the ground.

Standing over them, John fumbled to find the safety on the gun he now held in his hand. Much to his relief, he saw that Roger had landed on top of Bill who, from his loud gasps of air and the grunts he was making, had had the wind knocked out of him.

John continued his frantic search as Bill struggled to push himself out from under his partner. Finally freeing himself, Bill scrambled to his knees and, without even looking at John, began searching for the gun he had dropped in his fall. Spotting it partially buried in the mud, he scooped it up and pointed it toward John, who stood there looking at the mud caked barrel.

John wondered if it would go off if the trigger were pulled or if, like in those old frontier movies he liked to watch, it would blow up.

"Drop it," screamed the detective pointing the gun at John's chest.

"No way."

"Drop it or I'll shoot."

"No," said John who had finally pushed something on his gun which had moved, making him hope it was the missing safety. Feeding off the wave of relief that had come over him John said, "Put your gun down and let's end this thing." He then strained to hear the sound of people rushing across the field to his rescue, but all remained quiet.

Bill Stewart had not moved off his knees or lowered his gun in response to John's order. Realizing this could not go on, John stood there pondering what to do next. All he could come up with was to stall for time and hope the people behind the distant cars would wake up and hurry over. "Why'd you do this?" he blurted out.

"Why, what?" said Bill rapidly moving his eyes between the gun in John's hand and the open field behind him.

"Why did you do this? What's in the papers that's so important that you needed to kill to get them back?" John had decided to go for broke, "live for the answer, die for the answer" he said to himself. Although in the situation he now found himself in that, somehow, seemed like an inappropriate choice of outcomes.

Bill tried to wipe his face with his free hand leaving streaks of mud on his forehead and left cheek. Finished, he began to shake his head. "I've asked myself that a thousand times," he said, looking down at Roger. "To give up everything, including my freedom; was it that important? I don't have an answer - at least one I can use to justify what's occurred. I – we – never planned it like this - things just took on a life of their own. All I ever wanted back was the paper."

"What paper?" asked John.

"The one in your car."

"But what's in it, why is it so important?"

Bill now lifted his gaze off the gun John was holding and looked up at his face, before beginning to laugh. "Didn't Gilley bring the documents with him to your office?" he asked.

"How'd you know he was there – how'd you know?" shouted John at this unexpected question.

"What difference does it make? He was there and brought some papers with him," said Bill.

John felt on the defensive and began to search back through his memory of that meeting. He remembered Gilley had brought some papers with him, papers which he, John, had reviewed and given back. That's all he could recall, so he said, "I looked at some papers, but they were routine and I gave them back."

"So you don't know," said Bill laughing again. "It figures," he said shaking his head.

John felt his face getting hot. He didn't like the way he was being put down and for what, a bunch of papers the likes of which he looked at every day.

"Do you even have them – are they even in your car?" Bill now asked.

"They're all there, don't worry," said John, unable to look at Bill as he lied to him.

"Where'd you get them if you gave them back?" Bill now shot back.

John hesitated as he tried to figure out what to say next.

Bill had stopped laughing and the smile on his face faded away. "No answer – just as I thought. So it all comes down to this - there's nothing in the back of your car and you don't even know what I'm talking about. Isn't that true?" he said shaking his head again. "All for nothing, all for nothing," he said letting his voice trail off.

"What do you mean?" said John still keeping his eyes on Bill's hand holding the gun.

"All this," said Bill waiving the gun around. "Today, this weekend, being down here in hillbilly land. Everything. That's what I mean by nothing."

"And that couple, you thought they were us, didn't you?" asked John. Realizing he had just put his foot in his mouth he immediately added, "Forget it - I don't want to know."

"Yes." The answer hung in the suddenly still air. Bill then leaned over toward Roger and said, "You hear that Roger? He doesn't have the papers and he doesn't know where they are – or even why we want them."

Roger didn't say anything.

Bill spoke up again. "Did you hear that, Roger? He just told us he hasn't got a clue, the lawyer doesn't have a clue. We know about the *Miranda* warnings, but he looked at the documents and didn't figure it out. It was all for nothing – Roger, you hearing this?"

This time Roger stirred at the mention of his name and then tried to roll on his side. His face and his clothes were covered in mud. "I hear you," he whispered spitting bits of mud out of his mouth as he spoke.

It was obvious to John that Roger was in more pain and that his skin, what wasn't covered in mud, was turning a lighter color. Finding his best lawyerly manner, John proceeded on with his next question, "What about the *Miranda* warnings?"

Bill started to rise up, but changed his mind, and, instead, in a voice filled with contempt shouted, "Didn't he bring a copy of his waiver of rights form? Didn't you look at it? How many warnings were on the form? I'll save you the trouble of thinking – there were only four. Not five, remember the new Supreme Court case that just came down? Of course you don't. I'll spell it out, five good, four bad. Defendant's statement's not admissible. Got it?"

"I remember it," retorted John. "I read it. So that's what this is all about, you gave him the wrong form?"

Bill ignored him and went on, "My whole life – my whole life had been dedicated to ridding the earth of scum like Lonnie Gilley. And now look at me; I'm no better than them. Except everyone knew they were destined for jail. And what about me, counselor? Can you see me in jail? Where would I be safe? And my family, who's going to take care of them?"

John didn't have answers to Detective Stewart's questions because the realization had just struck him that two people died yesterday because a form was missing a sentence and it made him dizzy.

Slowly John began to talk, but it was to the gun, as he had grown more afraid of it. "Those people who died on the river yesterday, isn't that enough? Look, let's call an end to this, and I guarantee you that I'll testify you treated me okay. Think of your family. Don't you want to see them?" Then, lowering his voice, John pleaded, "But, please, please, let's stop before someone else gets hurt."

Bill Stewart seemed to be listening. As John was talking, he nodded several times in agreement - but said nothing. The gun John was holding was getting heavier by the moment and, in his opinion, now weighed at least fifty pounds. He had taken to slowly moving his elbow in a circle in an attempt to make his arm feel better.

"What's the use," said Bill speaking out loud to no one in particular. "What's the use?" he said, repeating himself again. "Do you know what will happen to me in prison?" he said looking directly at John.

"Yes," said John, trying to make a connection with the man in front of him.

Bill continued on as if in a trance, "I'll tell you the reality. They'll segregate me in any institution they put me in because inmates that I've put in there would love to see me. So I'll be housed by myself and the rest of my life will still be spent looking over my shoulder, waiting for the other shoe to drop. That's what will happen – because no one on either side of the bars in a jail can be trusted. I'll never get into general population - I'd be dead within a day."

"You probably just meant to scare them – the two people in the canoe," said John offering up an excuse, an out, anything for the detective to hang some hope.

Bill looked down at his friend, who was lying still and making no effort to speak or get up. "He's hurt badly," he said. "If I give up my gun, they'll come and take him away to fix up for trial. Fix him up just so he can stand beside me when we're sentenced. No thanks to me. Here, let's ask Roger, 'you want to go do forty years Roger?'"

The figure on the ground spoke so softly John had to strain to hear what he was saying. "Can't do it. We – could – death." His voice had faded out at the end, but John knew what he was trying to say.

Bill nodded. "Thank you; I forgot that for some reason, probably because I hate this state. They have the death penalty in Missouri. Yes, we could then be forced to spend all our money on lawyers to protect us from that. And our families, what would be left for them? Nothing would be left - because we would have spent it all. Oh, yes, but how we'd make the lawyers happy. They'd get their names in the paper and they'd be on TV – free advertising so they could get other clients. But there would be nothing left to give our families."

Roger opened his eyes and was trying to smile, although one side of his mouth was caked shut with drying mud. Glancing down at him, Bill then went on, "There's only one solution really - only one. I win, my family wins, and the lawyers lose. It's perfect."

"What's that?" asked John, whose eyes were still on the gun in Bill's hand.

"You're not as smart as I thought, counselor. Reach back into your small mind, what have I been talking about? And all this over a piece of paper." And then as if he were summing up his case in a courtroom Bill raised his voice and said, "Oh, well, as someone once said 'nothing's more beautiful than death.'"

The sound of the gun going off reverberated off the nearby trees. John had watched Bill's hand begin to lower and had begun to relax when the cloud of smoke and fire sent him reeling backwards. The gun roared again and the ground around Roger's head began to turn red.

"I'm sorry, Roger, I'm so sorry," said Bill, sticking the gun in his mouth and pulling the trigger.

John stood motionless and watched as the detective fell backwards and hit the ground. A persistent ringing continued in his ears as he watched the cloud of smoke around the detective slowly disappear.

He was unable to hear the people running up behind him, but felt the gun being taken from his hand. Just as silently someone began leading him back across the field.

"You blocked our line of sight," said the officer beside him. John kept walking, unable to hear what he had just been told. In his mind he was replaying different parts of the last twenty-four hours in no apparent order.

Suddenly Anne appeared in front of him and said something, then put her arms around him. He felt the warmth of her body as she kissed him and it felt good. "I love you, Anne," he said. "I never want to leave you."

Anne continued crying as she held on tightly to John, "I know," she said. "I love you too."

About the Author

J. Patrick Flanigan has practiced law in Johnson County, Kansas, for over 20 years. He is also a part time public defender for a local city, as well as a Guardian *ad litem* in state court cases.